"Jane Rule explores with delicate precision the interpersonal and sexual relationships between men and women, men and men, women and women. She takes as her difficult theme the many meanings and manifestations of love and friendship, their hazards, their sometime grace, and she realizes this theme splendidly. A beautiful, ironic, civilized novel."

Margaret Laurence

"Of all the post-war American novels I have read, *This Is Not for You* is by far the most elegant."

George P. Elliott

"I have read Jane Rule's engrossing novel and think it brilliant. It has what so many novels now lack: narrative sweep, compassion, sensitivity and humor. Few who read it will ever forget the narrator.

Faith Baldwin

"Intellectually stimulating and emotionally poignant."

Pearl Schiff, *Boston Globe*

"This elegant, powerful novel . . . told me to stop playing an Esther to her Kate."

Nancy M. Ruthchild, *Mother Jones*

"The title is right: this book is not for me . . . If you think it's for you, reader beware!"

Sr. M. Marguerite, RSM; *Best Sellers*

BOOKS BY JANE RULE

THIS IS NOT FOR YOU

a novel by
JANE RULE

the NAIAD PRESS inc.
1982

THIS IS NOT FOR YOU

Originally published by The McCall Publishing Company, New York.

Printed in the United States of America.

Cover, back cover photograph, and title page design by Tee A. Corinne.
The front cover is based on a photograph by Lynn Vardeman. The same
image was used on the original McCall edition in 1970. This image also
appeared on the cover of the June/July 1970 issue of *The Ladder*.

Printed by the Iowa City Women's Press. Bound by A Fine Bind.
ISBN 0-930044-25-8

Another Naiad Press book by Jane Rule: OUTLANDER

About the Author

JANE RULE was born in Plainfield, New Jersey, in 1931, grew up in the midwest and in California, and graduated from Mills College, California, in 1952. In 1956 she moved to Vancouver, British Columbia, where she and Helen Sonthoff lived, teaching and writing, for twenty years, spending summers in England, Greece, or New England. They have spend the last five years on Galiano Island, off the coast of British Columbia, taking a winter month or two on the southern deserts of California or Arizona. A Canadian citizen for some years, Jane Rule is active in the writers', women's, and gay communities, reviewing books, writing articles, and serving on government committees; but writing fiction continues to be her chief occupation.

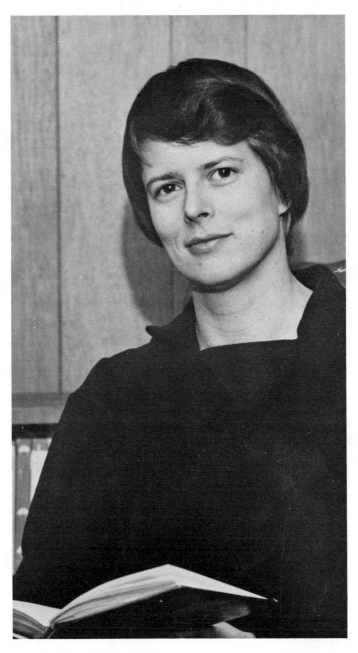

Portrait of Jane Rule by Leon Tuey, 1963, about the time *This Is Not for You* was written.

I

This is not a letter. I wrote you for the last time over a year ago to offer the little understanding I had, to say good-by. I could have written again, but somehow your forsaking the world for the sake of the world left me nothing to say. Your vow of silence must also stop my tongue, or so it seemed. What a way to win an argument! Now I find I can't keep your vow, not having taken it. Each of us has his own way to God, I used to say; there is no direct relationship, except through Him. But also, in the last hour of an examination we were both writing, I disproved the existence of evil. You must have written on the nature of salvation, starting down one of my untaken roads as I started down one of yours. For a long time, we could call back and forth, offering insults and encouragement. Not now. This is not a letter.

I sit surrounded by your trophies and treasures: old photographs, first editions, objects of stone and bone. Relics. I, who have complained half way round a world with you because you *would* clutter and burden the way with such things, now live in the little museum of what you finally left behind. What is it you want me to fall heir to? Surely you don't expect me to write with this quill pen or make real Jell-O in that seventeenth-century mold. And, as for the Milton, I will give it shelf room for your novice years, but the moment I hear you have taken your perpetual vows, into a library it goes where such things belong. I will keep the jewelry, the heavy paw of Mexican stone that lies at my throat, just as your beloved Rousseau's lion weighs down his sleeping man. And I will keep the photographs, taken in England, in Spain, in California, in New York. Why? Because I like to remember. I have not been reborn. I have changed neither my last name for a husband, as you did, nor my whole name for God, as you now have.

Funny, Monk, who seems to make a drama and a romance of you, still minds this second change of name. "She's giving up her given name. How can that be?" Given or not, biblical enough, "Esther" wasn't Christian for some time, was it? "Surely," I say, "it's no stranger than marrying any other way." So Monk tries to combine a notion of your marrying and being reborn. Soon she'll begin to call you by your new name, Mary Whatever-It-Is. And she is also threatening to send scented soap and colored sugar to that biblical address of yours in swampy New Jersey. You don't need to be called anything by me because I don't intend to call you. In these old photographs you are Esther Woolf, "E.," "little dog"; I was Katherine George, "Kate," and still am. And here's Monk, not yet twenty: Ramona Ridley. And Andrew Belshaw and Peter Jackson. I suppose I shared as few of your friends as you did of mine. And even those few we often shared uncomfortably.

"I never see why you like the men you like," you said once.

"Why?"

"They're all such . . . brutes."

"It's not so much that I like them. They like me. I've never gone out with anyone for long who didn't bring me some sort of dead animal as an offering. You inspire poems and songs; Monk gets diamonds; I'm brought home the kill."

"How awful! What do you do?"

"I pluck, skin, clean, and cook—with wine."

There's a picture here of the small octopus Andy brought me straight out of the Mediterranean Sea, not quite dead, still winding itself down his spear. Brute? No, Andy was not a brute, as far as I knew. He had, along with his intelligence, which you did admire, simple masculine vanities and appetites, attractive enough in so extremely attractive a man. I have always been drawn to good looks in men, something quite beneath your understanding. You were serious in all your relationships. I was not. If Andrew Belshaw was a brute, I had no intention of discovering it.

And you were patient, too, which often made me impatient with you. I was ready to make a soap opera out of Monk's problems: "Will the history instructor, Richard Dick, finally leave his wife and three children for his beautiful Ramona?" "Will Ramona Ridley throw over Dick Dick for the handsome social worker who interviewed her after her brother was booked on a narcotics charge?" "Will Ramona Ridley sacrifice all her loves for a career?"

"But it's serious, Kate. A number of people are involved. Monk doesn't want to be unethical. That's very important to her."

"Then she should take her red curls to the back row and stop raising questions about historical inevitability."

"But she may be in love with him, and if she is, isn't that the highest ethic?"

You would still think so, I imagine, but I argued that, since Monk didn't know how she felt, ethics had very little to do with it.

"But it isn't all that easy to tell. He says she'll simply have to go to bed with him to find out, which is out of the question if she can't feel committed. It would just be adultery then."

"It would be adultery anyway."

5

"Well, and the other thing is that Monk really feels she's got to live a little first."

"And what does she mean by that?"

"Work, try for the stage. It's pretty sheltered if you're going to move right from college and your parents' health insurance policy to someone else's without ever taking care of yourself at all."

"Ramona Ridley faces life with her own health insurance policy."

"But you know what I mean, Kate."

Yes, in those days at college I almost always did know, but your truthfulness, which I called oversimplification, sometimes embarrassed me. I was not prepared to reduce ethics to practical decisions. I had a personal investment in maintaining the gap. Perhaps I still do. And so I would gesture to the typewriter set up on the sleeping porch waiting for the last paragraphs of a paper on seventeenth-century prose or to the typewriter set up in the study with, as yet, nothing but the title, "The Metaphysical Necessity of Incarnation," typed across the top of the page.

"You're getting at that early. I haven't even finished reading Whitehead for mine on symbolism. But I have an angle for it. I want to talk about symbol as analogous experience."

"Misleading. Hocking says God is first known through sensation in nature. Now, if you approach that as analogy . . ."

Sometimes you were reluctant because you hadn't thought enough and didn't want so tentative an idea taken from you. The trouble was that you had to argue not only for analogy but by means of it, something I always mistrusted, moving as I do directly from fact to abstraction.

"It's all your poetic clutter," I would protest.

"And you don't care how any of it applies."

"All right, you apply it to . . . let's see . . . health insurance policies."

"Everything's relative. . . ."

"Relevant."

"That too," you would agree. "You never get caught up in it, do you?"

"Caught up in what?"

"Believing before you think."

You were so terribly loyal, translating my unkind satire into good judgment, my bad temper into righteous indignation, my defensive arrogance into natural superiority. I won all our arguments in those days, didn't I? I won our chess games, too, played in the spring sun at the college shop where everyone could see us, a motive you would have admitted freely. Not I. For you there was a romance about scholarship which permitted gestures and poses. You called us, in all seriousness, "Artists," "Intellectuals," "Young Saints." So I wrote you *Portrait of the Artist as a Young Bitch* and dedicated it to "little dog." Instead of being irritated, you illustrated it, illuminated it, and claimed it would one day be a collector's item. Now it is. I have put it on the shelf by the Milton.

In that green enclosure of young women, ungenerously supported by parents who wanted to preserve our virginity and their sanity a while longer, where only a few dozen concerned themselves at all with what you quite unself-consciously called "the life of the mind," you modeled our friendship in so lofty and extravagant a vocabulary that no responsible person could have been suspicious. There is, at a women's college, always some emancipating encouragement for those with masculine tastes for such things as mathematics, philosophy, and friendship. You had to model it. I could not. I knew better, which forced me to be occasionally condescending, protective, inadequate. But I don't want to confess to all these things. I want, rather, to describe them.

What, after all, did I know when I was seventeen and you were eighteen? Perhaps quite a lot. I knew what was right, and I knew I wanted to be right, and I knew I could not. Things irreconcilable have to be separated. I envied the flatworm its ability to be

7

cut in half and grow itself two new selves. I should have liked to do just that. Since I could not, I came upon a way to cut my life in half. Not quite, for winter, whatever the weather, is longer than summer. I wintered in California in the mild, academic climate with you. I went to Europe in the summer for a very different sort of life, which I never spoke of, from which I only gradually recovered each fall in your company and in work. But I had a recurring nightmare that a path through a narrow wood and across a shallow stream was all that separated those two worlds. And in that dream you were always about to discover it.

"Mother says I can go to Europe this summer if I can go with you. . . ."

"Is that a condition?"

"Yes," you said with such confidence that for the moment I could find no way to say that it would be inconvenient for me.

There never was a moment for saying so. All that spring while you planned our summer, I unplanned my own. It was not easy. But I didn't know, until we had actually set out, that it would be impossible.

Parts of that trip have become such set pieces over the years that it's hard to recall actually living through them. The humor was added after the fact, like salt at the table for those who must eat. I do remember clearly, because I haven't told it over and over again, the real beginning—lunch with your mother in a palm-infested hotel dining room in New York.

"You must have some idea how long you'll be away. You must have some itinerary."

"We're thinking of bicycling down the Nile in August," you said.

Seeing you there, opposite your mother, sulking in the city elegance she chose naturally for herself and unnaturally for you, I understood why you could have believed yourself to be an ugly little girl with too small a head for the heaviness of feature and hair, hands and feet too large for the slight body.

"You must promise me you won't go to Egypt."

"It's against my principles to promise. You have to learn to trust."

"Katherine, will you promise me?" she asked, turning to me in charming distress.

"That's not fair, Mother!"

"To a mother, there are things more important than being fair. You'd promise your mother if she asked, wouldn't you, Katherine?"

"She wouldn't ask," I answered honestly.

My mother—my adopted mother, old enough to be my grandmother—knew too little about the world to discover the promises to exact. In fairness, you and I should have traded guardians to pair innocence and appetite. Your mother suspected a great deal you were incapable of. Mine imagined a simplicity only you were capable of. But I did not want to trade.

"You are not a Jew," she said to me.

"Neither am I," you said, "and neither are you, except for the paranoia."

"Don't you understand that I'm concerned for your safety?"

Jason was there, too, the first of the arrogant, delicate boys who always attracted you. I can't remember that he did anything but blot the mayonnaise on his tender beard. It was Saul's arrival that did not so much break the tension as shift it.

"Have you had lunch, darling?" Mrs. Woolf asked, in a doubled mother's voice.

"Yep." He stood, refusing to give space to a branch of palm that crossed his brow like an awkward salute, his hands hanging loose, folders climbing out of his jacket pockets to his arm pits.

"Where have you been?"

"To the Cloisters."

"I love the Cloisters," you said, regretfully.

"Doing what?"

"Feeding peanuts to the unicorns," Saul answered, slumping into the chair a waiter had brought.

"I thought unicorns ate nothing but virgins," I said.

9

"That's why unicorns are starving in New York," Saul answered with pure, fourteen-year-old cynicism.

"Did you buy any prints?" you asked.

"Two, a little one for you and a big one for me. I don't know about taking unicorns to Britain, like coals to Newcastle maybe." Saul shrugged and began to sprinkle salt on the table in front of him.

"You're so nervous, darling."

"It's my Oedipus complex."

It was time then to feel sorry for your mother. She had two such unsuitable children, no matter how interesting. And, say what you like about the persecution of children by parents, the parents are finally the victims. They are not expected to rebel, even though they are the dominated ones for the real length of most parent-child relationships. Your mother was at the beginning of that domination, and no one had taught her any handsome or generous way to suffer. She has since learned a lot.

During that meeting, for all her failure with you, she did succeed in adding weight to the burden of responsibility I already felt. Why, with you, did I always feel responsible? You were a year older than I (that year we were nineteen and twenty), and you were neither stupid nor reckless. Impractical, yes, and trusting.

I keep speaking of your qualities as if I were writing a letter of recommendation. But people did—and probably still do—misunderstand you. Or at least they misunderstood what you have done and are doing. I should not pretend to be any different from the others. It is not that I have superior insight. It is not even that I have cared more. Simply, I was more important than the others to you, failed you in ways you could rationalize, an ability which may be one basis for a lasting friendship.

I have wondered what might have happened if you had not, from the first day we met, placed me on so high a pedestal that I couldn't get down. You were not entirely to blame. I often liked it up there, and, when I didn't, all I had to do was to move to the edge to see what a long way I had to fall. For you, I was not alone. Over the years, you had quite a number of us, self-conscious heroes and heroines, disdainful of each other's stances in your garden of honor. Jason was the first I met that day at lunch, and, if I was not impressed with his mayonnaise-threatened beard, he was as unresponsive to my raw-boned, bird-eyed suspiciousness. Your friends usually didn't like each other because embarrassment is not an interest to be shared.

If I had been a little older, a little less frightened, I might at least have been able to sit down, let my feet dangle over the edge, send you a rueful whistle through my teeth, and then say, little dog, listen. What I had to confess was no more than ordinarily grotesque. That was the trouble for me. I suffered so uncommonly from such common fears.

When you spoke of being called a Jew for nothing more than a last name and a dark complexion, guilty with wanting to reject a label which did not identify you, why did I listen in such superior, if also sympathetic, silence? I had my own stories to tell, being the illegitimate child of an Indian woman and a white man, a half-breed, adopted by an Episcopal minister and his wife who had already raised their own daughter. As a child, I was never called an Indian, a half-breed, or any of the variety of crude, colloquial terms every region has for its natives. My background was never mentioned to me by my adopted parents on the theory that I was to be made to feel no separation from them. And I half forgot it myself, growing up in the world given me. If I could have said to you, we suffer from opposite uncertainties, opposite guilts, I would have said it; but that was not really true. Yours was essentially a religious problem, no matter how else it was presented to you from the outside as a question of racial identity, integrity, courage. I believed you could establish your innocence, your freedom to choose. You wanted to. You did not secretly cherish the suffering you felt false heir to. I did.

And you talked with candor about your ugliness. Mildly, you envied Monk her sexual trials in parked cars, though, in those

11

days, you believed in the old-fashioned romance of giving yourself once, wholly, to someone wholly chosen. Perhaps accepting ugliness is the beginning of beauty. Monk never was given the opportunity, limited from the age of fifteen by prizes from beauty contests, fulfilling the myth that the American female now skips the awkward age. You were old-fashioned, suffering the sexual change which at first coarsens the features, corrupts the skin, violates the appetite, and finally establishes a humility which the spirit struggles with long after the body has survived. And you were further protected—or discriminated against—because you were born into a culture that does not recognize your kind of beauty, can be suspicious of it, even occasionally repelled. Only once before you were twenty was your ugliness clearly denied.

You had been working in the sculpture studio on one of those unconsciously comic female thinkers which in those days obsessed you when the instructor, an impatient middle European, suddenly shouted, "Always swollen heads and fallen tits! Why? Have you no mirror, Cleopatra? Look at *yourself*. See what a woman is!"

You told me about it with his accent and his gestures.

"It is the high breasts," shaking your own fists at your collar bones, "the small head for beauty," turning your chin as if with his hand. "Egypt."

You paused then, looking at yourself doubtfully in the long mirror on my closet door.

"Kate, I couldn't possibly be beautiful."

Standing there in blue jeans and one of Saul's old shirts, your dead father's watch hanging on your wrist, clay drying in the circles of your finger nails, you didn't believe him. What should I have said? I could not say anything, nor could I turn away, caught by what you couldn't see.

"Mirror, mirror on the wall," you chanted, "who's the fairest of them all? Not you, little dog."

It was a bad nickname, one only I used, having given it to you because you would walk just half a step behind me with a shorter stride, with a trot if I hurried. Like so much else that you could have found offensive, it amused you.

That night, after we had argued about art as imitation or incarnation, you giving in to the temptation of a Christian esthetic, I looked at myself in the same mirror, but did not ask the same question, not looking for your kind of answer. I liked my face well enough, its high cheekbones and strong nose, the dark, carefully remote eyes. I hardly noticed my body, instrument not object. "How am I to use myself? What am I to do?"

At college, where we had roommates and lectures to go to and papers to write, we could discuss your problems and ignore mine. Traveling, we had to encounter each other's difficulties, your vagueness and my obsession with details, your fear of most adults and my reluctance with strangers, your exhaustion and my restlessness. We had to encounter each other. And I had not wanted to.

I tried to explain my adopted sister and brother-in-law to you before we arrived in London; but, because they were old enough to be my parents, they were automatically your enemies, not in the real way they might have been, but simply dismissed into the dull world of authority and responsibility. Any man who went to the office, any woman who went shopping and dealt with servants and had her hair done could not possibly have anything to say to you. Frank, who is not easily offended, was the first man I saw suffer from your childishness. Doris was curious at first, then bewildered, but she never quite gave up. Last time I saw her, she asked about you. She said, when I told her what you'd done, "Well, He's the one grown-up Who will let her go on being a child." Doris, like so many children of ministers, had found having two fathers a bit much. I had more in common with you, having lost the only human father I knew when I was twelve, but I did not allow us to make common cause over that, either. Frank had been an unintrusive but willing substitute for official purposes. I think he was genuinely fond of me. It was gaining a second mother in Doris that was difficult. She was capable of being as suspicious as your mother, but she had never learned to be fearful. She invaded my privacy with more shrewd concern and indulgent affection than I could understand or handle. It might have been better for me if she had either never appeared or had been home more often.

Except for the war years, Doris visited Mother and me in the Bay Area once a year when Frank came to the States on business. She always brought me new novels and plays, and I did like discussing them with her, but I was as uneasy as I was flattered by the value she placed on my opinions, which were often based on experience she credited me with rather than experience I had had. With everyone else I had a more certain role.

In my last year in high school, I was captain of the debating team, captain of the swimming team, my top drawer rattling with medals for good attendance, good sportsmanship, good scholarship, good Godliness—a joy to my teachers and my elderly mother, a pain in the ass to my classmates, who were, just the same, never rude. I was at that time threatening to be a national swimming champion, which awed them a little and worried me a lot. I liked the prestige, but I hated racing. I was of two minds about entering a qualifying meet, but the coach, who had offered to take me to Carmel for it, persuaded my mother and Doris that I should go.

We drove down the afternoon before, checked in to a guest house my mother was fond of, walked on the beach for an hour, then went out for an early dinner. The town was full of Rotarians. At the third restaurant we tried, we finally agreed to wait an hour in the bar. When my age wasn't questioned and the coach suggested I have a cocktail, I agreed. Unlike you, I had always wanted to be an adult and was willing to make any of the appropriate gestures. Somehow we got into a friendly argument with four men at the next table. The coach was a Democrat; they were Republicans. That's how it seemed to me then, but, of course, the coach was also a young woman, healthily attractive as gym teachers are supposed to be. More drinks came, and more. We did finally eat, and our Rotarians delivered us to our guest house rather too noisily, shouting Republican slogans at our window long after they should have gone home.

I had not been drunk before, never having had the opportunity. I did not intend to be drunk then, and I was concerned about the noise we were making, troubled by the heavy uncertainty of my feet and tongue. My companion decided to take a bath. I was left with the complicated task of undressing myself. It must have taken me a long time. Finally I stood at the basin, thinking of brushing my teeth, washing my face, then trying to find my pajamas. As I stood there, a glass on the shelf fell into the basin and smashed. There were four glasses, and one by one they all fell while I stood watching. It seemed to me incredibly sad that every one should break. I began to cry. Perhaps her embrace began as a gesture of comfort. I was not surprised by it, nor by being put to bed. I was surprised by what she was saying, words I had read on fences and in literature but had never heard pronounced before.

"That's what they say: give a little clootch whiskey, and what you've got is nothing but a piece of fucking tail, a little redskin cunt."

I listened, so close to unconsciousness that it was easier to seem so than to sort out the appropriate response. I wanted to solve the problem about the broken glasses and I wanted to be sure the Rotarians had really gone home and I wanted to listen for stress, for accurate pronunciation just as I did in German class, and I wanted to go on trying to feel what I had begun to feel. The glasses began to fall again, but slowly this time, and they broke slowly in showers of light.

"Don't cry. Don't cry. It's nothing to cry about."

The next morning we did not discuss anything that had happened the night before. We agreed that breakfast was not a good idea. I had to swim at ten o'clock; we'd eat afterwards. It did not occur to me to refuse to swim. It was important to behave as if nothing unusual had happened.

I could not make myself go into the pool to warm up. I stood in my dry suit, my feet and hands blue in the warm morning sun, waiting to be forced by the gun. Only after I hit the water did I discover that it was salt. I swam eight lengths of the pool, my teeth clenched against my rebelling guts, touched in, lifted myself half out of the pool, and vomited with fountain force to the cheering crowd. It is the only record I have ever set. I never swam in a race again. If that had been the humiliating end of it, I would have felt punished enough for my sins, but we had a three-hour drive home after that, and the lead item on the sports page the next day would be NEW NATIONAL RECORD SET under a picture of me retching up the whole of the night before.

" 'Flu," the coach said to my mother and Doris, delivering me into their hands, but just half an hour before we arrived, she had persuaded me to try the only cure she knew, a little hair of the dog; and, as Doris held my protesting head fifteen minutes after I got home, she said, " 'Flu, my foot. You're drunk." I was too busy proving it to deny it.

Then she sat on the bed, wiping my face with a cool wash cloth, smiling and shaking her head, talking to me. "So, okay, how long has this been going on?" She didn't expect any answer, and she didn't get one, but she had a captive audience and enjoyed it, imagining both my fears and my sins in exaggerated generalities which were, nevertheless, alarmingly accurate. I have never told Doris anything. She always tells what I'm up to. And, if she's troubled by her imagination, she never admits it.

But you weren't aware of Doris at all, except as she was one of the authorities to be placated with childish good manners. You stood when she came into the room with the memory of a curtsy stammering in your knees, made any request with an apologetic preface, answered any direct question as if you had been called on to recite. Frank suffered from your behavior even more than Doris. In your hands his good manners turned into willful attacks on your independence. He found himself at the brink of a real argument over carrying your suitcase. You would not go through a door before him, a problem he finally solved by forcibly taking your arm and escorting you through. His tactful compliments were received with such surprise and suspicion that he gradually gave up any attempt to talk with you. Then he felt rude in his own house, uneasy. If you had been twelve, he would have known what to do. He would perhaps have taken on your instruction as he had his own daughter's, and to some extent mine. But you were twenty and now so close to being a woman that it was impossible to treat you like the child you also were.

"E.," I suggested finally, "why don't you relax with Frank and Doris? Try to get to know them a little bit."

"Why?" you asked, surprised.

"Because they're human beings. You might even find you like them."

"I do like them, Kate," you protested. "It's just that we don't have anything in common."

"Don't be silly," I said. "Find things in common. Take some interest in what they care about."

"What do they care about?"

Put that way, the question had no real answer. For you there was one source of identity, the measure of commitment one had to people and ideas, out of which should come the work one did. Neither Doris nor Frank was put together so tidily. Frank was a successful but not dedicated banker, a theoretical liberal who took his conservative social responsibilities seriously. He had a wine cellar, a rose garden, season tickets to chamber music concerts, a wife and two children, perhaps occasionally a mistress, but certainly not in London. About most of these subjects he was pleased to speak briefly, and he was also interested in listening, but obsession with anything was for him a breach of good taste. In your terms, therefore, he cared about nothing. Doris was even

17

more difficult to identify. The measure of her efficiency in any job was the measure of her boredom with it. What she enjoyed, she dawdled over and rarely finished, part of her pleasure being the freedom to be inaccurate and incomplete. There was never an error in her household books, but often flower arrangements waited for their final greenery until blooms were falling on the carpet. She made a similar division between people, careful and exacting of her own kindness with those to whom she was bound by nothing but duty, casual and sometimes wittily critical of the friends she chose and obviously loved. Even if you had been able to distinguish this pattern, you would have judged it shallowly perverse and missed the point, at least the human point. I could not answer your question; however, you heard my complaint and wanted to please me.

"Doris," you began the next night at the dinner table, forcing yourself to call her by her first name, "how long does it take to have a baby?"

Frank looked up surprised.

"Why," Doris said carefully, "nine months."

"No, I know that. I don't mean that. I mean really how long, how long out of a life, two years? Five years?"

"That depends, doesn't it?"

"But on what?" you persisted.

"On how much money you have, on how much of a mother you want to be, on what kind of a life you mean to interrupt."

"But it's no good having a child physically, just that, is it? That isn't what people mean when they talk about being fulfilled as a woman. You'd want to know your child. How long does it take to know your child?"

"It depends on the child," Frank offered, sensing the opportunity you were offering, no matter how grossly. "How long did it take your mother to know you?"

"She doesn't," you answered. "And she's never tried. She spends all her time trying to turn me into someone she'd like to know. So I have no measuring stick. How long did it take you?"

"With my son," Frank answered, "I think I sin as your mother does. With my daughter . . . well, what man would dare to claim he understood a woman, even a very young one?"

"But that's stupid," you said. "Women are people. You could certainly understand me."

"Surely, what Esther wants to know is how much time there's left for being something other than a mother," Doris said quickly.

"Yes," you said. "You see, first of all I want to understand the nature of the world. Then I want to marry and have a child to fulfill myself as a woman. After that I want to be a sculptor, a great sculptor. When I'm old, I'll join a contemplative order of some kind to serve God. I have to figure out the number of years each thing will take."

"I see," Doris said. "Well, I'd say five for the child, wouldn't you, dear?"

"Five or six at the most," Frank answered.

I was tempted to share their stifled hilarity because you were ridiculous, sitting there outlining your life, but I was also tempted to believe that you might, in your willful innocence, actually keep destiny in your own hands. There was about you such insensitive integrity.

After dinner, when you had gone to your room to write letters, I sat with Frank for a while.

"She thinks of herself as an emerging nation, as in need of five-year plans as India or Russia," he said.

"She has a lot of natural resources to develop," I said.

"True. But I don't see any place in her plan for a course in investments. Does she know that one day she's going to be one of the richest women in America?"

"I don't know. I didn't."

"I can't help knowing," he said. "Be careful of her, Kate, won't you?"

19

"How . . . careful?"

"I don't mean anything personal. It's just that she wants so much and doesn't know what she already has to offer."

I couldn't be with you every moment. I didn't want to be. There were other people to see. If I left you alone for a few hours, I never knew what you would find and bring back. Sometimes it was only a first edition or a seventeenth-century amber ring (which I wouldn't accept then, and, of course, have now), but more often it was a young composer or painter or actor, awed and irritated by the ample comfort of Doris' and Frank's living, fortunately unaware of how modest it was compared to your own. But for all the irritations of those first weeks, I was more independent of you in London than I could be once we left for the Continent, and there were the selling galleries to discover together, the late Turners at the Tate, the good arguments about T. S. Eliot and Christopher Fry. If the summer had gone on like that, I might have been able to cope.

Why was it that we decided to bicycle? I had never been enthusiastic, though I'd taken a couple of bicycling trips in southern England two summers before. It was probably your idea. I didn't find out until we were trying to get our new bicycles from one side of London to the other that you hadn't been on one since you were twelve. I was ready to leave them with Frank and Doris, but you insisted that you would practice in the three days we had left. Off down the crescent you'd wobble, dressed in blue jean pedal pushers, pale blue windbreaker, and white baseball cap, your dark hair more horse's mane than pony tail, vanishing between double decker buses.

"Don't watch," Doris said kindly, as I stood on the drawing room balcony.

"It's a sick fascination."

"You worry too much. I've never seen you so motherly."

"She's such an idiot," I said. "Who do you suppose she'll find to bring home today?"

"You don't have to be jealous of her young men. They're all homosexuals."

"Do you think so?"

"Yes, blatant or latent. It's hard on Frank. He finds her very attractive. 'What a waste!' he keeps saying. Are you serious about her, Kate?"

"It's nothing like that. In any case, I'm never serious about people."

"She's rather remarkably beautiful."

"Or ugly," I said.

By the morning we were to leave, you claimed to be able to ride with no hands through the traffic at Hyde Park Corner, which, even in those days, was terrible. We planned to leave a lot of our belongings with Frank and Doris, either to be shipped to us later or to be collected on our way home. Clothes never mattered to you anyway, unless they had about them the character of costume. I remember the first time you wore your academic gown at the Freshman assembly.

"Gosh, this is the life of the mind, all right. I really feel it, and I want to feel it all the time. In England, students do, don't they?"

"Feel the life of the mind all the time?" I asked.

"Wear gowns."

"They were monks once, too," I said.

"And thinking ought to be holy," you decided. "Or reverent. I wish I had a religious vocabulary. What's the difference between holy and reverent?"

" 'Holy' comes from the same root as 'whole'; taken over by the church, it means coming from God, therefore pure or sinless. To be reverent is to be loving and respectful at once. I don't know how I could think about history or philosophy, for instance, if I had to think like that."

"But you do think like that, Kate. Maybe I should be a Christian. Do you think I could be?"

"The vocabulary's free in any dictionary."

"But to have it mean something . . ."

"Well, save religious box tops and see."

As I inspected your double pack that morning in London, I thought perhaps you had taken my advice. There were pamphlets and postcards, deer antlers and junk jewelry, books and notebooks, all packed round with Kotex and toilet paper, emblems of one of your shynesses.

"But, little dog, you have to take some clothes."

"I was going to," you said, "but there isn't room. I can tie my coat onto the back."

The performance that followed reminded me of Fish, a card game I played as a child. "I have two pairs of shoes," I would say, and you'd answer, "I have none." You would have liked to add, "Go fish!" But I changed the rules. Out of your pack would have to come the antlers, into it the required shoes. In the end, this long-disputed first edition of Milton was the only thing I allowed you to take because you insisted that you needed it. One of your summer projects was to memorize the whole of *Paradise Lost*. I never heard anything beyond the first book, but I can hear that still:

> Of Man's First Disobedience, and the Fruit
> Of that Forbidden Tree, whose mortal taste
> Brought Death into the World, and all our woe . . . .

Through summer France you chanted:

> Is this the Region, this the Soil, the Clime,
> Said then the lost Arch-Angel, this the seat
> That we must change for Heav'n, this mournful gloom
> For that celestial light?

I woke to:

22

                    . . . from Morn
to Noon he fell, from Noon to dewy Eve,
A Summer's day; and with the setting Sun
Dropt from the Zenith like a falling Star . . .

and slept to:

For Spirits when they please
Can either Sex assume, or both; so soft
And uncompounded is their Essence pure . . .
And works of love or enmity fulfill.

At times I regretted not letting you take the antlers instead; you
couldn't have done much but wear them to anticipate your
Oberon period when you gave all creatures horns. But there are
worse things to live with than Book I of *Paradise Lost*. And
worse things we did discover.

The hazards of bicycling were not really among them. We
rode only to Victoria Station. Finding ourselves in Dieppe at
dusk, we hitchhiked to Rouen on a truck delivering toilets to farm
houses. We took a train from Rouen to Paris where you sold your
bicycle to a redheaded American boy. I stored mine. Years later I
gave it away to a young woman who didn't really look very
much like you.

And I have told that story too often, the last time to your
mother in a taxi after Monk's wedding to keep her from other
kinds of discussion about you. She laughed a great deal, if uncertainly. That's enough. This is not intended to be a 1950s version
of *Innocents Abroad*.

We were intent on silly pilgrimages. Fortunately, in search of
Rodin you also found Henry Moore. On the trail of Alice B.
Toklas, we learned to eat snails and read Henry Miller. It was a
summer of Henrys until we set out for Valla de Mosa to find
George Sands and Chopin, encountering instead Andrew Belshaw
and Peter Jackson on a train stalled between the French border

23

and Barcelona. We had been on our way all night, you very cheerful at first, trading sandwiches and jokes with five railroad workers who shared our third-class carriage, accepting lessons in drinking from their goat skin flasks; but, when morning came and you found yourself stained with red wine, a little sick with indigestible good fellowship and no sleep, you were simply miserable. The train stopped, and there was nothing to see but the flat heat of a flat landscape through the dirty train window. You were near tears, I near speaking my now almost constant irritation, but I suggested the dining car as a distraction for us both. Officials stood along the tracks on the shady side of the train, smoking cigarettes, obviously in no hurry to solve whatever the problem was. We climbed over armed guards, slumped down over their knives, bayoneted rifles, and pistols, enjoying a short and uncomfortable sleep along the corridors. We climbed with other foreigners, all crowding to the dining car to complain. Only the Spaniards stayed in their places, slicing melon and cleaning their fingernails with pocket knives. There we found or were found by Andrew and Peter. It was the first time I was more enthusiastic about strangers than you. You sat by the window, sulking, just as Peter did on the other side of the aisle. Andrew offered me an American cigarette. We exchanged unpleasantries about the train, Spanish customs officials, Spanish beer.

"We're on our way to Mallorca," Andrew explained. "I hope to hell we get to Barcelona in time to make the nine o'clock boat."

"We are, too," I said, "but we'd been thinking about staying a day or two in Barcelona."

"Why, in this heat?"

"Just to look around."

"Have you got an address for Mallorca?"

I did not want to admit that we were on our way to Valla de Mosa. I didn't even know that it was a place to stay. "No, not really."

"Because I've got a good one, out of town, cheap, right by the sea. Would you like it?"

24

"It sounds like just what we're looking for."

You were taking no interest in the conversation; Peter's silence was more hostile than indifferent. In these moods, you were both as responsible as Andrew for convincing me that it was a good idea. I wanted to be relieved of our isolation, of your devotion and dependence, your soaring and tumbling moods; but I also felt guilty. Because Andrew was not the person I would have ordered, because Peter seemed as difficult for him as you were for me, the solution had enough discomfort in it to be acceptable. While we were in the dining car, the train began to move again. Before we returned to our own compartments, we agreed to meet on the platform at Barcelona to decide what we would do.

"I thought you said we were going to Valla de Mosa," you said, lurching along the corridor behind me.

"We still can. We haven't decided anything."

"But you want to go with them, don't you?"

"It sounded like a good place, that's all."

"I don't think that one guy was so keen on having us along. And he's the one who seemed nice."

"What is it about you that makes good looks and decent manners so repellent to you?"

"They scare me," you said bleakly.

But arriving in Barcelona and walking down to the square where Columbus looks so intently out over the wrong sea revived you. We sat with the boys at a sidewalk café, drinking brandy and eating popcorn, unable to talk sensibly against the songs, threats, dances and fights of two dozen beggar children for whom we were the most likely carrion in the neighborhood. You had not seen beggars before and in your distress encouraged them with small change against Andrew's advice. Their number doubled; their anger increased. Two waiters beat them off a dozen yards. Cowed but still insolent, they jeered at us across the forbidden space.

"I can't stand this any longer," Peter said suddenly. "Let's get aboard ship."

"Before dinner?" Andrew asked.

"We can eat on board."

Without ever actually having decided to go with them, we went. Standing on deck, looking back at the square and the children, I heard Peter say to you, "Why do they have to be ugly with our greed? Why can't we suffer for our own sins?"

"I don't know," you said. "I've never even thought about it."

"Don't then," Peter said, stepping away from the railing. "Let's look at the sea, instead."

As you crossed to the other side of the deck, I felt Andrew beside me relax.

"I'm glad you decided to come along," he said.

He was still watching the children when I turned to answer him. There was hardness in his face, but it seemed to me in conflict with a stronger, less certain gentleness. Aware that I was looking at him, he smiled.

"It's hard to have no decent answer," I said.

"It certainly is, and that could be the slogan of my life."

A rough sea and the smell of rancid oil discouraged our appetites. Rain made the deck uncomfortable. We were very tired from sitting up all the night before and so decided to go to bed. I wonder now why we all so unquestioningly always traveled third class. You and I had plenty of money to travel comfortably. Andrew, as it turned out, was the son of an oil-rich Albertan who provided all his children with handsome allowances. Only Peter, living on the G.I. Bill in Paris and scrounging for painting materials, had any reason for such economy. Andrew would have explained it in one of his terrible lapses into sociological jargon as "dedication to peer group values," I suppose. We were students and therefore traveled like students. That night you and I found ourselves in adjacent upper berths in a cabin for a dozen women. I was too tired to object to the sour smelling straw mattress, the heat or the noise. I lay down in my clothes and was asleep at once, but several times in the night I woke to the retching of an unhappy traveler. And once I saw that several men had invaded the cabin and were dressing themselves in the underwear of women who had bothered to get undressed. I slept again without reaction. I had even forgotten that you slept just across the gulf of aisle. It was not until morning that I realized you had been sick in the night.

We found our way up into the air and stood gray-faced in the gray morning, staring out at the line of shore which was Mallorca.

"Doesn't look very promising," Andrew said, appearing beside us. "I've just heard that we've been through the worst storm in ten years. It's supposed to start clearing at noon."

Peter had obviously had no better a night than you. The pallor he always had was luminous that morning, and he shook a little under his thin jacket though it was not really cold. But he seemed easier with Andrew as well as with us. He was the only one who had been to Mallorca before, and his confident anticipation reassured us.

The streets of Palma were shallow streams of mud, and Peter's friend who was to get him black-market money and cigarettes had left the island, and the bus we got on to take us to the north coast of the island bogged down twice in water holes. We all had to get out, help unload the heavier luggage, trunks, crates of live chickens, a bass fiddle, wade out of the mud to higher ground, back again to push, reload, and climb back to sit, wet and filthy on hard benches. It took over five hours to cover the few miles up over the mountain and north to the inland town of San Telmo which was as far as we could go by public transportation. We had been told we could get a taxi to take us from there back over the coastal hills to the village which was our destination. But there was no taxi. We walked the last four miles, grateful to have nothing but our bicycle packs to carry. The sky had cleared, and already, under the intense sun, the road surface had dried to dust. We passed tiny, slow-moving burros loaded with wood, then rested on large rocks and watched them pass us. Peter found a harmonica in his pocket, which he was soon teaching you to play.

We arrived at the hotel about seven o'clock in the evening to find that it was, truly, on the sea. Waves broke against its rock foundations, and the terrace hung out over the sea like a deck. We were greeted with enthusiasm by the owner and his wife. We were the only guests in the hotel and therefore chose our rooms among the twelve available. Somehow our simple luggage was scrambled, mine with Andrew's, yours with Peter's. No one joked about it. Peter returned mine and claimed his own.

When we discovered that there was no water for bathing, we changed into our suits immediately and went to the beach. It was a clear, warm evening, but the sea was still rough with the storm we had traveled through. We played hard in the surf, returned to the beach more scratched and bruised than we intended. You or Peter began to build a sand castle which we were to rebuild almost every day with greater elaborateness. At last you could be a child. We were all as intent and as isolated from each other as children. And we did not return to the hotel until we were called from play like children. It was eleven o'clock at night when we sat down to an eight-course dinner, the first real meal we'd had in two days. Immediately afterwards we went to our rooms.

You and I tried to write letters, but our lamp sputtered against a sea wind that blew even through closed shutters; so we turned it out, opened the window to the sound of the sea and lay down. Almost at once I also heard the sound of someone crying.

"E.?" I said quietly.

"I think it's Peter," you answered.

"Why?"

"I don't know," you said.

We listened again, but the crying had stopped or had been taken in to the sound of the sea.

"I feel guilty to feel so happy," you said. "Are you glad we came?"

"I think so," I said. "Yes."

"Thank you for being patient with me. . . ."

"E.," I said, "don't . . ."

"I know. I just mean . . . thanks."

28

By the time we arrived on the terrace the next morning, Andrew and Peter had finished a breakfast of tea and dry toast.

"Kate, what is 'flush' in Spanish?" Andrew asked.

I shook my head.

"Or in French?"

" '*La toilette ne march pas*' will do," Peter said. "The point is that they just don't want to understand. I've already given an imitation of a toilet flushing that would have gotten me into RADA. They don't want us to use the water."

"Why?" you asked.

"Because it's the dry season. They have to have it hauled over the mountain."

"All right," Andrew said. "We'll pay to have it hauled over the mountain," and he went back into the kitchen to see if he could make the necessary arrangements.

"The tycoon," Peter said, but not unkindly. "All I want is a boat, and I think I've got one. Look."

We followed him to the edge of the terrace and looked down at a small row boat, moored in a rock pool just beyond the steps.

"I've got one spear gun, one mask, one pair of flippers, but we can take turns if you're interested."

We were interested, you because there was no new skill you did not want to acquire, having taken your progressive school education seriously, I because I knew I would be good at it.

"Good news," Andrew said, coming back with a breakfast tray for us. "For the enormous sum of twenty cents a day, we can have working toilets and baths. I've told them to put it on my bill."

"No," you said. "Five cents apiece."

"Oh Esther, please—" he said.

"Five cents apiece," you insisted.

"Don't argue with her, Andy," Peter said. "It's a good point. Now get on with your breakfast and let's try the boat."

Andrew did not like being crossed, but he shrugged off his irritation. I was sorry. It seemed to me stupid to make an issue of so simple a generosity. But the simple was always what mattered to you.

"Dailiness, the Eternal Now Moment," you would argue to defend yourself against my exasperation.

No vocabulary obscured the fact that your primitive sense of fairness came directly from nursery school.

"Oh grow up, E.," was my standard retort, but you never did.

Peter, who unlike Andrew had his hands full protecting himself, found your odd little assertions of independence reassuring. He never really encouraged the attention you increasingly gave him, but he accepted your company as he never accepted mine. He gave you a sketching pad and took you with him several mornings when he rowed out to a small island in the bay. Andrew and I encouraged these expeditions not because we wanted to be together but because we wanted to be away from each of you. Often we exchanged no more than a few words after you left, then sat in companionable silence reading, writing letters, or simply watching the sea. Occasionally Andrew suggested a walk, but more often we waited for you both to come back before we did anything. For as much as we liked the relief of those mornings, we missed the enthusiasm you and Peter brought to any project. Peter was physically frail, obviously often not feeling well, though he never spoke of it, but often he had enormous energy, too. Climbing a steep hill, the rest of us fell silent, but Peter almost always sang or played his harmonica or recited patriotic speeches or made up poems of encouragement for us. At the top, he'd hurl himself to the ground in comic exaggeration of his breathlessness, but, while we rested, he could never sit still. He was finding rocks and flowers, exclaiming over the shapes of clouds. Occasionally he would begin to dance, awkward and serious, stop suddenly, squint at us, and then begin to laugh.

"Don't play the fool," Andrew would say, a little uneasily.

"Esther, let's make ourselves caps with bells on so that people won't mistake us for our serious friends."

And you would join him in inventions, sometimes no more than pure mime, sometimes elaborate with props, branches from the stunted bushes that grew out of rock, grass, flowers, the paper which you always carried. Once, in one of the strange, raised-stone graveyards, you played leapfrog tag together. Andrew and I were always audience to your demented innocence. But we were not very good at entertaining ourselves without you.

Andrew looked up from his book to watch you coming in from the island. Peter had handed you the oars, then wrapped himself in a blanket. He stood in the bow of the boat, playing "For Those in Peril on the Sea" on his harmonica. Then he gave the sign of the blessing and shouted, "Peace be with this hotel."

"They make me feel old," Andrew said, but like me he did not altogether dislike the feeling.

Peter's enthusiasms could be suddenly cut off by a complicated reticence which you accepted without question, but which obviously troubled Andrew, perhaps even angered him.

"Why is Andy so impatient with Pete?" you asked one night. "Pete admires him so much, and it hurts his feelings."

"It's when Pete goes quiet," I said.

"Well, he can't be sociable all the time."

"But sometimes he does it to get at Andy, don't you think?"

"Maybe," you said. "It's not a good sort of friendship. People shouldn't have to get at each other or explain anything. They should accept each other."

The next morning Peter suggested that we all go out to the island together to spearfish. Andrew was reluctant, but, when he saw that I wanted to go, he agreed. We anchored just south of the island in about thirty feet of water. Peter began to put on the fins and mask.

"Why don't you let one of the girls have the first go?" Andrew suggested quietly.

"You be the man of the family, darling," Peter said. "Just let me be myself."

In the moment afterwards, when no one spoke, Peter stood up and dived into the water, almost capsizing the boat. I was not honestly surprised, and for you nothing had really been revealed.

"Let's swim."

More carefully each one of us went over the side, and then we swam rather self-consciously together to the island. Peter stayed out beyond the boat for a while, but then he came over to us and very deliberately offered the equipment to me. I felt unreasonably angry with him, as critical as I might have been, perhaps was, of myself. I accepted the gun, the mask, the fins, each with careful politeness. I suppose I was responsible for the competitive mood that developed. I was the strongest swimmer of the four, but I knew nothing about spearfishing. It is so easy to misjudge distance and size in the reflecting clarity of that water. More or less by accident I caught the first fish. You did not want to be bested, were always willing to test yourself against whatever I had achieved, but you expected to lose, and losing always increased your admiration of your opponent rather than your uncertainty about yourself. Peter, on the other hand, needed to put me in my place, and he could not. When Andrew snagged a small octopus by mistake and brought it to me with mock ceremony, he was content, but Peter went down again and again until his lips were gray. It was time for lunch, but he would not stop.

"Pete, come on," Andrew shouted.

"I'm not hungry," he answered. "Go on in if you want to."

It did not seem sensible to leave him, but after a few minutes we swam back to the boat to wait. Finally Andrew decided we must go in to lunch. We had not eaten in five hours, and breakfast had been the usual tea and toast. Andrew shouted again and got no answer; so he pulled on the anchor. It was snagged in coral, thirty feet below. Each of us had a turn, but it would not budge.

"Pete, could you come give us a hand?" you called, and for you he came.

After we had all pulled together, the anchor seemed more firmly lodged than ever.

"We'd better go down the rope," I said.

"It's too deep," Andrew said.

"Why don't I try?" I said.

"I'll go down," Peter said and disappeared before anyone could protest.

He surfaced once, gasping, and went down again. We could see him, working his way down hand over hand on the rope. It was hard to judge whether he had reached the anchor or simply paused a few feet above it.

"I think he's in trouble," I said.

Andrew went down ahead of me, but he had not waited for breath and let go at twenty feet, Peter hanging in the water just five feet below him. I kept to the rope and, gripping it with one hand, reached an arm around Peter's waist. Then you were there, helping, and Andrew again. When we surfaced, Andrew rolled into the boat; and, while we lifted from the water, he pulled. Then Andrew had his mouth against Peter's, breathing his breath into Peter's lungs. I cut the anchor rope, and we were moving toward shore.

Peter began to breathe almost at once and was conscious and able to stand by the time we reached the shore. We took him down to his room, wrapped him in blankets and gave him some brandy. He slept most of the afternoon while we sat, Andrew reading with determination, you sketching, I trying to reason myself out of rage. I did not want to suffer either for or with Peter. I wanted to get out.

"Cocktail time," Peter said, standing at the top of the steps looking not much grayer than he always did.

We all turned to look at the vine that grew up over the wall and onto the roof of the hotel. The first moon flower was open. The second trembled suddenly; then the petals sprang wide and white. As each flower opened, giant hummingbird moths came across the terrace to hover about them. A moment later the owner of the hotel appeared with a tray of cocktails. It was a ritual we were now familiar with. As we sat drinking, the darkness closed in. There was no moon.

"How can I love you all?" Peter asked with quiet drama. "But I do . . . even you, Kate."

"We're going to eat the octopus," you said.

Andrew and I said nothing. I wondered if he felt as tempted to crude retort as I did, but I did not want to be even that curious.

I was reluctant the next morning when Andrew suggested that he and I walk into San Telmo for cigarettes. I was tired and wanted to be alone. But, if I had stayed, you would have kept me company.

Andrew and I started out briskly, but we hadn't reached the top of the first hill before he suggested a rest. We climbed onto a rock from which we could look down onto the bay and the hotel. We could even see you and Peter, sitting on the terrace.

"Kate, there are things I ought to explain," Andrew began.

"I don't much like explanations," I said.

"Why?"

"They diminish things so."

"There's nothing to diminish," he insisted. "There's nothing between Peter and me, at least as far as I'm concerned."

"How unfortunate for Peter," I said.

"And for me," he said. "I don't enjoy it. I didn't realize it until this trip. I didn't know him very well. We were drinking one night in Paris and just decided to go—very casually. It wasn't until the first night . . . I should have pulled out right then, but I didn't want to hurt him. Now, I don't know what to do. Sometimes it seems to be perfectly all right with him. Then it's just terrible. I get fed up. I think I'll leave, and then I'm afraid to leave him."

"So you asked us to join you."

"Yes, but not just because—"

"It's reason enough," I said.

"You don't like to be involved, do you?"

34

"I don't like being on the edgy edge of things like this, no."

"And Esther doesn't even know what's going on. She doesn't even see that Pete's indifferent to her."

"He's not, in the way she cares about," I said.

"But why would a woman . . . ?"

"Are you a little jealous?" I asked.

"Don't be silly," he said too quickly.

"All right, but let's go," I said, getting up.

"Wait a minute, Kate. Why do you always run away?"

"To keep from hurting people who aren't bright enough to protect themselves. I'm not interested—in the way you care about. It's a ridiculous situation for you, isn't it? But why do you choose two people like Peter and me?"

"Peter and you?" he asked. "You're not—you and Esther aren't—"

"No, Esther has nothing to do with it, except that she seems to have your talent for picking the wrong companions."

"I wish we could talk. I wish we could talk until I understood. I always pretend to, but I don't. It's as if I'm always into a conversation at the place where it ends. In two weeks I know practically nothing about you, and you don't know very much about me, either. We're a couple of strangers marooned with an issue. Why don't we ever really talk, Kate?"

But we didn't talk. He talked, first about his father, the kind of self-made man who must then make other people in his own image. Andrew was his only son, whose interests he both indulged and raged about. Languages, social anthropology, and painting were all so much bullock shitting nonsense. Andrew should be in engineering or at least in business school if he hadn't any real aptitude. In another five years he would be expected to take over the family millions.

"It's just my luck not to have a younger brother—better still to be a younger brother. Then I could be given to charity."

"Second sons go into the Army," I said.

"A third son then, assigned to killing off dragons in Alberta."

Andrew could not help sometimes suspecting his own rebellion, for it did not include giving up the family millions. He saw himself as something of a scholar, a traveler, a collector. He could live simply enough, as he did now and as he had when he stayed for a time in a monastery in India, but he could not have endured such a life if it were not a free choice. He wanted the freedom of money, and he wanted the power of money.

"There's something weak about a poor man, something distasteful."

In the next sentence he began to speak of Peter, at first with kindness but gradually with impatience.

"Will a man like that ever really paint, really accomplish anything? He's beginning to talk about leaving Paris, moving down here where it's really cheap to live. There are hundreds of people like him. They move from Paris to Spain. Pretty soon they run out of money even in Spain, go on to North Africa for a while to work on construction jobs, drift back to Spain again. Why does anyone choose to live like a victim? Why does a man want another man on top of him, Kate? I don't want to be a prude. I want to understand, but I just don't. I had a friend once in the Army. He wasn't anything like Pete. He was tough. There was nothing too tough for him, but he'd go down on his belly for any pansy he could find. He wanted to be humiliated. And that's what Pete wants. I can't stand it. It's different for a woman. It doesn't seem to me the same thing at all. Physical things are different."

" 'Jill goes down on her back,' " I said, but he didn't hear me.

He was discovering how he felt as he talked, and he was fascinated by his acceptance of natural inferiority. The sun was very hot, the floury dust too soft and deep for easy walking. Don't blame the Indian at the bootlegger's, the Negro with the switchblade, the Jew in his brother's pocket, the woman in her sister's bed. Morality is a luxury which only the Anglo-Saxon male can afford. Being able to afford it, he must buy it, judge others who can and don't, excuse the rest of the world with condescending kindness. But Andrew neither was nor felt that safe. The rich are also a persecuted minority, and the moral burden was heavy. The more difficult it grew to interrupt his monologue, the harder he found it to tolerate my silence. I could feel his growing frustration, but there was nothing I could say. I had to protect myself. It takes confidence to exchange confidences. Before the morning was over, it seemed to us both that it would never end.

Could all these remembered fragments explain to you now why it was that I left you there? I made no attempt to explain at the time.

"I want to go back to England in the morning."

"All right," you said.

"You want to go on to Madrid with the boys."

"You mean . . . without you?"

"With them," I said.

"All right."

"I have to go, E."

"Then you must."

And that was all. You were not a letter writer. I did not know how you were or where you were for the rest of the summer, but, when we met in the fall, nothing in your behavior ever suggested that I had done anything reprehensible. "People shouldn't have to explain anything. They should accept each other."

It was a bad winter for me, that last winter at college. I had lost my enthusiasm for philosophy, for the history of myth, for poetry. I wanted to go on studying, but I wanted to be involved in the present, to learn something useful about politics, economics. The system did not allow for so radical a change of mind. I had to go on discovering biblical footnotes for Donne's poems, Doppelgänger images from Zoroaster to Eliot, arguments for various transcendent realities which now seemed to me dully unreal.

If you hadn't begun to go to chapel with me that fall, I might not have gone myself. I wore that kind of piety with more and more discomfort. I didn't mind explaining the ritual to you, but discussions about the nature of belief troubled me. I wanted to turn away from all that, but it was as awkward to change one's Sunday habits as one's major in the last year at college. The chaplain often asked me to read, and the chaplain's wife expected me to help with coffee because I always had. When I was asked to give the student sermon that spring, I could think of no easy way to refuse.

"There's no point in being a nominal Christian," I said as we walked to class one morning after breakfast.

"No," you said, "but I suppose it's very hard to be more than that. It's a hard faith."

"Do you think so?" I was somehow surprised to hear you say it. "Are you going to join the Church, E.?"

"Someday. I hope so."

"I've been asked to give the student sermon just after spring vacation. I'd like you to be my reader."

"Could I?"

The word of God is certainly safer with you than with me, I wanted to answer, but I didn't. It would only have prompted admiring protests which were increasingly difficult to tolerate. Or was it simply having an audience to them that made me impatient? Monk was your almost constant companion that winter, and she found your devotion even more tedious than I did, perhaps because it was not directed at her. I did not particularly like Monk in those days. She seemed to me silly; yet often one of her quick remarks was either very shrewd or accidentally frightening. Even after all these years I am sometimes not sure with Monk. Then I never was. She would chatter about her professor, her social worker, and the lesser men in her life until you and I were so tired of that we could even welcome her taunting us about our own conversations.

"Let's have a little something pithy on the nature of existence, Kate," she'd suggest.

"That's a big question, Monk," you'd answer, protective of me or of her.

"And that's a big answer!" Monk would say. "Come on. Put

your minds to it. You see, I don't really believe this place really exists. It's just a series of slogans about education for womanhood or catastrophe or life, all of which amount to the same thing. But where's the world to live in? It's not here, is it?"

"It's not supposed to be," you said.

"Then what is it supposed to be?"

"A retreat, a place for study . . . whatever you make of it."

"A vacuum, but maybe a vacuum's real. You can't make anything out of it, but it can do something to you. It's done something to you, Kate, hasn't it?"

"Probably," I said, not about to be drawn into the conversation, but remembering "all is void, lucid, and self-illuminating."

"It's a nothing place with no answers. Am I going to wear a girdle tonight or not? Now what good is any education if it doesn't help a girl decide that?"

"You mean . . . as a chastity belt?" you asked.

"Isn't she quaint? And that's the truth; a quaint vocabulary so out of date it can't deal with moral problems past the fifteenth century. How can I talk about my 'virtue'?"

"How, indeed," I said.

"You're such a prude, Kate. Well, give me some prudish advice. Tell me what to wear tonight."

Before I could answer her flippancy in kind, I had to censor a sudden obscenity, and you, as usual, answered the question for me.

"Your girdle," you said. "After all, he's a married man with three children."

"But that's the barrel I'm over," she protested. "He can always just go home—" She must have caught my impatience because she shifted quickly. "And Whitehead doesn't talk about that. Plato does, of course, but he was a fairy, wasn't he?"

"Wear your diaphragm," I said.

"That's another thing I haven't got. They ought to be handed out like free milk at recess, but no—textbooks on all the positions, instead. Are you teasing me, Kate?"

39

"No. I think you ought to sleep with him because your not is beginning to be a bore."

"But, Kate, I thought you thought—" you began, but I had hailed another friend and was excusing myself.

"Isn't Kate a virgin, then?" I heard Monk ask as I walked away.

I should have been sympathetic with Monk's restlessness, suffering so badly from it myself. The rigid division I had made was breaking down, perhaps because I had had so little of the summer for myself, perhaps because I had so little to give to the work there was to be done. Often, as we sat together over coffee at the shop, I would lose track of the conversation between you and Monk and find myself watching two or three students who had not elected my careful circumspection. They were not attractive to me; neither was my need. I indulged it only in my imagination, hoping I was relatively safe, unrecognizable.

Watching, I was aware long before you were of the interest Sandra Mentchen (called "Honorable" occasionally, more often Sandy) had begun to take in you. It was casual enough at first, a nod, a brief exchange of conversation at our table before she moved to her own. She was a small, slight, intense girl, a musician who disciplined her talent and nothing else. In the first two years at college she was always in some kind of trouble, staying out all night or drinking in her room or failing her required English courses. And from the beginning there were rumors about sexual peculiarities. We had no reason to know her well because she took none of the courses we did and lived in another dormitory, but everyone knew her a little. Because you admired anyone with real gifts, you were flattered by the small attentions. Perhaps it was only part of the general tendency of seniors to be more of a group in their last spring. We all shared the pressure of comprehensive examinations and almost too immediate futures.

"Everybody's going to Europe," Monk said glumly.

"Everybody?"

"Well, aren't you? Isn't Esther?"

"Mother hasn't okayed Slade yet," you said, "and I haven't been accepted, anyway."

"But you will be, and Kate will get a Fulbright for the London School of Economics. It isn't fair. You ought to have brains *or* talent *or* money and leave something for me."

"I didn't know you wanted to go," I said.

"Everybody wants to go. Not everybody can be as casual about it as you are. I suppose you're going over for Easter as well."

"No," I said. "Mother's going to London to be with Doris and Frank, though, so I'm going to stay on campus. I did that last year, too."

"Oh yes, it was Christmas in Rome, wasn't it?"

"That's right," I said.

"All three of us will be here for Easter vacation," you said. "I think lots of the seniors will be around."

"Too bad," I said. "It was so beautifully quiet last year. Not a soul around. If being a nun were like that, I'd be tempted."

"Wouldn't it be something like that?" you asked.

"No, nothing at all. What I want is an enclosed order with everyone else, or almost everyone else, on perpetual spring vacation."

"That would suit me, too," Monk said with such odd seriousness that I did not respond with any of the obvious remarks.

Monk could not have gotten permission to stay at college without the excuse that she must help supervise rehearsals for the spring play, which was her own. She was the only daughter of a successful farmer among numerous sons. It was unusual for a man in her father's position to choose to educate a daughter—he was cynical about a son who had wanted to study agriculture—but Mr. Ridley had recognized in Ramona just what he recognized in prize cattle. He had, therefore, determined to raise her carefully and breed her well. The crowns and cups from beauty contests, which he kept in his own den, were evidence that she should be sent to college for the final prize, a rich husband. Any other honors along the way, plays produced, degrees granted, were acceptable, but he did not want any accidental trophies for her beauty. He did not approve of independent holidays either at home or abroad. He apparently did not realize that Ramona was more apt to catch a married professor than a young millionaire at a small women's college, no matter how richly attended by other young women whose suitable brothers were sent east to college. In any case, a haven for rich young women attracts more fortune-hunters than fortunes. Ramona's father, strict but unaware, went on sacrificing his steers for his higher hopes, while Ramona debated girdles with the history professor or a modest future with the social worker and prepared her play for production.

You had no difficulty persuading your mother that you needed time to work during spring vacation. She was serious in wanting to do the right thing for you, but, if it involved your being at home, it was always the wrong thing for her.

I was probably the only one a little sorry not to be going home. It was the only place where I could work without interruption. My comfort was quietly arranged by a housekeeper who took impersonal pleasure in her task, and my mother's vague, affectionate company was always peaceful. But she often traveled now to give me more freedom from her loneliness or a more interesting holiday. I could never have told her that I did sometimes miss the innocent and reasonable life we lived together for the first few years after my father's death. It was probably true only because I was free to miss it. And I had found a substitute in the orderly life at college, particularly when I could stay there after most of the students had left. I tried not to resent the number of other people who also chose to stay, but I was disappointed.

"I won't come knocking at your door," you said. "I'm going to work all day in the studio and read all night. And Monk's going to be tied up with rehearsals and her private life."

"Good."

"Was Sandy here last year?"

"Yes, she was, rehearsing for the Bartok concerts. She wasn't around much."

"She's staying this year, too, working on her proficiency concert. . . ."

"And . . . ?" I said.

"I had a long, strange sort of talk with her the other day—the day you didn't come in for coffee. She asked a lot of questions about you. When she heard you were staying on campus, she suddenly said, 'Well, that's that,' and got up and walked off."

"Then *let* it be," I said.

"Do you think she's queer, Kate? That's what people say. And it did sort of seem . . . I don't know."

"That would be all you'd need, E."

"Then you do think she is."

"I don't think anything at all. But then she's never propositioned me."

"Well, she didn't me. Monk's just terrified of her."

"Why?"

"She heard a rumor that it was Sandy's ambition to sleep with every senior on our corridor, and about two weeks ago Monk saw her leaving the room right next to Monk's about three in the morning. Monk kept saying, 'I'm next. I'm next.' When I laughed at her, she said hadn't I noticed how friendly Sandy had been with her when we were all having coffee. Of course, she has been. . . ."

"Monk has only one thing on her mind, and that's her problem. Maybe Sandy's got another. You've got a sculpture show to get on and two papers to write. That's enough."

"More than enough," you said, but you weren't finished. You sat, folding an empty match book into a flower. "Do you think I could be queer, Kate?"

"Why?"

"I don't know—only it doesn't seem to me odd for one woman to love another. I love you. It's not sex or anything like that, but, if it were, I don't know—I wouldn't be shocked. When I thought that, thinking about Sandy, I suddenly wondered about me."

"E., don't get involved with Sandy."

"Did you know Pete was queer?"

"Yes."

"I didn't. Andy had to tell me. I don't mind about that, either. Maybe sex isn't very important to me."

"Maybe not," I said. "Not by itself, anyway."

You sat there, your face turned a little away, thinking, your cheek still softly curving like a child's, your woman's beauty still half sleeping in your eyes and mouth, but in your throat, in the line of your shoulder, breast, it woke, and you couldn't ignore it much longer. I watched you, thinking, you are not to spend yourself on a Sandra Mentchen. I haven't saved you from myself for that. If stopping it meant encouraging Sandy to think that you were already involved with me, that risk might better be taken. It would be strange, perhaps even difficult, after four years of being so careful about small details to be just as consciously careless, to allow an occasional gesture of affection, to adopt the pronoun "we." I said no more to you about it, but I never missed morning coffee after that. When Sandy stopped at the table, I was friendly with her, so friendly that she could rarely have a conversation with you. I talked of "our" plans for next year. I occasionally let my hand rest lightly on your shoulder. And I watched Sandy withdraw a little until, by the time spring vacation began, I felt I could relax.

Or perhaps nervousness about my work simply distracted me. I had promised to give a sermon. I had to write it. It's hard to remember now just why I chose the subject I did. It must have come out of a conversation with you, a play I'd read by Dorothy Sayers, one of my mother's favorite writers, or some of my father's marginal notes in a commentary, and the hope that, very indirectly, I might deal with some of my own doubts. Anyway, on that first Saturday morning, when the dormitory was as deserted as I had hoped it would be, I sat down at my desk, surrounded by books, making notes on various interpretations of the story of Cain and Abel. When the phone rang and rang down the empty corridor, I finally had no defense against it.

"Kate?"

"Andy! Where are you?"

"In the city. I just got in."

"How long are you going to be here?"

"That somewhat depends—look, can I see you?"

"Of course."

"This afternoon?"

"Well . . . yes, sure."

"Is Esther around?"

"Yes, shall I see if she's free?"

"No, better not. I'll get in touch with her later. Do you look as good as you sound?"

"No, but I'm sure you do."

"For that, I'll change my tie."

"Tie? I don't think I've ever seen you in a shirt!"

"What a disappointment I'm going to be. I haven't been out of long underwear all the Canadian winter. Why did you want to go to Spain when you live in a place like this?"

"As you'll remember, I don't know myself."

"Are you free for dinner as well? I know that's a very bad boy-girl thing, calling Saturday morning for Saturday night—"

"Don't waffle. Just come along."

I was surprised that Andrew Belshaw would call me rather than you, for though I'd had several whimsical letters from him during the year and one rather drunken and amiable phone call from Calgary, I assumed that he must have made a closer friend of you in the weeks you traveled together after I left. We had talked very little about those weeks, but now I remembered that, if his name came up in casual conversation, you rarely said much. Perhaps, out of loyalty to Peter, you had gone on mistrusting him.

I remembered, too, just for a moment, that last, long morning which I had used to myself as the final excuse for being driven away from all of you. I didn't really believe it at the time, and now, caught by my own pleasure at the sound of Andrew's voice, I let go of unnecessary defenses against him. I quite simply wanted to see him.

I worked peacefully for the rest of the morning, intending to make only casual preparations for his arrival. "Don't spend all day on a meal you don't intend to serve," Doris would say. I'd let vanity rest in the high cheekbones and coloring of an unknown mother and in the handsome burnt-orange cotton dress my known mother had recently sent to me. I would be all one color.

"You're gorgeous, Kate," Andrew said, in almost surprised approval, and I thought that he had never seen me in a dress before.

"So are you—the sky-eyed boy, all dressed up in clothes."

Perhaps the reason I liked Andrew's handsomeness so was that it made him a little less real to me, a little less accessible; for I had nothing to offer that could belong to the other half of his silverware ad. Meeting him there in the large, empty living room, I was even sorry there was no one else around to admire him, for he looked as at home in his well-tailored suit as he had in his perpetual swimming trunks or old khaki trousers.

"How many times did I sew up that back belt loop on your old trousers? You must have someone very faithful and clever to turn you out like this."

"Mother, sisters, and Papa's charge accounts, but I've got my trunks in the car—just in case you didn't recognize me."

We went to the pool, which we had to ourselves, except for the white-haired custodian who issued locker keys and towels before she disappeared again to the company of her newspaper and never-quite-finished cup of tea.

Lying in the California sun, we talked about the Mediterranean, remembering the beautiful bell we had found in a derelict chapel, a half-wild hunting dog that looked like a deer, an English professor and his mistress who had come to the hotel one night for dinner.

"Where's Pete now?" I finally asked.

"Back in Paris or in Spain, I suppose. We don't write." When I didn't comment, Andrew propped himself up on his elbow to look down at me. "Did you leave because of Pete and me or just because of me?"

"Neither," I said.

"I guess Esther's told you all the humiliating details."

"None at all, humiliating or otherwise. Oh, I heard about a dinner in Madrid, a show opening in Paris, that kind of thing."

"That was kind of her, I suppose. After you left—oh, it was comic really, Esther running after Pete, Pete running after me, me running after Esther. It kept us together, anyway, but it was a magic circle before you left, Kate. Why did you go?"

"I had some chasing of my own to do," I said.

"Did you catch anything?" he asked amiably.

I held up my hands to measure a fish. "How's the dragon slaying been in Alberta?"

"Bad," he said. "I want to be at Cambridge next year for my Ph.D. This time the whole family's against it, but I'll go finally, after a lot of unpleasantness. Are you going over?"

"I think so, to LSE. Esther wants to go to Slade."

"What do you plan to do, Kate?"

"Work. Salvation through work."

"At what, though?"

"I'm not sure, but I've got to get out of the theoretical and into the real world. It's teach and write articles, or be a spy and a humanitarian. I'll have to see."

"But never a princess."

"Certainly not," I said, smiling. "In real life there's a difference between a bastard and a king's daughter. Are you going to take me out to dinner?"

"I am."

Andrew took me out to dinner not only that night but on Sunday night and Monday night as well.

"Now look," I said as I got into the car on Monday night, "I

47

want no more of this south sea island curry with Hungarian violins at two hundred dollars a martini. Let's go to the local steak house."

"All right," Andrew agreed, "but in Calgary there's not much else. It's nice not to have to struggle to spend money for a change. I'll go to the steak house with you tonight if you'll drive to the ocean with me on Wednesday."

"I can't, Andy. I have to work. Aren't you going to get in touch with Esther? Why don't you ask her?"

"Canadian social customs," he said, a little embarrassed. "I didn't think it was the thing to date two girls at once, particularly if they were friends. You wouldn't mind?"

"Of course not. Why should I?"

"I sometimes wonder why you don't completely destroy my ego," Andrew said, sighing. "I thought maybe at least I was a status symbol: rich, handsome—"

"Ah, you are, but there never seems to be anyone around to admire you. It's a pity."

As if to contradict me, Monk hailed us as we walked into the steak house. She was on what she called "public mating business," with Robin Clark, her brother's social worker, "And, of course, my own."

"Are you Andy . . . the Andy of Spanish fame?" she asked at once.

"I'm afraid so."

He and Robin shook hands, Robin at an awkwardly balanced disadvantage behind the table, while Monk and I measured them against each other. I let myself enjoy the advantage for the moment I had it. I was no more competition for Monk than Robin was for Andrew.

"I was going to ask you to join us, but if this is a real lovers' reunion—"

I protested while Andrew and Robin reached for extra chairs. Without ignoring Monk, in fact making it seem a subtle compliment, Andrew turned at once to Robin with questions which would give Robin authority in the conversation.

"What I know is out of a course in sociology, but you've been there, and you know really. . . ."

But he did not let either Monk or me relax into listening.

"I wonder if you'd say, Monk" or "Kate, what about the church and social work? Do ministers know enough to get involved with drug cases?"

We talked about morality and the law, church and state, freedom and the imagination, earnestly at first but no conversation in which Monk is involved is unleavened for long. Andrew did not strain to match her humor, more pleasantly enjoyed it. I had not seen him in so entirely social a role before. That he should be as graceful as he was handsome seemed almost unfair.

"But I like the unfairly endowed," I said at a point when the remark was not out of keeping with the discussion.

Andrew did not miss the compliment or the implication that I knew very well what he was doing. Even my comrade's smile of encouragement didn't rattle him. I did not intend it to really, though it occurred to me that Monk's life was complicated enough without Andrew.

"I hate to break this up," Monk said finally, "but I've got to get back to a rehearsal. Are you going to be around a while, Andy? Maybe we could do this again."

"If Kate really won't elope to Mexico with me, I'll probably be around until the end of next week."

"Doesn't he say the sweetest things, Kate?" Monk asked, turning to me with one of her brilliant burlesques of a smile. "Are you tempted?"

"I haven't checked on what Whitehead would say about it yet," I answered. "Do you know where Esther is tonight?"

"She's gone beer-drinking with Sandy."

"Seriously?"

"Well, I hope not, but she doesn't have much sense of humor, does she?"

49

"Why did you let her go?"

"I'm not her mother," Monk answered sweetly. "I leave that sort of thing to you."

Robin and Andrew were standing patiently. Monk turned again to Andrew to say good night, and they were gone.

"Who's Sandy?" Andrew asked, as he sat down and poured the last of the wine into our glasses.

I shrugged.

"Do you mother Esther too much?"

"Probably," I said. "And then I'm not around or, if I am, I walk off."

"She's safer than you know," he said. "I should know."

When you dropped in the next day just before lunch, I waited for you to mention your evening with Sandy. But your nervousness, which always took form in objects made of matchbooks, bits of paper, anything at hand, apparently had another source. When the table by your chair had been turned into a zoo of mythical animals and we had exhausted complaints about work and college gossip, you fell silent with whatever it was you were about to say. I waited.

"Would you like me to spend the day with Andy tomorrow?" you asked finally.

"What do you mean, 'Would I like it?' "

"Well, you care about him, and so I suppose I should try to get to know him better . . . if you'd like me to."

"I should think you already know him better than I do. If you don't want to go, don't."

"But I'd like to like him, Kate, if you do."

"Why?"

"Because, if he matters to you, I've obviously not been fair about him. We had a bad kind of disagreement this summer, but it was probably a misunderstanding all round. I guess I will go."

"Don't do it for me, E. I do like Andy well enough, but that doesn't mean you have to."

"No. I want to. Anyway, I can't work yet. I'd like to go to the ocean."

It was about the same time on Wednesday that there was another, unfamiliar knock on my door. I was not really surprised when Sandra Mentchen came in.

"I've practiced myself into blood blisters," she said. "Are you in a mood to drive out for lunch?"

"Sure . . . just one more paragraph, and I'd love a break."

"Good. Can I just wait for you here?"

"Sit down," I said, turning back to my typewriter.

My chess game isn't really good with an audience. Neither is my cooking. Still I am ambivalent about showing off because what I lose in concentration I gain in energy. I finished a difficult transitional paragraph with odd confidence.

"I wish I could write that quickly," she said, as I finished.

"So do I," I said. "We aren't going anywhere that needs a skirt, are we?"

"No, I just want to pick up a hamburger and eat it on top of a hill somewhere. I had a lesson this morning," she added, explaining her own clothes.

Sandra Mentchen always dressed well, whether for the concert stage or for tennis. She chose what you called "no-colors"— beige, stone, or very pale, muddy greens or black. She had the fair skin of a redhead, which she was not, brows and lashes pale, a thin, triangular face that would strengthen as it aged. She was all texture rather than color: leather, raw silk, roughly woven wool, linen. That day she had on an Irish sweater with leather buttons which I coveted.

She drove a sports car which most people coveted, pale in color, elegant in line, powerful. Everything matched. And she drove with the same hard, accurate skill that she used on the concert stage, like a man. It is what the reviews still say of her: a masculine strength. They usually add a phrase about feminine sensibility or, more negatively, lack of masculine intelligence. "Not bright but sometimes brilliant," was her teacher's evaluation of her. She had and has the force of discipline. These things are enough.

"On top of a hill somewhere" was obviously a vague reference to a specific place. There was nothing happenstance about the rock-shadowed parking place, then the small meadow we walked down to, protected from the road by the steep incline, lined with trees to the north and south, open only to the view in the west so that, as we ate, we could watch the city, clear in a sea wind, white.

"I don't think Esther's a sculptor, do you?" Sandy asked abruptly.

"I don't know," I said, quick to be irritated by the arrogance of tone. "It's not something like music that you do know early."

"Oh, I don't mean talent. She's probably got lots of that. But she doesn't think of it as a life. She's full of a lot of nonsense about fulfilling herself as a woman and serving God, as if they were something else again."

"Maybe for her they are."

"Then she's not a sculptor, and she never will be."

"What will she be?"

"Somebody's wife," Sandy said.

"Perhaps."

"You aren't sure?"

"How could I be?"

"Very easily. All you'd have to do is ask her."

"Ask her what?"

"Don't put me off, Kate. Do you want her or don't you? Because if you don't, I do. I wouldn't even bother to ask if I couldn't see how she feels about you. I want you to take her or let her go. At the moment, she's just going to waste."

"And you're looking for 'a wife'?"

"That's right," she said, and then she turned to me, "aren't you?"

"No . . . I don't even like the vocabulary."

"Who said anything about liking it? What are you going to do —join her in a nunnery in your old age?"

"Leave her alone, Sandy."

"Why? Give me one good reason."

"Esther."

"Do you want me to feel sorry for you, Kate?"

"No," I said. "There's no reason to. It's just not her world, not her sort of thing."

Sandy was silent for a while then. Finally she said, "How do you stand it?"

"I don't even find it very difficult," I said, but the tightening of her face made me regret it. "I don't know. I go away. In the winter—this winter—I don't know."

"This is where I always come," she said, "with a new one every week. But not Esther, you say."

"No."

"Then you," she said simply.

"Are you bargaining?"

"In a way," she said.

"Now?"

"You *are* girlish."

"And you're bloody childish," I said, sounding to myself like Doris. "Come on. I have to get back to work."

I sat at my desk all afternoon, trying to contemplate gifts acceptable and unacceptable to God. "Where is your brother?" Well, where was God? Whose keeper is He? Are all the rest of us meant simply to serve the chosen few, those beloved? And if that is true, should I have bargained? No. It would not have been for you. I wanted her. It was no bargain.

The transitional paragraph was glib. What followed was turning into an obscure private joke. Before dinner I tore it all up.

After dinner I began again. At midnight Sandy, in a velvet shirt and linen trousers, did not bother to knock.

"I'm sorry," I said, "but it's awfully late."

"Please."

"Aren't any of your friends around?"

"Esther's just gone to bed."

"This is an odd sort of blackmail."

"It's not blackmail."

I was surprised by her body, surprised by its ignorance of itself and therefore of mine. She must always before have done all the teaching of the very little she knew, physically too shy to be curious, simply needy. I would like to have been relieved, but I was disappointed. We lay in the dark, silent. Then Sandy got up.

"I can't stand much more of this," she said.

"Oh? I'd heard you were determined to make everyone in the graduating class."

"Don't, Kate. Help me."

How? In the dark, particularly, words are important, as graphic and repetitive as the body's rhythm, but anticipating it so that nothing is uncertain or clumsy. While touch is gentle, exploring, let words invade, startle so that crude touch does not. Then speak gently so that breasts do not forget what thighs open for now. Talk to desire, call to it, make it come to you all together. Now.

"There," I said. "That's something worth feeling guilty about, anyway."

"You're incredible."

Not bad for a girl, I wanted to say, or it's nothing really, or all I'm after is a credible performance; but I didn't say anything. After a moment, I turned on the light to find a cigarette. "Don't hide. You've got a lovely body."

"Aren't you ever afraid?"

"Of this? No."

Now get out, I wanted to say, but I didn't. We talked awkwardly for a little while before she finally dressed and left. It was three in the morning.

That was a different kind of bad day for you, too, wasn't it? And, though Andy was the villain, I don't suppose he enjoyed it, either. Years later he said to me, "Why did I feel I had to have her? Why did she make me so angry?" Because he wouldn't actually force you, he had to commit some other violence.

"You and your purity! The only thing that keeps you a virgin is your stupidity. You think I was brutal to Pete, and you don't even know what you do to Kate. You didn't even know why she left you."

"I haven't come to ask you if it's true, Kate. I just have to tell you what he told me. Otherwise I would feel I'd betrayed you."

"It's true and it's not true," I said. "I've never minded your not knowing, and I don't mind your knowing now."

"Did you . . . want me?"

"No," I said, "not ever."

"It sounds so crude to ask . . . why not?"

"Because I don't want to want you. It's as simple as that."

"Oh," you said. "Well, one thing is true. I am stupid."

Before I could say anything more, you had left.

Andrew did telephone before he left town. Neither of us said anything about you, but he didn't burden me with reasons for his change of plans.

"Maybe I'll see you in the fall, in London."

I gave him Frank's and Doris' address. I didn't want to be angry, but the control I thought of as a virtue might have been fear. I could not afford to feel frightened.

I went back to my desk to write the final paragraph of the sermon. "We are the betrayer and the betrayed. We are Cain and Abel."

Monk announced her engagement to Robin Clark at the party after the opening performance of her play. Her parents were not there, and, because you were as surprised as everyone else, I decided that it was an impromptu gesture, its motives despair over the obvious failure of the play and perhaps revenge against Richard Dick, who was there with his wife. The party was very like the play, sad and silly and confused, everyone with ponderously intelligent lines dealing with true confession circumstances. Yet the only difference between that very bad play and Monk's recently very good ones is that she is now conscious of her view of the world.

"Do you think we could leave?" you asked before I did think so, but I agreed at once.

"When did she decide to do that?" I asked as we walked back to the dormitory.

"She didn't. And she won't be able to make it stick. Her father will never let her go through with it."

"If one kind of performance fails, try another."

"I think so," you said. "What's going to happen to Monk?"

"She's going to be a rich man's wife," I said, and then I remembered what Sandy had said about you. "Or not."

"But she does have talent, Kate. She just doesn't know yet who she is."

I began to laugh, not being able to help it.

"What?" you asked, still urgently serious.

"Oh, I don't know, little dog. Do you know who you are yet?"

"Well, I know this much—that right at the bottom of me there's one strong word, 'yes.' "

And at the bottom of me an even stronger one, "no," but the sweetness of your confidence did touch me. I did not want to mock you, ever.

"Is your show just about ready?" I asked.

"No. I'm never ready until the day after things are due, but I still have three weeks. So much of the old stuff is junk, Kate—swollen heads and fallen tits. I wish I had enough to show only what I've done since I got back. I had a good title for it all, 'Holey, Wholly, Holy,' but I can't use it."

56

"Thank God for that."

"Nobody likes my jokes but me."

"They aren't jokes," I said.

"When are you going to walk me through the service? That's more pressing. What a weekend it's going to be, Sandy's proficiency concert Saturday night and your sermon Sunday."

"I haven't seen Sandy lately."

"Nobody has. I just caught sight of her between classes a couple of days ago and she said, 'You and Kate are coming to my concert, aren't you?' It's funny, but I think it matters to her a lot, our going. I do like her. Do you?"

"Yes," I said.

It is hard to believe that anyone was important to Sandy on the night of her concert. When she came onto the stage, the black Grecian folds of her dress making her stiffness appropriate, her pale, triangular face was grave, preoccupied. She turned not away from the audience but toward the piano, which was what she had come to find. She sat down, making no nervous adjustments of bench or dress. She was perfectly still, waiting with perhaps no awareness at all that an audience waited with her. Then she began. The music she played was chosen to display the range of her skill, technical and interpretive. The professional critics were there because Sandy had already begun her career as a concert pianist. They could be picked out among the music students and faculty members, who also made occasional notes on their programs. This was as much an examination as a concert, and at first I found it hard not to listen with some anticipation of the criticism. She was precise, almost automatic, a perfect machine, the emotion there, but programmed in advance, memorized. Then first in Bach and again in Bartok, she played as if she were discovering rather than recalling, and the sound opened into the present, into the audience, new and requiring. There. There it is, whatever it is, the power.

"What will she do now?" you asked, as we waited for space in the crowd.

"You mean, tonight?"

"Yes."

"Well, there's the reception."

"But afterwards."

"Do you want to be with her?"

"I'd be inadequate," you said.

"For what?" Monk asked, suddenly at my elbow. She had been sitting with Robin a few rows behind us. "Are you going to the reception?"

"No," I said.

"Of course, you have to be Jesus Christ tomorrow morning," Monk said, and then she turned to you, "and you have to be Jesus' little helper."

"Sun beam," you said. "I guess I won't go, either. If you have a chance, tell Sandy it was just great, will you?"

I had none of Sandra Mentchen's preoccupation with the performance itself. I felt very much the way I had on the morning I had stood at the edge of a pool waiting to disgrace myself. "Talent without discipline, courage without moral intent are deformities, not gifts," I could hear my father say, and I agreed with him; yet I very much hoped that just those deformities would carry me through the hour that was about to begin. You waited beside me with a different kind of nervousness, which had to do with particular uncertainties: standing at the wrong time, mispronouncing a word, reading a prayer designated for me. But you weren't worried about failing anyone but me. And there was something else for you, more important. Over your cherished black academic gown was the white surplice, "the life of the spirit."

"Try it on for size, little dog," I had said and helped you on with it, just as more recently you must have been helped into your second bridal gown by one of your sisters, who call you by God's nicknames now.

Then, unconverted Jew and reverting half breed, we stood in the unorthodox costumes invented for essentially Espiscopalian variations, about to conduct a service which would have a Hindu prayer or two along with the general confession and thanksgiving, in honor of the Brotherhood of Man: Cain and Abel. The choir was in place; the candles were being lighted; there were only a few people in the congregation still offering private prayers. When the organ began the introduction to the processional hymn, the congregation stood, and, as they began to sing "Once to Every Man and Nation," we walked slowly down the aisle, seeing nothing but the familiar backs of heads until the procession parted before us and we stopped to bow to the cross, given to the chapel by my family in memory of my father. Then I had to face the congregation with the call to worship.

"Create in me a clean heart, O God, and renew a right spirit within me. . . ."

But immediately I could kneel for the general confession, for the Lord's Prayer, and, when I stood again, I could turn my back on them for "Glory be to the Father, and to the Son and to the Holy Ghost."

The responsive reading, according to the printed program, was adapted from *The Just Vengeance*—mine, but you had to carry it out. You read out clearly:

"Brother, what is your name?"

"My name is Cain and Abel," the congregation was forced to reply.

"Brother, what is your name?"

"My name is Cain and Abel."

"Brother, what is your name?"

"My name is Cain and Abel."

"God send justice! The blood of Abel cries out from the ground."

I had put into your mouth all that I didn't dare to say or could no longer say. You read the St. Paul passage: "Who wilt not suffer you to be tempted above that ye are able, but wilt with the temptation also make a way to escape, that ye may be able to bear it . . ." and "for thou madest us for thyself, and our heart is restless, until it find rest in thee. . . ."

I read the sermon quietly enough, except inside the voice of Judas:

"Can anything clear me in my own eyes? or release me from the horror of myself? I tell you, there is no escape from God's innocence."

And on into the last paragraph:

"We are Cain and Abel, we are the betrayer and the betrayed, gaining, with an awareness of our double nature, humility and—perhaps—salvation. Let us pray."

Yours was the prayer before the benediction.

"O life-giving sun, offspring of the lord of creation, solitary seer of heaven! . . . By the path of good lead us to final bliss. . . . Deliver us from wandering evil. . . ."

After all these years, your voice is what I remember more than my own. They were the last prayers I ever offered. And you offered them, your own and your first. If I had not so certainly turned away from the Church then, would your own detour have taken so many years? Probably I had nothing to do with it.

"What a performance," Sandy said, as she shook hands with both of us after the service. "I wish I wanted to be saved. What I ought to do is write a couple of hymns. I could get along without 'Once to Every Man and Nation.' When you're ordained, Kate, that's what I'll do."

"A safe promise," I said, being pleasant, waiting for some reference to my other talents.

"That was a great concert last night," you said.

"Well, I passed," Sandy said quietly, "on the strength of Bach and Bartok. I wish you'd both been around for a drink afterwards, but I knew you had this to do this morning."

"Why don't you come drinking with us after my show?" you suggested.

Sandy looked at me, and then she said, "I'd like that, but I've got to go to Los Angeles. Maybe some time before it's all over. . . ."

That night I went to find Sandy. She was in the living room of her dormitory, talking with a couple of friends.

"Hi," she called. "We were just arguing about your sermon. These people don't want Cain and Abel one nature. They want the sheep and the goats separated."

"You're really a Zoroastrian, aren't you?" one of them asked.

"No," I said. "Just a bad Christian. Have you got an hour or so, Sandy?"

"Sure."

We excused ourselves.

"Where do you want to go?" she asked.

"Anywhere that's private."

"Let's drive then."

After we had left the campus and the town and were driving in the hills above the city, I was not sure I could or would say anything. Perhaps I had never intended to.

"What do you want from me, Kate . . . anything?"

"Just this probably . . . getting out. That was bad this morning."

"So was the night before, mostly. You can't mind much about that. You did what you thought you had to, didn't you?"

"I think so."

"Well, that's enough. I'm glad you came. There's something I wanted to say to you, and I couldn't have unless you'd come. I've been trying to figure out ever since that night what it was between us that made everything so bad, even what was good. I sat there in chapel this morning, ready to be furious, you two all dressed up in tents, going down the aisle like a couple of newlyweds, and I thought what a mucked-up fucking waste it was. I still think so. But that's not it. While you were up there doing it, it was like me the night before: no mistakes, but nothing else either, except once or twice. And I thought, 'I know what's wrong between us. We're friends, and I didn't know it.' Then af-

61

terwards, when you were just waiting for me to take a crack or try to make time with Esther, I saw that you didn't know it, either. So I think you're out of your head, and you think I am. It doesn't matter. I could have a drink with you and Esther. It would be okay. Yes?"

"Yes," I said, but I felt just a little the way I did when all those glasses began to fall, sad, helplessly sad.

I wonder if the reason so many adolescents love Fitzgerald is that he never outgrew that kind of sadness. It takes some measure of innocence to mix honor and depravity that way, and a setting is also necessary—the heavy night scent of eucalyptus, for instance, and the far, small, bright towers of a city. He would have remembered the tune playing on the car radio. I don't, but it might have been "You'll Never Walk Alone." Those were the days before privately financed good music stations, which we would have felt required to listen to. They were also the days before it was popular to support persecuted minorities, better still to belong to one. Neither Sandy nor I knew that we were making an emotional investment which fifteen years later would give us almost Negro status with very little Negro pain. The attitudes we were developing and the decisions we were making were based on an older morality for populating those coastal hills and inland valleys. Though the Jews had already been burned and the smog already sometimes smarted in our eyes, we were still prepared to be the victims rather than the heroines of a population explosion so violent, its fallout of conformity so deadly that even the conservative Church would begin to question its doctrines of moral sickness and health. What a waste all Sandy's angry aggressiveness now turns out to be. And how many silly years it took me to discover that I was playing my game of hide-and-seek mostly by and with myself. But we didn't know then. Sandy still doesn't.

Last year, when I had a drink with her after a concert, she asked me to send money to another of those amateur little magazines she has been supporting for years.

"Isn't it time that people with freckles stopped forming leper colonies?"

"Is that why you live alone?"

It's not as easy as that. Once, briefly, not even true. Habit. Like not going to church. I gave it up on that Sunday as people give up smoking, and, though I have been occasionally since, I am not a practicing Christian. The second Sunday I missed chapel I had a phone call from the chaplain. Would I like to have sherry with him and his wife that afternoon at five? Certainly I would not, but I went. And after the sherry was poured, the chaplain's wife arranged to be in the kitchen attending to supper.

"I didn't really have time to tell you," he said, "what a fine service that was, not just the sermon, the whole service. The president said he was going to write you a note. Did he?"

"Yes," I said. "It was very nice of him."

"But something went wrong for you," the chaplain said.

"I'm frantic about my other work," I said. "It took more time than I had."

He started to say something and then stopped, but he wasn't waiting for me to say anything more. He was testing the bridge he was going to try to walk.

"I have left the Church twice," he said finally, "to sin in peace. I didn't come back frightened. I came back tired, tired of myself."

Tiredness of myself is what's driving me away, I might have said, but I didn't. I let his offer lie between us. We talked around it about my work, about plans for next year, about your show which was scheduled for the middle of the week.

"Performances and occasions," I said. "Robin Clark told me a story the other day about a youngster just out of reform school. He'd been sent to the Catholic farm. When Robin asked him how it was, he said, 'All day long we dug potatoes, eight hours a day, and what did we get at the end of it? Communion. Starving to death and nothing to eat but communion.'"

"Which is what this spring is for you."

"Pretty well," I said.

He had the kindness and good sense to leave me alone after that. I meant to go to call on him and his wife at the end of term, but I never did find or make the time to do it.

It was easy enough for you to find no time for chapel when I didn't. For the week before your show, you rarely attended lectures, and often Monk or I would take both lunch and dinner to the studio for you. I didn't confess then to a mild envy of both Monk and you, for you both had places for work, tools, and props. I liked the studio better than the theater, which always seemed to me a little seedy, too crassly make-believe. The studio was a simple shack by the creek, always either too hot or too cold, corners filled with rags, half a dozen dusts pooling and sifting under the wrapped-up work of the day, all in a strong glare of critical light. Occasionally after dinner, if no one else was in the studio, I'd stay a while with a book, liking your absorbed company, the occasional fragments of conversation. In this way I had seen stages of most of your work. I did not expect your show to surprise me, but it did.

There I saw the four years I had known you gathered together in one place, beginning with the figures whose heads were the right size for their hands and feet in postures our bodies have learned only from their clothes, idealized bulk of matriarchal virgins naked at a movie. Then what you called the shrunken head series, which were all very small, military, naked lead soldiers marching off to war. Next came the mythical animals with Miltonic morals, gargoyles ready to brush their teeth and be put to bed. Surely, you were the one who should have disproved the existence of evil. Then came what Monk called donuts for Henry Moore, circles and figure eights whose loose ends sometimes flowered into faces. I had seen them all, and I had known that resemblances were sometimes strong. What I hadn't seen was the progress your concept of yourself had made against my static face. Whether my face was perched on top of a young body already stiffly suffering vaginal senility, was a death's head in the mouth of a gargoyle, or bloomed at the end of a fragile stalk, it was the same serene mask.

"I've envied you," Sandy said quietly, as we stood together waiting for you to be able to leave. "I still do, but I don't envy her. I can see you better than that in the dark."

"Not better," I corrected. "More clearly."

Your work had never been taken very seriously by your teachers, who found you both too easily influenced and unconsciously distorting. Technically you were both ham-handed and picky so that small areas of obsessively careful detail often lived in a large carelessness of design. None of them imagined that you'd amount to much; yet they were puzzled by your almost humble confidence that you would and weren't willing, quite, to disabuse you of it. Perhaps that was why the party after your show, unlike any of the others, turned into a mild sort of orgy.

Twenty of us started out, and we picked up others along the way, some connected with the college or the neighborhood, others friendly strangers, mostly men to balance the party. I found myself with a grotesquely tall medical student who chinned himself on street signs. Sandy settled with the young music librarian who looked enough like her to be her brother. I think they may have been dimly related. It was a musical family. You spent the earlier part of the evening trying to deal with Richard Dick, who had turned up without his wife and was telling you that he'd made an awful mistake: you were really the one he'd cared for all this time. We had begun with beer, but gradually more and more orders of whiskey came to the tables. Some people were trying to dance in a space entirely canceled if people came out of the men's and women's toilets at the same time. Richard and Robin were preparing to have words. A stray freshman was sick. Someone began to ask for identification cards. Just before we were thrown out, the sculpture instructor suggested that we go back to his house where there was wine and room to dance. In a sorting out of cars, we lost a few of the drunkest and strangest, but it was still a large and boisterous party as it continued in private, more united now in celebrating the night for you.

You rarely drank very much, but I was not surprised to see you uncertain of your footing and giggling. You'd had very little sleep for several weeks and enough to drink to let yourself be as tired and relieved and foolish as you felt. Richard was now too drunk to be more than a superficial nuisance, and there were a number of others who insisted on dancing with you, on taking you out to the terrace, where the drugs of eucalyptus and bright distant city helped the cheap wine to make no one feel responsible for nothing very important.

Wanting a rest from my acrobatic giant, I took my turn with Richard, who decided now with gallant lack of focus that really I was the one he had wanted all these years, but he mistook a wine bottle for me and followed it out into the kitchen. I moved toward the door and met you in it.

"Absolutely everybody's kissed me tonight but you," you said, your face very solemn and childish.

"Then it's probably time to go home," I said, not seeing Sandy until I tried to move past you out onto the terrace. "Is this everybody?"

"Somebody," you said.

Sandy met my anger with a shake of her head and a hand on my arm. "You have such a bad memory, Kate. Kiss the girl. It's a game everybody's playing on the terrace."

"Kiss the girl," someone else called, and it became a chorus, a song.

And so, there in the doorway, I kissed you on the mouth, for the crowd. And you moved on into the room of dancers.

"I'm going to take her home and come back for you," Sandy said. "All right?"

"I should have brought my car," I said.

"And your sense of humor. I haven't had a drink since we got here."

"All right," I said.

I had begun helping to clean up by the time Sandy came back, and she stayed to dry glasses.

"I am too tired," our host admitted. "You finish. I sleep. Have coffee if you like."

We did, taking our cups out onto the terrace.

"Did she get back all right?"

"Yes, and Monk was right behind us so I left her to put Esther to bed."

"Quite a night."

"Kate—"

"Don't start, Sandy."

"But she was crying."

"She was tired and had too much to drink. All right. It's hard on her."

"It's a little hard on you too, isn't it?"

"But I enjoy it," I said.

"You don't, you know. But I suppose you think you'll last. It's only a couple of weeks now, isn't it? But then she's going to be in London, too."

"That will be different. There wasn't any problem here until about a month ago."

"Well, come on. Let's go. Say, what happened to your flagpole?"

"Five men carried him out some time ago, same ones who took Richard."

"Men."

"Men," I said to you the next day over a 4 P.M. breakfast. "It's time you met some men."

"All right, Kate."

"We're not going to share a flat in London. In fact, we're not going to see much of each other for a while."

"All right."

"Little dog, don't you understand?"

67

"I guess so. Anyway, it doesn't matter. It's what you want."

"That's right," I said.

And there was nothing left then of our college days together except what is recorded in too many home movies and too many albums, yours among them here on the shelf, our young faces under Oxford caps, across our throats and shoulders gold hoods against black academic gowns: Ramona Ridley, Sandra Mentchen, you and I.

II

THROUGH CONNECTIONS at the bank, Frank found me a flat in the neighborhood of the British Museum, and Doris furnished it for me with things from their attic. I hadn't much mind for my surroundings in those days, and I paid almost as little attention to my bank account, into which Frank or Mother seemed to have put a substantial supplement to my Fulbright money. I was not what they or I considered extravagant. I was expected to live comfortably. It was arranged. By the middle of August, my trunks had arrived to be unpacked into waiting book shelves and drawers. I had established myself with the butcher and green grocer, found a char who would come in two mornings a week, and bought my first picture to hang in the front hall, a Picasso line drawing of two female nudes in passive company.

"Do you really want to live alone?" Doris asked, turning from the drawing, her arms full of parcels.

"Yes, I think so. At least, I don't mind at all."

"When does Esther arrive?"

"The end of the month. She's going to Edinburgh first, for the festival."

"And she'll stay with you until she finds a place," Doris said.

"Yes."

"You should have taken the double bed."

"She can sleep on the couch," I said.

"Darling, you really ought to cover up that bite on your neck."

"It isn't a bite," I said, covering it quickly with my hand.

"Well, nibble then. The teeth marks show." She had put her parcels down and was rummaging in her handbag. "There." She had found a Band-Aid. "All these years in London, and I've never met a cannibal. I lead a sheltered life."

"Do you?" I said, letting her put the Band-Aid on my neck.

"Umhum," she said. "I never did have the fear of God put in me, but I don't like the look of the v.d. clinics or jail."

"Are you going to start worrying about me and nagging me after all these years?"

"I suppose not," Doris said, "though somebody should. It's the only part of being loved that you've missed. You might even like it."

"No," I said. "I wouldn't like it."

"Put these eggs in the frig, and get me a vase for the flowers. Don't make a face. You don't have to do anything about them. The char will pitch them when they're finished."

"Do you want a drink?" I asked. "Frank sent over a bottle of Scotch, a bottle of gin, and half a dozen bottles of wine yesterday."

"Well, yes. I'm glad he remembered. Do you notice he's a bit dopey these days?"

"I hadn't, no," I called, in the kitchen by this time.

70

"It's usually a woman," Doris said, following me out. "But sometimes it's just business."

"Do you mind, Doris?"

"As little as I can manage, and he's very discreet, which is thoughtful of him. Sensible, too. If I ever met one of them, I'd kill her."

Doris had found the vase for herself and was arranging rust and violet snapdragons. She did not seem at all distressed.

"I never really know how you feel," I said.

"That's because I tell you, which is always confusing. You never tell me a thing. I can make you up for myself, whole cloth, and never be uncertain."

"What would you like me to tell you?" I asked.

Doris went on arranging flowers until her silence made me wonder if she'd heard my question. I didn't want to repeat it.

"What I'd really like to know you can't tell me. You don't know yourself," she said finally. "Don't put any more gin in that. It doesn't save steps. I'll still want another."

That was always the way conversations were between Doris and me, sparring and scatty with more flavor of intimacy than intimacy itself. I almost always enjoyed them because I could be as frank or as frankly evasive as I liked, but after she'd gone I sometimes felt heavily lonely for an ease between us that there never really was.

What was it that she wanted to know? Had it to do with you? But there was no point in discussing you with Doris. There was nothing to say.

Rather early in the morning on the first of September, you phoned from Paddington Station. I could hear the inevitable Scottish cold in your voice and the inevitable uncertainty.

"Come right over," I said. "There's plenty of room for you."

"What will I do with all my stuff?" you asked, relaxing into plaintiveness.

"Check your trunk and bring everything else."

"How do I get there?"

71

"By cab."

"There's a queue ten miles long," you said, your voice fading away as you looked to confirm your own statement.

"Jump it," I said.

"Jump it?"

"All right, don't jump it. People will move along. I'll have coffee waiting."

An hour later I opened the door to you and a cab driver and a corridor full of luggage. You looked simply awful.

"You look wonderful," you said, as all three of us shifted suitcases into the sitting room. "You look marvelous. You have no idea how marvelous you look."

"I'll take care of the cab driver," I said.

When I came back into the room, you were sitting on the couch without having bothered to take off your coat.

"God, it's good to be here. Up all night on the train. Exhausted. Filthy cold. It rained every bloody day we were there. We swam everywhere we went. Spent the family fortune in taxis."

"We?"

"John," you said. "I'll have to tell you about John. He's going to phone. What time is it?" and before I could answer, "Are you sure it's all right to be here? Are you sure you have room?"

"You're sitting on your bed."

"I'll just stay tonight. I'll find myself a room tomorrow. I really could look this afternoon—"

"Stop it, little dog. Stay for a week. Stay as long as you need to. There's no problem."

"No problem," you repeated, rubbing your forehead.

"No, so take off your coat while I get coffee. How was the festival?"

"It rained," you said. "It was all right. It was good. Just nobody there. I mean I didn't meet anybody until John turned up, and I didn't meet him until three days before I left."

"And who's he?"

"A director. He had a play on up there. He came back to London yesterday and said he'd phone here around noon. He's going to help me move my stuff."

Between getting coffee and moving suitcases out of the way, I heard a few more details.

"He's sort of old—well, bald, and he knows simply everybody."

"Everybody?"

"Gielgud and that whole crowd."

I stalled a moment in the kitchen so that I wouldn't have to comment on that remark.

"Oh, I've had a letter from Monk," you called. "She's coming over. She'll be here in three or four weeks."

That returned me to the sitting room at once. "How on earth . . . ?"

"I even wonder if she didn't plan it that way from the first," you said, half grinning. "Her father is sending her to England to get her away from Robin."

"I'll be damned."

"John says he can help her get into RADA. She's going to be awfully late, but I think that's what she wants to do. Oh, that coffee really tastes like home." You drank it and then looked around you for the first time. "You're so settled here, Kate. It's really . . . your own place, isn't it?"

"Doris did it for me."

"I'll have to find something less . . ." You didn't finish your sentence.

"You'll need some place to work," I said. "It may not be easy to find."

"John has some leads," you said without much confidence. "You cook and everything like that, don't you?"

"A little," I said. "I've got a woman to clean and iron."

"I mustn't do that. Mother's given me a household book. How to get clay off the carpet and tomato stains off the pillow cases, I hope. It's my do-it-yourself year."

73

"Maybe you and Monk—"

"No," you said. "You're not going to hold my hand, and I'm not going to hold hers. Everybody has to be independent."

The phone rang: a careful English voice asking for you.

"Ask him to lunch if you like," I said.

You always had an odd, alert expression when you were listening on the phone, as if the message coming through were in code. Whenever I telephoned you, I tried not to imagine your face, mouth a little open, eyelids blinking rapidly. If I did, I had to control the temptation to speak in riddles and numbers. "Come to lunch" or "I have an extra ticket for the theater" never seemed worthy of your concentration. John had probably not known you long enough to notice and was suffering from nothing more than your pauses and apologies.

"Maybe that wasn't a good idea," you said, as you hung up. "Maybe we're too much trouble. Maybe you won't like him."

"I'll like him," I said.

But I didn't. He was a tall, pale man with a sharp face and thinning blond hair, so mannered in his politeness that I was as suspicious of him as you usually were of "grown-up" men, as you called them. He was not a flatterer, however; instead he fed you names of important people he knew, another each time your attention wandered, which it did occasionally from tiredness and uncertainty. He treated you rather as if you were a parking meter with the time always running out. I was a problem he hadn't the attention to calculate. With perverse sympathy, I watched him making that basic mistake.

The first three days of what turned out to be a ten-day visit, you slept a good deal of the day, woke in time to stir through your suitcases for something to put on, drink a cup of coffee, and rush off to meet John. You got home long after I'd gone to bed, though not always after I'd gone to sleep. I would lie, listening to you stumbling about over your scattered luggage, coughing, finally settling to the heavy sleep I'd find you in the next morning. I would pick up a still damp velvet raincoat and shoes, hang up a

74

dress, pitch underwear into the bathroom hamper to make a path for myself into the kitchen. After you'd complained about the char's stacking your luggage so that you couldn't find anything, I didn't bother with that. I don't like untidiness, but I felt indulgent at first. It was a small flat, too small for two people. Some confusion was inevitable, and I expected each day that you'd look for and finally find a place of your own.

On the fourth day, I woke you when I came in from shopping, tripping over a record player you had apparently bought the day before.

"Sorry," I said, "but this is getting to be an obstacle course."

"I'm in the way," you said mournfully. "I knew I would be."

"You're not," I said. "Your clutter is. Why don't we put just one or two of these things in the hall closet?"

"I'll move out today," you said, sitting up in bed with an effort.

"Is that easier than putting your record player away?"

"That's for you," you said. "I've got some Deller records, too. I wanted to play them for you last night, but then it got late with John . . ."

"Oh, E., you're not supposed to buy me things like that."

"I'm not supposed to do anything for you, with you, or about you."

"Okay, I'm delighted. And I wouldn't even mind seeing you for an hour or two every other day or so."

"He wants me to sleep with him," you said.

"And?"

"He says that I'm still a virgin at twenty-two out of some kind of pride or weird masculinity. I shouldn't wear my father's wristwatch."

"So he's a psychologist as well?"

"He's honest. That's what I like about him. And he does understand people, all kinds of people."

"Why don't you have some coffee and wake up?" I suggested.

I moved with deliberate slowness in the kitchen, putting the groceries away while I waited for the coffee. I wanted to ask if you'd gone for your ration book, but I knew you hadn't. I knew you hadn't been looking for a room, either. I spoke firmly to myself about not being a nag. In the other room I heard Deller's voice singing "Fine Knacks for Ladies."

"Though all my wares be trash, the heart is true, the heart is true . . ."

"John says most women don't like Deller's voice. Those who do—"

"I know," I said, "Have some sort of weird masculinity. Forgive me, but John sounds a little like a Penguin Classic."

"You don't like him."

"I don't know him. I can think of more appealing arguments for getting you into bed, but perhaps this one will be more effective."

"He's not trying to argue me into anything, Kate. He's just trying to point out why I'm reluctant."

"Oh."

"I don't want to be a professional virgin."

"Well, who's paying you to be one?"

"Nobody," you said meekly. "Maybe I just want someone to want something of me . . . anything." The phone rang. "Damn! That will be John. I'm supposed to be meeting him for lunch."

It was another three days before we had as long a conversation again. During that time I had a silly argument with Doris; the char threatened to quit; and I was out one night later than you were.

"Wait a minute, Esther," I began this next conversation.

"I'm late," you said.

"For what?"

"John, he's—"

"Taking you to look for a flat? Or to get your ration book?"

"Actually, no," you said. "These friends of his out of London have asked us down for the day, and—"

"Have you looked for a flat at all?"

76

"I'm going to tomorrow. I was going to today, but this came up."

"No," I said. "Call John and tell him you're not going."

"But I have to, Kate."

"No, you don't. You have to get your ration book and you have to look for a place to live. The time's up."

"But I don't know how . . . without him."

"I'll take you," I said.

"You don't want to. You told me. You told me I had to be independent."

"And *this* is independence, using my living room like a hotel room, me like a personal maid, and trailing around after John, picking up all the names he drops until he lets you into bed, Daddy's wristwatch and all?"

"I'll call him," you said.

I went into my bedroom and shut the door. I could hear your voice uncertainly explaining in the other room. Then you knocked on the door.

"You're the only person I really care about in the world," you said quietly. "I'm not going to do all the apologizing you hate. I'm going to clean up the living room. Then I want you to tell me how to get to the ration board. I want to go by myself. I'll bring the book back here for you. Then I'll look for a place. May I stay tonight?"

"Oh, little dog," I said. "Let me apologize for once, just for the novelty of the thing."

"You have nothing to apologize for. You never do. You only get angry when I can't hear any other way. Now I'm going to clean up."

I am not good, I wanted to shout after you. I am jealous and hurt and frightened. But those aren't things to shout at a child. They are not even things children shout at each other. I had already shouted what I could. Now I had to bear your being contrite.

John, for all his offers, was not available for flat hunting, and I was not allowed to go until after you'd made your decision. Even then, you were reluctant to have me see the place.

"I like it all right, but it's sort of awful."

Off Sloane Square, at a good address, Lady Alice's house was as worn and unable to keep up with its neighbors as her face, which unpaid bills and alcohol and forgetful friends had weathered into an odd combination of bloat and gauntness. In strained Mayfair she shouted instructions at you as we followed her up four flights of stairs. She rented out the two main floors to a doctor and his wife, kept the third floor for herself, offering you the attic which, aside from a box room and rather primitive bath to be shared with her, was one large room, low-ceilinged with two small dormer windows. Down the center of it, like a path, lay a decaying hall runner. The only other floor covering was an enormous bear rug, more hide than fur, mounted awkwardly by the side of a small bed, a child's bed probably, painted white. The few other pieces of furniture were enormous, a carved dining-room sideboard and dinner table with two matching chairs, the master chairs, and a wardrobe with two full-length mirrors. On the chimney wall, there was an old gas fire with a cooking ring that crooked out from one side.

"It's bigger than any room I've ever had," you said, "and she's even given me dishes and pans and things like that."

"You won't need many pans," I said.

"I'd never be able to learn to cook more than one thing at a time, anyway. Isn't it a great table? I can have my desk at this end, work at the other end and eat in the middle."

"Has she told you the name of the bear?"

"Pooh," you said, and even you cringed.

"It's a terrible place, E.," I said, laughing. "I can't imagine anyone but you living in it."

"My own," you said, looking around curiously.

Frank's notion (shared by other people) that you were purposely rebelling against your mother didn't really explain your choice. The way you lived in any setting was not as conscious as that. You were, in fact, so little separated from your childhood that Lady Alice's sad snobbery and exiled dining-room furniture probably reminded you of home and gave you some comfort. You had always spent more time in maids' quarters than in your own, and this room might have been the attic of your mother's town house where you and your brother played on rainy days, a place where you had learned to order people's trunks and old rockers and bedsprings into your own design. Far from being rebellious, you had looked for and found just the kind of playroom you were accustomed to. The only difference, admittedly a happy one, was that you never had to go downstairs to eat, say hello to guests or good night to your mother. You could even sleep among the inventions of your day.

"But she'll be so cold," Doris protested when I described the place to her. "And she won't eat properly. Isn't her mother giving her enough money?"

"She's bought herself a complete, very expensive mountaineering outfit and two cases of baked beans," I said. "And she has a record player just like the one she gave me, so she must have some money."

"Is she just slightly feeble-minded?"

"It's her tree house, Doris. I expect one day I'll find her with a blanket draped over the chairs, sitting under it on the floor reading something wicked out of *Godey's Lady's Book*."

"That goes back to my generation's older generation—and farther."

"Esther's old-fashioned."

"Will she be all right?"

"I imagine so. She can have dinner with me a couple of times a week. Slade's practically around the corner from me."

"I meant to pass on a compliment from Frank the other night. He wanted to know where on earth you'd learned to cook."

"That certainly doesn't sound a compliment."

"But it is. He was really quite nervous about having dinner

79

with you before we came. I saw him putting stomach pills into his pill box. You really are a very good cook, Kate, and I can't think where you learned."

"I've always been fed well, and I can read."

"I suppose, if anybody had ever let me—or if it had ever occurred to me to go out on my own the way all you kids seem to —I would have been more like Esther—made a kind of mud pie party out of the whole thing. So the question is, where did you get the confidence you have about ordinary living?"

"It doesn't seem important enough to me to be bad at it."

"Is there anything important like that?"

Loving, I might have said, but I probably didn't really know that much at the time.

"I have a project for you," I said. "I want you to ask me and a young man named Andrew Belshaw to dinner next week."

"Fine. Who is he?"

"I met him in Spain and saw something of him in California last spring. He's Canadian—Alberta oil, here for a Ph.D. at Cambridge. I think Frank would like him, and I'm sure you would."

"And you do?"

"Yes," I said.

I did not meet Andrew's boat train. He telephoned after he had checked in at the Cumberland and asked me to meet him there for a drink. I caught a bus along Oxford Street and sat down, by mistake, next to a woman with pale red hair and a neatly trimmed red beard and mustache. No one looked at either one of us which, under the circumstances, was unnerving because it left me isolated with what seemed after a time to be my own fantasy. When I got up to get off at Marble Arch, she followed me down the sidewalk and right into the hotel lobby. I saw Andrew standing by the counter at the theater ticket agency. As I hesitated, she did, too, just at my elbow. Andrew looked up, saw us and hesitated. I ran to him.

"For a minute there, I thought you'd brought a friend," he said.

"She's real then?" I asked, turning quickly to look back.

"It must be some sort of circus," he said. "There. She's going over to join that company of dwarfs."

"Get me a drink," I said, "before they get out the feathers and ask me to join."

"Not a chance," Andrew said smiling. "This cowboy saw you first."

We didn't stay at the Cumberland. Andrew wanted to go to Chelsea to a pub, then on to a little restaurant he had discovered several years before. We took a bus, then walked along the Embankment in a warm, late afternoon, Andrew liking the ground under his feet after five days aboard ship.

"Isn't it marvelous?" he said, taking my arm. "You aren't at work yet, and I have a week before I have to be at Cambridge. I want to really *do* London. I've only been here a day or two at a time since the war."

"Were you here in the war?"

"Down in Sussex mostly, then into Holland, but I got into London quite a bit, and I always thought I'd come back here after the war to see what it was really like. It's still a sad, war city, though, isn't it?"

We were looking at a great crater in the earth that has since been turned into a garden. In 1952 the tidying and high-fence building were still going on.

"Was it as bad as you thought, getting away from home?" I asked, perhaps because the sadness in his face seemed abstracted; he wasn't really looking at what he saw.

"Yes. I had a badly symbolic thirtieth birthday just before I left."

"You're thirty? It never occurred to me that you were that old."

"Oh, don't you begin at it, too!"

"It's just that you don't look . . . or seem . . ."

"My father's words exactly. A case of retarded development. Here I am, thirty years old with nothing to my credit but a B.A. in philosophy, some Boy Scout badges for an occupation war, and some business experience as my father's ashtray emptier and my mother's barman at charity luncheons. He's quite right, of course. I'm not trained to *do* anything, and he doesn't dare imagine what my experience would recommend me for. I'm not even married."

"Then he shouldn't object to your getting a Ph.D. That will train you—"

"But not for the job I'll have to do. I told the old bastard he'd live forever and never turn over anything to anybody. And that's true, but it's not the way he sees it. 'Poor old England,' he said, 'now the remittance men are going the other way.'"

"I'm afraid I'd like your father," I said.

"How can that reassure me?" Andrew asked, "but it does. Come on. I'm thirsty for one of those filthy English gins."

While we drank, Andrew got out his appointment book and a fan of tickets he had bought while he was waiting for me. Around those he began to block out our "doing" of London, as careful of our feet and our stomachs and the variable English weather as he was of the interests we were willing to share. I did remember to reserve an evening for seeing you, but you had already promised John you'd go to an important party with him. Between us, we managed not to see each other for the week Andrew was in London. We were not exactly awkward about him. You had no patience with negative loyalty of any kind. If anything, I think you were comforted by my being able to go on liking him during the time that you couldn't. But our experiences of Andrew were so different that it was hard to talk about him.

I was not really bewildered by the violence in Andrew which in those days I never saw. He spoke of it himself occasionally, sometimes bitterly self-critical, sometimes justifying himself. His temper wasn't always simply an expression of his own frustration. He could lose it to other people's stupidity and brutality as well.

And I understood why I never saw him do it. With me, Andrew took a deliberate holiday from aspects of himself. I was neither a woman to win nor a friend to compete with. For me, our relationship had the same kind of ease. I hid from myself in his handsome protection, refusing to see any harm in it or in him for either of us. I didn't tire of Andrew as I did of other company, particularly yours.

Doris could not have been more enthusiastic about Andrew than Frank, who surprised me with his almost immediate and candid approval. Frank's own son was a fiercely ambitious young man, impatient with his father's unstraining success, with his father's love for England. They had disagreed as much as Frank would allow it. Finally he had given his permission for young Frank to finish his education in the States. But he would never understand why his son could not be glad of the freedom from ambition Frank could have given him. It was what Frank would have liked himself. He might have been, if he had not had to sacrifice his comfort for it, a minor botanist or music critic. But he was first a gentleman, and that was expensive. To recognize in Andrew the same tastes and temperament was a sharpened pleasure because of his recent failures with his son.

Doris did not usually leave men to port and cigars except at large, formal dinners because Frank was a man who often found other men's company gross and tedious. Even when the custom was observed, the ladies hardly had time to powder their noses and compliment each other on their hair styles before Frank raised the men from the gusts of digestion and manly good humor in the dining room to the clearer, upper air of the drawing room. But on the evening Andrew and I had dinner with them, Doris signaled to me at the end of the meal as if it were ritual.

"I hope you don't mind," she said. "It's all I can do to be generous with Andy myself, but I haven't seen Frank so happy in months. And it makes me feel guilty for suspecting him of other things. I don't think they'll be long."

"It doesn't matter," I said. "Frank really does like him, doesn't he?"

"It's not hard," Doris said. "I've seen Arrow shirt ads before, but usually they're stuffed. This boy's an absolute delight. He's intelligent."

"I knew you'd like him."

"Oh, Kate, you're not going to waste him, are you?" Doris asked with some real distress.

"Of course not. I'll give him away long before he's spoiled."

"But he's so good with you."

"Better than he really is, he claims. So am I. But wouldn't it be awful to live with someone who always brought out the best in you? Exhausting!"

"Don't you . . . aren't you interested in him at all?"

"Well . . . no," I said.

"But how about him?"

"He doesn't really strike you as the sort of person who'd pine, does he? We're a lovely rest for each other. And, God knows, we both occasionally need it."

"Frank is going to insist that you marry him," Doris decided.

"But he isn't even pregnant!"

"You're impossible, Kate."

"Yes," I said. "Why don't we have some port and cigars? I'm sure Frank and Andy won't, and we need to amuse ourselves with something."

Doris was so near true distress that I had to work hard on distracting and entertaining her. I was afraid for a moment that she might ask me if I wanted to go to a psychiatrist or a minister of my choice, but by the time Frank and Andrew joined us again, she had settled to a civilized and entertaining distance.

"That was almost more than I'd bargained for," I said to Andrew after we'd left. "You're sometimes so lovely as to be a trial to me."

"Why?"

"Well, Frank obviously wants to adopt you, and Doris thinks I ought to make a dishonest man of you at once."

"I do like Doris!"

"I'm glad. I do, too. It's odd. I think I am a little vain about you. I like showing you off. It doesn't embarrass you, but it does embarrass me."

"Why should it?"

"I don't want to even look tempted."

"Are you ever?"

"No . . . not really."

"Because I am," he said, quite matter-of-factly.

"But it doesn't really matter to you," I said.

"No, it doesn't."

"If it ever did," I said, "I'd go to bed with you."

"Generously."

"I'm afraid so." And then I grinned. "But I can't ever imagine you desperate."

"What's really unfair is that, if you were desperate, I couldn't do anything about it. And that embarrasses me."

"Let's make a pact about never being desperate in each other's company."

"No," Andrew said, "because someday we might outgrow being embarrassed."

"How is it that Esther didn't fall in love with you? I don't really understand that."

"Simply insensitive," Andrew said, but it was a hard joke for him.

The day Andrew left London I was restless with the reading I had planned to do. When I phoned, you were out; so I went to call on Doris, planning to stop at Sloane Square on my way home.

"I've been thinking about Christmas," Doris said. "With young Frank away and Ann threatening to accept an invitation to

France, Frank and I must either go away or find another family. Would you like to have your friends here for a sort of house party? Don't say yes as a favor to us, only if you'd really like it."

"I'd love it," I said. "Who and how many have you got in mind?"

"Well, Esther, of course, and Andrew? And—"

"You don't think Mother will come over?"

"No, not until spring. And what about this other college friend of yours?"

"Monk? Yes," I said.

"And if she and Esther have young men about—"

"Monk would think a real English house party almost too much to hope for. It's a marvelous idea."

"Shall I ask them?"

"Yes," I said. "Let's be very proper. You do so many things that please me, Doris. I wish I were a better sort of sister-daughter for you."

"You please me," Doris said, a quick, affectionate hand on my cheek, "and always have. The only person you find hard to please is yourself."

What a comfort she would have been if what she had said were true. Just the same, I set off to find you in an uncommonly happy mood, the sort that catches up the human details of a street as if they were all as bright and free as the autumn leaves that also fall, noticed and rejoiced in. I took the stairs, two at a time, forgetting that I had no use for my body, banged loudly on your door, shouting, "You must be in, E. I won't be disappointed!"

I heard you moving about inside, but it took you a long time to come to the door.

"I was asleep," you said.

"Well, wake up. It's a glorious day. We're in London. We should do something—at least go for a walk in the park."

You contemplated my mood out of a face white and still from sleep. "I'll have to get dressed. Come in."

It was the first time I noticed with any shock the physical

chaos you lived in, perhaps because here it was complicated by your sleeping, eating, and working all in one room. Days of changes of clothes were piled on one chair. Dirty dishes and plates of butter and jars of jam were visible under opened mail, books, sketches. At the far end of the table there was an unfinished head of John, which apparently had fallen over. It hadn't been wrapped and was drying, while its rags curled stiffly over the arms and back of the other chair. The room smelled oddly of peanut butter, Imperial Leather, and clay. I wandered around, picking up books and sketches, not watching you hunt for something to put on. You went off to the bathroom to dress, leaving me to tend my ailing pleasure.

"Let's go out for lunch," I said, when you came back, dressed in black trousers and a black sweater, your face unmade-up, "and then walk. What's the matter, E.?"

"John's married," you said quietly. "He has two children."

"When did you find that out?"

"Two days ago. He didn't tell me. One of his friends did. When I asked him about it, he was embarrassed. Then he got mad. What did I think his spending all this time and money on me meant, anyway?"

"What did you say?"

"Nothing. Why am I so stupid, Kate? Why do people have to keep telling me things that I ought to see for myself?"

"It's not your fault," I said. "I'm so sorry, E."

"No, don't sit down in this mess. Let's go out. Let's go to the park. And we won't talk about it. I swore I wouldn't, and that's the first thing I say. But that's all. Come on."

There was no conversation to be made as we sat side by side in a dull, cramped little snack bar eating gray tomato sandwiches. I didn't want to talk about Andrew, and it didn't seem the right time either to mention Doris' Christmas plan. We finally did chat about Monk, about a play I'd seen, about registration at Slade and LSE. And I watched your face in the mirror before us, the bold strokes of dark hair and brows against the paleness of skin, even your lips pale, your whole head part of a collage of ads pasted on the mirror, meat pies congealing on open shelves, steam from a kettle dampening the reflection of your temple. I wanted to get you out of there into the bright, clean autumn day of the park. Once we were walking it was right for me again, but you didn't notice where we went. You didn't see the bright red double decker bus, caught in a shower of leaves, like a paperweight snow scene, just as we crossed the road, or the five young boys in a ballet war under a statue, or the long-legged girl lying beside her bicycle in the tall grass, reading a leather-bound book, or the chrysanthemums. You did not see all the people seeing you, sleep-walking through the park. You did not even see me, walking carefully beside you until we were almost at the band stand and the band suddenly began to play. You looked up, smiled, and put your hand on my wrist.

"There," you said. "There you are."

How many times in that long English winter, during which we were learning to live single and singular lives, did I look up to think—more accurately feel—"There, there you are"? If I didn't invest you with the same powers of safety and strength you always so generously gave me, if I never had the candor to speak the simple relief and pleasure of recognizing you again among so many strangers, I did, just the same, more often seek you out than you did me. I could, of course, because I was the one who also imposed the restrictions. And I moved in the world you were discovering because I did not want you to discover mine. I made no friends at the London School of Economics. Instead I made casual use of yours at Slade and Monk's at the Royal Academy of Dramatic Art. I should probably have been more generous with my flat because it was in the neighborhood, because I could afford heat and had access to Frank's supply of drink, but too many of the art and drama students both bored and frightened me, willing, as they were, to be themselves in whatever mood or need they happened to be. I liked better going to the cafes and pubs where gossip and arguments always had a public flavor, where friendliness, not friendship, was all that was required.

Occasionally I went to your room for one of your parties, which were never really planned, happened instead gradually and gradually ended, defined in time by the possibilities of public transportation rather than by night or day. I didn't much like them, noisy with ill-informed theories around your large, never-cleared table, awkward with stayed orgasms on child's bed and bear rug. You were never a hostess, feeling responsible for nothing that went on around you except whatever intent conversation you were the other half of. A crowd, whether on the street or in your room, was as much background noise as a radio. Under the protection of it you talked or listened to one other always. If Lady Alice complained, you let someone else deal with her. If she decided to lock herself into the bathroom for a long, leisurely soak while ten beer-strained boys waited in line, you let them threaten her with the consequences. I stayed long enough to attach faces to the names and backgrounds you talked of and then left, sometimes alone, sometimes with Monk, who, for reasons of her own, often found these gatherings as tedious and depressing as I did.

At first I didn't imagine that I would see much of Monk, certainly not unless you were around and wanted her with us. But it was to my flat rather than your room that she came. And I went alone to the boat train to meet her because you had a class or an appointment or simply a need not to meet her. I can't quite remember. I only remember being surprised that I was left to be concerned about her. After failing so badly in hospitality with you, I was determined both to be more patient and to define the limits more clearly with Monk. She would understand the problems of food rationing from the beginning, and she would know the hours I was committed to my own work, which had begun. But I would be more helpful, too. Monk, after all, had never traveled out of her own country before.

89

From the moment we greeted each other, we might have been reading a carefully reversed script.

"Kate, you look simply awful!" she exclaimed, shining at me out from the frame of her glorious red hair which offered its own lights even in the vaulted grayness of Waterloo Station, lights by which not one but two young men had also found their way along the platform. "My beasts of burden," she said by way of explanation as she took cartons of cigarettes, which she did not smoke, out of their mackintosh pockets to offer to me.

Monk had no questions about what to do with her luggage. The beasts had arranged all that. They also arranged us very carefully in a taxi with Monk's one necessary suitcase and a couple of parcels which turned out to be household supplies, cans of butter and meat, sugar, cake mixes, coffee. There was even a bottle of whiskey, but that evening we weren't to open anything, because the beasts, on their way to Edinburgh, were staying over to take us both out to dinner. It was ladies' night at their club, which happened also to be Frank's club where he and Doris were having cocktails, as if expecting us. Frank knew one of our escorts, knew the family of the other, and was reassured for a second time in a few weeks about his ability to be pleased by the younger generation. Doris, who always tried so hard with you, was effortless with Monk, at her hopeless best that night in making hilariously tactless remarks, encouraged by all of us. It was the first time I entertained the possibility that Monk was a fool on purpose.

We were all asked back to Frank and Doris' for a nightcap and accepted. Frank told the driver to take us through the park so that Monk could see Buckingham Palace.

"There's the Queen!" Monk exclaimed at an elderly, ordinary woman walking her dog. "Doesn't she look English? I was told Philip wears lipstick, but that can't be true, can it?"

"I told you, only for state occasions," one of the beasts reminded her.

"Isn't it lucky that you found these two to prepare you so well for England?" Doris asked, amused.

"I didn't find them!" Monk protested. "They found me. I decided I wouldn't talk to anybody. I cried all the first day out, and then I was sick all the second day. I had a book to read after that, but these two came down and got the stewardess to introduce us. I told them I was engaged—it's only officially broken, not really —but they said they were both thinking of becoming priests; so we spent the rest of the trip together."

"All very proper," Doris agreed.

"But I had no idea, Sidney," Frank said in a heavy tone, "that you were thinking of renouncing the world."

"The sea air and the red hair," Sidney explained.

I wondered why the manner that had so often irritated me at college amused me now. Perhaps it was my faithless comparing of your two arrivals, you so isolated in your apologetic uncertainty, Monk so confident that she could not offend. Occasionally on that first evening, confronted with the silverware at dinner, with the butler at Frank and Doris' front door, Monk faltered, but she clowned past her fear with, "Do the English have unusually big mouths?" about a dessert spoon and "Butlers do make a place feel more homey, don't they?"

"She's simply marvelous," Doris said to me quietly. "She's a riot."

"I'm not always sure she knows she's funny until after someone else has laughed," I said.

"Nonsense! It's simply perfect timing."

Once or twice over the Christmas holidays, Doris shared my doubts, but she and Frank were by then so much Monk addicts that it didn't matter.

Monk stayed with me only four days. During that time she somehow persuaded the officials at RADA that she should be allowed to register late, found herself a bed-sitting-room and cooking privileges in the flat of an elderly woman who traveled a lot, and got herself established with ration book and shops. She was also around the house enough to learn the few English house-keeping tricks I had at my command.

"What's that?" she asked, watching me in the kitchen.

"Toad-in-the-hole. Something English for your supper."

"Is it really toad?"

"You'll love it."

"But what's in it?"

Carefully she copied down my meatless or unrationed meat recipes.

"Now," she said, firm against her own embarrassment, "I can't flush your . . . thing. If I'm going to stay, you'd better let me in on the trick unless it's like a secret, family recipe."

Knowing how to cook the food and flush the toilets in a for-eign country is the basis for sanity, for people like Monk and me, anyway. You were more concerned with learning to ask for a ticket to Sloane Square with an English accent, a talent which embarrassed Monk and me so much that we always walked away to avoid hearing it. Monk's capacity for embarrassment, along with her surprising ability to deal with practical problems, se-cured our new friendship. Occasionally she offered quick insights into herself which were not so reassuring.

"Being engaged is a marvelous convention. I don't have to think about marrying anybody, not even Robin."

"Don't you want to marry him?"

"I'm too frightened of the idea to think about what I might want."

But Monk never settled to talk about herself as you did. Be-cause I couldn't expect from her your reticence about requiring a return of confidences, I was grateful to Monk. She was extraor-dinarily easy for me to be with.

You went on worrying about her just as you had at college. Apparently she went on talking to you just as she had at college.

"She gets so depressed," you said, "and she won't think anything out. What's she going to do about Robin? She can't just leave him waiting indefinitely."

"Perhaps he simply won't wait indefinitely."

"For Monk he will. She has a terrible effect on men."

She's not the only one, I might have answered, but I didn't. After your experience with John, you were being very careful to avoid the sort of man who would make any demands on you. How conscious it was I don't know, for Slade offered you so many opportunities to meet young men more reluctant than you. Marcus and Clide and a boy we all called Purple Bell gradually formed a kind of gang around you for mutual protection. You admired their work, and they admired you. Not long ago, when I was in London, I went to a show of Marcus', and in one of the sketches I saw the prototype woman he was beginning to understand when he sketched you. I would like to have bought it, but I am enough surrounded by the world you made or were made into. "Laying ghosts" is an unfortunate expression. I trust that's not what I'm doing now.

As had been true at college, you and Monk both seemed to have worlds to work in. I did not. My studies were really not much less theoretical than they had been. I was learning a new vocabulary and imposing the same discipline on new raw material. I still despaired of finally putting knowledge to some real use. And, because I no longer shared the books I read with you, I could not even talk much about what I was doing. When I heard in casual conversation with a friend of Doris' that a large reception center for orphans was terribly shorthanded, I decided working a few hours a week was what I needed.

"You're always paying debts of one sort or other," Doris said.

"I'm sorry it's an orphanage," I said. "It just happened that way. I need something ordinary to do."

"Why not take up beagling?"

"Monk has. Her accounts are enough, thanks. Twenty people and thirty dogs after one rabbit. Besides, I have the only set of long underwear, and she has to wear it."

"You work too hard, Kate."

"I don't. I work too much at one sort of thing."

It was an hour's ride on the underground and a ten-minute walk, most of it through orphanage property, past the office buildings and hospital along a row of cottages where some of the children were housed, eight or ten together with a couple in charge. There were dormitories, too, for those who would not be staying more than a few days. None of the children, except for those seriously ill or handicapped, stayed longer than a month or six weeks. Once they had been examined and tested and observed, they were sent elsewhere to foster homes or schools. A few were returned to homes of their own when parents recovered from illness or financial difficulty and could deal with them again, but most of them were abandoned children, either there for the first time having been found wandering the streets, camped in bombed buildings, or there again not having been placed happily the first time. I went twice a week for two hours in the late afternoon to supervise a recreation period for boys and girls between the ages of twelve and fifteen. Sometimes I had as few as a dozen, but more often there were thirty or more. At the end of each session I met with one of the officials to report what I had observed of certain children, to drink a strong cup of tea, to listen to complaints about the shortage of staff. In that small room off the recreation hall, crowded with a couch, several chairs, and boxes of equipment, I often felt a terrible, physical apathy, an infant's helplessness of body in which I was more aware of the antiseptic smell, the metallic taste of tea, an aggressive spring in my thigh than of the conversations I was supposed to contribute to. Perhaps they were attacks of memory. They served as a kind of defense against a despair of spirit, for I learned quickly that what I observed was really useless information. There wasn't time; there wasn't energy of imagination to do more than sort the children out generally and keep them daily out of trouble until they were sent on somewhere else. The talk about them was an outlet for tired human beings who wanted to complain.

"That one's not epileptic at all! The psychologist says it's hysteria," the matron reported angrily. "So don't let him fool you."

Sometimes I protested, tried to explain the psychological terms I had been trained to trust, but it only made them suspicious of me; and part of my job was to relieve them for a little of the burden of these children. There was little else I could do. With new faces each time, as strange to each other as they were to me, there was not much hope of organizing any elaborate group activity. The games they knew, prostitution and thieving, were not appropriate. The games I tried to teach them were complicated by their refusal to accept the convention of teams. In a relay race, the boys stole the shoes of their own team mates. At darts, they liked each other for targets. Any game with a ball quickly turned into one-man-keep-away and mob violence. Only two means of discipline worked: brutal threats occasionally carried out and physical tenderness. The first I was reluctant to use; the second there were too many for. I was reduced to sometimes frighteningly unsuccessful attempts at simply keeping them from hurting themselves badly for two hours twice a week. There were children who were not violent. They sat passively or tried to press themselves into corners to keep themselves from harm. One little boy, who must have been twelve but looked no more than seven, sat pulling out and eating his hair. One side of his head was absolutely bald.

"You need helpers," Monk decided. "Esther and I'd better come with you."

"Sure," you agreed, but you looked doubtful. "I don't know much about children."

The first time you both came you were less than useless. The boys fought for curls of Monk's hair until she had to be rescued, and a girl who begged to wear your ring then stole it from you. Neither of you would be discouraged, however, and gradually the three of us learned to control the children. We began then to have positive ideas. Monk played the piano, and you knew a hundred dances, which some of the children were willing to learn while others stamped and whirled and leaped and fell in their own inventions. We even managed to organize a fast, undisciplined sort of volley ball, two of us always playing with the children, the third giving time and attention to the ones too frightened to play.

Neither of you would deal with the officials as I did, and sometimes we had fiercer arguments among ourselves than we had with them.

"There's no point in antagonizing people," I'd try to explain on the long ride home in the tube.

"They need to be told it's wrong," Monk would say, "even if it doesn't do any practical good."

"I think we can explain," you'd insist. "After all, these people work there because they care about children. It's just that they don't know any better."

"I don't think three rich American girls with a freshman course in psychology are going to be looked upon as experts."

"I'm not rich," Monk protested. "And they can't fire us because they don't pay us. They have to listen to us whether they like it or not."

"And then take it out on the kids we've shown sympathy for—been conned by, as far as they're concerned. And we are conned some of the time, you know."

"Sometimes I think you're a cynical person, Kate," Monk said.

"No, I'm not. I just don't want to fight until I can get somewhere by it. That takes power."

"Knowledge is power," you said.

"Not unless you mean the sort that teaches you to use money and political position."

"That is cynical," Monk decided with some satisfaction.

While I stored up frustration as if it were fuel or canned goods, Monk began to write protest plays as lucidly silly as her "psychological dramas" had been. It wasn't in your nature to protest, and, though you may have begun with explanation, the work that came out of those afternoons was as individual as your attention always was. You spent an afternoon talking with a boy who was learning to be a bell ringer, and for weeks after that you worked on the extended body, weight that would seem to hang and float at once. Sometimes it was butchershop carcass; sometimes there were shoulder blades as sharp and delicate as butterfly wings. Figures groped or reached, leapt or swung. It was the first time in your life you had found a problem that was both technical and aesthetic. Years later, when you finally did your Christ, His beginnings were in that boy bell ringer, who had been able to tell you how notes were run through the muscle and bone of his reaching, hanging weight. There was no protest, no explanation; the note, the statement, that was all.

I liked our conversations on the way to the orphanage better than those on the way back. Monk usually entertained us with stories of catastrophic rehearsals or her latest discoveries about the habits of the natives. After she gave up beagling, she took up rowing. I think one of the beasts had been stroke of the Cambridge crew when he was an undergraduate, and she wanted to know what it was like. She described practice hours in what she called "the tank" before anyone was allowed out on the river, but before that day came, Monk had to withdraw.

"I was getting absolutely lopsided!" she announced, "really," to us and several other passengers who had given up trying not to overhear. "I don't suppose men have that problem."

Not to be outdone by Monk, you explored your talent for mimicry, which included not only half a dozen accents but an ability to suggest bodies totally unlike your own. You could in a stance or gesture recall dozens of our college friends and introduce us to people at Slade whom we'd never met.

I was aware that sometimes our traveling companions did not find us as entertaining as we found ourselves. We had to travel at the beginning of the rush hour. We met at a fish and chips shop always, then rushed down escalators with a newspaperful each, stood for the first twenty minutes, eating and talking and laughing, falling about a bit because our hands were always too busy with other things to be hanging on as well. The last forty minutes, there was always more room, but we made too much gay use of it for the tired, end of the day newspaper readers. I tried to quiet us sometimes, but I never wanted to. I depended on those borrowed high spirits for my own.

Andrew came unexpectedly on his first visit late one Saturday afternoon in November. Because a fog had settled, I persuaded him to stay at the flat for the evening. I had a bottle or two of red wine. There must be a can of something that would do for dinner, but at six o'clock there was another knock on the door. Monk, her hair tangled into curls by the dampness, stood holding up a small, bleeding, paper bag.

"Liver!" she said in a regal voice.

"How did you get it?" I asked.

"I simply said to the butcher, 'But what do you do when you've spent your week's ration and are still thin and hungry?'" She did not see Andrew until I'd welcomed her in. "Oh dear, a love nest. I didn't know. Really I didn't."

"There's enough here for three," I said.

"But I've invited Esther," she said sadly. "I should have phoned first."

"I should have," Andrew said.

"There's enough for four," I said, dumping the liver out onto a plate. "Plenty."

"But Esther won't want to come with you here," Monk said to Andrew, then smiled helplessly. "Why don't you and Esther go out to dinner, and I'll stay home and cook for Andy?"

"Making it worse only makes it worse," I said. "Can't you ever learn?"

"No," Monk admitted. "What will I do?"

"Take off your coat. Wash the blood off your hands. And have a glass of wine."

"And I?" Andrew asked.

"More or less the same thing," I said. "It's time peace was made. Liver is as good an excuse as any."

And it turned out to be. You never had any human awkward-
ness. You greeted Andrew not as if you had expected him to be
there but as if it were the natural place for him to be. And you
settled at once to talk with him because there really were questions you had to ask about Cambridge and his Ph.D. program.
Monk and I listened for a while, my attention shifting from what
Andrew had to say to the attentive loveliness not only of your
face but of your whole body. You sat on the floor near the gas
fire, one knee up to support both hands and chin, your long hair
pulled back, then caught before it fell, heavy and dark against a
pale blue sweater. There was nothing delicate about you, the
bold bones of your hands under your strong chin, full, almost
Negroid mouth, flat cheek bones, black eyes and brows. It was a
face meant for repose, the fact of it animation enough. Beside you,
Monk's prettiness was not even a distraction, and that night she
did not try to compete. She went with me into the kitchen to help
prepare dinner, leaving you and Andrew to a peace that did not
seem to have to be made.

You left soon after dinner, on your way to a gang party the
rest of us could not be persuaded to go to. At around ten o'clock,
when Monk also decided that she had taken up enough of our
evening, Andrew and I walked her home. I could feel how careful they were being of each other because Monk's badly timed
jokes had stopped, because Andrew paid too much attention to
his conversation with me. After we left her, I let the conversation
stop, and we walked for several blocks in silence.

"We had a conversation about Canadian social customs once
before," I said.

"Yes, and I should have taken my own advice then."

"Well, but don't now, just to try to pay a bad debt. You'd be
good for Monk."

"How?"

"Don't be irritated with me, Andy."

"I'm not. It's just that sometimes I don't get the hang of being
friendly."

"I have to work tomorrow evening."

"Okay," he said, with enough resignation in his voice so that we could both feel the game was being played properly.

I had not really thought about Monk until she telephoned the next day just before I was going out to meet Andrew for lunch.

"That bastard's asked me out tonight!" she announced. "What did he tell you, that he was going back to Cambridge?"

"Of course not. I told him I had to work tonight. You didn't refuse, did you?"

"Well . . . yes, damn it."

"Never mind. I'm about to have lunch with him. What time will you be ready tonight?"

"Kate, hasn't anyone ever told you that lending men is a dangerous game?"

"I'm not lending him to you, Monk. I'm giving him to you, to return the favor for the liver."

"What's the matter with him?" she asked suspiciously.

"He has an addiction to redheads."

"Harems more likely," she said, "a brunette, a redhead, and a . . . blonde?"

"Not quite. What time?"

"Seven."

I did not work that night. I barely escaped being paid, however. Amateur standing in some sports is hard to maintain if you're twenty-one and in good training.

After that Andrew came to London almost every weekend. I often had lunch with him. His work and mine had moved closer together, and I talked with him as I had once talked with you. I was testing patterns in the economics of underdeveloped countries, as they were then called. It is still a more accurate, if less tactful euphemism than "emerging nations." Andrew had a great deal of information about primitive cultures which threatened to be relevant. We argued a lot, really because Andrew's interest was theoretical, mine more and more urgently practical.

"You *are* going to be a spy and a humanitarian," he said with some disapproval.

Occasionally I also went to the theater with Andrew and Monk, but it wasn't long before they began to isolate themselves, however reluctantly. Andrew didn't talk with me about Monk until just before Christmas when he dropped by for a drink.

"Kate, I'm going to have to marry her."

"Who?"

"Ramona." He had stopped calling her Monk almost at once, but I wasn't used to her real name. He might have been talking about someone else.

"Have to?"

He smiled. "She's not pregnant, no. And she may have to be pregnant before she will marry me."

"Has she broken off with Robin?"

"No."

"Well, don't hurry it. She is in love with you, as much as she knows how to be."

"Love's something none of my 'harem,' as she insists on calling you and Esther and herself, learned much about, it seems to me."

"She's right, you know. You are a harem thinker," I said before I could check my anger.

"I should have let us make that pact about not being together when we're desperate."

"You're not desperate," I said, trying to recover amiability.

"No," he said, "but I am embarrassed. Sometimes I feel a little too much like community property. I hear, for instance, that I was once traded for a bag of liver."

"You were, yes," I admitted. "That was a bit of face-saving that shouldn't have been necessary. I'm sorry."

"We're making each other earnest," he said.

"Just don't make me nervous, that's all. Is there anything you want me to do?"

"Come out to dinner with me."

"What about Monk?"

"She's tangled up with a late rehearsal."

Andrew had not been as candid in his explanations with Monk as he had been with you, and, though she was not openly jealous of the time he and I spent together, she was not easy about it. After that particular evening, she wondered if I didn't owe her a bag of liver ("I can be an Indian giver, too"), but she took the reassurance in a return of rough teasing. When she was feeling particularly safe, she was even generous.

"You know, Kate, you shouldn't always talk shop with men. They aren't really terrified of intellectual women if they know how to be women, too. It isn't that you aren't attractive enough. You could do something more interesting with your hair."

"Kate doesn't need the entire male population in love with her," you answered angrily.

"I wasn't suggesting that she did. One would do."

"One would be too many," I said. "I haven't time for that sort of thing."

"Do you know what I think?" Monk asked. "I think you've got a secret lover. Andy thinks so, too. He doesn't go along with my theory that he's some sort of important spy or a married man with a tragically insane wife. Andy says it's sure to be subtler than that, but he's poor at specific guesses. Where were you last Friday night, for instance?"

"If she wanted you to know," you said, "she'd tell you."

"And why wouldn't she want me to know? I tell both of you where I go."

"You'd be so disappointed if you knew," I said. "I have a duty to your imagination. After all, you're a writer."

"But I'm supposed to create the mystery, not be baffled by it myself. You don't behave as if you were in love. But you might have a secret sorrow."

"Tell us," you said, "are *you* in love?"

"Oh, perhaps a little," Monk said. "And don't give me a lecture about keeping two men on the string. You have three."

"That's different," you said.

"Yes, it is," Monk agreed. "It's absolutely regressive."

"What's regressive about friendship?"

I could have answered that one, but I didn't. I wanted to get off the topic entirely.

"Doris wants to know if there are to be more than the four of us for Christmas," I said.

"Marcus and Clide are both going home," you said. "But Purple's going to be on his own."

"Shall we ask him?"

"Sure."

"I think one of the beasts is going to be in town, too—Sidney," Monk said. "That would make us even and give Andy a little competition in all directions."

"Let's not have anyone else," you said suddenly. "Just the four of us."

"What about poor Purple?"

"He wouldn't fit, not really. He'd rather spend Christmas in a pub."

Sidney wasn't even reconsidered, and the number was settled at four.

"Fine," Doris said. "Then we won't bother to open the top floor. I can give Andy young Frank's room. I suppose you want Ann's room, do you?"

"No, put Monk in Ann's room and Esther and me into the guest room."

"I've written to Andy to suggest he spend the whole of his holiday with us. It seems silly for him to go to a hotel at all. Wouldn't you like a real holiday from housekeeping, too? The other two could come for five or six days—"

"No," I said. "We'll all three come at the same time. And you must promise me one thing right now—no negative conniving. Andy wants to marry Monk."

"Does he," Doris said, not really surprised, simply thinking about it. "All right. It is all right, isn't it?"

"I think so," I said. "I think it might be a very good thing for both of them."

"Such altruism!"

"Masochism," I said, smiling.

"You tell the truth often enough and someone may believe you."

I did finally go over a few days before you and Monk arrived because Doris wanted help and companionship while Frank and Andrew played chess, listened to Bach, and talked about what had happened to some of the great European wine cellars during the war. Neither of them in either principle or habit excluded women from their conversation, but they were so content together we often chose to exclude ourselves. I didn't miss young Frank, whose defense against his father was usually pompous aggressiveness, a tone he couldn't drop while he was at home; but I did miss Ann, who was perhaps too dully typical of the nicest sort of English daughter, but she had an affectionate grace with her parents that I found charming. I couldn't imitate it. I didn't try. And I felt less inadequate because Andrew made himself so attractively at home. Perhaps Frank's occasionally referring to us as "the children" gave Andrew the right sort of convention to move in with me, one that would be protective of both Monk and me. We went Christmas shopping together for Frank and Doris, Andrew with the addresses of several wine merchants, I with the name of a shop where we could find French gloves, and we gave them the presents we had found jointly, deciding to sign our cards "the children." I went with him, too, to approve the amber necklace he had found for Monk on a day he and Frank had gone off together. Immediately, when we got home, he went to Doris for her approval, helping her over her uncertain loyalties. By the time you and Monk arrived, we were a solidly established family who could turn our attention entirely to our guests.

If I had not seen Doris working carefully with a calendar, I would have thought that the following five days simply developed with extraordinary natural pacing. Monk, less absorbed in playing her part, could have learned a great deal about playwriting. Doris, however, had generously given her a number of important scenes, hours in the day when she and Andrew would find themselves alone together on leisurely errands or in front of the fire with glasses of champagne while other people seemed to be still dressing or not yet back from calling on elderly relatives and business friends. If Monk did not agree to marry Andrew on the last day of the house party, it was not Doris' fault.

She planned as carefully for all of us. She invited you to suggest inventive ornaments for the tree, then went off with you to Woolworth's and Harrod's and two or three art supply shops for the necessary materials. She might have been mildly surprised that you chose to work under rather than on the library table, but she did not show it. Occasionally we would find you both sitting on the floor, Doris as intent as you on starching and dyeing, cutting and painting. When people dropped in for drinks and Doris had to be hostess, she took them into the library to see you in the workshop. You'd nod out from under the table and behind a growing pile of invented flowers, star-winged angels, and apparently Easter eggs. On Christmas Eve, during cocktails, the decorating began. Frank followed your directions, threading dozens of tiny white lights through the branches. The rest of us followed with ornaments, but none was placed until you had decided where it would go. When we had finished, Doris was the first to speak.

"Esther, it's marvelous. It's a barbaric prophecy, as if we really were waiting for the Birth."

You turned to her, seeing her for the first time. At that moment, dinner was announced. We were reluctant to leave the tree, which was, as Doris described it, crudely splendid.

"Kate," you said, calling me back for a moment, "do you think I could go back to my place for a few minutes tonight?"

"Of course, if you need to."

105

"It's just that I'd like to give Doris one of my bell ringers. I think maybe she'd like it."

"I know she would," I said. "Are you going to want to go to midnight mass?"

"Will you go?"

"For you."

"No, then," you said. "Let's stay with the others."

At dinner you asked Andrew if he'd mind going back to your room with you for a few minutes. You had treated each other as friends for weeks, but you had both been careful not ever to be alone together. Andrew would have liked a quick gesture of approval from Monk, but he could not risk it. He agreed at once.

When you had gone, we all went to our rooms to begin collecting presents to put under the tree. I was wrapping a last-minute present for Andrew, a book on dragons I had found, when Monk came into the room. She sat down on your bed and watched me for a moment without speaking.

"I've never known anything about Christmas before," she said finally. "In my family Christmas is just hell. Andy says it's the same way in his family, too. Do you know how lucky you are?"

"Yes," I said.

"Or do you get mixed up about it the way I do? Most of the time I'm just enjoying myself, but sometimes it's so nice it makes me feel sad because this isn't my family and because I could never learn how to live like this. Does it feel to you really your family?"

"In a way," I said, "but part of it is having all of you here. When Frank and Ann are home, when Mother's here, it's not as easy."

"No, but still it wouldn't be like my family. And I didn't mean that. Have you ever wished Doris and Frank really were your parents?"

"No," I said. "You see, there is Mother still. If they were all my real family, it would be different, but I'm not sure it would be better."

"Doris thinks it would. She told me she'd often wished you were her daughter."

"Doris is very motherly," I said. "She'd like to adopt you and Andy and Esther, too."

"I wish she could."

"Are you a bit homesick?"

"Just for something I never had, and, if you've never had it, how can you make it? Andy doesn't know any more about this kind of living than I do."

"I suppose not."

"He's been the only son just the way I've been the only daughter, spoiled and fought over and forced to be something he's not until he doesn't really know who he is or what he wants."

It was not exactly the image I would have made of Andrew, but I recognized him in it. Monk could not afford to be as uncritical as I was. She was obviously contemplating what kind of a husband he would make.

As if she'd read my thoughts, she said, "I sometimes wish I could be a friend of Andrew's the way you are, but it never works that way for me."

"It's regressive," I said, without looking up from my wrapping.

"Well, yes, but it's a regressive season. Isn't Esther's tree terrible?"

"No. It's wonderful. I love it."

"Should Andy have gone off with her?"

"Oh, Monk, you're not worried about that, are you? I sometimes think you may really be in love with him."

"I am," she said bleakly, "but don't tell him!"

"You'd be the obvious one to break the news."

"I can't. He'd lose interest in a minute, Kate. That's the way men are. As long as they don't know, as long as they're uncertain, they're marvelous, but the minute they're sure, they're all bastards."

"And you call me a cynic!"

"But it's true."

"Then you aren't in love with him," I said primly.

" 'I love him not because he's rich and handsome, Nelly,' " she said in a comically theatrical tone, " 'but because he's more myself than I am.' "

"And would you lose interest?"

"I don't know. I don't think so. I can't imagine it. He is beautiful, isn't he? I mean, even his teeth."

"Even his teeth," I agreed. "Now, that's enough. Go get your presents."

We went to bed well after midnight, Doris cautioning us all to sleep late in the morning because these years were a brief respite between being children and having children which we should enjoy. She stood with Frank, her hand cupped round his elbow, an odd, masculine gesture, more personal for that, because it is the kind only years can teach and permit. They saw us upstairs as if they were going to fill stockings for us all before they went to bed; we countered with dignified behavior, prompted by an uncertain amount of brandy, which is always sobering to the young.

"How are you?" I asked, when we got to our room. "I don't seem to see much of you, seeing you all the time."

"Fine," you said. "You were right about Doris. I should get to know her. I'm still pretty hopeless with Frank."

"You're fine with everyone. You've made a beautiful tree."

"Monk thinks it's awful," you said, amused. "Then she's never really looked at Christmas trees to see how awful they traditionally are. Doris likes it, though, doesn't she?"

"And Frank and Andy and I."

"Do you think she's going to marry Andy?"

"I wouldn't be surprised."

"But what would happen if they ever stepped out of the silverware ad and started trying to live together?"

"What happens to a lot of people, I suppose."

"That's a terrible thought."

"I didn't mean it that way," I said.

"Probably I'm jealous," you said.

"Of whom?"

"Both of them. If I were a man, what a Christmas I'd make this for you!"

"What a ghastly idea!"

"I don't know. I wouldn't make such a bad man, do you think?"

You were standing in your bra and pants by this time, but your hair was still done up in a large soft shape at the back of your finely shaped head.

"You make a beautiful woman. I'd settle for that."

"You would?"

"I mean," I said quickly, "you should."

You got into your pajamas and went off to wash, leaving your father's watch carefully on the bedside table, your clothes scattered about the room. I picked them up and put them away. Then I turned off the overhead light and opened the window, loving the smell of earth and trees even at this time of year in the crescent.

"What are you looking at?" you asked.

"Nothing really. I was smelling." You came and stood beside me. "You smell lovely, too."

"Doris has marvelous soaps. It's cold."

"Hmm. Get into bed."

I followed you to your bed, covered you as if you were a child, then sat with you for a moment. You took my hand tentatively and put it to your mouth.

"Merry Christmas, Kate."

"Merry Christmas," I said. "You do make it fine for me. Sleep well."

I lay awake for a while, wondering if Mother, left to herself, would go to midnight service. She was vague in her letters about what her plans were for Christmas, but then she was always vague. She did refer to people and places by their names, but there was never an identifying phrase, a reminder. Doris and I had to guess or not bother to guess. She fades, I thought. Or

109

dreamed. I woke, expecting and missing the uncertain sweetness of her voice, the wry, shy morning moment which began any of our days together.

"I miss Mother today," I said to Doris.

"So do I," Doris admitted. "It always seems odd if I'm not introducing myself to her on Christmas morning of all mornings."

"Introducing yourself?" Andrew asked.

"Mother never seems to know anyone very certainly in the morning," Doris explained. "It's not that she's senile. She's always been that way. Once you've established yourself with her again, it's fine, but it always has to be done."

"How unnerving!" Andrew said.

I would have said *no* if Doris hadn't said *yes* so promptly. The ritual of being reestablished had always been reassuring to me, as if Mother considered again and accepted again the responsibility I was to her. For Doris, her natural child, to be considered again and again must have seemed an unnecessary strain. I didn't say these things, either. If Doris ever presented a view of Mother, that view took precedence over mine, for I had neither the length of experience nor the blood claim to speak with her authority.

After Mother had been brought, with reservations, into the breakfast conversation, Frank reminded us of their absent children, then of the absent families of all our guests. It was a graceful substitute for a real blessing and probably more accurately expressed the feelings of everyone at the table who, not able to depend on God to love those well whom they loved badly, carried the burden with some sense of responsibility.

Christmas morning without the very young and the very old, without God Himself, is simpler. From under our nearly pagan tree, we took the gifts, not quite one at a time, and measured again the degree of perception there is in giving. It was one of Andrew's extraordinary talents. I have never had a present from him that didn't serve the image I hope I hold up to the world: a book I would like to be thought of as reading, a blouse neither so tailored as it fit my private taste and public shoulders nor so feminine as to embarrass me, a sketch either a little subtler or a little bolder than I would risk buying for myself. Your gifts were your own. You always gave yourself away to anyone you trusted or wanted to trust, not always in the work you were seriously doing however. I have gross enamel cuff links with my initials on them from your brief enthusiasm for learning to make them. I have a mosaic ashtray—the very first thing you tried—which is a ridged and fractured attempt at a candle and book, I think, and perhaps my name is on that, too, though it would be hard to prove in the inaccurate cuttings and smeared plaster. I would not have been surprised by a pen wiper or pot holder, though I don't remember those particular kindergarten items on any of the many Christmases we exchanged presents. Monk had a flare for the outrageous and useful, but did she know that giving you a cook book was outrageous? The card on my lounging pajamas said, "to encourage you to entertain more at home." When Frank opened his shaving mirror, he asked if he wasn't too old to look that closely at himself.

"Oh no," Monk protested. "I just hope I look like you when I'm your age."

"For all our sakes, I devoutly hope you don't," he answered.

There weren't many embarrassing moments that Christmas. Robin's Care packages, set next to Andrew's amber necklace, troubled everyone else more than they seemed to trouble Monk, who talked about "hands across the water" and offered to bake us all tollhouse cookies when she next had the kitchen in her flat to herself. Andrew tried not to look as if he'd be poisoned by them, and Doris quickly opened another present to distract us all. Andrew and Monk had the majority of Christmas horrors from younger brothers and sisters, amateur scarves, glass-encrusted bottle openers, pictures of horses, a bow tie that lit up, and a bird whistle. You opened more presents than you wanted to from your mother, a winter wardrobe almost entirely unsuitable for the life you were leading, but Doris admired her taste, and you were glad not to complain, in fact to be elegantly dressed for the final few days of the house party, though the number of young bankers and lawyers and politicians you attracted were a nuisance to you for weeks afterwards.

"Most of them are dull," Frank admitted to me, "but most responsible people are, and she's got to find someone who will take care of her."

"I suppose so," I said, "but somehow I can't imagine Esther wife to anyone like that."

Wife to anyone, I might have said. You were simply no good at the ordinary encounter, the physical and emotional details of a day. You could have kept a man's principles and hopes in very good order, but not his house and his children. Monk tried to advise you as she did me.

"People don't always want to be talking about their souls and their visions," she said to you impatiently. "As for the Slade uniform, which year is it that you learn the difference between boys and girls?"

"With clothes on, I'm not sure," you answered.

"Well, socially that happens to be important."

More important and sometimes more difficult than Monk would have imagined. I often was not sure through the first pint of beer whether a companion was male or female. That doubt one night made me reticent with a tall Negro for longer than pleased her. Later, when I was certain and friendly, she accused me of prejudice. "Look if you're a nigger, I'm a—" clootch, squaw, I would have gone on to say, if my nose hadn't been broken in the middle of the sentence and my two front teeth knocked out shortly after that. Yes, grotesque. That part of my living was. Spoken of at all. I had to speak of this, lie about it, because I was in the hospital for a week with those and other painful but fortunately not serious injuries. I quite unreasonably wanted to keep Frank and Doris from knowing that I had been in any trouble at all. You pointed out to me that, even if I could keep them ignorant for the week I was in the hospital, my face would not heal completely for some weeks after that.

"What am I going to tell them?" I asked. It was difficult to talk.

"A car accident?" you suggested . . . or perhaps asked.

"Frank would want to check that out, legally," I said.

"A fall?"

"Does it look like a fall?"

"No," you admitted.

I couldn't really see to judge because my eyes were badly swollen. I hadn't told you what had happened, but I gathered from your silence that it was pretty obvious.

"I've already told the police I won't lay charges. Thank God I'm twenty-one."

"Couldn't you just not tell them—I mean, just say you don't want to talk about it?"

"Maybe, but try to put them off for a little while, E., would you? I haven't the face to face them with just yet."

The next day, when I couldn't see at all, Doris came.

"Don't blame Esther, darling. She begged me not to come for at least two or three days. She said you didn't want to see anyone. You can't see anyone, can you?"

"I didn't want you to see me," I said.

"It's not a pretty sight. Your doctor said you were badly but inexpertly beaten—no permanent damage."

"That's right," I said. "Good as new in a few days."

"Weeks. Hurt pretty badly?"

"Some. Can you keep Frank out of it?"

"He's in Scotland this week."

"Thank God for that."

"I'll have to tell him something sooner or later."

"I'm not awfully good at talking at the moment."

"Of course not."

She had taken the hand that wasn't bandaged and stayed quiet for a while. Then she gave me bits of news about the children and friends.

"I mustn't stay too long, but I'll be back tomorrow."

I nodded, wondering if I could hide behind my swollen mask long enough to make the raising of the subject finally too awkward for her. Monk was told I had been in some kind of accident which I was still vague about and was too sick for visitors. But on the fifth day, when my eyes were really beginning to open again, Andrew arrived, bringing a bed jacket made like a cape so that I didn't have to struggle into it, the catalogue of a show in Paris we had talked about going over for, and a precious box of chocolates for the nurses. He didn't stay with pleasantries long.

"You've got to put your mind to what you're going to tell Doris—and everyone else, Kate. Make it a blatant lie, if you want, but you've got to say something. Doris is simply beside herself."

"Tell me what to say," I said. "What can I say?"

"Was it someone you knew?"

"What difference does it make, Andy? It's not a paternity case, after all."

"It does make a difference. It could happen again, Kate. You could get yourself killed."

"Possibly, but not probably. I made a mistake, a very stupid mistake. It was my own fault. It won't happen again."

"Why did it happen at all?"

"You imagine, Andy. You make up something."

"You were restless," he said. "You went out for a walk and went too far into Soho. It seemed quiet enough, so you stopped for a drink. Stupid, of course, dressed in dollar signs the way you are, but you didn't think of that. On the street you were followed. Somebody tried to grab your purse, and, stupid again, you didn't simply let go. You put up a fight and were beaten up."

"If I'd said that in the first place—"

"Well, they were young kids. They didn't get your money. You thought of the kids at the orphanage. And you felt the whole thing was your own fault, wandering around on your own at that time of night. It isn't as if you could think very clearly right afterwards."

"Can you tell Doris that and make her believe it?"

"I can try. I will try. But, Kate, you ought to try to tell somebody what really happened."

"Why?"

"It could help."

"I'll be more careful, Andy. I didn't like it much myself."

"No," he said. "And I wish you wouldn't risk it again . . . ever. There are other solutions."

"How's dragon slaying?" I asked.

"Pretty good, actually. Slow, but that's as well. You'd be a hell of a looking bridesmaid at the moment."

"And work?"

"Slow, too. And that's not so good, but there's time."

You came to the hospital every day to tell me about your classes, about parties with Marcus and Clide and Purple Bell, who sent a bunch of flowers. You didn't want to tell me about the orphanage, but, after I'd asked several times, you admitted that the recreation hour had been canceled until I was well enough to go again.

"What happened?"

"A minor sort of riot," you said, trying to grin. "Monk and I just couldn't control them. Nobody was hurt finally, but I don't know why. It took three of the permanent staff to calm them down again. After that we got our temporary walking papers."

"After Monk told them just what was wrong and why it really happened."

"Well, a bit."

"It must have been frightening," I said.

"It was, partly because of what might have happened, but it was more than that. It was being helpless. It was knowing that good will doesn't mean a thing. Why is that, Kate?"

"They don't understand the language."

"But you could control them."

"Only sometimes, and that will doesn't have anything to do with good will."

The thought of going back there depressed me terribly. I was, of course, afraid, not of the physical violence, which never seemed quite real, even after it happened, but of the aggressive pointlessness of it all, whether the assault of my will or theirs. And I wondered what real difference there was between the state of my face now and the state of my mind on other brief if not so abrupt occasions. Perhaps there had been no misunderstanding at all between you and the children, between me and the Negro. This possibility I could not discuss with you or with Andrew because it infected my sense of all relationships, not as an idea but as a fear.

At first, when I didn't leave my flat, everyone understood that I must feel shy about my face. You and Monk brought me books. Doris did my shopping. But after the bruises turned green, then yellow, and finally faded altogether, leaving my face only slightly swollen, after my new teeth were fitted, still I didn't go back to lectures or suggest new plans for the orphanage. Frank invited me to go along on a business trip to Paris, but I refused. Andrew's extra theater tickets went to you or Doris or one of the boys. Then I began not always to answer the phone or door bell.

Monk telephoned one morning while the cleaning woman was there.

"Warn Miss George that I'll be over in about half an hour," she said.

I hadn't the energy to go out to avoid her, and, anyway, I was trying to keep to myself, calling as little notice to the habit as I could. Monk arrived with two suitcases.

"Where are you off to?"

"Here," she said, setting the cases down.

"Here?"

"That's right. My landlady has gone to Greece for three weeks, and I simply can't stay alone there. It's too easy. I'm not asking you if I can stay. I'm telling you. And don't suggest I go to Frank's and Doris' because it's just as easy there."

"Why not be easy?" I suggested.

"Really, Kate! Is that kind advice for a friend in distress?"

"I'm not good at kind advice, and I'm nobody to spend three weeks with just now, Monk."

"I wouldn't say that. Your cheerful best is always pretty exhausting. I really like morbid people. I grew up with a whole crowd of them."

I couldn't discourage her. I hadn't enough interest in my own comfort to be forceful. Once I realized how determined she was, whether she stayed or not didn't seem to matter. I made no effort to make her feel welcome, but she didn't seem to need it. When the cleaning woman had gone, Monk unpacked her clothes and books, finding places to put everything away. Then she explored the kitchen, which was well stocked with food I hadn't bothered to eat.

"This is going to be fascinating," she said. "I've never watched slow starvation before. It's a perfect idea for a TV play."

I sat with a book I had been holding when she came in and ignored her. She found the extra key and went off to an afternoon class. I had not moved when she got back, but I began to feel just a little foolish in my sullenness. When she brought in sherry, I tried to be civil.

"No, now don't strain yourself. I have plenty to sulk about myself. We'll just sulk together."

She stared at the gas fire in such a ridiculously accurate imitation of me that I felt a weak threat of amusement, then a stronger sense of irritation. I did nothing but drink my sherry. After a few minutes Monk went back to the kitchen. She was a quiet cook, one of the few I've known. The occasional opening of a drawer or cupboard, the gentle scraping of a spoon in a saucepan were undisturbing sounds. She came back into the sitting room, poured me another glass of sherry, and then pulled out the dropleaf table, which I hadn't bothered to set for weeks. After she went back to the kitchen, I noticed candles and five daffodils. I got up, went into the bathroom, washed and made up my still slightly blurred face. Then I went into the bedroom and put on my lounging pajamas.

"Well," Monk said. "Who's coming? Do I have to go out for the evening, or can I sit in the bathroom and read?"

"You'll do whatever you please," I said, "obviously."

It was a light, delicious meal. Monk had discovered the French habit of serving things one at a time so that no plate was ever crowded, and she had a flare for seasonings so that ordinary white fish could taste as delicate as sole, a green salad be worth the trouble of eating it. She bothered with bright garnishes, not so much things like parsley, which was, she said, nothing but an adjective; hers had the strength of prepositional phrases. I ate without real pleasure, but I was not put off.

"Now, how about a little brandy with your coffee?" she suggested.

"There isn't any brandy."

"But there is. I brought over the last of a bottle Frank gave me last month."

We moved over to the fire, leaving the candles burning, and sat in unself-conscious silence for some time.

"Would you like me to put on a record?" Monk asked finally. "Yes."

When she chose Deller singing "In Darkness Let Me Dwell," I did not know whether she mocked or consoled me. It didn't matter. It was all the same thing, and that sort of reducing of gesture was a possible revelation, one that could be lived with.

It was a week after Monk moved in that I returned to lectures, but we never did go back to the orphanage. It remained a debt, collecting different kinds of emotional interest for each of us.

At the end of the second week, I was recognizable enough to Monk for her to risk raising the subject of Andrew, who had been noticeably absent.

"He told me I had to make up my mind," she said.

"And you can't?"

"I couldn't imagine being married to anyone else."

"What about Robin?"

"Poor Robin. Think of all those food parcels!"

"You only have to return the ring."

"And I'll miss that. I like to look at it sitting there in the drawer. And it's been awfully useful at some of those parties Esther gives."

"I suppose Andy'd give you another."

"Anyway, I can't really send it back. He'd probably have to pay duty on it."

"Give it to Mother to take back. She'll be here in a couple of weeks."

"Does Andy love me, Kate?"

"Yes."

"Is he too good for me?"

"You said yourself that you were very much alike in lots of ways."

"I don't mean that. Is he too rich for me? Is he too handsome?"

I don't know why I was surprised by the question. Just those attributes had made it possible for me to make friends with Andrew, put him out of reach enough to be a friend. But I didn't say that.

"Those aren't the sorts of things you have to live up to," I said.

"Those are the sorts of things you can lose," Monk said, "or have taken away from you by another woman."

"He can lose them himself, of course."

"I hadn't thought of that."

I don't know what it was that finally made Monk decide, but on the last weekend she was with me, she came home late Saturday night with the news that she and Andrew were engaged. She was wearing his ring. The following weekend Frank and Doris gave them a party, the Monday after which Monk received a letter from her father ordering her to break her engagement or be disowned.

"Here we go again," you said. "What more can he want in a son-in-law?"

"Apparently he objects because Andy's a foreigner," I explained.

"A Canadian's a foreigner?"

"Well, yes, and you see, they weren't supposed to be. They were cowards—I suppose from Mr. Ridley's point of view, traitors during the Revolution."

"Holy God!"

"It is pretty ridiculous. Andy's just furious, but Frank was marvelous with him, told him not to lose his head. Frank has asked Monk if he can write to her father."

Nobody ever saw the letter that Frank wrote. Even Doris did not know what was in it, but I imagine, along with the praise Frank could genuinely offer for a young man he would have liked as a son, he used a banker's language about the financial facts of Andrew's life. The letter was followed by several telephone calls. The Ridleys did not accept an invitation from Frank and Doris to come to England for the wedding, but in all else they were not only cooperative but enthusiastic. The date was set for the first of May. Andrew sacrificed Frank as best man so that he could give Monk away. You were to be maid of honor, Ann, and a friend of Monk's from RADA and I bridesmaids.

We expected Mother to be there for the wedding, but just a week before she had planned to arrive she wrote to say that she was having a little trouble with her legs. Her doctor did not think she should travel. Telephone calls to her gave us no more information. She felt perfectly well. Nothing was seriously wrong. She was sorry she couldn't keep all the medical names straight, but the point was that she shouldn't travel just now. Perhaps she could still come for the coronation in June. Your mother, whom no one expected, suddenly wired to have her plane met.

The role your mother chose to play is hard to describe: Paris dress designer, Negro mammy, Queen Mother, wicked step-sister to the maid of honor. They don't add up, but your mother never did. She would work at one part until long after it failed, then switch to its opposite with the same result. The only constant thing about her was her aggressive uncertainty, whether she was deciding to keep her suite at the hotel or move in with you so that she could understand your life better, whether she was being a surprised foreigner who found all the customs charming and quaint or was telling everyone just how things ought to be done. Doris, after the first ten minutes, stiffened into pleasantries and played by those hard rules from then on. Frank courted her with some irony; Andrew nearly ignored her, and Monk hid from her. I did what I could to protect you, but you had your own defensive devices. Occasionally you had "talks" with her, in which you tried very earnestly to present your own views; three or four times you lost your temper with her; but mostly you sulked, eyes blank, mouth a little open, until anyone who didn't know you might have wondered about brain damage. Stupidity may be the deadliest sort of passive resistance.

Though there was plenty of money from all sources to put on the not very elaborate wedding Andrew and Monk wanted, Mrs. Woolf insisted on treating both Andrew and Monk like poor relatives. She wanted to buy not only all the dresses for the attendants but Monk's wedding dress as well. When she heard that Doris and Frank were having the reception, she offered to pay for it. And she tried to give Andrew a check for the honeymoon. Frank twice tried to explain that the Ridleys were paying for the wedding and wanted to, that Andrew was neither reluctant nor incapable of paying the traditional expenses of the groom, but he could neither comfort nor distract her.

"Katherine, is there nothing I'm to be allowed to do? Have I come all this way to be rejected and scorned?"

Doris said, when I repeated this comment to her, asking for suggestions, "Tell her she's doing a marvelous job of being all the hellish relatives who weren't able to attend. Without her it wouldn't even feel like a wedding."

"Why don't we accept the bridesmaids' dresses?"

"And have her decide what they're going to be?"

"Even that would be better than more scenes."

"Well, ask Monk."

Monk said dismally, "Andy and I are going to elope, if we get married at all. Why don't you marry him? I won't even ask a bit of liver."

"Just the bridesmaids' dresses, Monk," I pleaded.

"She'll make Esther wear white. It's all part of a plot. You'll all be in white, and Andy won't know which is which. He'll get his harem after all."

But once Mrs. Woolf had that much of her way, she was suddenly cooperative. The only thing she insisted on, when Monk and she went to choose the dresses, was that Monk not be shown the prices. The dresses were simple, becoming to us all, and probably shockingly expensive.

"You're a real P.R. man, Katie," Andrew said, not much approving. "I should send you to Canada to deal with my family."

"They're not coming, I gather."

"No," he said.

"They're all right about it, aren't they?"

"Just fine," he said. "My father sent me a check for ten thousand dollars."

"Lovely."

"And told me that was that. It was a grand letter, a 'good luck, son, now that you've become a man' letter."

"What does he mean?"

"That now, whether I know it or not, I've chosen to be independent."

"What are you going to do?"

"Go right on as if nothing had happened. I'll get as far along with the Ph.D. as I can. Then I'll raise hell."

"Will that work?"

"It always has," he said. "Now, I haven't said a word to you about any of this. Ramona doesn't know, and I don't want her to. There's no point in worrying anyone about it."

That evening you and your mother came to my flat for dinner. It was part of the "getting to know how you live" program "without actually moving in" program that I was trying to run.

"Now, this is a perfectly pleasant place to live, Esther," your mother commented at once.

"But no Lady Alice," I said.

"Thank heavens. That woman hasn't any real rank. No one who drinks like that could have."

"But in other ways she's very proper," I said to head off a more violent protest from you.

You shrugged, picked up one of my textbooks, and sat down on the floor to read.

"Always interested in books," Mrs. Woolf said cheerfully. "That's what I admire most in you young people. And envy you, too. I was never encouraged to be serious about anything, but I mustn't complain. I can live it all through Esther and you . . . and Ramona, too, of course. Do you think Andrew's just a little bit cold, a little bit hard?"

"He's a man," you said, looking up from your book.

"I've known other men willing to accept wedding presents."

You gave me your drowning dog look and went back to your reading.

"He's a bit proud, that's all," I said. "And, you know, I think your idea of giving them a check is a marvelous one. Why don't you make it out to both of them and not be very specific about how they should spend it? Then, when they get around to setting up a real house, they could buy something with it."

"And just how much had you in mind?" Mrs. Woolf asked, her tone suddenly hard, her face candidly inquiring.

"You be a bitch with Kate, Mother, and that's the end!" you said, slamming your book shut.

"Darling, you misunderstand. Katherine's giving me advice, very good advice. You're too emotional. I find artists are, don't you, Katherine? It's been a great relief to me that Esther had the good sense to make a friend of you, someone sensible and practical.

I asked Katherine how much I should give because I want to be generous without being embarrassing, dear. It seems so easy to make a mistake."

I could have forgiven her everything but the dissolving of your face. You wanted to believe her. You wanted to be mistaken. That left you no choice but to betray your own understanding. You must have been manipulated into mistrusting yourself from the time you were a little girl. No wonder you had no ordinary sense of an emotional climate. But, of course, it was the same training that made you able to tolerate me.

The wedding occurred and is recorded, just as yours is, along with all the other public occasions of our living, in photographs and clippings, stored on the shelf. I do not want to be our social historian. I remember perversely what wasn't the dramatic center, the heel of your shoe breaking off at the reception, your mother's imperious search for strawberry tea when the reception was over and it was time for dinner, the late night phone call from Monk, who had left her passport behind.

Two days later I left England myself, called home for the first time and the last.

III

Mother's first stroke only temporarily handicapped her. The slight drag of mouth, the droop of eyelid, and the occasionally scrambled sentence were less and less noticeable as the days passed. Because I was at home and could share the extra chores with the housekeeper, a nurse wasn't needed. And Mother submitted to my personal tending of her much more easily than I expected her to, for she had always been physically a very private person. It was as if she simply withdrew her identity from her body, treated it and let other people treat it more as if it were something that belonged to her, yes, but like her clothes and her furniture which someone else had always been allowed to keep clean and repair. She was grateful for each thing she was again able to do for herself, but it was the pleasure of returning independence, not modesty or dignity which she had never lost.

Doris, who at first had planned to follow me in a day or two, postponed and finally canceled her trip as the reports grew more encouraging and Mother made it clear that she would rather spend time with Doris when she was really well again. I was a little surprised that Doris could be so easily persuaded to stay away. I couldn't have been, but my relationship with Mother wasn't at all what Doris' was with her. They were never openly unpleasant with each other, but there was always tension between them which in Doris was a quick impatience, in Mother a tone of doubting surprise or willful bewilderment. Between Mother and me there had always been an odd consideration. We did not want to get in each other's emotional way, and we never did, sharing a strong, negative sensitivity to each other. But we were both very much aware of the duties we had to each other, and we both liked duty. While I did what a daughter should do for an ailing mother, she accepted my attentions, whatever they had to be. But, as she recovered, she gradually withdrew until I could feel her preparing to dismiss or set me free. I had been there a month when she suggested that it was time for me to return to England.

"Would I be awfully in your way if I didn't go back until fall?"

"Of course not, dear. But what about your work?"

I didn't know how much of my wanting to stay at home was a disenchantment with my work, how much a reluctance to go back to London itself, how much a realization that Mother was now old and frail and therefore temporary. In that month there had been a slow healing going on in me, too. I wanted it to continue, as if there were a stage beyond being restored that I could discover in that quiet house, in that wall-enclosed garden with my healing, dying mother. I gave a simple explanation and was given permission to stay.

Informative postcards from Andrew and disgraceful ones from Monk made it clear that they were enjoying Europe and were not planning to be back in England before the autumn themselves. I tried not to calculate the expense of those months for

Andrew, but it was obvious that he was refusing to accept his father's word as the last. I simply hoped he was right.

There was no word from you until late in June when I had three pages of your child's hand, filled with exclamation marks, faces, and date lines to indicate the number of times you had tried to begin again or go on. Nothing in the letter brought me any sense of your work, your mood, your living. The fact of it suggested that you were lonely, as well you might have been with both Monk and me gone. Because I could have gone back and didn't want to, I chose to be irritated with your inability to write a letter and did not answer it at once. I press the point now to make it seem an important failure. For you I'm sure it wasn't.

I did not write to you until nearly the end of August, and that was no more than a brief, sharp note to say I would not be going back to England at all. Mother had had a second, more severe stroke, and this time Doris came.

"You're as brown as a whole Indian," Doris said when we met at the airport. "It's nice of you to look so well. It makes me feel less guilty."

"There's nothing to be guilty about. I've done nothing but please myself all summer."

Driving from the airport to the hospital, Doris wanted to be told just what to expect, and I tried to be accurate, but nothing could really prepare or protect her from her first sight of Mother, whom she hadn't seen for more than a year. There was no introduction now, no renewed recognition. Mother lay, partially paralyzed, invaded by tubes, eyes tracking nothing but her interior dilemma, brain receiving little but the garbled messages of its own catastrophe. My throat tightened, but not for her who seemed too isolated to expect and therefore inspire sympathy. Doris held her hand, stroked her forehead, spoke to her quietly.

"Mother? Mother, darling, it's Doris. I'm here, Mother. I'm here with Kate. It's Doris, Mother."

I walked over to the window and watched a man in a wheelchair being taken to a car in the parking lot.

"She doesn't know me, either," Doris said to my back.

"It's too soon," I said. "She will."

"You try."

I did not want to, but I couldn't refuse. I went to the other side of the bed, touched the insensitive, paralyzed hand, and spoke very softly. Saliva suddenly spilled from the drawn corner of Mother's mouth. I wiped her face. She did not respond.

"Tomorrow or the next day or the next," I said to Doris.

"Hasn't she known you at all?"

"I don't think so. It's hard to tell. She may not have any way of showing what she knows yet."

At first I waited for Doris to suggest that we leave. Finally, trying not to be uneasy about the slight shift in authority, I made the suggestion myself.

"She can't live through this!" Doris said as we walked toward the car. "I don't care what the doctors say. She could never be right again, could she?"

"It's hard to know."

"Oh, Kate, pray she has another in the night."

She did not. The following morning she was much the same. Her color was perhaps a little better. She seemed to be differently restless, as if she might sometimes be aware of vague shadows outside her own mind, but these were not yet signs for Doris, who needed some shocking, normal occurrence, like the sound of Mother's conscious voice.

We spent a great deal of time at the hospital, not always in Mother's room. We went to the cafeteria for snacks, to the lounge for magazines, even sometimes out beyond the parking lot to the eucalyptus groves for a short walk. Doris did not talk much. When she did, she talked about Mother, but they were short, specific observations which, gathered together, made no more sense than they did separately. Doris obviously wanted to come to some conclusions, but, until she had really taken in the facts and accepted them, she could not.

Without being able to mark the precise moment of it, we

began to be certain that Mother did sometimes recognize us. Her noises became attempts to speak, then speech itself, our names. The pain she was now in was definitely again a healing pain. The doctors continued to say exactly what they had said before: that she could gradually recover or die in the night; but Doris, who had prayed for the simpler solution, now turned her mind to the problems of Mother's less and less theoretical life.

"When she's stronger, she should go into a nursing home," Doris decided.

"She'll want to come home," I said.

"Well, she can't. I can't stay with her indefinitely, and neither can you."

"I can," I said, but carefully. "Doris, I'd like to."

"It's not something I'll let you do whether you want to or not."

"Why?"

"Katie, you don't owe her anything. You've given her more than she had any right to expect."

"It's not true, Doris, but anyway that's not the point. I simply want to."

"Why?"

"I love her."

Doris looked away from me, hesitated, and then said, without turning back, "I should be glad that someone does."

"Doris?"

"I have a different problem. I love you, and you're only twenty-two years old, and she could go on living for years."

"I don't think she will, you know. If only for a little while . . . a few months, and, if it's too hard or if it begins not to make sense, then—"

"You'd never admit it."

"I would, Doris. I promise. Will you let me try?"

She would not agree then, but it was still a decision that could be put off. Mother would have to be in the hospital at least another month, perhaps a good deal longer, and, while she was there, neither Doris nor I could think what we might do but visit her daily and settle less tentatively to a domestic routine of our own. During Mother's first illness the legal steps had been taken for me to handle her routine financial business, and I continued with it now. Because I had also made the decisions for the household, I found myself naturally in charge of those, too. If I had not been intent on proving to Doris that I could take charge, I might have been shyer of doing what was more naturally hers to do. But she had never really lived in the house and could not have run it without alarming the housekeeper, cleaning woman, and gardener. Mother's fear of fire had made a cold, decorative hearth in the living room, a chimney clogged with birds' nests, and odd rituals for emptying ashtrays. Her love of privacy had inspired an elaborate system of door answering, during which even an invited guest was thoroughly inspected through the peep hole before bolts were shifted and the second inspection carried out in the hall. In every aspect of the domestic day, there were the quirks of Mother's quiet life to which I had grown so accustomed that I hardly noticed them; for Doris they were a constant irritation. Yet she never made a direct complaint. And, when she did complain to me, she suggested good-humoredly wild alternatives. Together we let the house go on as if Mother were still at the center of it, and perhaps that, as much as anything else, let Doris drift gradually into accepting Mother's return to it. Perhaps, too, it made Doris restless enough so that she finally agreed to go back to England before Mother was allowed to come home.

"You will stay, Kate," she said for the last time.

"Yes, I will, and I'll let you know how it's going. With nurses, there's going to be so little for me to do, I'll probably take a course or two here. It would be simple enough."

"That's a good idea. And, if you need me—"

"I'll tell you. Give my love to young Frank when you see him in New York."

Doris was set free to a future she could feel responsible for, I to a past that I felt relieved not to share with anyone.

Mother's return home was delayed several times, but finally just after the new year, the doctor gave his permission. Her own bed had been moved out of her room and replaced by a hospital bed. I had hired three nurses and a young helper for the aging housekeeper, who would not have minded my waiting on my mother but would have been distressed if I had also helped her look after the nurses. I enjoyed all these preparations, the anticipating and solving of problems before they occurred. And Mother, whom I saw in the mornings at her most lucid, was very happy at the prospect.

I knew that her mind still short-circuited occasionally, but I imagined being at home would be less confusing for her. I was not frightened by the temper tantrum she had when she discovered that she was to be carried into the house on a stretcher rather than wheeled in in a chair. And, because she had been upset, I was not really alarmed by her bewilderment when she was finally settled in her own room.

"Where's Mother? Where's Grace?" she asked over and over again.

I did mind the nurses' humoring of her, accepting her confusion. I was patient with it, but I wanted to assert myself against it with rational reassurances. Because she did know me, because clear questions about the running of the house did occur to her, I was sure that gradually her own childhood would settle again into memory. But, as the days passed, she more and more often begged me to take her home. I had promised, she reminded me, and, though this hotel was pleasant enough—she had no serious complaints about the service—she really wasn't well enough to stay. I always answered with the explanation that she was at home. Sometimes she agreed, admitted that her mind was unclear. Sometimes she simply turned away. Gradually she developed craft in her persuasion. She would ask me about particular flowers and trees in the garden, and, when I answered inaccurately, she was triumphant with proof that she was not at home, but that pleasure would almost immediately dissolve into a child's pleading, "I want to go home, I want to go home, I want to go home."

As her mind grew more and more confused, her body grew stronger. She was able to get out of bed, and, though she dragged her left leg and had no strong use of her left arm, she could work her way around the furniture of her room and out into the hall without help. It was not safe to leave her alone for even a few minutes, and she was strong and willful enough so that neither the housekeeper nor the maid by themselves could control her. Sometimes even one of the nurses had to call for help. Mother seemed most restless in the early hours of the morning. The night nurse, a small, nervous woman, occasionally called me at four in the morning to calm Mother down. I was usually already awake because, too directly crossed, Mother would shout. Sometimes she threatened to commit suicide, but more often she was full of accusations. The night nurse was a pervert. I had at least three men in my room every night, and she simply couldn't sleep. Her father was on the roof killing eagles and cats. I could quiet her if I could distract her. I often sang to her songs she had sung to me when I was a child. I talked to the doctor about sedatives. We had to balance carefully the dangers to her heart of more medication and more emotional strain.

Yet, after one of these nights, when I couldn't believe her heart could stand her tantrums of confusion and fear a moment longer, I would find her in the morning, lying quietly in bed chatting with the nurse about what she might put on for the afternoon. I would bring her her jewelry cases just as I had when I was a child, and we'd sit together, trying on rings, bracelets, earrings, pins.

"It's a nuisance not being able to do this for myself any more," she'd say, "but, on the other hand, I feel rather queenly having it done for me. Do you want this sapphire when I'm dead, Kate, or shall we give it to Ann?"

I'd go off to afternoon lectures I was attending reassured, but by dinnertime she had mild complaints about the number of animals that had been in her room.

"I never knew you to be so interested in zoos when you were a child, Kate. I don't really mind, but we are going home soon, aren't we?"

It must have been early March, a time when I had begun to accept and despair of Mother's condition, that you telephoned from New York.

"I've been home since Christmas," you said. "I kept meaning to write, but the point is that I needed to talk with you. I think I want to be in California, and Mother's agreeable. Anyway, I'd like to come out and look around. Could you see me?"

I didn't know whether to ask you to stay or not, for your sake really. Mother was by now accustomed enough to the comings and goings of nurses so that one more person would probably not upset her. But I wondered how hard her sometimes extraordinary conversations would be for you, how alarming the occasional scenes in the middle of the night. Perhaps I felt a little protective of Mother, too. You had met her only briefly on several occasions. The possibility of your seeing her the way she was now sharpened my own sight, but exposing Mother to you was less important than seeing you myself.

For all the things you weren't able to do, for all the problems you couldn't understand or deal with, you had with my mother's madness no difficulty at all. The morning you arrived, she remembered that you were coming. She sat in the chair by her window, the uncertain side of her face away from the light, her hair combed, perhaps even a little rouge on her cheeks, in a new, pale blue dressing gown. When I brought you in to her, I saw for a moment the person I had already lost. She greeted you with the gentle tentativeness and curiosity she had always had and remembered all the ritual questions a hostess asks of a guest. It was the first time she seemed quite certain that she was at home. It didn't last, but in those more difficult conversations you neither humored her as the nurses did nor asserted your reality against hers as I did. Rather you shared her interests and concerns. You agreed that living in a hotel was difficult without ever agreeing that she now lived in one. You asked her to tell stories about her sister, Grace, and her mother when she called for them or said she had just seen them. But the most extraordinary thing you did was to sketch her hallucinations for her or make them out of cardboard, paper clips, and bits of jewelry. These representations of what she saw comforted and delighted her as nothing else could. With you she found a way out of her loneliness. She sometimes called you Grace or Mother, and once, when she heard me call you little dog, she laughed and said, "We have an everybody in the house." And then deliberately she called you by many names, knowing it was a game.

She did not have a bad night until nearly two weeks after you arrived, but that was very bad. When it was over, the night nurse gave notice, explaining to me that I needed to find someone stronger, someone with more psychiatric training if I intended to keep my mother at home. Intend I did, and within a week I had hired Olga Hanser, a German woman in her forties who was strong and sensible and gruffly kind. Mother treated her to a number of verbal abuses and wild stories for the first several nights, but after that she seemed content enough, gradually even fond, for she called Olga Hanser "Mac" with some amusement. I began to call her Mac, too. We all did.

During those days which turned into weeks, I began to hear about your life in London after I left, even before I left; and I could imagine, as I had refused to before, how hard it had been because now we were together again, leading as orderly and pub-lic a life as we had at college. I needed to do nothing but listen. You did not make a soul's trial of it, though it had been a soul's trial. Instead you were taking what you had learned from it to plan something better.

"I think I can live alone here, and I know I can work alone. That's what I want to do."

"But not yet, E."

You knew that I was not being generous, that I wanted and needed you with me. Our chess games now were for the benefit of no audience. They could take my mind off Mother, off my uncertainty about my own work, off all the decisions I could not make. You brought home books and records I would otherwise not have had the mind for. And because you were there, I could even sit in the sun sometimes, doing nothing but keeping you company. Occasionally we went to a movie, but I never liked to be away from the house for long. You set up a workshop in the garage where you occupied yourself when I was with Mother or doing my own work. The housekeeper liked you because you had an appetite for the cookies she loved to bake, and the maid didn't mind the chaos of your room because you let her talk to you about her boy friends. The nurses, of course, loved you because you were so good with Mother.

"That friend of yours should be a psychiatrist," Mac said to me one night when I went in to check for the last time before going to bed.

The idea amused me, but I answered seriously enough.

"It's too bad she can't draw a few pictures for you," Mac said.

"You have one patient, Mac."

"Well, I'll soon have two if you don't begin to get a little sleep. Your light was on until three-thirty again last night, and you were up before I left in the morning."

"I never sleep a lot."

"Obviously."

"Do you?"

Mac gave me a look that was both amused and reprimanding. "Why don't you go to bed before I put you to bed?"

Once I was in my room I thought of bundling a quilt over the crack under my door or turning out the light and reading by my radio light as I had when I was a child. In my nightgown and robe, I started into the hall to go to the bathroom just as you came out of your room. Mac, sitting at a small desk at the other end of the hall, looked up and smiled at our confusion. You retreated. I went into the bathroom furious. I sat on the toilet, staring at myself in the chrome knobs of the built-in chest in front of me. I began to make faces, wide mouths vanishing into my ears, fat-eyed squints. The old monster! When I left the bathroom, I turned and glared at Mac's profile and said, in a very soft voice, "Bugger you!" She did not look up. I went back into my bedroom and tried, in no louder a voice, "You're fired." Then I got into bed and snapped out the light. You went into the bathroom. When you came out, I could hear your voice with Mac's. Suddenly I tightened into a different kind of anger—fright. Was there no safety anywhere? I heard your bedroom door click shut and relaxed again. I was talking to myself. I was telling myself all the sane, quiet things I knew to tell. That kind of lecture always takes a while, and I was wide awake when it was finished. I was calm, but I wanted a cigarette. I turned my light back on, smoked and began to read.

In the morning I did not get up until after Mac had left. I avoided her out of embarrassment. But the next night she was as gruff and amiable as ever. I was impressively adult, friendly, but with an order or two framed as suggestions, one of which was that we set up the desk in Mother's dressing room where there was more space and also a comfortable chair.

"Good idea," she agreed.

It was two or three days before I could force myself to begin the process of sending you away. I did not know how I would cope, once you were gone, with a house run to accommodate madness. As we sat with Mother playing therapeutic games, I had rested in your immunity to her sudden sexual references, cats copulating on her dresser, the mailman naked at the door, our own night adventures. I could let them seem as natural a part of the conversation as references to travel, friends, the garden, and the weather. When we weren't with her, we could talk of other things, but I wasn't immune to such a permissive limbo. My mind and body ached with obscenities of their own.

"E.," I finally did say, "you've given me six weeks. I don't have to tell you how much you've helped. But you mustn't stay any longer. This is going to get worse. And, when it does, it would be better for me, too, if you had a place nearby, some place I could get away to occasionally."

You looked at me as if you were going to protest, but you didn't. Two evenings later, at dinner, you told me you'd found an apartment with a marvelous space for work about ten minutes' walk away. I canceled the pain, which was almost panic, at the old ease of parting. It was going to be as simple as that. Did you see it? Probably. You came into my room late that night, no more than a trace of apology in your voice.

"I think we should talk about it, just once," you said. "I think you should tell me about it, just once. And I think you should tell me the truth. I won't argue with you about anything, but I have to know. I have to know why I'm being sent away, because it's the last time."

Had I somehow imagined that there wouldn't be a last time, that always you'd be there when I looked for you, unquestioning, undemanding? Of course not. Had I imagined then that I would resist this confrontation until it occurred and then resist no longer, let all the years of resistance go to pay whatever impossible debt there would be? Perhaps. For I reached out to you as if to touch, to embrace, just as I heard myself say, "I'll lie to you as long as I live, little dog, and you'll go on believing me."

"You do love me. You do want me."

"No."

"Or you would have let me come to you years ago."

"No."

"How do I begin. Where do I touch you? Kiss you?"

I took you in my arms to stop you, held you gently until you were a crying child to be comforted. We did talk then for an hour or more, but I didn't explain anything. We talked our way back to where we had always been, simply a little more firmly established there than before.

On the twenty-fifth of May (it was your twenty-fourth birthday), you moved into the apartment you had found, again without my help, though you did take a small truckload of furniture from the storage room—chairs, card tables, bookcases, another single bed.

Already in that incredible apartment were two refrigerators, a hot plate, a grand piano, and a double bed mattress, things forceably left behind by the previous tenant who had not paid his rent and finally, the legend went, shot it out with the FBI. There were bullet holes in the wall. Space the place did have. There were a large living room, a kitchen, two bedrooms, and two baths. The rent was fifty dollars a month, which was too much. I don't know what floor the apartment was on because I was never able to figure out the basic structure of the building. It sat just behind a row of shops with an outside staircase, at the bottom stone and then metal and then wood, which didn't open onto all levels. Most of the windows of the apartment opened onto something between the fifth and sixth floors of a hotel on the other side of the block. One of the problems was that not only the windows opened that way but the whole wall of the shower in one of the bathrooms. There simply wasn't an outer wall, but you weren't troubled because there was another bathroom to use. The kitchen must have been twenty feet long, but it was only three or four feet wide. Opening the door of a refrigerator completely shut off one end of the room. That was convenient. You could leave the door open to shut off the area that became your study, at the end of which was a stained-glass window. There was no heat, and the roof leaked, but you had dealt with both these problems in London where the climate was not nearly so kind. Space was what you wanted, the kind you didn't have to worry about, and no one had ever worried about this. You had running water and electricity. These were all you needed. You left the piano and the double bed mattress in the larger of the two bedrooms, tucked the single bed into the smaller one (which was really no more than a storage space under the eaves to be shared with the spiders), furnished one end of the living room with chairs, table, and book-cases, and left the largest space for your work.

Soon after you were settled you enrolled in several courses, not at the university but at the trade school where you intended to learn to use power tools. Before you had been settled a month, you had permission from the landlord to install heavier wiring to accommodate your new collection of drills and saws and soldering irons. Questioned about the noise, you explained that the young man just below you was a composer of electronic music and not only didn't mind but was delighted by the opportunity to extend as well as demand patience. Sound, you said, was your new dimension, and you bought a motorcycle. The costumes for these new skills were elaborate. You had half a dozen kinds of helmets, variously inarticulate gloves, boots of several heights and resistances. But even in these alarming garments, you were never a dykish terror. You were a little girl playing Buck Rogers with the humorless intensity that belongs to an imaginative child.

If I had ever hoped for a haven of escape from my own decorous madhouse, this was not it, but I went there often enough just the same. I never climbed into your apartment without for a moment thinking that you were in the process of moving. It was simply not the sort of mess I could get used to. One day the furniture would all be piled right at the head of the stairs, perhaps because you had decided to scrub the floor and then forgot about it or had been interrupted by something more important; or you were making room for a large building project; or you were having a party. When the furniture was in place (a loose idiom for how objects ever lived with you), there were large piles of scrap metal, wood, glass. One day I found all your clothes on top of the piano because you had temporarily turned the closet into a darkroom for a friend.

Most of the people you discovered came first to the apartment below you, which was even larger than yours and not quite as disreputable because the young man in it seemed to have a num-

ber of ex-wives who occasionally cleaned the place up. I suppose
most of those visitors were harmless enough or grew up to be. I
might not have taken them so seriously if you hadn't. I probably
wouldn't have taken them at all. But I have never chosen my
human environment. I have always borrowed it from someone
like you or Monk or Doris. I should, therefore, try not to complain.

They all seemed to do a lot of talking. The vocabulary resembled our own in some catagories. More of the proper names
were French and many more of the superlatives were improper.
Their subject matter was different. God had only negative things
to do with it. They were interested in a kind of petty criminality
that they called freedom. Stealing was a basic act, but there were
individual rules about it. One stole only food he didn't need, another only food he did. Some bought nothing but materials for
their work; others stole nothing but. Some restricted their victims
to people they knew, others to strangers. One would not take anything for himself. Another sold all he took. What mattered was
the existential rule-making, the creative morality. You and I
began to argue about it when you began to defend it, and that
happened almost immediately.

"It isn't just a game," you insisted. "It's a philosophy, a serious
philosophy. I mean, have you really read Gide?"

"I've been even more experimental than that. I've stolen light
bulbs and American flags and road signs, but not since I was ten."

"There is innocence in it," you said thoughtfully.

"You know, conversations around here are beginning to compete with Mother's."

"You can't want everyone to accept your reality, Kate."

"It's not *mine*. There's an objective difference between halluci-
nation and fact."

"But is there a moral one? What's art?"

"I'm not talking about morality. I'm talking about sanity."

"Sanity's a convention," you said.

So it may be and one that hasn't found easy acceptance since the Victorian period. I could not argue that I lived with insanity and knew what you did not. You still came often to the house, bringing Mother sawed, soldered, and wired objects, and you went on learning the names of her dead relatives and imaginary companions and torturers just as you went on learning the names of the friends of your downstairs neighbor. You didn't have to deal with stocks and bonds, nurses, servants, and old friends of Mother's who were still alive. Those were the realities or conventions you chose to ignore.

I cannot say that the "sanity" of the old ladies who did occasionally come to call was any comfort to me. Their propriety and sympathy sometimes seemed more grotesque than Mother's violence of imagination. When she was obviously out of her mind, I didn't let them upstairs to see her. I would invite them into the living room for tea, all of us carefully avoiding the chair Mother habitually sat in, and I would ask them questions about their grandchildren and their clubs and their travels, letting them punctuate the conversation occasionally with, "She's much the same, is she?" and "It's such a pity." But on the days when she was calm and rational enough to receive guests, I always waited with a terrible tension for one of her disconnected comments. The old ladies did not humor or argue or engage with Mother at those moments. They ignored her. The sins against good behavior she committed did not exist. She did not even have to be forgiven. And so she became, like their own passing of wind, unreal to them. It took an age I didn't have to so discipline nose and heart. Perhaps all of us have trouble admitting what we have no control over.

My own sanity had to lie outside both households. I attended summer session, and in September I committed myself seriously to completing the masters degree requirements in economics and government. At about the same time you made another kind of important decision.

"I want to tell you, Kate, that I've decided to take a lover."

"Oh? Anyone I know?"

"You may have seen him around. His name is Christopher Marlowe Smith. He's married, but he didn't have enough money on his grant to bring his wife and child west with him. He'll go back to them in a year. We've made a perfectly rational agreement. He has needs and so do I."

"Is he going to live here?"

"More or less. He'll keep his other address for a while, but he'll move in on Tuesday after I'm fitted for my diaphragm."

"You're not at all in love with him or anything like that?" I asked carefully.

"He's an intelligent person. He's attracted to me. That's all, but we've agreed that that's enough, all either of us wants right now."

"What if you find you're getting more involved than that?"

"I won't," you said simply. "I'm going to treat it as something like a training period, a learning experiment."

"Sex and cooperative living," I said.

"Yes."

You were nervous. You were trying not to be defensive. You were trying not to ask either my permission or my blessing. You did not even risk the suggestion that I would like this Christopher Marlowe Smith. I made some attempt not to treat him like an invention or a joke, though either of those was preferable to considering him as a fact. I postponed that trial for over a week.

By the time I did call, dressed in dark linen and looking rather like the local social worker come to make a report on the moral and sanitary conditions of the building, Christopher Marlowe Smith was as well settled as anyone could be in that tangle of used auto parts, pianos, and refrigerators. He was not much older than you, had a broad-faced, ordinary handsomeness, an uncertainly loud voice, a way of rubbing his hands together as if he were going to make a meal of whatever was put before him. At that time he had not yet got over his surprising good fortune, and his laughter had a startled, self-satisfied tone that was not unpleasant. He obviously thought the whole thing was quite a lark, though his own cliché for it was "fucking great," in military manliness. He'd served his year otherwise innocently. You looked a little tired, a little bewildered by the amount of human noise after living with nothing but drills and saws, and you were mildly embarrassed by his frank and expressive enthusiasm for your tits, cunt, tail, in fact every four-letter part of you but your mind which there had not, admittedly, been time to discover. I generously considered the possibility that you had lost it anyway. Yet who but a hardy, insensitive, cheerfully argumentative, simple-hearted sponger could have lived with you like that? If I wasn't kind in my private summary of your Christopher Marlowe Smith, I was kind enough to him. And he was to me, too. As long as no one asked for money and offered it freely, he worked on the buddy system with everyone.

"Here's our Katie," he'd say, giving me a one-armed hug, "with a case of beer and the second best-looking legs in town. And I've got that paper for you, though old Charlie claims it isn't worth its weight in shit. Why don't you just once stay for dinner? Ah, I know. Mom. Well . . ."

Blurred. You were. I was.

"So Charlie knocks on the door, and I say, 'Look, Charlie baby, we're at it just now, having a lesson, so why don't you come back in an hour, eh?' So he goes back downstairs and turns up the volume on the most God-awful, I mean erotic machine noises. That man's got an inhuman sense of humor."

The lessons weren't going all that well, you admitted with no more than hopeful concern.

"I'm slow, he says, but I'm getting a bit better."

Progress. The same thing could be said for Mother. The housekeeper and maid suggested that we didn't need the day nurse. I was home enough during the day to keep an eye on things, and I would still be free to go out in the evening. I decided to ask Mother herself about it.

"As long as it doesn't interfere with your work, dear, but it's true, I don't have many needs. I could have my bath after four."

I had learned not to count on the permanence of the smallest agreement. I knew explanations might have to be made over and over again, but so great a step forward was encouraging to me and would be to Doris, too. The night before the new routine began, I spoke to Mac about it.

"You can just check out with me in the morning."

"And you're not interested in my opinion."

"The doctor's agreed. He thinks it may be a morale booster for Mother."

"Mmmm."

"Well, anyway, we're going to try it."

I tried to sleep at once in order to be fresh in the morning, and, of course, I couldn't sleep at all. I heard the clock in the downstairs hall strike five before I finally napped. I woke startled at what I thought was the striking of nine. My own clock confirmed it. Damn Mac! I fumbled into my robe and rushed into the hall. There at the other end of it stood Mac in the door of Mother's room, talking to the housekeeper.

"Good morning," she said.

"Why didn't you wake me?"

"I was near the end of a good murder," she said.

"Is everything all right?"

"Fine."

I looked into Mother's room, and there she sat tidily enjoying her breakfast tray.

"Good morning, Mother."

She looked up, paused, and then said, "Katherine, you haven't combed your hair."

"I overslept," I said, grinning.

"It's not like you."

"No."

"Well, go make yourself look like yourself, dear. I don't like shocks with my breakfast."

By the time I had washed and dressed, Mac was gone and Mother was watching television. The maid was in her room dusting. I went down for my own breakfast in the dining room.

"That wasn't a very good beginning," I said to the house-keeper.

"Miss Hanser didn't mind. She said she could always stay over a bit if you were having a sleep."

"Well, she won't have to again. It was nice of her, but she should have called me."

"Doesn't hurt to learn to take a little along with the giving, Miss Kate."

I knew that Mac and the housekeeper had had a nice, long chat about just what would be good for me. I couldn't resent it. In fact, I felt more in charge of the household that morning than I usually did and could even indulge myself a little in their concern. When the housekeeper told me she had a number of "sit-down" jobs that morning and wouldn't need me to be with Mother at all, I went to my own work without protest. I didn't see Mother until lunchtime. She was serene and attentive.

Perhaps it was the long strain of the year that had passed which had become too much of a habit for me. I couldn't accept the reassurance of Mother's continuing quietness and clarity. I was more reluctant than ever to be away from the house for long, and I was, in dozens of small ways, nervously overprotective until Mother herself grew mildly impatient with me.

"You do hang about, Kate. Haven't you got work to do? Don't you want to go out to see some of your friends? Or have Esther in for dinner."

I did go out then, walked as far as your apartment, but I remembered the story about Charlie, and I didn't want to be greeted by the interrupted Christopher Marlowe Smith. Even if you were involved in no more than one of your long, incoherent arguments which never had a focus narrower than the nature of Man, I didn't want to join it. I would like to have found you alone, but really alone as you had been before his vocabulary, even his voice stress and gestures became your own. I certainly didn't want to know how the lessons were going now. I didn't want to go to the library, either. I knew where I would have gone if I had been any place but in the town where I had grown up. Nearly two years away from that. My hand felt the still unaccustomed thickness at the ridge of my nose. What I really needed was an evening with Monk or Andrew. Monk and Andrew. I walked the quiet blocks home and went to my room to write them a letter.

It crossed one from Andrew, in which he tried to speak of work and the haphazardly happy domestic life he shared with Monk in Cambridge, but the central fact of the letter was Peter Jackson's suicide at the hotel where we had all stayed on Mallorca. "Nobody who knows anybody else well ever needs to ask why," his letter said.

"Why?" you asked.

Nobody who ever loves anybody else well can help asking. Christopher Marlowe Smith sat very still. For all his boisterousness, for all his sharing of other people's wealth, he had an instinctive delicacy about emotions not his own.

"And why there?"

For some reason I suddenly thought of Sandy Mentchen and her meadow. It was not the first time Peter had gone to Mallorca. In the years between he might have stayed several times in that hotel, but I wasn't much comforted by the fact that we only numbered among his griefs . . . that Andrew and I only numbered among them. Surely you were . . .

"Stupid," you said. "Why was I so stupid?"

"You weren't, E. You were the only one who wasn't."

"Do you remember what he said about those children? 'Why do they have to be ugly with our greed?' I'd never thought about it. I still haven't. I haven't even thought about Pete for months. He needed other people to keep him alive. He needed that."

"What was he like?" Christopher Marlowe Smith asked.

How eager we were to make him up again in words, to bring him back to life, flinging himself up mountains, playing his harmonica, being priest in a row boat—but not crying in the night, not nearly drowning himself, not declaring his hard love. We spared ourselves those things, as we had tried to at the time, you in ignorance and I in anger. We were giving him a proper burial, until you did say, "He was queer."

"Oh," Christopher Marlowe Smith said.

That doesn't explain it, I wanted to protest, but I was probably the only one among us who really was afraid that it did. And I felt a returning, almost soothing anger for Peter Jackson. It honored him better than my attempt at guilt. With it came an impatience with your wanting to have a share of the responsibility. It was his own life; he took it, helped himself to the lot. We ended our conversation in unspoken disagreement.

That night I tried half a dozen ways of writing to Andrew. There was nothing decent to say. We had never talked about Peter Jackson except as a way of talking about ourselves. A moment's silence then, a moment's shutting up. I stood, deciding to get a drink. When I opened the door, Mac took a step back.

"Is something wrong?"

"No. She's asleep."

"Then . . . ?"

"I've been wondering about how much longer you . . . she'll really need me. I thought we probably ought to discuss it some time soon. Your light was on . . ."

"Yes, I suppose we should. Come in." She did and stood awkwardly, looking at the crumpled paper on my desk. "I was trying to write a letter. Sit down."

"You'd hear her if she called," Mac said without moving.

"If the doors were both open . . . Mac, don't go. I couldn't manage it."

"Manage what?"

"I'm nearly out of my mind now," I said, beginning to shake. "At least I know you're there."

"As a possibility?"

I didn't answer.

"Kate." She took my head in her hands.

"Be careful of my face. Be careful of me."

147

"You'll fire me in the morning."

"Yes, I will."

But I was asleep when she left in the morning. There was a note at my place at the breakfast table giving a formal week's notice. During that week, we exchanged only a few words. After she had really gone, I found her card with address and phone number on my desk. Across the back of it was written, "As a possibility." I never saw her again. But I kept the card.

"What are the dates of your spring vacation?" Mother asked one morning.

"I'm not sure," I said. "Why?"

"It's time for me to see Doris, and I want her to be here so that you can get away for a week or two."

"I don't really need a holiday."

"You do. Anyway, it would make me feel better."

"I wonder where I'd go," I said, trying to be agreeable.

"Why not Carmel? You haven't been there in years."

"No," I said.

"Well, begin to think about it."

"All right."

"I'm going to talk to Doris about finding myself a companion. There's no hurry about it. You want to be here until you finish your work in June, but after that we must make some other arrangement."

"Mother, don't send me away." I was appalled to hear tears in my voice.

"My dear child!" Mother said. "I had no intention of *sending* you away, but you must want to go. You have things to do with your life. I know I won't live forever, but I don't want you to think it's forever. Now, go get your calendar, and let's think about Easter."

You and Christopher Marlowe Smith had also been thinking about Easter. He wasn't sure he shouldn't go east to visit his wife and child since he'd not managed it at Christmas. He hadn't the money to go, of course, but perhaps he could borrow it.

"You're not going to pay for his trip, are you?" I asked, as we sat over coffee in a shop just down the street from your apartment where we now often met.

"I think I should," you said. "I think he ought to go, and he can't afford it himself. The only thing is that I don't want him to feel indebted to me. Do you think he would?"

"No more than he already must," I said.

"A clean break in the summer is important. It's what we agreed on at the beginning. But, if I just give it to him . . . yes, that's the way to do it."

Christopher Marlowe Smith didn't agree. In fact, he was uncharacteristically adamant about it. Borrow, yes. Take, no.

"I can't have that," he said to me. "I'd rather steal it from her —or anyone."

I made myself leave my purse sitting within his reach, but I advised you later that you'd better let him have the money on the terms that made him comfortable.

"Otherwise I think he might steal it from you," I said, trying for lightness of tone.

"Maybe he should. Then I wouldn't be involved at all."

"Just leave two hundred dollars or so lying around for him to pick up?"

"Oh, no. He'd have to figure out how. That wouldn't be my affair."

"E., you don't really take this stealing thing seriously, do you?"

When you hesitated, I terribly regretted having asked the question.

"I stole these saddle shoes," you said, moving one foot out from under the table to display a shoe that looked at least five years old.

"When?" I asked with bored irritation.

"A couple of weeks ago at a church bazaar."

"Have you gone right out of your mind, Esther?"

"I don't know. At first I thought I might just shift the price tags. That's what I've done before, but this time I thought, no, I must take them outright. They were marked at twenty-five cents. They fit perfectly."

"But why?"

"I'm not a Christian," you said. "It would be hypocritical to support a church bazaar."

"But there's a difference between supporting something and . . . and that!"

"Yes. There's being passive. I've always been passive. Now I'm learning to make real choices, to admit my condition. . . ." Your voice had begun to sound very like Christopher Marlowe Smith's. "To act." You were nearly rubbing your hands together.

"I don't even know where to begin to disagree," I said.

I saw your eyes rim with tears. "Then you know how I've felt with you for all these years."

"But, E.—"

"Morality is creative," you said. "Each of us makes his own."

I didn't point out that you were begging, borrowing, and stealing yours. I did not know how to attack from my own indefensible position. I was also suffering from a failure of imagination. It was so difficult to believe that you actually had carefully worked out a principle for stealing rummage. After you had drawn my attention to the saddle shoes, I began to take nervous notice of all your clothes. Those worn that I hadn't before seen you wearing were obviously part of your growing moral wardrobe. It was not handsome. You looked more like a penitent than a crook.

"Esther doesn't look well to me," Mother said after you had been to dinner one night.

"She's just in a seedy mood," I said.

"Why don't you take her along with you when you go off next month?"

"I might," I said, not really having thought about it. "I'll ask her."

We agreed to take a trip, but neither of us could decide just where to go.

"Why don't we just drive?" you suggested.

"We might have trouble with reservations."

"We could put sleeping bags in the car."

That kind of vagueness reminded me too much of our summer in Europe. Having to make a dozen decisions a day for want of having made one before hand would put me in a restless, bad temper the whole time. When I read in the paper that Sandra Mentchen was giving a concert in Los Angeles, she provided the arbitrary destination we needed.

Doris arrived conveniently just an hour after Christopher Marlowe Smith left the same airport with borrowed, not stolen, funds. She had an album full of photographs of Ann's wedding which, for all the months it had dominated her letters, hadn't really occurred to me until I caught quick glimpses as you and Doris handed the photographs back and forth across the front seat on the drive home.

"Were parts of it appalling?"

"Oh, yes, but Frank and Frank got on surprisingly well, and Ann was amused and relaxed about it."

"What's he like?" you asked.

"Like the young men Frank wanted you to marry—tall, proper, responsible."

"Don't you like him?"

"Very much," Doris said, smiling. "He's just the sort of person Ann should have married. She's orderly that way, always has been."

"I admire that," you said. "She looks beautiful, doesn't she?"

Your shyness about and obvious interest in Ann's wedding made me wonder how uneasy you might be with your own circumstance.

"A woman shouldn't be over thirty," you said in a decisive tone.

"Ever?" Doris asked.

"To marry," you clarified. "I'll marry before I'm thirty."

"How are all your other projects going?"

"All right," you said. "I read a poem the other day about Persephone who was called, 'for hell too fair, for earth too wise.' It made me wonder if certain kinds of knowledge do disqualify."

"Disqualify for what?" I asked.

"Life," you answered.

I felt Doris watching me, and I knew the question in her mind was how far changed the relationship between you and me might be.

" 'Whose mortal taste brought death into the world, and all our woe,' " I recited.

"You two leave me behind," Doris complained.

"I was teasing E. about Milton," I said. "She thinks so much pure doctrine for an anti-Christian. Do you want to be dropped off at your place, E.?"

When you had left us, Doris said at once, "How can she dress like that?"

"It's a new sort of costume—stolen sack cloth and ashes."

"But why?"

"I don't know, Doris. The character she's living with has some odd ideas."

"Who's she?"

"He. Christopher Marlowe Smith."

"You're making him up!"

"That sometimes occurs to me, but only when I'm trying to comfort myself."

"Is she going to marry him?"

"Oh, no. She's taking him like a course, that's all."

"Passing or failing?"

"I'm not sure."

"How are you, Kate?"

"Pretty well. But I'm afraid Mother's about to fire me. She wants to talk to you about finding a companion."

"How marvelous! Here I am braced for a long argument, and there's not going to be one."

"I guess not," I said.

This time I wasn't prepared for Doris' shock when she saw Mother, who seemed to me so very well.

"She looks a hundred years old, Kate! And she's so slow and so vague. I hardly recognized her. How do you manage? What can it have been like for you?"

I checked my first reply which would have been, "But she's so much better," and said instead, "She's really no trouble. She can do almost everything for herself."

"But she's turned into a vegetable!"

There was anger in this, which I could have met with an anger that startled my own nerves. I didn't risk a reply. Doris was too caught up in her own emotion to notice mine, or perhaps she took my silence as a sharing of how she felt. She was sympathizing with me guiltily. I went into the kitchen for drinks before the housekeeper wanted me to. The hot clam snacks weren't ready.

"Aren't you going to have your cocktail upstairs with your mother?"

"Not this one," I said. "We'll have several."

"You've had no tea," she said, which was as much reproof as she dared.

"Tell me about Monk and Andy," I said, as I took the drinks back into the living room. "I haven't heard from either of them for a while."

"That news is all bad," Doris said. "Did you know Andy's father had stopped his allowance?"

"I'd heard something about it."

"He's not going to be able to finish his degree. Frank offered to lend him the money, but Andy says he can't accept it. He's not gotten along very fast with his research. It would take him too long. And Ramona's pregnant."

"What are they going to do?"

153

"Go to New York. Andy has contacts there, and the salaries are better than in England."

"Can he work in the States?"

"I should think so. I think Mr. Belshaw ought to be shot!"

"How's Monk taking it?"

"Oh, she's treating the whole thing like a lovely new adventure, which is lucky for Andy, but I don't think she can really have imagined what it's going to be like if he doesn't find a job right away or if he doesn't find a good one. Andy has some very expensive tastes. And with a baby—"

"When's the baby due?"

"In August, I think."

"That might change Mr. Belshaw's mind," I said.

"I doubt it. It sounds to me as if that's just the kind of mess he wants Andy to be in. And I can't believe that he really thinks of making a man of Andy. He wants revenge. He's smart enough to know that financial difficulty is like sickness—it doesn't improve most people."

"Shall we take the next one up and have it with Mother?" I suggested as I picked up Doris' glass.

"If we have to," Doris said, making no attempt to hide her reluctance.

I had too much invested in Doris as an adult to be able to bear being her childish accomplice against Mother. And I had too much invested in Mother. I did not want to leave them together, but I had no choice, and perhaps, once I was not around for Doris to complain to, she'd get accustomed to Mother as she was now and be more patient with her. But Doris had never been patient with Mother or Mother with her. It was their relationship, their problem. I had to leave it behind.

In the morning, as I drove over to pick you up, I felt suddenly really glad to be getting away—and not just away. I was glad to be taking a trip with you. As I turned into your block, I caught sight of you sitting on your suitcase out on the sidewalk. You had on a yellow cotton knit suit you certainly hadn't stolen from a rummage sale. Your hair was up in the soft, held shape that gave you elegance. In fact, you looked posed there on the street, an ad for expensive youth.

"Let's go south," I called, reaching over to open the door for you.

"I thought you'd never come and you're ten minutes early."

"How long have you been waiting?"

"Let's see," you said, swinging your suitcase into the back seat and then looking at your watch, "about six years," but it was a cheerful tease, one I could almost answer.

"Shall we go the coast and take a couple of days?"

"Lovely."

Lovely. It didn't take us long to leave the urgent, interrupting traffic of the freeway, to be up and over the coastal hills to the cooler, subtler spring of the shore and the ocean. We talked a great deal in the familiar, argumentative vocabulary we had learned at college. I remember the paradox of our discussion about subjects in art—the machine and the metropolis—as we drove through miles of almost unpopulated land, forests and rocks and dunes. I talked about the misconceptions in foreign aid and international social work. You talked about the relation of sculpture to public values. We decided to go to Greece. We told each other familiar stories. We turned our friends into ideas. And gradually we talked a little of our problems, mine with Doris and Mother, yours with Christopher Marlowe Smith, but somehow, in the undemanding intimacy of a car moving through that enormous landscape, difficulties diminished to their proper size. On the second afternoon we arrived in Los Angeles not only not tired from our trip but refreshed by it.

"Are we going to try to get in touch with Sandy before the concert?" you asked.

"I hadn't thought about it. Is there any way we could?"

"I think she's made Los Angeles home base. She's probably in the phone book."

And so she was. You decided, with greater awareness of emotional subtleties than I was accustomed to in you, that I should make the call. Perhaps living with Christopher Marlowe Smith had some positive educational value after all.

"We've driven down for your concert, at least used it as an excuse," I explained to a surprised and obviously pleased Sandy.

"Come right on over," she insisted. "We're free this evening. Isn't that luck?"

Before we left the motel, which was really too far out of the center of things to suit us, I telephoned home to say that we had arrived safely but wouldn't have a contact address until the next day.

"Kate, darling," Doris said, amused, "the number of urgent messages around here in forty-eight hours needn't swell profits for Bell Telephone. Unplug us for a while. Have a good, thoughtless time."

"Well, I'll check in in a day or two."

"If you're homesick," she said.

She didn't offer to let me speak to Mother, and I somehow couldn't ask to. I put the phone down, irritated.

"It isn't really all that odd of me to call home, is it? It's the first time I've been away over night in eighteen months."

"I'm sure she didn't mean that," you said. "She just wants you to have a real vacation."

"I suppose so, and I've gotten neurotic about Mother. I know that."

"Doris doesn't know—" you began.

"Why has she got more right to hate Mother than I have to love her?"

"She doesn't, Kate."

"Doesn't hate. I can't earn a mother. Why do I try? Why should it matter?"

"I don't know," you said.

I was embarrassed, not before you really because you were absolutely uncritical. I was exposed to myself, and I was ashamed of an envy I could do no more than hide. I was ashamed of the moral currency I used to buy myself a place in the world, but I couldn't have borne the greater shame of behaving like the bastard I was. I took my purse and retreated to the bathroom to readjust the mask which I wore even more for the mirror than I did for the world. Okay, scarface, apologize to Doris, your big sister, permissive parent figure, bloody rival. There are enough un-Freudian facts to be getting on with, or at least another set of them.

"Is this going to be awkward?" you asked as we drove to meet Sandy.

"I don't know," I said. "It's not like you to think so. Are you wishing we weren't going?"

"Oh no," you answered quickly.

"Out with it. What are you thinking?"

"I don't want to make you angry."

"E., if you don't want to make me angry—"

"Won't it look like . . . I mean, won't Sandy think, because we're together—"

"Probably."

"I don't care. I mean, I do care. But you wouldn't like it, would you? So, what shall I say? Or just not say?"

I felt terribly tired, terribly depressed, as if every decent, sane thing I did were almost comically irrelevant. I tried to imagine your carefully speaking of Christopher Marlowe Smith, and I couldn't bear the incredulous or pitying expression on Sandy's face. I tried to imagine myself in the same pose I'd taken at college, but it seemed unbecomingly grotesque, perhaps even cruel. Why didn't we simply let her think what she wanted to think? But I couldn't suggest what amounted to pretense to you.

"It would be easier for me with Sandy if she did think—I don't mean to lie. I don't mean that," you said, "but—"

"We don't have to get that involved, anyway," I said. "We haven't been invited to an orgy or a bull session. We're just having dinner with a friend. Let's keep it simple."

"Right," you said.

Unspoken collusion, our little vanity. It made us self-conscious with each other, peculiarly lighthearted. We were laughing at an unpromising joke together when Sandy opened the door. Her look of amused indulgence should have stiffened my back. It didn't. I kissed her and watched her offer the same greeting to you, noticing the stronger definition of her face, your confident beauty. Then we followed her into a large, piano-dominated living room, furnished expensively and quietly in textures rather than colors. She took the hand of the girl who had stood to greet us. She was not really good-looking, but she had an extraordinarily lively face, full of light and change. She wore loose raw silk, gathered sleeveless at her shoulders, falling straight to the floor, a present from Sandy, I imagined.

"Esther, this is Esther. And Kate."

We could comment at once on your shared name, but we didn't need to look for conversation. There were so many questions to be asked and answered. And Esther Wilson kept us from feeling guilty about a shared world because she knew a great deal about it herself and because she also moved in and out bringing drinks and snacks, tending the cooking dinner. I did watch her, not only because I was curious but because she asked for my attention and approval. Once, as she left the room, I turned back to your conversation and met Sandy's eyes. I smiled, wanting to say something, but you were talking urgently about creative morality.

"Have you given up God then?" Sandy asked.

"It's not exactly that," you said. "It's being free enough of doctrine to discover God or whatever there is to discover."

"There's a lot to discover," Sandy said.

"You're happy, aren't you?" you asked suddenly.

"Yes, in some ways very. Are you?"

You turned to me uncertainly.

"We've had a bad year," I said, "with my mother."

Esther came back into the room with questions about how we liked roast beef.

"Could I see the kitchen?" you asked, "and maybe help?"

Sandy handed me a cigarette and was slow and mannerly about lighting it. Then she said, "How did you break your nose?"

"Dyke fight in Soho a couple of years ago," I answered, wondering as I spoke why I had to be crudely inaccurate now.

"It makes you look sad. What is it about your mother?"

I explained briefly, but, when Sandy didn't comment at once, I added details, the rerouting of Mother's fears, the preadolescent obscenities, the conscious inhibitions of her mind lifted like the front wall of a doll's house.

"So you've been being her wall, as well as your own," Sandy said.

"Like that a little, yes."

"But there's Esther."

"Yes," I said.

"And no," Sandy concluded. "She's not living with you."

"It's not been a house for living with—"

"Neither's mine," Sandy said, smiling. "I'm not in it more than three or four months of the year. I have a smaller place in New York, too, but I'm there even less."

"What does Esther do while you're away?"

"Teaches in the winter. She travels with me sometimes in the summer. I want her to give up teaching. . . ."

You and Esther had come back into the room. Esther went to Sandy, kissed her lightly and then turned to me.

"She'd get tired of me, and I don't want that."

"But I do," Sandy said. "Being tired of you occasionally is just the way I want to live."

"Sandy has an ambition to be middle-class and middle-aged. Do you, too, Kate? Are you tired of being young and wildly attractive to women?"

"Am I wildly attractive to women?" I asked, smiling.

"Of course you are, isn't she, Esther? I worry about Sandy on tour, but, if I had *you* on my hands—"

"When are you going to feed us?" Sandy demanded.

"Now, darling. That's what we came in to say. Come and serve."

You had watched like a shy child at too noisy a birthday party and looked at me now with all the appeal of uncertainty. I wanted to make some protective, even possessive gesture, but I was afraid to. It was Sandy who took your arm as we went into the dinner table. I was uneasy for a moment at the table, wondering if I would be expected to hold a chair. I had no real knowledge of the manners of this world.

"We don't say grace," Sandy said to my hesitation.

The wine at dinner was almost too much for you, but perhaps you needed it to find your way into the imitative candor you usually offered when you were sober. What surprised me—and perhaps it shouldn't have because of your oddly assertive independence with most men—was that you began to court Esther, not Sandy. If I had had less to drink myself, it would have made me uncomfortable. If I had had fewer months of dislocated living, I would have had stronger defenses against the erotic good humor over coffee and brandy. Sandy did control it, but with amused indulgence. She was not drinking as much as the rest of us. I finally did refuse the second brandy both for myself and for you.

"More coffee," I said, "before I'm completely demoralized."

"You don't get demoralized," Esther said sadly.

"No," you agreed, as sadly, "Kate's permanently moralized. You know, I haven't been this drunk since that party after my show. About the last thing I remember was saying to Kate, 'Everybody's kissed me but you,' and do you know what she said?"

Sandy laughed and said, " 'Then I think it's time to go home.' "

"You didn't!" Esther said.

"I'm afraid I did."

"What did happen after that?" you asked.

"I kissed you," I said.

"And I took you home."

"Sandy took you home?"

"Apparently."

"And Monk put you to bed."

"Well, probably you deserve three," Esther decided, "but I do think it's sad that you don't remember any of them." She leaned over quickly and kissed you on the mouth. "Will you remember that?"

"Coffee!" Sandy ordered. "I am not running a bawdy house." Esther moved at once, if a little unsteadily.

"And then, again, I think it's time to go home," I said.

"I think I'll stay here," you said, sleepily.

"Why don't you stay?" Sandy said, turning to me. "This turns into a double bed."

"Kate only allows me to sleep with men," you said, and then you were dozing.

I lit a cigarette for myself while Sandy watched me.

"Is that true?"

"It's crudely put," I answered. "She's been living with one Christopher Marlowe Smith for about six months now. He's gone east for his vacation to visit his wife."

"I don't understand it," Sandy said.

"It's simple enough really."

"But what are you doing here with her now?"

"I don't know," I said. "Creative morality."

"You're the most indecent prude I've ever known, and I've known plenty," Sandy said, my head held between her hands. "You really are."

"It's a rare talent."

"I'll go see about that coffee."

I moved over to you, put my hand on your forehead, and spoke to you. You turned your face into my shoulder.

"E., come on. You have to wake up."

"I can't bear to," you said.

"Why?"

"I can't bear to."

"Yes, you can. There'll be coffee in a minute."

"I'll wash my face."

You had left the room by the time Sandy and Esther came into it with fresh coffee. It was only eleven o'clock, but it seemed to me nearly dawn.

"I'm sorry," I said. "E. just doesn't drink well."

"Is she all right?" Esther asked.

"Oh yes."

"Shall I go see?" she asked Sandy.

"No," Sandy said.

You apologized for yourself a moment later, seeming nearly sober and terribly white. You didn't want coffee. You didn't want me to stay for it. It was an awkward leave-taking, during which I began to wonder what had actually happened to make us all so very uneasy. As soon as we got into the car, you began to cry. You cried all the way back to the motel.

"I'm terribly sorry, E.," I said, once we were in our room. "I should have known better."

"How can you speak to me at all?"

"What do you mean?"

"Humiliating you like that. Why did I do it?"

"We all had too much to drink, that's all."

"You're not indecent. You're the finest person I know."

"E., it was really rather fun. You mostly enjoyed it, and so did I."

"Did you? Did you think Esther was . . . attractive?"

"Yes. Didn't you?"

"Yes. I don't know. I didn't want to be out of it. I felt so terribly out of it. You don't ever feel that way, do you?"

"Of course I do."

"You are wildly attractive to women. It made me so confused. It was like a nightmare. I thought you'd do something. I was so frightened you'd do something, and I'd have to just stand there and watch."

"And so you thought you'd better do something and have me just stand there and watch?"

"Was I awful?"

"You were lovely. How in hell did we get into this?"

The phone rang. I reached for it, thinking of Mother. It was Sandy.

"You got back all right then," she said. "I wanted to apologize . . ."

"Oh, Sandy, will somebody please laugh? What's the matter with all of us?"

"Drink," Sandy said. "Was it funny?"

"Yes, it was funny, and it was very nice, and E. and I have both decided that your Esther is wildly attractive, and E. wishes she were queer and I'm glad I am. Now let's all go to sleep."

"All right, but how about a milder sort of drinking after the concert Wednesday night?"

"We'd love it."

I hung up then. I was shaking.

"Is that true?" you asked.

"I don't know," I said. "I don't even care. Sort it out for yourself."

As I went into the bathroom to undress, I thought I heard you say, "I've had five orgasms with Chris," but as a glass smashed into the sink, it might have been, "I'd never get beyond a kiss."

"Are you all right?"

"Yes, I'm all right. Just clumsy."

The next day we found another motel, and we found two selling galleries. We even chatted about the night before as if it had been what it really was, a rather drunken, ordinary social occasion.

"I'm glad we're going to see them again," you said.

On Wednesday evening, while you finished dressing for the concert, I telephoned home. I think the housekeeper answered. I don't quite remember the order of things. I only know that by the time I hung up, you were asking when Mother had died.

"Nearly two days ago. You'll have to drive me to the airport."

Somewhere in the years in between I've lost the flair for stoic heroism. In those days out of a composite of Ingrid Bergman films and that one scene in the Duchess of Malfi—"I am the Duchess of Malfi still"—I played everything with marvelous understatement. At least it seemed so to me. From the outside, I may have more resembled one of Francis Bacon's silent screamers. Melodrama doesn't have to be noisy. All of which means simply that I still can't speak with any emotional candor about that trip home. If this were really for you, I should try. It was the last of our abortive holidays. But I didn't think of you walking into the concert late and alone, meeting Sandy and Esther afterwards, nor did I think of your driving the car back alone the next day. Great presence of mind requires some absence of mind. You were always so easy to sacrifice.

Doris met me in a chauffeur-driven car, lent to her by one of Mother's friends.

"I've had so many tranquilizers I didn't dare drive."

She did seem not so much calm as becalmed. And there were traces of a recent storm, fragments of sentences and unrelated laughter. Mostly, however, she reported the facts as we rode in hearselike quiet and importance down the highway toward home.

"The morning after you telephoned, while she was watching television. The housekeeper was with her. She simply said, 'Oh,' as if she were mildly surprised, and that was all."

"Where is she now?"

"I had the body cremated that evening. She wouldn't have wanted that sort of funeral. There's going to be a memorial service tomorrow."

I didn't really take any of it in until I was in the front hall. Then I couldn't think what to do. I simply stood, bewildered.

"Take your suitcase up," Doris suggested gently. "I'll get us both a drink."

I passed Mother's door, which was shut, and went on to my own room, which was offensively ordinary. I put my suitcase down, went into the bathroom, washed and combed my hair. Then I went back down the hall to Mother's room, which had not been without a night light for eighteen months. The darkness startled me less than the glare of light when I turned on the overhead switch. Even the bed was gone. I was looking at the empty blue of the Chinese rug. I started over to Mother's chair and heard, "Pull the door to. The heat register blisters the paint." I turned and closed the door behind me, seeing, as I did, the large portrait of me at about seven, which hung over the dresser, on which were the young faces of Frank and Doris. The top drawer was still open a couple of inches as it always was for Mother to use as a grip for pulling herself up. A terrible drawer since my childhood for finding things: matching gloves, hairnets, compacts, an old bit of jerky wrapped in tissue paper. The better drawer was underneath it, where rings were kept in old coin purses, necklaces wrapped in lace, stray beads in pill boxes, earrings in jars. I reluctantly turned around to face the empty room again. No message here. No last instructions. No blessing. The accidents of birth and death. "Oh," I said aloud, just trying it. Then I turned away, closing the door quietly behind me.

At the edge of the living room I stopped. The furniture had been completely rearranged. Doris sat on the couch now facing the fireplace in which a fire blazed. She turned and saw me.

"Come have your drink, Kate. Don't worry. I had the chimney cleaned out this morning. I was determined that you weren't going to come home again to a tomb of a house. Doesn't it make a difference?"

I cried then briefly in speechless anger while Doris said, "I know. I know. It's such an awful relief after all these months. But you don't have to do any more. It's over."

I saw in the flames her hair catch and wither. I saw her flesh respond, then fall away. A log broke and sagged into soft ashes. I closed my eyes and felt a child's shaking sigh through my body, which Doris held and went on speaking to.

. . .

Both Frank and young Frank arrived the following morning on the same plane from New York. There were other relatives. We had forgotten to pick up the ashes, which had to be signed for and redirected to the storage area. I went with Frank to the funeral parlor just across the street from the primary school I had attended. We used to play tag and ghost in the parking lot. Frank took the small, heavy brass box that held both Mother's ashes and those of the required coffin. As an afterthought, the funeral parlor director handed me a pill-sized envelope.

"Her wedding ring."

Frank carried the box, wrapped in brown paper, tied with string, the release papers (and perhaps the bill?) tucked under the string, like the purchase it was. I was not confused. She was not in the box. She was not in the house. She was in my mind, a heavy thought, a terrible joke, an old tenderness, and I did not have to share any of those things with anyone. I felt nothing but curious at witnessing the placing of the box in the slot next to the one that held my father's ashes. I was glad Doris had wanted no ceremony, had not wanted even to be there for the absurd fact. Frank and I didn't have to talk about it. When we got back into the car, he sat for a moment. Then he took my hand.

"Is there anything you'd like to do before we go back?"

"We're due back for lunch in half an hour," I said.

"There's time for a chocolate milkshake," he said.

"How very like you you are," I said, smiling. "Let's."

And I watched the relief on his tired, aging face. When we did get back, ten minutes late, Doris asked at once whatever had kept us so long.

"We had a milkshake," I said.

"Oh, Frank, really!"

"I've ruined the child's appetite," he admitted, "and my own."

It somehow got us through the rest of the day, which had a formal Episcopalian sanity about it. Young Frank left that night. I had hardly spoken to him, paired as we were, he with his mother, I with Frank. Frank stayed on another day to meet with lawyers.

There was nothing either surprising or complicated about the will. The estate was divided equally between Doris and me. The only problem was the house.

"We'll have to sell it," Doris said. "It would be ridiculous for either one of us to keep it."

Because we were both there to agree, we did not have to wait for the settlement of the estate to sell it. It was put on the market at once and sold almost at once, furnished. I did take my desk, some antique tables, and Mother's living-room chair, but I was too uncertain of my own future to put very much in storage. Doris didn't want anything. The shipping problems were simply too great. Anyway, she shared few of Mother's tastes.

"I've lived without my childhood for all these years. There's no reason to go back to it now."

We divided the jewelry among us. Young Frank was sent Mother's only fine painting to balance rings and bracelets sent to Ann.

The house was ready to be left in a little over three weeks.

"I don't much like your living in a hotel," Doris said, "but I do see with only a couple of months—"

"It makes sense."

"And you'll come to London for at least part of the summer?"

"I'll see, Doris. Probably. I'll let you know."

"Kate, I never have really thanked you because I don't know how. I couldn't have done what you did for Mother."

"I wanted to do it."

"Have you forgiven me?"

"For what?"

"Not wanting to. And not really wanting you to, either. I simply let it happen."

"It was a different sort of thing for me."

It was the third time since Mother's death that we had tried to say something to each other, but neither of us could finally risk it. There was too much that might have destroyed the agreement between us. Doris would have had to tell me how she really felt about my replacing her all those years ago. I would have had to tell her something of my guilt and envy. We were burdened enough—and perhaps kind enough—not to ask anything new or more of each other.

I did see you during those weeks, not when you returned the car because I was out with Frank and Doris, meeting lawyers. We had a brief cup of coffee the day before Christopher Marlowe Smith came back. I did all the dull talking. I had dinner with you and him one evening when Doris was out seeing friends, but you and I were both audience that night. Once Doris had gone and I had moved into the hotel just across the block from you, I saw you almost daily, but I was preoccupied with finishing my thesis, with writing applications for jobs with Washington agencies. I didn't ask much about your living or your plans, and you offered nothing.

It was the first week in June, after my thesis had been submitted, that I did think to ask when Christopher Marlowe Smith would be leaving.

"The end of this month."

"What are you going to do then?"

"I'll keep the apartment to work in," you said and then hesitated.

"What's that paper napkin going to be?" I asked.

"I'm moving downstairs when Chris goes. I'm moving in with Charlie."

"With *Charlie?*"

"I had a long talk with Charlie the night I got back from Los Angeles. I told him a lot of things about you and Sandy and Esther and Chris . . . really about me. He said I was trying to figure out too much on too little evidence. How did I know Chris wasn't just lousy in bed? Well, I found out. He is, and I'm not . . . at least not with the right person."

"Have you been sleeping with Charlie all along?"

"No, just the time Chris was away."

"Does Chris know?"

"Sort of. But we made a perfectly straight agreement. I mean, there's nothing complicated. He'll go back to his wife the end of the month, and I'll move in with Charlie."

"What about Charlie's wife—wives?"

"Well, he's through with marriage, that's obvious."

"But what about you, little dog? Didn't I hear you say that you were going to get married before you were thirty?"

"Yes, and I will, but, since I'm not going to be a virgin, I might as well have some experience that's worth something, and this is worth something. I'll never have to be uncertain about how much of a woman I am."

"Graduate school," I said.

"And I've started to work again, really work. I hadn't done anything all year until after Easter. I'm back to sound with Charlie."

Christopher Marlowe Smith had been a possible sort of trial for me. Charlie was a different matter. He really was bright. He shone like Lucifer, and, if I had not disproved the existence of evil, I would have feared for him. I could not afford to be afraid for you. In the heterosexual code I had recommended to you, you were, if not saved, on your way to it. At least, at the time, that's how it seemed to you. I had to accept it.

Christopher Marlowe Smith was not so persuaded. In fact, he behaved very badly, according to the terms of the agreement. He offered and then threatened to divorce his wife. He cried. He suggested killing Charlie or at least turning him over to the police for failure to support his children, for drug addiction, and finally even for theft. You were simply bewildered. You tried to remind him that the terms of the relationship were his idea. He roared with protesting pain.

"Hasn't she got any feelings? Don't I mean anything to her? I taught her everything she knows. I made a woman of her. She can't just throw me out. Katie, she can't."

But you did. I drove the still incredulous Christopher Marlowe Smith to the airport. I don't think he believed he was leaving until he was actually boarding the plane. He turned at the top of the ramp, raised a sad hand, and was gone. On the quiet drive home, I realized that I shared some of his bewilderment. After ten months you were so simply untouched by him, not cold really. What, then? Rational maybe, but that was too calculating a word. You were innocent of him, having done him no wrong.

It was the way I wanted to leave you. I had notice of a job in Washington, D.C., and I could have gone to it at once, but I delayed the appointment for a month. There was no point in it. You had no time for anyone but Charlie. It was true that you had begun to work again, but you were not sculpting. You were making machines for Charlie. When you weren't out together collecting old motors and parts of motors at the town dump or buying expensive tape recorders or stealing wire from hi fi shops, you were together in the apartment that was now entirely a workshop. I could drop in if I liked. Charlie didn't notice, but anything beyond his notice was beyond yours, too. Among the parts and sounds, you spent your days, Charlie's servant and accomplice. I ducked under and climbed over wires, listened a while, sometimes even cooked a meal which we would eat together, sitting cross-legged on the floor, but I wasn't really there. Or was, in a dimension I wasn't prepared to accept. Charlie would explain to anyone, but he was really telling the steps he was taking to himself. It didn't matter who overheard. He was the first intelligent person I knew to make what has now become a cult virtue of inarticulate speech, one-man jargon. I understood nearly nothing about his work. He was somewhat clearer in his talking about you.

One day I found you sitting on a pile of scrap metal, having your hair cut. Charlie waved the scissors to direct rather than greet me. I sat down on the chair he indicated and watched until your hair was as short as his, which was as dark as yours and long for a man's.

"There," he said. "We need this. Now we change clothes."

He was taller than you but finer boned. I watched you trade

shirts and then trousers, quite decently. He looked at you and smiled.

"You're enough woman still—even for me. You have a witness."

"How does it look?" you asked.

"As he says, like a bad disguise," I answered, getting up.

"I'll call you 'brother cunt' until it grows back again," he said.

I started toward the door.

"Kate?"

"I came to say good-by. I leave for Washington in the morning."

"I'll walk you back," you said.

You looked at yourself in every shop window along the way, not vainly or nervously as most people do. You were curious. And, as I looked with you, I had to admit a sharp, new attractiveness in you, not crude, except in the sense of primitive. I looked away and let myself record the familiar street instead.

"You don't like it, do you?" you asked finally.

"You should have made some sort of agreement with him, E."

"I have. No limits. No barriers."

"Whatever he wants whenever he wants it."

"But I can want, too," you said, nearly hostile. "I can take. I can be his lover. He's not afraid."

"His whore and his master. His slave and his keeper," I declaimed, but quietly.

"And I would have been for you."

We were standing in front of my hotel, shoppers pushing past us.

"You look like your own little brother," I said, trying to smile. "Somehow, take care of yourself, will you?" I touched your hand, your chin. "Don't shoot it out with the cops."

I had not really planned to leave for Washington in the morning, but I knew I had to leave town. My trunk had already been shipped. I'd sold the car. It wouldn't take me more than a couple of hours to pack. I picked up the phone and called Los Angeles, not really expecting Sandy and Esther to be at home. Esther answered the phone.

"I'm on my way east," I said. "I wondered if I'd go by way of Los Angeles."

"We'll be here for at least another week. When can you come?"

"In the morning?"

She called to Sandy, who came to the telephone. "What plane shall I meet?"

"I don't know," I said. "I'll make my own way."

"Is Esther coming with you?"

"No," I said. "No, she's staying here."

As is so often true for me, the urge to talk vanished as soon as the opportunity offered itself. I arrived at Sandy's apartment soon after lunch and allowed myself to be persuaded to stay that night and the next, but, as soon as that was settled, I felt embarrassed and uneasy, regretting the impulsiveness of my trip. Esther, reading my nervousness as a need to talk with Sandy alone, went out to shop, probably for the second time that day. All the time she was gone, I asked political questions about the South American countries Sandy had toured recently. Because she was interested and well informed, I gradually began to relax. I asked her then what she knew about electronic music.

"I'm a prejudiced performer, not a musicologist," she said, but it was a preface rather than a closing remark.

After two hours, Esther returned with one small parcel.

"Well, you don't have to do that again," Sandy said, grinning. "It isn't you Kate's shy of. Is it late enough for a drink? Or do you want to drink with us?"

"I do," I said. "I want to talk, too. I just don't know exactly what's on my mind."

"Let me get the drinks," Sandy said, "and I'll tell you."

"She sometimes sounds a lot smarter than she really is," Esther said, "but then you probably know that."

I noticed again the receptive liveliness of her face. I wanted to say something pleasant to her or something amusing, but I did not know how to be either in the assumed intimacy I could feel. I didn't say anything.

"I made a fool of myself last time you were here. Don't let me do it again, will you?"

"You weren't foolish."

"I was. I think I must have been frightened of you, and I wasn't really prepared for Esther at all."

"People rarely are," I said.

"And she was so completely different the next time we saw her. That must have been simply terrible for you."

"Yes," I said. "She did come back here, did she?"

"Oh yes. She spent the night and left from here in the morning."

"I'd forgotten."

"Esther?" Sandy called. "Where are the onions?"

"I'll get them."

Sandy came into the room with a pitcher of martinis.

"Now. What happened when Esther got back? And what's happened since?"

"She had a long talk with a man named Charlie, finished off her contract with Christopher Marlowe Smith, and is now living with Charlie."

"And how do you feel about it?"

"Awful," I said.

"And how does she feel?"

"Properly had. Marvelous."

"So what's the trouble? I thought that was the goal. No, don't tell me. I know—he's not good enough for her."

"He's had three wives, a handful of children, and probably not the balancing number of divorces. He steals. He takes drugs, apparently."

"We're none of us perfect," Sandy said. "At least he's not a homosexual."

I didn't answer, resting in the pain I suppose I'd been waiting to have inflicted. Esther was handing around onions.

"What are you going to do with your private life now?" Sandy asked.

"Give it to charity," I said.

"A lay sister?"

"Why didn't you love her, Kate?" Esther asked suddenly. "She loves you so very much."

"A wrong sort of question," Sandy said. "Kate can't answer it in front of us. She's, for one thing, too polite. Anyway, I've already explained it to you."

"But you can't really think that going to bed with a woman is wrong," Esther persisted. "What about Sandy and me?"

Esther left Sandy the end of that summer. Or perhaps Sandy ordered her out. Esther was not the sort of girl to leave alone, even in a room, much less in a city. And Sandy, who had so thoroughly and unhappily explored the kind of living Esther apparently enjoyed, could not stay indulgent. A good many marriages are no better and last no longer. At least there were no legal delays and expenses. At the time Esther asked her question, I had no answer. What happened to them afterwards doesn't really prove the point I didn't make. For one with my nervous, negative morality, risking failure is less terrifying than risking success. I could more easily have died for you than lived with you, and I know how ridiculous that is.

IV

THE FIRST MONTHS in Washington were my trial by cold water for saving the world. I was not really surprised, but nothing could adequately have prepared me for that sort of endurance test, except perhaps reading C. S. Lewis, which I had. How often I thought of Ransom's night under the tree with the devil calling over and over again, "Ransom, Ransom," until, when he finally replied, "What?" the answer was always "Nothing." Survival in climates of boredom and futility where the greatest temptations are extending the coffee break, losing the last twenty memos, and playing jokes on the telephone is the most uncelebrated and even mocked virtue of our time. I was fortunate in two things, a natural earnestness about duty and a boss who found my good manners helpful at her official luncheons. There was plenty that was useful, if depressing, to learn.

When I was not at the office, I was at home reading official documents. Because there was no one to provide a human world for me, I had none, not even a chess partner. Shopping for a record player, I discovered kits for the first time. For my present occupation, they were an even better power fantasy than chess. When I hooked up and turned on the first amplifier I ever wired, watched the light come on and then heard the sound, I believed for an unserious moment that all my careful following of Washington directions might one day make a policy machine I could control. There was that about it, but, of course, there was also a soldering iron. And there were the wires. One corner of my otherwise serene apartment was probably, more than anything else, a shrine to you. It's too bad we couldn't have played amplifiers as some people play chess, by mail. I did write you a letter or two, but I had no answers. Perhaps that's why it is so easy to write this now, out of a long habit of nearly futile pages. What I never supposed you really read I don't quite believe you won't read now. It comes to the same thing.

Andrew and Monk did answer my letters with more and more insistent invitations to visit them in New York. Much as I wanted to see them, I delayed the trip because seeing them again would be a kind of confrontation I wasn't prepared for. It was one thing to talk a little about you with Sandy, quite another to talk with Andrew and Monk. And I was not ready to admit either my boredom or disappointment with my job. Andrew's letters, in particular, were urgent, finally almost angry. I telephoned in the early spring to say I had a long weekend.

"You should have your third-year home leave by now," Andrew said, but he was pleased just the same.

"Wouldn't it be better if you got me a hotel room?"

"Better for you maybe, but not for us."

He met my train, which I hadn't expected because it got in at around four on a Friday afternoon. The surprise of seeing him there covered my surprise at the change in his looks. At twenty-five, I had not yet begun to expect my friends to age. And Andrew had never really seemed the nine years older than I that he was. He was still an unusually handsome man, but the light had gone out of his skin and hair. His face was thinner, yet he carried himself as if aware of a new and burdensome weight with unexpected mannerisms of trouser hoisting and hair smoothing, a man nervous about his looks as Andrew had never been.

"I told Ramona we'd have a drink before we came home to give her a chance to get things organized with the baby."

Once we were in a bar, sitting at a small table, he seemed more familiar to me. Something of the boy of the world had grown into a man of the world in the still easy good manners, a confident pleasantness with people who did him some service. But his face warned me against open questions, which no longer seemed possible. I thought of Doris, who was convinced that this was no way to make a man of Andrew, while I answered perfectly safe, technical questions about my job.

"How are you really, Kate?" he asked suddenly.

"A bit uncertain," I said. "A bit lonely."

"Does it make sense, what you're doing?"

"I'm not sure yet, Andy. It's too soon to tell."

"Not for me it isn't," he said. "I've got to talk, Kate. We may not get another chance this weekend. I can't talk with Ramona. She just can't or won't understand."

"Then talk," I said.

Through his four and my two whiskeys I listened to a monologue so reminiscent of the one I had heard all those years ago on a walk to San Telmo that again I couldn't even interrupt to reply. Oh, some of the basic subject matter was different. Peter was never mentioned, and homosexuality was only a minor reference in a new context. But Mr. Belshaw was still at the center of it, more monstrous than ever, and the rage against the victims of this life was simply redirected to himself.

"For two months, Kate, I was first asking and then begging for a job, anything finally. I couldn't even pay the rent. 'Thirty-four years old? Never worked?' I had to go to my father's friends. I felt as if I were asking for charity, and that's exactly what they'd been told to give me. Do you know, one of those bastards even suggested that I be a sort of gigolo for his daughter? 'Take her to shows and things, my boy. Just the one to do it with all that travel and culture.' "

He had finally found a job in an advertising agency, but he was more or less an office boy, even sent out to get coffee for the twenty-five-year-old junior executives nearly fresh from M.A.'s in sociology at Columbia.

"And when I try to explain to Ramona that it's just not possible, she talks about having to begin at the bottom. Do you know, she isn't even ashamed of me. That's what I can't bear, Kate. That's what I simply can't bear."

There had been no nurse when Monk came home from the hospital with Lissa, which for Andrew seemed as primitive as letting Monk drop her baby in a field. They had no money for new clothes, for theater tickets, for entertaining friends.

"What's the point to living if you have to live like this? Ramona says lots of people do. Do you know what she says, Kate? Can you imagine? She says, 'The honeymoon's over.' I've married Kathleen Norris in disguise! If only she'd bitch about it, if only she'd come out with one ordinary complaint. . . . I sit there and disintegrate before her eyes. Look at me: hair and teeth falling out, bloated with drinking up my child's piggy bank future. And Ramona says she really doesn't mind doing her own hair. She doesn't. And she looks marvelous. She doesn't look old enough to have a child. People think I'm her father. And all the time that bastard sits up there gloating over my freedom, my dignity, my sanity. He doesn't give a damn that I have a wife and child."

"What are you going to do about it, Andy?" I was finally able to ask.

"Something," he said. "I'm going to do something."

"Don't have another drink. Being alcoholic isn't your style."

"I'm learning to adjust."

"A Lawrence father figure."

"A New York City coal miner—at least that has flair to it. Let me tell you about the psychological principles of the irritating commercial."

But he allowed himself to be taken home, which was a pleasant two-bedroom apartment north of the George Washington Bridge, sparsely but handsomely furnished, the walls crowded with Andrew's extraordinary collection of paintings, two or three of which he'd sold to buy all the furniture they needed. Monk was not exactly prepared for us. The moment when she could have left the baby with a bottle and the dinner in the oven and greeted us serenely had passed some time ago. We walked in to Lissa's howling and Monk's frantic, last-minute preparations of a meal no sane, young mother would try to cook. I hoped her unreasonable gesture was more for Andrew than for me. I had not had enough married friends to feel comfortable about the hour and a half I had just spent listening to Andrew's unhappiness, though his criticism of Monk was nothing but a complaint about her kindness and good humor. I am never good at being late. Andrew went to Monk first, who ordered him to deal with the baby, which he did, picking her up and bringing her to me. She was as appealing a combination of them both as I had imagined, the beginning wisps of her mother's red hair, her father's almost shocking blue eyes. She gave me an indignant look and turned her face away.

"Hey!" her father said, holding her out from him. "What's that all about?"

She glared at him, grabbed his nose and squealed a primitive satisfaction.

"Try not to get her too excited," Monk called from the kitchen.

A moment later she came in, and what Andrew had said about her was true. I could have thought that what the last four years had done to him had not marked her at all, except that an unaltered face is as much a defense as one too quickly eroding. And there was in her manner, as the evening passed, all the experience of her once theoretical doubts. She was uncertain not only with Andrew but with the baby, almost unfamiliar, as if she'd been called in that afternoon to play the part. They tried very hard not to disagree about what to do with Lissa, who woke and cried every hour. Andrew obviously thought she was old enough to be disciplined. Monk couldn't bear the idea.

"Don't you think it's unfair of God to have arranged it this way?" she asked brightly. "I mean, she's so helpless in the hands of absolutely amateur parents."

I don't suppose Monk meant that they needed a nurse, but Andrew, convinced that they did, suffered such remarks with only superficial patience. That he was better than Monk with Lissa gave him no comfort and was certainly not reassuring for Monk. She was more in awe of him than I could understand, helplessly inept and eager in her attempts to please him. He did try to be pleased, but much of what she did he did not want to see his wife doing. Her "thrifty, witty" curtains, her delicious but inexpensive meals, her cleverly revised wardrobe all depressed him. Though it was easy to be furious with him, it was hard not to feel sorry, too.

"Maybe I should try to be unhappy," Monk said when we were alone together. "I can be unhappy for him, but I never expected to live in a great house with servants. I wouldn't even know how. And that's what irritates him—I'm a good wife for the bad world he lives in."

"It's not really that, Monk," I said, trying to reassure. "He's frightened of being a failure.'

"Andy? He couldn't be," she said with energetic certainty. "He's just impatient because he has so much confidence. He thinks he can run a firm before six months is up. It's not a bad job he's got, you know, Kate. Robin never dreamed of making the salary Andy's begun with. And we're not exactly slum dwellers. It's just that Andy goes into a major depression because he can't buy a Jackson Pollock or go to Bermuda for the weekend. In five years' time he'll probably be able to. Then it will be my turn to be miserable. I don't even want to be rich. The whole idea scares me."

In the next room Lissa woke in an immediate rage.

"She's got her father's temper," Monk said, hurrying off with a look of defeat even before she'd tried to cope with the baby.

Andrew came in with the shopping, took the baby from Monk and soon had her changed and eating contentedly. Monk put away the groceries with comments like, "Oh, how nice! Lobster," and "Were we really out of caviar?" I would like to have thought it funny, but I had outgrown the gallows humor of adolescence. Life was burdensomely serious, even dangerous. I could only be afraid. That fear perversely pleased Andrew. He had found someone to take him seriously. He burdened nearly all the weekend conversations with psychological and economic statistics to indicate the inevitable destruction of the individual and therefore of art. Pompous and panicked, he lectured on the failure of Western Man while Monk blinked and yawned over knitting and I filled ashtrays and emptied glasses.

"It's *your* crisis, Andy," I finally said. "You just confuse the issue with generalities."

He walked out, slamming the door. Monk went on knitting for the moment before Lissa began to cry. We took turns walking her until she fell asleep again on her mother's shoulder.

"Well, you just can't let him go on being an angry bore," I said defensively. "He could make a habit of it."

"The prince in his frog phase," Monk explained, resigned. "You know, he's always been a little like this. It's just that he was always on his good behavior with you. He shouted about his thesis sometimes, and he can talk for hours about the failure of Cambridge, in fact the whole educational system in England."

"How long will he stay out?"

"I don't know. Sometimes he's away for a day or two, but with you here he'll just have a couple of drinks around the corner."

"How do you stand it, Monk?"

"That's not the problem. It's Andy who can't stand it. I get more and more afraid that he'll simply leave—but let's not talk about it. Isn't there something a little sordid in your life that we could talk about for comic relief?"

"Not at the moment," I said, "but Esther's doing pretty well."

I tried to entertain Monk at your expense, so grateful for a topic that I forgot to feel guilty.

"But that's immoral, Kate, and it's illegal as well. I can't believe it. Is he attractive?"

"To some people, he must be. And I think he's probably very talented."

"We should rescue her," Monk decided. "We should get her to come east."

"To her mother?"

"Ah . . . I'd forgotten about her. A block. But she could live in Washington with you."

"I think you could put Lissa down now," I said.

Andrew came in while Monk was in the bedroom with Lissa and I in the kitchen getting myself another drink.

"I probably need a good psychiatrist," he said to my back.

"Or wise, kinder friends," I said, turning to him. He looked terribly tired. "Andy, it's a bad time, that's all. You'll figure it out."

He nodded.

"I'm sorry," he said to Monk as she came into the room to join us.

She kissed him tentatively, then stepped back to look at him. "Red and blue are my favorite colors, but I'm not as mad about pale green. Shouldn't we go to bed?"

I listened to their brief love-making, which was no more reassuring than the faint sirens of New York. Petty, private disasters.

We talked once again before I went back to Washington about saving you, but none of us seriously considered it. The idea was simply an idiom for fond disapproval.

"We haven't really heard anything about you at all," Monk said as I was getting ready to leave.

"Nothing much to say. Aside from doing my work and being my boss's social secretary, I build amplifiers."

"But aren't you meeting all sorts of important people?"

"Yes," I said. "I helped Mrs. Roosevelt on with her coat. She wears the same powder Mother did."

"And what's she like?"

"Human."

"Rare," Andrew said.

"In a way. But I felt awfully hopeful, as if one really might finally grow up to be human."

"Well, it's a marvelous job for you," Monk said. "You're so good with old ladies and people like that."

I made a face.

"But you are. You never say the wrong sort of thing. It's no way to save the world, of course, but somebody's got to be pleasant."

"And being an Indian is such a political asset as well," I said.

I said good-by to Lissa with whom I had become intimate enough so that she was willing to pull my hair and chew at my watch band, but she was still indifferent to social customs. It was another year before she learned to call me Crow, the only appropriate nickname I've ever been given.

Andrew took me to my train, missing another half day's work, but he was sober and gentle and apologetic.

"Being in the prime of life is a hell of a letdown after being young, but I'll sort it out somehow. Meanwhile, keep on being brave and useful for us, won't you?"

"Take care of your redheads."

"Yes."

He settled my suitcase on the rack, handed me a newspaper and a candy bar, kissed me and was gone. It wasn't the candy bar that made me cry. I was terribly tired.

. . .

"Long weekends don't seem to be your sort of hobby," Joyce Lowe said to me the next morning when I went into her office to answer some questions about a report.

"Friends with a teething baby," I said.

"Not the sort of friends to have."

I shrugged agreeably. I liked Joyce Lowe. She worked hard and had a practical, but not cynical view of what could be accomplished. She had a quick temper about unimportant details, but she could be patient for months to make a real point. She had been patient with me while I learned. The occasional, sharp correction now and the slightly acid personal comments were signs of approval. I failed her only in never misinterpreting them and therefore never giving her the opportunity to be kind or confiding.

"We're having lunch with private agencies on Thursday. Wear a hat."

I nodded.

"And not the gray one if you don't look any better than you do today."

"I'd better take the agency folders home tonight," I said.

"No. Get some rest or sex or something. I'll do the talking."

I took the folders home on Wednesday night, and Thursday morning I was in Joyce's office when a telephone call came through for me from New York.

"Take it in here if you like," Joyce said.

It was Mrs. Woolf, asking if I could have lunch with her.

"Today?"

Yes. She would be at the Washington airport at noon. She wanted me to meet her there.

"I can't today," I explained. "I have a business luncheon."

She wanted to know how soon that would be over.

"I really don't know, but I won't be free until around six this evening."

But she had to see me. It was urgent. She was leaving for

California in the afternoon. Couldn't I cancel the luncheon? Or anyway meet her by two o'clock? Her plane left Washington at three.

"I don't see how I can," I said. "Is there anything wrong, Mrs. Woolf?"

Yes, there certainly was. She couldn't talk about it over the phone. That was the point, but she assured me that something was terribly wrong, and she had to see me before she left for the West. It was a matter of . . .

"Life and death?" I prompted when her voice faltered.

Yes.

"Could you hold on a minute?" I said, cupping my hand over the phone. "Joyce, this seems to be an emergency. I need to be at the airport at noon for a couple of hours."

"Then go," Joyce said.

"What's the flight number?" I asked Mrs. Woolf. "I'll meet the plane."

Joyce was handing me a lighted cigarette when I hung up.

"I'm awfully sorry," I said to her. "I couldn't think what else to do."

"Then there probably isn't anything else to do. Can you be back at the office by three, or do you need the afternoon off?"

"Oh no, I'm sure I can be back by three."

"That would help. But if not, just give me a ring. I'm not a matter of 'life and death.' "

"Good," I said.

"Is it bad, Kate?"

"I really don't know," I said. "I think a good friend of mine must be in trouble."

"Are you involved?"

"No," I said. "There will be no reflection on the office."

"I didn't mean that," she said. "Surely I don't have to tell you . . ."

"No, you don't. I was making a bad joke."

"Be careful you don't pick up any of my other bad habits," she said. "You owe me a cigarette."

"I'll write it down."

I stood, watching Mrs. Woolf walk toward me as if she were the arresting officer, for I was sure that whatever had happened to you was somehow my fault. It was a natural guilt your mother had carefully nourished in me. She looked more like a lady lawyer than a policewoman in her elegant suit and short fur cape, but she was neither calm nor aggressive. She had been crying and she was relieved to see me there, even grateful, so candidly so that she didn't offer to pay for cab fare, time off, or our drink in the bar before we had lunch.

"She's in jail, charged with possession of drugs. Or was this morning, anyway. Bail's being arranged. And there's a young man involved, a person named—"

"Charlie," I said.

"That's the one. You know him, then."

"Yes," I said.

"Katherine, I don't want you to betray any confidence that you feel you can't, but it would be a great help to me to know as much about this as I can before I arrive. Esther and I haven't had a very easy relationship over these last few years. I don't blame her. I blame myself. I have tried, but obviously—"

She couldn't go on talking for a moment. I waited, oddly expecting small paper animals and flowers to appear on the table. Your mother had never reminded me of you before, and she didn't really now, but, however badly and ordinarily she put it, she was your mother; this was hard for her.

"I'm sorry," she said.

"How much do you know about the circumstances?" I asked.

"Nearly nothing. She and this young man were picked up by the police."

"Where?"

"At her apartment."

"What kind of drugs?"

"Marijuana."

There was a lot I didn't know, and I told her so. What I did know or could guess was hard to say. If you had been experimenting with drugs, you would not easily be persuaded to deny it. And, since stealing from a church had seemed to you sensible, a little marijuana certainly could fall within the range of your morality. But even if you hadn't been tempted to extensions of perception, you would probably want to share the blame with Charlie or even take it to yourself. And Charlie was not the sort to turn down that kind of sacrifice. He lived on it. I didn't tell your mother that.

"Charlie lives downstairs," I said. "In fact, they've been living together, so it's possible that he can be charged alone. It's not his first arrest. If Esther is involved, the worst is probably a suspended sentence."

"It will ruin her life," Mrs. Woolf said.

Now that a jail sentence has become a status symbol in the civil rights movement, some of the general, social horror has been dissipated. In 1956, a record hadn't the same reality. We were too far away from the suffragette movement for it to be anything but an academic reference; nevertheless, I used it. I used everything I could think of to show that your life might not be entirely razed by such an experience.

"She won't ever be able to hold any position of responsibility. She won't be able to vote."

"It's not good," I admitted, "and maybe it won't happen, but Esther hasn't ever wanted to be anything but a sculptor, and she wouldn't know how to vote anyway, I'm sure never has . . ." but I faltered because such penalties seemed dreadful to me. "Look, the point is to try to understand her view so that you can persuade her to take the advice of the best lawyer available."

"I brought her up . . . I brought both my children up to respect the law."

"The trouble with that is, if she has broken the law, she ought to accept the punishment."

"Not while I can fight it. I'll take it to the Supreme Court!"

"That won't be Esther's notion of respecting the law," I said, and I could just hear the kindergarten logic which would allow you to break the law but not to use the legal loopholes to set you free of it; your sort of creative morality would stop at avoiding consequences.

"I don't understand her. I simply don't understand her."

"Try, Mrs. Woolf."

We looked at each other.

"You blame me, don't you, Katherine?"

"What would be the logic of that? You could as easily blame me."

"And in a way I suppose I do. You could have protected her."

"How?" I demanded.

"I'm not blind, Katherine," your mother said. "Haven't I made that clear from the beginning? She needed someone like you, someone responsible."

"That's hardly fair," I said and heard, from all those years ago. "To a mother, there are things more important than being fair," without the Yiddish accent but with its emotional rhythms still.

"Well, it's past in any case. I have to decide what I'm going to do with Esther once I've gotten her out of this mess. I think perhaps we'll take a trip, and then she'd better come to live with me. As soon as I have her with me, I'm going to telephone. I want you to talk with her and tell her that you agree with me about what she's to do. Will you do that much?"

"No," I said. "I'll listen to what she has to say and try to understand her point of view. And you'd better do the same thing, Mrs. Woolf, if you want to be able to help her at all. Excuse me, but you've been an aggressive fool with her long enough to know that doesn't work. Now it's time you were practical."

"Why Katherine!"

I had gotten up from the table as the waitress came with the check. I took it from her.

"I can't allow—" Mrs. Woolf began.

"It's good practice," I said. "Give Esther my love."

On the way back to the office I was having a conversation in my head with Monk. There now: I don't have to be pleasant to people, and, if it doesn't save the world, what's the point? But I knew that being rude didn't save the world, either, and I couldn't shut off first embarrassment and then shame. Under both of those, of course, was the pain of her accusation. She had made her arrest after all.

"I'm not guilty," I said aloud, but what a comfortless thought that was when the heart also required, "Forgive me, E."

Joyce was just back from her luncheon and taking a long-distance call from her husband when I got to the office. I went to my own desk and pushed papers from one side of it to the other until Joyce called me in. I took her a lighted cigarette.

"How did it go?" I asked.

"The other end of the table went a bit thin and competitive without you there, but I got more or less what I wanted. Can you have dinner with me tonight? I'm going to stay in town to get some work done."

"Sure. I can come back with you if you like."

"I like," she said. "Now get hold of these five people for me for an afternoon meeting some time next week."

"Robertson's out of town until the first of the month," I said.

"We'll do without him then. Get his assistant."

"Anything else?"

"Not just at the moment."

I find it very difficult to concentrate on things that don't require it. I spent the rest of the afternoon with at least three stations of my mind turned up full volume, and I not only listened to them all but did a good deal of talking back while I also made telephone calls, proofread reports, and added a few memos of my own to external communications. At five-thirty Joyce was standing by my desk ready to go.

Over a drink a few minutes later, she asked, "How did your lunch go?"

"A bit thin and competitive, too," I said, "and I didn't seem to be much help."

"Does it matter?"

"I don't know. Is a new commission going to be set up, do you think?"

"You're usually smoother at changing the subject than that."

"It's just a boring story with an unhappy middle."

"Tell it to me, anyway," Joyce said. "I don't want to talk shop."

"Once upon a time," I said, "there was an ugly, little rich girl with a mean, real mother and a make-believe father who looked like a wristwatch. She was kept in a tower at the top of the house along with the second-best dining-room furniture and her ugly little brother until they both grew tall enough to be mistaken for beautiful grown-ups. They even fooled their mean, real mother, so she sent them out into the world to be fallen in love with, and they were."

"Who fell in love with them?" Joyce asked.

"I fell in love with one of them."

"Which one?"

"For the story it doesn't matter," I said. "It's just to establish authenticity. Anyway, the ugly, little rich girl who looked like a beautiful grown-up wasn't really interested in being fallen in love with, not at first, anyway. She wanted instead to understand the nature of the world. Then she wanted to be a great sculptor. After that—but maybe I haven't got the order straight—before she was thirty, anyway, she wanted to marry and have a child to fulfill herself as a woman. And after that she wanted to be a nun and serve God. The plan went pretty well for a while. She read some books, and she went to church, and she made some faces and other things for the world, but somehow the one, two, three of it all got multiplied. There were some giant steps to be taken, and, since she was really an ugly, little rich girl with a mean, real mother and not the beautiful grown-up she seemed to be, she landed once or twice a little short—short of understanding, short of being great, short of marriage into bed, and just now, in what ought to be the middle of the story, short of the nunnery into jail, not being wise enough or great enough or fulfilled enough to know the real difference between cells. And now her mean, real mother, who should have explained it to her in the first place, is looking for someone else to blame."

"Which of these characters did you have lunch with today?"

"The mean, real mother."

"And?"

"That's all of the story there is," I said. "Are we going to have another drink?"

"Sure," Joyce said. "But which one of the characters are you?"

"I'm the author," I said. "Authors have no place in their own stories, except to admit authenticity, and I did that."

"It's not much to admit," Joyce said, signaling a waiter for two more martinis.

"I'm not guilty," I said.

"What a limited way to live," Joyce said. "You know, I haven't played this sort of game for ten years, not since I was your age. I wasn't very good at it then, either."

"I'm sorry," I said. "I was just trying to be entertaining."

"Do you have a mother?"

"No," I said. "She died last year."

"Father?"

"No."

"Do you have any friends here?"

"No."

"Why not?"

"I don't know," I said. "Probably I'm resting. I'm not very good with people."

"No, of course not."

"I'm really not," I said, "except at a distance."

"All right," Joyce said, smiling. "I should have kept mine, but you are entertaining. Shall I tell you a story now?"

"You don't owe me one. They're not like cigarettes or working days."

"You'd better explain what that means," Joyce said sharply.

"Nothing," I said, feeling frantic and miserable.

"You had a rotten day, didn't you?"

"Yes, the sort of day that makes it unbearable to be around people . . . people I care about, anyway."

"Do you want to go home?"

"If we could just not—" I tried to explain.

"Not talk? Not risk anything? I'm not as good at that after five-thirty. Why don't we have dinner some other night?"

"But what about the work?"

"Katherine George, you didn't really think—"

"I'm told I'm a good cook," I said, finishing my drink.

I did cook dinner that night but not until after midnight. Joyce, in my robe, was looking around the apartment. She was curious about the hi fi equipment, the books, and the paintings.

"You're not going to be with me for long, are you?" she asked.

"Why?"

"You don't need the job. You're using it. I'm not surprised. Not exactly. Oh, I do regret the last six months. This isn't going to be a one-night stand, is it?"

"What about your husband?"

"He's away a lot. We spare each other details."

I did not make up my mind; a decision didn't really seem relevant, or the time for it had passed. It was not a circumstance I was accustomed to. The despairing rebellion of my appetite hadn't ever before resulted in this kind of midnight snack, in conversation which could accommodate problems at the office, personal history, physical intimacy. I had come near it only once before with Sandy, but the minute we began to talk we stopped considering each other as sexual objects. For Joyce it was natural enough, for most people probably. For me, it was very awkward at first, politeness and crudity in comic collision in the same sentence or gesture. I felt as embarrassed as I might if I'd found myself serving chocolate milk and brandy with rare roast beef. And sometimes as much put off. But being put off helped in a way just as the fact of Joyce's husband helped. It was slower and less physically painful than a broken nose but no less punishing finally. I don't mean to suggest that I suffered. My own clumsiness and occasional distaste more often interested than frightened me. And I was more simply impatient than jealous when Joyce spent time with her husband. When I built him an amplifier, guilt had nothing to do with it. I was glad of ways to kill time. It was, like all my other experiences, one I could afford, but I speak only of the price. That's all that should interest me now.

That and the connection there obviously was between those first hours I spent with Joyce and the hours you were waiting for bail. The telephone call your mother had suggested was not put through. I didn't really expect it, but I did send off an urgent note to you, asking you to phone when you could. As the days passed and there was no news, I tried to think what else I could do.

"Isn't there anyone else you could get in touch with?" Joyce asked.

"No one I know well enough or Esther knows well enough."

"Why doesn't she let you know?"

"She might not have got my letter. She might not know anything yet herself. Her mother may not even have told her that I know. In fact, that's likely."

"But I thought her mother approved of you."

"She did. If I hadn't been so stupid—"

"It's a good thing *I* wasn't there. I would have thrown something at her. All you did was buy her lunch."

"That was worse," I said, "and I knew it."

"You're a calculating girl," Joyce said. "You deal the same way with me in the office, don't you?"

"How do you mean?"

"You figure people's emotional angles and usually give them plenty of space. My secretary's never noticed, for instance, that there's a large sharp-edged coffee table called 'I can't stand typographical errors until after eleven A.M.' She doesn't even know where her bruises come from. You never run into anything like that, or, if you do, you know it."

"I'm not that smart," I said. "I do it by walking around a lot of furniture that isn't even there."

"Yes, it's true," Joyce said, thinking about it. "But that's flattering—for people who don't want to go to bed with you, anyway. Months of nothing but a very wide, single berth!"

"I didn't know," I said.

"You didn't know!"

"It's true."

"That's not flattering because it suggests that the idea simply didn't occur to you."

"That's not true," I said.

"Well, anyway, it occurs to you now, doesn't it?"

I let her gentle, curious confidence control my response. If she wanted me to work, I worked. If she wanted me to vanish, I vanished. I talked when she asked questions, and I let her distract me from the subjects she raised. That asking about you almost always turned into a sexual ploy didn't surprise me. Joyce wasn't really conscious of it; she played with the seasonings of jealousy and sympathy, that was all. Occasionally she told me about other people she'd made love with, always women. And she had a continuing curiosity about my sexual experience. She wanted details.

"I don't know why men like pictures. Stories are much better. I can look at you."

"I like pictures," I said to tease.

While she protested, I heard you protesting about Christopher

Marlowe Smith's collection which he insisted was simply educational. But you were earnest and embarrassed, trying to explain that learning by doing was better; professional demonstration, even in photographs, made you feel too inadequate to try. Joyce was gloriously scornful, treating me to the comic obscenity of various poses, a demonstration lecture which finally required audience participation.

"Well, you fucked that up nicely," Joyce complained, nearly asleep.

"But I'm converted," I said.

She was satisfied, and why shouldn't she have been? She received in fact all the fantasy tenderness, desire, ease I had refused you. And I should have been satisfied, too, in being so wholly taken, so wholly delighted in, the parts of my life gathered up in her pleasure. I was, sometimes for days at a time. I was glad of her, grateful for her, as I am sure I couldn't have been if I had really loved Joyce as I loved you.

Love is a hard word, but one can't go on being adolescently embarrassed by it. Admit it to the vocabulary at all, and it has to play some part in a lot of relationships. I told Joyce often, a dozen times a meeting, that I loved her, and I did, in a way that I could afford. I never told you. It's simple enough. I couldn't be guilty of you. I hadn't that kind of courage.

And where in hell were you all those weeks? Did you ever get my letter? Did you ever know that I had seen your mother? Three months had gone by before the first of all those postcards arrived. This one, the picture of a temple, had carefully and clearly printed across the back, "I don't like Japan." (It's a good thing you never tried for the Peace Corps.) They arrived fairly regularly after that, almost always temples. You seemed to be avoiding sculpture, the gods themselves, but you must have stood at the gates several times a day, while your mother read the endless guidebook facts, chanting against the chanting you strained to hear.

I never did hear anything from you of your arrest or the final dropping of charges against you. It was Christopher Marlowe Smith, sight-seeing in Washington, who invited himself for a drink and pieced the story together from a few facts, a few more rumors, what was becoming part of the legend of Charlie.

"Yes, he went to jail all right, two years, I think it is," Christopher Marlowe Smith confirmed with some satisfaction. "Esther's mother bought her off, charges and all. Christ! You know I didn't have any idea there was that kind of money involved. Probably just as well. I would have killed the guy, and getting off a murder charge can be pretty expensive. Just the same—"

"It wouldn't have made any difference," I said.

"Maybe not. I'm a chiseler all right, but I'm strictly small change. Do you know a funny thing, though? When I first heard about it, I felt guilty. Why in hell should I feel guilty? I didn't exactly give her to him, but she was so clueless about things and people. Charlie's a very smart guy, Kate. To tell the truth, he scared me shitless. And shitless I went, home to the wife and kiddy. I was really glad when I heard she was out of it with nothing, not even a charge. I was relieved. You know, there's one story going around that she was asked if she'd lived with Charlie as man and wife. She said, no. 'Do you deny that you've had sexual intercourse with this man?' 'Of course not,' she says, 'you asked me if I was pretending to be married to him.' It's probably not true. I mean, I don't think she was ever even questioned like that, but it does sound like her, doesn't it? It's a damned good thing she didn't ever get into court. She'd be serving terms for everything from stealing out of the collection plate to sucking off. Her mother did the right thing."

"I wonder how her mother persuaded her," I said.

"She probably didn't even have to. When Esther's scared enough, she does what she's told. You know, in a lot of ways she's like my little kid, defiant as hell on the way through the plate glass, but sadly docile on the other side."

"But leaving Charlie there—"

"Katie, from what I've heard, nobody has ever been so glad to leave anybody since the damsel got away from the ape."

"A pretty highly developed ape."

"Yeah," Christopher Marlowe Smith agreed. "Fucked up enough to be a genius, but I don't like queers so confused they like women—'like' used advisedly here. I wonder how much he knew about her money."

"If he didn't know any more than she did, he'd be pretty ignorant."

"Anyway, Mama's finally come to, and she better not let that one roam the streets again until she's bought her a marriage license. Next time she's picked up, they might notify the wrong owner."

"How are things with you, Chris?"

"I think I've got another grant going for me. If my system works, I should last until 1964. It's order that matters."

He stayed for dinner and tried to invite himself to stay for the night.

"You've been so nice to me, Kate. Isn't there anything I can do for you? Can't I go to bed with you?"

"Thanks just the same, Chris, but it's not necessary."

He protested mildly for the sake of gallantry, but he was not hard to get rid of.

That night I had uneasy occupation for my insomnia. I had always worried that Charlie would somehow get you into difficulty you couldn't cope with, but I had never imagined that you might be unhappy with him, perhaps even frightened of him, hurt by him. Christopher Marlowe Smith didn't know any but the primary colors, had a funny book morality, in which heroes could have all the ladies they liked as long as they kept to the missionary positions. He was quite simply jealous of Charlie. Remembering how easily you let Christopher Marlowe Smith out of your life, I had a sudden image of you walking away from the jail, Charlie blurring like a bad photograph at a barred window, shouting, but the sounds were not human; they were supersonic chords, sustained as the sound of machines, finally falling in the natural drift which was sleep. I woke a few minutes later, knowing that I identified not with you but with Charlie. Whatever he might have done to you, I was suffering his pain, not yours. My own pain, of course, in his invented person.

There was a postcard in the morning from Athens: the Parthenon. Across the back of it was printed, "I've found Athena."

"You know, I don't even know who Athena is," Joyce said. "When I'm around you, I sometimes feel culturally deprived."

"She's all kinds of things—virgin goddess of wisdom and war, mother of gods, a weaver, an owl lover, the patroness of Athens, daughter of Zeus who sprang full grown from her father's forehead. For Esther she is Reason which directs Creative Energy, and it's about time she rediscovered that."

"Oh," Joyce said.

"Don't be put off," I said. "It's only a game we play with Greek gods instead of baseball players."

"Like chess and wiring amplifiers."

"And cooking," I added to defend myself.

"Let's not both be defensive at the same time. I get afraid of boring you, that's all."

"Only because I bore you," I said. "People with odd interests can be pretty tedious."

"Why can't you get a TV, Kate? Or subscribe to *Playboy*? Something my speed."

"I thought you didn't like pictures."

"I don't like you when you're being so goddamned superior."

"Insubordinate?"

Her hand lifted, then stopped. "Darling, what is it?" She was taking my hands away from my face. "I wouldn't hurt you. I was only bored . . . tired, a little bit jealous. Kate?"

"It's just battle fatigue."

"No rough stuff, darling, ever. I promise. If I'm going to feel guilty about you, I'll just feel guilty, that's all. I just keep thinking you're not only bored rigid at the office but with me, too. The only more interesting job in that office is mine. So I ought to help you find something else, shouldn't I? But what would I do? You're such a lovely habit."

"Let me worry about it. I'm not worried about it. I'll buy a TV."

"A kit?" Joyce teased.

"No, instant TV, all right?"

I was meeting more people, joining Joyce on the cocktail as well as the luncheon circuit. I was being brought to the official attention of heads of various offices. I was glad of the connections but not because I was looking for another job in Washington. I turned down two offers, which both pleased and troubled Joyce.

"We'd still see a lot of each other," she encouraged.

"Let me worry about it," I said again.

I didn't worry really. I was busy worrying about other people. Andrew had quit—been fired from?—his job and was, as far as I could understand, trying to set up a small business of his own with a friend, a selling gallery that would support itself at first by a curio corner, Japanese paper kites and camel saddles. It didn't sound to me a hopeful way of raising the capital they needed in the first place. I offered to invest some money in it, but Andrew refused. He had his own collection of paintings to fall back on, and he was quite confident. After all, they had turned out to be a very good investment. There was no reason why he shouldn't be able to use the same judgment in New York that he had in Europe. But, by the time I saw Andrew and Monk in July, he had sold nothing but his own paintings to buy what no one else was yet willing to invest in. He was still cheerful. But he was nervous.

"New York's a good market," he said, as he showed me some of the work of the young painters he was interested in, "in some ways, too good. There's too much stampeding. Innovation is too important. There aren't trends here so much as explosions. This man, for instance, has plenty of talent, and he's got his own vision of cool, lonely, oddly intimate space. Isn't that a nice canvas?

He's Canadian. But look at this one—he's jumped on the band wagon since he's come to New York. By the time he paints his way off it, there will be another one to get on, so out of a year's work, there will probably be only one or two things that are his own. That's not enough to make a painter. But somebody else, who isolates himself, stays with his own landscape, may take years, may not make it at all except for accidents of taste. It's too much of a gamble. It's getting to be like mining stocks. It shouldn't be."

"How much do you buy outright?"

"Very little," he said. "There's not the money for it. What I really need is money for promotion."

"How long can you last, Andy?"

"I'm not thinking about it that way."

"Has Dan got money?"

"Some. He ought to be in in a few minutes. The thing is that he's got contacts, very good ones. He doesn't know as much about painting yet as he should, but he's learning."

"Married?"

"No, he's not interested in women."

We were looking at kites and camel saddles when Dan Karno arrived. He was younger than Andrew by two or three years, had a clown's startled and curly face, a neat, strong body, a manner that was attentive, engaging. I found him easy to talk to. When we left, I had the impression that he liked me.

"That's what Ramona says," Andrew commented. "You know, it used to irritate me that women felt flattered by men like Dan and Pete, until I understood how tired a woman gets of being a sexual object. Mind you, it would be a pretty thin party for Ramona if she didn't get her share of good heterosexual aggressiveness, but she says Dan makes her feel like a person. I can see that."

"It's not just a homosexual talent," I said. "You have it, too."

"I work at it," Andrew said, "sometimes. But I'm really a bottom pincher by nature."

"Are you?"

"Of course. Once I outgrow my Canadian reserve, I'm going to be a dirty, old man. Just what happened to Yeats."

"I wonder what I'll be," I said.

"I used to think some sort of North American Sitwell, less fey, more missionary."

"But not now?"

"You've got very relaxed, Katie," Andrew said, looking at my hand on his arm. "It's becoming."

"I've got myself a TV," I said.

"And a friend?"

"Yes," I said.

"Good."

After that, I could speak of Joyce naturally enough, quote her views on the relationship between private and public agencies dealing with foreign aid, talk about a couple of good restaurants we'd discovered, explain her official entertainment schedule. I tried not to notice that I did not mention her husband, that I did not correct Andrew when he made a comment which assumed that she was not married. After we got to the apartment, the subject was dropped.

Monk greeted us with a list of the things Lissa had eaten or tried to eat that day: the soap in the bathroom, the kitten's catnip mouse, Andrew's mail.

"She's more like a dog than a human being," Monk complained. "She even barks."

Lissa, on all fours in the hall, barked to demonstrate. The kitten stayed well under the couch.

"What time's the baby-sitter due?" Andrew asked.

"Why don't you make a drink first and then let me tell you about it?" Monk suggested with a melodramatically bright smile.

"Why?"

"I don't want to be beaten in front of Kate. It's so embarrassing for her."

"She can't come," Andrew said.

"No," Monk admitted. "She's got the flu or something."

"Why didn't you find someone else? In all of New York City—"

"I tried, Andy. I can't get anyone we know. But I can stay home. I called the gallery just after you left, and Dan says he has a friend who would take my ticket."

"I'll stay home," Andrew said, but it was not a kindly offer; it was a threat.

It was no time for me to make a third offer. I took a small, cloth book out of my purse and gave it to Lissa, who immediately put it on her head and made a number of inquiring and assertive noises which were extremely useful.

"You can get up off the floor now, Kate," Monk said. "Andy and I have decided to be pleasant to each other until later. You know, you look marvelous."

Monk looked all eyeteeth and eyelashes, an ironic commercial for young motherhood. The apartment showed more signs of her industry and talent, two tall, handsome string lamp shades which dominated one now nearly bare wall, strongly patterned drapes, an invented, hanging bookshelf. When I admired these things, she looked uncertain.

"It's a bit too 'homey' for Andy. He says we need Granny in the corner, so I took back a rocking chair I was going to refinish. I'm not being so domestic these days. I'm writing a play."

"Which is why," Andrew said, coming back into the room with drinks, "you should go tonight and I should stay home," this time quite pleasantly.

"But, if I could finish the third scene tonight, maybe I could show it to Kate while she's here."

"Then I think you should stay home," I said, knowing the decision was already made.

"I can't seem to make Ramona understand how important it is for us both to go out, to be seen at things, to meet people," Andrew said as we were on our way to the theater. "This baby-sitter thing is ridiculous. I bet this happens twice a week."

Monk explained later what hadn't been hard for me to guess. Andrew wanted to go out at least four times a week, sometimes to a show opening or cocktail party that cost no more than the baby-sitter and transportation at the time but put them in professional and social debt that Andrew would determinedly and generously repay, sometimes out to dinner or the theater with friends.

"There isn't any money," Monk said. "I know it's a crude thing to say, but people who don't have it have to talk about it now and then. Not Andy. No, that's inaccurate. He'll talk about thousands of dollars. What he can't deal with is not having cash for the baby-sitter. Dan sold my ticket last night so that I could pay her for last week. But the trouble with Dan is that he understands very well about baby-sitter money and doesn't have a clue about business money. They can't last another two months. Andy won't face it, and Dan doesn't understand it. Kate, I don't know what to do. I don't know what we're going to do. I made the terrible mistake of suggesting to Andy that I get a job, just to help us along while the gallery got started. He was gone for nearly a week. But somebody has to do something."

"I wonder if I could talk to him."

"He's not talkable to. You know, he was angry when you wrote about investing in the gallery. When I said maybe you thought it was a good thing financially, he said, 'Don't be ridiculous!' You see, he does know. But then he begins talking about one good show, one good sale."

"Could I lend you some money?"

"I couldn't explain where I'd got it. I suppose we're just going to have to face ruin before he'll face ruin."

"Couldn't I—?"

Monk began to cry.

"I'm going to talk to him," I said. "This is simply ridiculous."

"Don't, Kate, please. He couldn't stand it. He'd leave. He'll leave anyway."

"I don't believe that," I said.

"We'd better read my play. That's what we're supposed to be doing. When he comes back with Lissa you'll be expected to make all sorts of intelligent remarks. Of course, that might be easier if you hadn't read it."

"I want to," I said, dreading it.

But the play was oddly good. There was a distance between the characters' and the author's perceptions so that their cliché-ridden circumstances were presented as cliché-ridden circumstances, so that their elaborate rationalizations were meant to be ponderous. It would have been depressing if there hadn't been a curious, garish humor that controlled the tone.

"Just a little Freudian fairy tale," Monk said nervously.

"But it works, Monk."

"Do you think so?"

"I do. What are you going to do with it?"

"Oh, I thought I'd get Andy to finance it at some good, small place off Broadway."

"Do you know anyone to show it to?"

"Maybe," she said. "Do you really think it's good enough?"

"Yes."

"I'd thought of TV. It's that sort of length. . . ." But her tone suggested that she had none of Andrew's desperate confidence in pipe dreams. She smiled suddenly. "There's no point in being sane about solutions. I might as well join the madmen."

I bought a painting called *Loon Spaces* by the Canadian Andrew was interested in. I would have bought two or three if Andrew hadn't been suspicious of my motives. I like to complain now because recently a Canadian gallery bought another painting of that period for nearly five times as much, and I don't admit that I was investing not so much in a painting as in Andrew. It's a good painting. Andrew's profit was no more than baby-sitting money, though I doubt that he spent it that way. There was nothing more I could do.

When I got back to Washington, the first of your cathedral cards had arrived. The message read, "Mother likes Italy," which meant, obviously, that you didn't. Or you were recovering your sense of security enough to find your mother's company increasingly difficult. I didn't envy her what I remembered of your sulking exhaustion in the heat of southern Europe.

The heat in Washington was more intolerable. I don't know why a laboring furnace is not as hard on the nerves as the endless exhaling hum of an air conditioner. I don't know why being nearly cold inside and soaked with heat outside is more uncomfortable and more unhealthy than more extreme changes of temperature in the winter, but everyone in the office was limp with lasting summer colds, irritable and inaccurate. Joyce, because of one important meeting, had not been able to take her vacation with her husband, who went alone to the New England coast. I might have suspected her of arranging the conflict if she hadn't seemed so genuinely disappointed. There was, of course, no question of our taking a vacation together later. Joyce would never have risked so much. I talked of going to England for a couple of weeks. That disappointed her, too.

"I suppose you'll meet Esther," she said.

"I might, if she's there. I'm going to see Doris and Frank—if I go."

"You've got to turn on the air conditioner again, Kate. It's just unbearable in here. Why don't we go to a movie? Why don't we do something?"

There wasn't a movie either of us wanted to see.

"Why do we stay in town?" Joyce asked. "Why don't you come home with me?"

I had been to Joyce's house several times when her husband was there. I had even once spent the night in the guest room. He was always very pleasant, but he found things to occupy himself,

205

work in the garden, an errand, and he always went to bed very early. I tried not to think about him, which was not as easy at their house as it was at my apartment; so I went as seldom as I could. There was, while he was away, no reason to refuse. And for Joyce it was more comfortable. She had her own entertainments, her own space. And perhaps a perverse sexual excitement, too.

"What household god are we going to offend today?" I got used to asking, feeling her restless, inventive moods.

"I like you reluctant, and you know it, don't you?"

"I get tired."

"No you don't. You get moral."

"That's right. The heat makes me moral."

"Well, you don't have to do anything. Just relax."

"Where did you get that idea?"

"I read about it. I read, too, you know. Sex can get as dull as conversation if you don't keep yourself informed."

"Yourself?"

"You're an absolutely standard type, you know—the crude prude. You need to be shocked."

"Joyce—"

"Shut up now, darling. I want to concentrate. I'll do the talking. You listen."

I listened to a great deal, demonstrated narratives from novels, reenactments of scenes with other women, pure fantasy, but in all that sexual story-telling there was never a reference to Joyce's husband or to any man. The world might have been one sex. I never asked. I didn't think about it. But I was glad when his vacation was nearly over and I could move back into town. I was tired.

You were sending French cathedrals now with such messages as, "What about the Catholic Church?" and "If I'm baptized in the Anglican Church, will you be my godmother?" There were fortunately never return addresses. I wasn't expected to answer any of these questions, not at once, anyway. Plotting your course, I asked for my vacation for the first two weeks in October. It was a miscalculation which might have looked to you deliberate. You and your mother boarded the *Queen Elizabeth* the day before I left Washington.

"Why didn't you come while Esther was here?" Doris asked.

"I tried. She doesn't bother with small details like dates," I said. "How is she?"

"Mother- and travel-weary and absolutely drugged with God."

"Even at the breakfast table," Frank offered wryly.

"Did they stay here?"

"Yes," Doris said. "Don't ask me why. I had a lapse of memory. Most parents really ought to be killed at birth, except the delightful ones like Frank and me."

"Don't count on testimonials from our children," Frank said.

"In fact, the house needs more using than it gets," Doris admitted.

"Well, Mrs. Woolf must have taken up a number of rooms," I said.

"Yes. I did feel sorry for her, in a way. She's awful to Esther, but she's inaccurate. Her blows don't often really land. Esther's do, particularly the Jewish ones—religion as positive choice rather than negative identity. The odd thing is that her mother almost encourages her."

"Not odd," I said. "Did either Esther or Mrs. Woolf say anything about Esther's experience in jail?"

"Not a word," Frank said. "What's that?"

It wasn't as easy to tell the story to Frank and Doris as it had been to invent for Joyce. They were more concerned and made some effort to understand.

"And I complain that young Frank gives me ulcers!" Frank said. "I can quite see that Mrs. Woolf would think Esther was best off as a nun, but what about the nunnery? A very superior mother superior it would take, don't you think?"

"Is E. talking about that?" I asked.

"Not really," Doris said. "She hasn't even joined yet. She's still got godmothers rather than mother superiors on her mind."

"Oh, and wasn't that a discussion!" Frank said. "Did you know that Esther wants you to be her godmother?"

"Yes," I said. "She sent me a postcard about it."

"How like her," Doris said. "What did it say?"

"Just that, with a picture of a cathedral, I forget which one."

"Have you refused?"

"There wasn't any return address," I said. "I will."

"We should find an appropriate postcard," Frank suggested.

Later, when the nervous hilarity died down a bit, we talked more seriously.

"I'm just not sure that the Church lends itself to any safer living than the existentialists," Doris said.

"Dear, that's not fair, safer surely, even if no more truly moral."

"What on earth is being truly moral?" I asked.

"That's a question worthy of Esther herself," Frank said.

"Trying to be truly moral is what got her into trouble in the first place," Doris said. "My point is that the Church is no sanctuary from that."

"No," I said. "I agree. In that sense, stealing from the collection plate is safer than contributing to it."

"Only daughters of a minister could talk like that," Frank said. "Of course there's a lot of rationalizing in the Church. Still, the values it represents—"

"Rationalizing isn't the point," I said. "E.'s never rationalized like that for her own comfort or pleasure or justification. She thinks up the act to demonstrate the idea, not the other way around. She didn't really want those saddle shoes, after all. She took them because she thought she should."

"What about Charlie?" Frank answered.

"Same thing."

"And now," Doris said, "she'll go around looking for things to give up."

"Because she wants to," Frank said.

"Well, yes," I said, "but 'wants' only in the sense that she wants to carry out an idea."

"I want to think she's safer," Frank protested. "Don't disabuse me. I don't know how to worry about it."

I didn't either. And like Frank I wanted to be reassured, but Doris wouldn't let the subject go. Over morning coffee at Fortnum's, she dealt with it again.

"Aren't you going to try to discourage her, Kate? After all, you've left the Church."

"But not on sound moral grounds," I said. "There was really nothing wrong with the Church."

"You thought there was something wrong with you."

"There is," I said.

"Nonsense!"

"I was tired of rationalizing it. I was tired of being a hypocrite."

"All right, but that was the Church's fault, not yours."

"No," I said.

"Look, the Church is morally so primitive—"

"It's not," I said firmly. "Some people in it are. Some people out of it, too. I'm a moral primitive myself. I think, for instance, that adultery's a bad idea. It's just that I happen to enjoy it. I left the Church so that I didn't have to take morality seriously."

"Well, then you'd better go back. It hasn't worked."

"What do you mean, it hasn't worked?"

"God's still watching you."

"Oh, sure. I'm just not watching Him."

"Why should you be persecuted? Why should you feel guilty?"

"Because I am guilty," I said. "And I don't feel persecuted. I'm out of E.'s danger, Doris. I'm in no fear of being truly moral."

"I'm not so sure," Doris said. "I'm not so sure."

Joyce telephoned twice while I was in London. Doris asked no questions, but she seemed relieved. I was not. I wanted a rest. I went to the theater. I called on the late Turners at the Tate. I saw the shows at the selling galleries. Doris and I went to call on Ann. Frank and I played chess. Still, it was not long enough. I went back to Washington, passive but reluctant.

Fortunately Joyce was very much involved with her husband at that time. We had only one evening together in two weeks. She was apologetic, suggesting but not explaining certain problems that she had. He would probably be out of town the second weekend in November. Would I save that and spend it with her at her house? That seemed comfortably far off, easy to agree to. About that time I had a telephone call from you inviting me to New York for Thanksgiving. It was that date I looked forward to. I didn't put my mind to much else.

It was Tuesday evening, the second week in November, that I came home to find Andrew waiting for me. He had obviously been drinking for several days, hadn't shaved or changed his clothes. What is worn and ill fitting is less derelict than an expensive suit so abused.

"It's a wonder you weren't picked up for vagrancy," I said. "Come inside."

He seemed more dazed than drunk. I didn't try to talk to him. I sent him into the bathroom with the suggestion that he shower while I shopped for dinner. I came back not only with food but with a pair of jeans, a sweat shirt, and a razor. He was in the bedroom, still in his clothes, asleep. I had a drink, read the evening paper, finally fixed myself a meal. At eleven o'clock he was still so deeply asleep that my taking off of his shoes, trousers, jacket, and shirt didn't disturb him. I made up the couch in the living room for myself. When I got up at seven, he still didn't wake. I began to wonder if something had happened to him, if he had been hurt, but, when I went in to him, his breathing was normal, his color good. He must simply be exhausted. I left a place set for him at the table, a note by his grapefruit, telling him about the jeans and the razor. Several times during the day, I thought of phoning, but, if he was there and awake to answer, I didn't know what we would say to each other. And the phone ringing on and on unanswered would be too specifically worrying.

"A quick drink tonight?" Joyce suggested.

"I can't. I'm expecting an old friend for dinner."

"Oh?"

"Andrew," I said, trying not to be irritated.

"Oh."

He was sitting in the living room, reading, when I got home. He had shaved and put on the jeans, the sweat shirt, and a pair of clogs I had left in the bathroom. The kitchen and bedroom had been tidied. His white shirt was drying on the shower curtain rod in the bathroom.

"I've made martinis," he said, as I hung up my coat and changed my shoes.

"Good. Why don't you pour while I get dinner started?"

"Langer isn't as good on the visual arts as she is on music and drama, is she?" he asked, his hand shaking as he filled the glasses.

I answered vaguely, openly, so that he could go on to make his specific point. He sat at the table with his drink while I cut up peppers and then mushrooms and made a salad. He spoke a sentence at a time with long, uncertain pauses.

"Come on," I said. "Let's go into the living room. I can ignore this for a while now."

We sat without talking then. I was not yet willing to ask questions, and Andrew was obviously not troubled by the silence, looking, as he must have been, for a way into or out of the story he expected himself to tell eventually.

"I may be here for a while," he said finally.

"Fine."

"I think I've probably left Ramona."

We both sat with that possibility until Andrew was prepared to explore it further. I got up to get the martini pitcher and turn down the vegetables.

"She'll be all right," he said. "You know her play?"

"Yes."

"She's sold it to TV. She's working on another. She says she's full of them."

"Is that why you left?"

"It's why I could leave."

"What about the gallery?"

"I have to think that through still. It's as good as finished now, but we've got debts. Dan wants to keep it open until after Christmas. I don't suppose another six weeks matters all that much."

"Does Dan know where you are?"

"No. I'll have to let him know."

"How long have you been gone?"

"I was trying to think. Since last Saturday, or maybe it was Sunday."

I had all sorts of comments to make, but they were either too harsh or too complicated for the moment. What Andrew needed, before any real sorting out was done, was food and rest. He ate uneasily that first night, but he didn't drink after dinner. We listened to music until it was time to go to bed.

"I'll make up the couch," he said. "I suppose that's where you slept last night."

I let him, though I could tell it was hard on his head to do so much leaning over. He needed to be thoughtful. I put Gelusil and aspirin in plain sight on the shelf above the bathroom basin.

"Don't get up until I'm gone in the morning," I said. "I'll leave you coffee and juice."

"Where's my suit, by the way?" he asked.

"At the cleaners around the corner. I can pick it up tomorrow night on my way home."

"I don't seem to have any money," Andrew said. "I could cash a check."

"Not to worry," I said.

I left him twenty dollars in the morning, but it was still on the table when I got home that night. Andrew was in the kitchen, inventing dinner from things he'd found in the refrigerator and cupboard. He was, in a quiet way, enjoying himself.

"I hope you don't mind," he said.

"I never have."

"No. Ramona does. Funny about that. She says she wouldn't mind if I were bad at it. But she's not bad at it, either. She's a very good cook."

"I put your suit in the hall closet."

"Thanks. I had an overcoat, too. I must have lost it. I think I left it on the train."

Over cocktails, I explained the problem I had about the weekend.

"I tried to put it off," I said, "but I'm supposed to go to New York to visit Esther over Thanksgiving, and Joyce was—"

"Go," he said.

"She suggested that you come, too."

"No, Kate. I'm fine here if you don't mind my staying."

"It would be a help to me if you did come."

"Seriously?"

"Seriously. If you don't mind coping."

He smiled. "I'd like to meet her."

I should have explained about Joyce's husband then, but it was awkward. It was not a time for my life to seem as complicated and unreasonable as Andrew's. I shifted the conversation to a couple of alarming, funny stories I had heard that day, typical of the sick humor Washington has always enjoyed. Andrew got up then to finish fixing dinner.

The dishes were done and we were on our second cup of coffee in the living room before Andrew settled to talk about himself. He was much easier, feeling much better than he had the night before, but he still did a lot of hesitating, a lot of sudden breathing. Much of what he said at first was petty and defensive. He was trying to convince himself that the problems of his marriage were caused by such a difference in tastes and values that solutions were impossible. He talked about their arguments over Lissa, over furnishing the apartment, over their social life, over his work.

"Ramona is, basically, a very nice girl who eventually wants a house in the suburbs, a bridge club, and a dog. If she never saw Europe again, if she never looked at another painting, she wouldn't be unhappy. She could even get along without the theater as long as she had a television set. And the books she reads are available in any bookmobile or drug store. I can't live with her, Kate. I can't even talk to her. I don't know why I ever thought I could. But in London she did seem interested in other things, not exactly well informed, but interested. And when she made ridiculous remarks, I thought she knew they were ridiculous. She doesn't. Nine-tenths of her humor is just accurate blundering. Dan said, after the first opening we had, she'd better stay home and baby-sit. But why should she be blamed for that? She can't change. She would if she could. The harder she tries the worse it gets. It's the same with Lissa and the house. And with me. You know, just a month ago, after I'd told her to stop being so cheap about her clothes, she went out and bought black underwear! When I said I hoped she didn't intend to impress prospective buyers with that, she cried. But, if your wife doesn't know, after you've been married four years, that black underwear isn't your sort of amusement, what hope is there?"

"She gets frightened, Andy. People are clueless when they're frightened."

"I know. But it isn't as if I beat her. And I try not to be critical, but, even when I don't say anything, she knows me too well. . . ."

She didn't understand him; she knew him too well. I didn't try to argue. I waited. Surely, he'd get restless enough with silly complaints to come to the point. He couldn't avoid talking about the problem of his work forever.

"I've tried to explain to Ramona that this gallery thing isn't just a matter of money. Maybe we'd have to go pretty deeply in debt at first, but it mattered to me. She didn't see why I couldn't take another job as well. Nothing has persuaded her that I have any real trouble getting a job. She thinks I'm just choosy. But, if I wouldn't work, she would, and I could stay home with Lissa. Can you imagine?"

I didn't say yes. I listened.

"Then she offered me the money from her play," Andrew said in a tone of such shock and anger that he might have been reporting an attempted murder.

"She wants to help, Andy," I finally said with some anger of my own. "What in hell is so shocking about that?"

"I'm not going to live off my wife!"

"But Andy—"

"I am not going to scrounge around with my little hobby while she pays the rent."

"Then why don't you pay the rent?"

He was quiet for a long moment. "Would you mind if I had a drink?" he asked finally.

"Of course not. I'll get it for you."

I poured us both strong Scotches. Andrew was staring at his hands when I went back into the living room.

"Maybe if I went west . . ." he said, after he'd taken a long drink. "Maybe if I went alone, I could get something. Then later, if Ramona wanted to, we could try it again. Maybe . . ." But he shook his head.

"Andy, you're running scared."

"You're damned right I am," he said. "You're damned right."

"So stop. Just stop a while. You don't have to go all the way west. There are jobs right here. I've got to know quite a lot of people."

"Can you picture me as a civil servant?"

"Well, I am."

"But you have the patience of a martyr, Kate. I haven't any."

"Because you thought you didn't need any, Andy. Now you do. You simply have to decide—"

"You young ones," he said. "I'm too old to jump through hoops. I'm too old."

"You're too stubborn and too bitter. Sometimes I think all you want to do is prove your father's point."

"I have," he said, finishing his drink. "That much I have done."

"Well, then, you'd better think up something else to do. You've still got half your life to live."

"Shall we have another?"

"One more," I said. "Then that's enough."

"And let's talk about you for a while. Ramona says . . ." but he hesitated.

"What does she say?"

"That we always talk about ourselves and our problems when you're around."

"You'll have enough of me and my private life over the weekend. Don't worry about that. Have you seen Esther?"

"Oh yes, quite a lot of her actually. Ramona has, anyway. She's pretty tedious just now. She's got only two subjects at the moment, neither of them in my range."

"Two?"

"God and John Kerry."

"Who's John Kerry?"

"A wretchedly ambitious young doctor she met on board ship. You'll meet him when you go to New York."

"Will I like him?"

"Maybe. He's pleasant enough. It's just that nobody seems to be there. He's very nice to Esther. And he's very patient with God, too."

"Christian?"

"I doubt it. I think he's one of those fellows who believes in himself."

"Is Esther serious about him?"

"As Ramona would say," he began, not noticing this time, "is Esther ever anything but serious? She even told me John reminded her a little of you, but the similarity is too subtle for me."

It was unreasonable to feel disappointed. It had been so many years since you'd been free of other people that I'd probably not have known how to deal with four days alone with you. But I had been imagining it.

I thought of trying to get back to the subject of Joyce before we went to bed, but she couldn't be easily introduced into the conversation. It was not until we were driving out to her house on Friday after work that I told Andrew a little about her. We were within two or three minutes of arriving when I mentioned that Joyce was married. Even then, it wasn't a direct statement.

"Her husband's away for the weekend, but maybe you'll meet him next week. A nice sort of guy."

"Husband?"

"Take the next right," I said. "It's the white house down at the end of the road."

Joyce was shy of Andrew at first. She made bright, uneasy conversation, her voice loud, her gestures exaggerated, but her nervousness was good for him. He liked that kind of requirement. As I watched his persistent approval and good humor, I remembered that he was a man with numerous sisters who must have been both competitive with him and in need of his good opinion. I wondered if they missed him, if they made any attempt to represent his cause with their father. But Mr. Belshaw didn't sound the kind of man anyone would persuade. He could be indulgent, but he was dictatorial. Andrew was not really unlike him. He used the power of taste rather than the power of money to assert himself, indulged people more often than he agreed with them, and that, in most circumstances, is more flattering. Joyce knew he could not possibly approve of the wall plaques and hanging pots of ivy, the bowls in the shapes of nut shells and strawberries, the paperbacks and old school texts that mixed on the book shelf. That he chose to make himself feel at home anyway was a compliment to something rarer and more important than shared tastes. His good looks, perhaps even more than his educated sensibility, gave him a power to use generously with women, and more men than are willing to admit it care about having handsome friends. Andrew knew how to use that power. I never heard anyone accuse him of being vain. He looked at people rather than mirrors, and I could see Joyce now reflecting his handsomeness with the feeling that perhaps she was, after all, more attractive than she sometimes thought. But I make Andrew sound more calculating than he was. He wanted to please Joyce, to put her at ease; therefore he gave her his attention.

Just this talent in Andrew, which I loved and so often rested in, made you suspicious of him from the first. The peace you made with him did not so much include his good looks and good manners as ignore them, which left him only the currency of his mind, fortunately sound in any theoretical discussion. It was a good thing that you never saw him floundering in near idiocy with practical problems.

Joyce was uncritical and delighting. She didn't suggest, or allow either of us to suggest, going to bed until well after midnight, and she and I didn't spend the morning, as we always had before, being characters in her sexual fictions. We had finished breakfast by ten o'clock, and Joyce was looking for shoes and warm sweaters among her husband's belongings so that we could take a long walk.

"Doesn't he make that sweater look marvelous?" Joyce asked, when Andrew had climbed ahead of us to the top of a small hill. "Have you ever met any of his sisters?"

"No."

"Good," she said, smiling.

Andrew was calling to Joyce to ask her the name of a tree. He had discovered that she liked to name things, and he did her the further courtesy of remembering what she told him so that on the way home he could test his new vocabulary to please both Joyce and himself.

Sunday it rained. We spent the day, as children might have, playing games of various sorts. Andrew was good at Scrabble, bad at Monopoly. Searching through the game box with Joyce, rejecting anything for two, he found jigsaw puzzles.

"Stand back," he said, delighted. "I'm an absolute genius with these."

His eye for color and shape, for emerging pattern, did make him very quick, and the process, which seemed to me tedious, gave him real pleasure. Joyce involved herself with him. I withdrew a little, watching his face, less strained now, younger. I remembered building sand castles on a beach. He looked up suddenly and smiled.

"Where did you go?"

"I was remembering sand castles," I said.

"Has Kate told you how we met, Joyce?" Andrew asked, careful that even so innocent a game for two be shifted.

We sat up until eleven, Andrew tending the fire and the drinks.

"Well, I don't have to work tomorrow," he said, standing up, "but I've got to see that my women do."

He had gone to bed, and Joyce and I were emptying ashtrays when the back door suddenly opened, and Joyce's husband called cheerfully from the kitchen. For a second Joyce did not respond. Then she answered his greeting as cheerfully.

"Isn't it nice you're home," she said. "Kate's just about to desert me, and I was longing for a nightcap."

"I'm glad you could keep Joyce company," he said to me, coming into the room. "Have you had a nice weekend?"

"Very," I said.

"But don't be polite now," Joyce said. "You go on to bed, and I'll do the explaining."

I stood, uncertain what to do.

"Do you want to take Andy a nightcap to bed?"

"Oh, I don't think so," I said. "Well, good night."

"Good night."

I stood outside the guest bedroom door for a moment, but I could hear Joyce and her husband getting ready to come upstairs. I knocked quietly.

"Come in," Andy called. He was sitting up in bed reading. "What's up?"

"Joyce's husband's home."

"Oh." He thought a moment. "Well, come on to bed then."

"Andy, I'm terribly sorry. I—"

"Just be grateful I'm here. At least nobody's going to break your nose."

There was another quick knock on the door, and Joyce was handing my suitcase to me.

"God! Aren't we lucky?" she said and was gone.

Andrew had pulled the second pillow out from behind him and moved to one side of the bed. He went on reading while I undressed, but he'd put his book away when I got back from the bathroom.

"I always meant to ask you if you slept with your teeth in," he said, grinning.

"Just for special occasions," I said.

I got into bed, trying to be neither stiff nor intrusive. Andrew turned out the light, and we lay listening to the sounds of the house.

"Well," Andrew said in a quiet, but very wakeful voice, "we've done everything else together." He took my hand, waited, then turned toward me. "Why not this, Kate?"

I understood the offer. It was no more than that. One gesture of reluctance from me and he would have turned kindly away. I did not make it. And perhaps curiosity, as much as the sad ridiculousness of the circumstance, required me. It was not physically unpleasant. It was curiously simple. And afterwards our bodies were related enough for sleep. Andrew slept almost at once. I lay awake, refusing the moral and emotional complexities that threatened to make important what I was sure was not.

I was awake when Joyce got up at six-thirty. I tried not to disturb Andrew as I got out of bed, but he woke.

"Go back to sleep," I said. "I'll go in with Joyce. You can drive my car in later."

"What about her husband?"

"No problem."

"All right," he said and turned over.

Joyce and I didn't attempt conversation until we were in the car and on our way to work.

"Silly damned thing, leaving the men asleep while we go off to earn the bread," she said. "I wonder if they'll have breakfast together."

"Maybe," I said.

"Andy must have been surprised."

"Mmm."

"Sorry to throw you at him that way, darling, but it was lucky, wasn't it? Another half hour—"

"You didn't know he was coming?"

"Of course not. He told me he probably wouldn't be back until Tuesday."

"Oh."

"You're not mad at me, are you, Kate?"

"No."

"It was a good weekend, wasn't it? Except for last night. I had such lovely plans for last night."

Andrew was in no more cheerful and sociable a mood than I by the time I got home for dinner. For the first hour we simply tried not to get in each other's way.

"Joyce's husband is quite a nice guy," Andrew said finally as we sat at the dinner table.

"I thought you'd like him," I said.

"I did."

The assertion lay between us for a moment before we both tried to pick it up at once. Andrew hesitated in automatic mannerliness. But I did, too.

"I think it's sort of a mess, Kate. Not just that he's a nice guy. Not just that. Your job's involved. Why Joyce, anyway?"

"I don't explain and defend well at the same time. They're two different activities."

"But why do you always get yourself into a sexual mess?"

"You're a great one to talk!"

"Well, you're a friend of Ramona's—or are supposed to be. Why did you let me do it?"

"Really, Andy, that's one cliché too many."

"A home truth," Andrew said, "but you wouldn't know much about that. You know how to use people and be used by them. Right out of the manual for social workers and humanitarians. It's too bad there's no course in being a human being. You've never cared enough about anybody to be really ugly or really beautiful. You're too damned tidy to think you've betrayed Ramona because it never occurred to you that you ought to be loyal. And, of course, making love with me matters so little to you that being upset by it seems to you a cliché."

"And what does it mean to you? Nothing humanitarian about it on your side? No small hope that you might have begun a conversion?"

"Thank God, girl, I don't suffer from any fear of kindness. I didn't want to do anything *for* you. I simply wanted you . . . for myself. That's probably ugly, but it's got some clean beauty to it, too. It's at least part of what love's all about. Have you ever wanted and taken somebody you also loved? No. You don't love Joyce. So why should you feel guilty about her husband? You don't love me, so why should you feel guilty about Ramona?"

"And you love me, and so you do feel guilty?"

"I love Ramona."

"I see."

"Why don't you hit back, Kate? Or cry? Or be unreasonably angry? Don't you really care at all?"

"For what?"

"For me. Am I really beneath your contempt?"

"Perhaps," I said. "Perhaps you are."

"Why? Am I really so inferior to you?"

"No, Andy, you're superior to me—born male, white, handsome, intelligent, and rich. Perhaps with so much, I would be as reckless . . . as loving . . . as ugly. My own sins are simply the ones I can afford. Maybe they don't include either love or contempt. Except in very rare, extravagant moments with you."

"You're not poor, Kate. You're stingy."

"I agree. Monk should have got something more for that bag of liver."

We were too shocked to stop, too miserable to be very accurate, accusing each other at random. You got involved in it. So did Peter. And poor Monk was set above us like a martyred referee.

"This is just too stupid," I finally protested in the tears he had accused me of being incapable of. "Tearing each other apart doesn't help any."

He stopped then and stared at nothing. "I don't know," he said finally. "Maybe it does. We're such shits, you and I, such real shits."

The word from Andrew had power because he never used it. For that moment I shared his despair, never mind that it was too easy, a gagging comfort that the sickness was communal. The story, as I would have told it about all of us at that time, would have been even more unbecoming than it is now. Shits, the lot of us. So much for your "artists," "scholars," "young saints."

We were listening to old Deller records when the phone rang. It was Monk.

"Dan had an idea that you might know where Andy is," she said. "I've got to reach him. His father died this morning."

"I do know where he is," I said. "I'll get in touch with him and have him call you back."

Andrew would have had no defense against the news at any time, but at that moment he was so raw he reacted immediately. He wept. It was a hard weeping that went on a long time. I wondered if it was the kind of weeping Doris had done. When it was over, he telephoned Monk. I put him on a plane for Calgary at one in the morning.

I spent the rest of the night writing two letters to Joyce, one an official, the other a personal, resignation. She accepted the first with an official acknowledgment; she accepted the second with no comment at all. She was, perhaps, as relieved as I was.

planation, I gathered that you and John Kerry had planned to announce your engagement at a party scheduled for Saturday evening. John Kerry's mother had been invited. She arrived from Louisville on Wednesday afternoon. She departed on Wednesday evening, accompanied by a disbelieving but dazed son. By the time I arrived on Thursday, your mother had retired to her rooms, leaving her secretary to telephone canceled invitations.

"I just can't believe it," you said over and over again.

"But what happened?"

"It was all perfectly pleasant through cocktails and dinner. Oh, a bit stiff with Mother being impressive and Mrs. Kerry not being impressed, but John and I had expected that. Then over coffee and brandy in the living room, Mrs. Kerry started talking about the old families of America. At first I didn't think anything about it. I mean, the Kerry family don't have money. John's father ran off with somebody else years ago. So his mother needs ancestors, and she's got lots. So she was betting ancestors against affluence—okay. But she kept using the word 'blood,' and she was obviously getting excited. John tried to interrupt her a couple of times, not rudely, just making a light remark, but she wasn't having any of that. Finally she said to him, 'You let me handle this, John.' Before anyone could say anything, she turned to me and said, 'And don't think you'll fool anyone with Christian baptism or changing your name. You're the sort of Jew even plastic surgery wouldn't fix.' I told her I wasn't trying to fool anyone. I'd been baptized because I'd accepted Christ as my salvation. She said that Christ couldn't save me, and, if there was anything more disgusting than a murderer of Christ, it was one who then tried to hide in the Church from the consequences. John tried to protest. So did Mother, but neither of them got more than two words into a sentence before she said to Mother, 'And, looking at her, I wonder how many niggers there've been in the wood pile.' That did it. Mother went right off her nut. She started calling John a gold digger, his mother poor white trash.

She ordered them both out of the house, but not before Mrs. Kerry called me a mongrel and Mother a bitch."

"And John left with his mother?"

"What else could he do? Mother said if he tried to contact me, she'd call the police and do what she could to ruin his 'little career.' The minute they were gone, Mother and I had a great row of our own. She hasn't appeared since."

The chauffeur opened the car door for us, the butler the front door, and a maid was waiting to take me to my room. You were more or less ordered into the library where tea would be served when I was ready for it, after I had given and taken instructions about my personal habits and wardrobe. There was a note from Mrs. Woolf, apologizing that she was not able to greet me, advising me to comfort and reassure and advise you. She would hope to join us for dinner. In other words, I was to make it possible for her to join us for dinner. I didn't feel like it. I should have gone and had a good shout at your mother myself, but I didn't feel like that, either. There had been no satisfaction in my last experience of being rude to her. And, though it seemed to me that she had behaved inexcusably, she'd been badly provoked. I turned to the maid who was unpacking my suitcase.

"Will people be dressing for dinner?"

"No, Miss George, not tonight. But everything will be pressed. Is there anything you'd like me to lay out?"

"The black wool, I guess. Thanks."

"Would you like your bath drawn at six?"

I smiled at her. "I really prefer a shower."

She returned the smile, offering just the degree of conspiracy I had invited. I wondered how people like Mrs. Woolf trained servants in the tact she was incapable of. Of course, she didn't. The housekeeper would take care of that. Yet no matter how much professional kindness she bought, Mrs. Woolf couldn't protect herself from the Mrs. Kerrys of this world or even from her own daughter. Or from me. I'd better choose to be kind to her.

"Your father used to say," I heard my mother's gentle, uncertain voice, "guest and host share the burden of hospitality, but each carries the whole weight."

You sat, sulking at the tea tray in the library, too tired and despairing to cope with ritual weight.

"I can't stand tea," you said.

"What would you like?"

"A Coke—in a bottle."

"So would I."

"Oh dear."

"E., ask for it," I said firmly. "You don't have to be a victim."

"But that's just what I am, Kate. I should have left here last night, just gone, but you were coming. Anyway, I can't."

"Why not?"

"No money, not a penny of my own. I signed everything over to Mother after California—for my own protection, she said. I've got nothing but charge accounts and pocket money."

"That's not the real problem, anyway, is it?"

"I don't suppose so," you said.

"What about John? What's going to happen?"

"I don't know."

"Will he get in touch with you?"

"I don't know."

You began to pour out the tea.

"Do you want to marry him?"

"Of course I do," you said, energy in your voice for the first time.

Then gradually you began to tell me about him, how you'd met aboard ship, he on his way home from two years at an eye clinic in Barcelona, staying over in New York for a convention where he gave a paper, staying on after that, postponing his return to Louisville first a week, then a month, until he'd asked you to marry him.

"He was going to go back with his mother, anyway. There's a practice in Louisville pretty well ready for him to walk into. We were going to be married here around the first of the year, and then I'd go to Louisville."

"Did you have any idea about his mother?"

"You know me, Kate. After the fact, sure. I mean, I think now about things he said, and I should have known or had an inkling. He's an only child without a father. She's a southern lady. She'd hate all Jews, 'niggers,' and Catholics on principle, and if one, both, or all three wanted to marry her son, well, she wouldn't like it. Isn't it a good thing I finally chose to be an Episcopalian?"

"Shouldn't John have known?"

"Well, I didn't know my mother was going to call him a gold digger and poor white trash, did I? I think he hoped my being a Christian—he was glad I was baptized before we were engaged—would do it. The 'nigger in the wood pile' bit caught him off guard. I wonder if there is one. But it hasn't seemed exactly the right time to ask Mother a disinterested question."

"The mongoloids," I said. "This is no time to feel tired of it, right at the beginning of the battle, but I do. I must have been born tired of it."

"I'm not," you said.

"How would you live in Louisville, anyway? How would you be a southern lady?"

"I could begin somewhere. John isn't like that. He says it's only a question of time because it's a question of economics. He's very practical and unemotional about everything, like you. It's funny. He's the first sort of ordinary man I could ever feel attracted to, ever really like. Love. Maybe it's because I feel surer of myself. He's polite and responsible and all the things I used to be afraid of, except in you, of course. When I told him I just wasn't interested in sex any more, that I wanted to be a Christian, he accepted that. He said he respected it. He said everybody our age had some experience, and that didn't have to be discussed. Now we should take things seriously. You know, from the minute I decided that I could become a Christian, it really was like being born again, a new life, and there was John to share it with. . . ."

As you talked, you obviously forgot for a moment what had happened the evening before. Your voice was full of a child's happiness. I had time to notice the new design of your hair, the quietly expensive dress that allowed for your taste for large, sculptured jewelry, the absence of your father's wristwatch, your engagement ring, but, when the picture was complete, the catastrophe reoccurred to you.

"What am I going to do, Kate?"

"I suppose you've got to wait for him to do something."

"But Mother's threatened him with the police."

"She likes him, doesn't she?"

"She did."

"Well, you need to deal with her."

"How?"

"Shall I?"

"I wish you would. Would you mind? Even when I try to be decent, I'm not."

When we had finished the tea neither of us wanted, I sent up a request to see Mrs. Woolf. I was invited to her apartment at five. I had expected to find her in operatic decline. Instead, she greeted me at the door of her sitting room with a firm voice and hand that drew me into a formally affectionate embrace. She had aged since I'd last seen her. Her makeup was less strained and really more becoming. It was a tired, sad face, but I liked it better.

"I'm sorry to include you in another crisis, Kate," she said, as she led me to the chair she had chosen for me. "It was planned to be a very pleasant weekend. Will you have a drink?"

"No thanks. We've just had tea."

"Do you mind if I do?" She poured herself a whiskey and soda. "Last time we met, you gave me some rather blunt advice. It may surprise you to know that I took it. Tried to, anyway. Before last night, I think Esther might have given a better account of me than you would have expected. However, that can't be undone."

"It must have been grim," I said.

"Yes, it was. The only thing to be said for me is that I didn't start it. The only thing. I lost my temper. It was more than that. I felt really quite out of my mind until this morning."

"I would have, too," I said.

"No, Kate, I don't think so. But it's nice of you to say so. Esther and I have now said things to each other that aren't new but should be old, should be passed. How many times can people begin again, do you suppose?"

"May I change my mind about that drink?"

"I'd be grateful," she said and poured me a scotch the way I like to drink it without asking.

"What are you going to do if John tries to get in touch with Esther?"

She didn't answer at once. "I don't see how he could," she said finally.

"You don't want him to."

"Does it make any sense to you, with all this in his background? Oh, I know. John isn't his mother. Esther shouldn't have to bear my sins either, but, if Mrs. Kerry is the worst example of Louisville—and I'm afraid she's not—what could it be like for Esther? And for John himself? After all, he's going to practice there. He has to have patients. I just can't conceive of it."

"But what if he and Esther can?"

"I don't know. I just don't know. What do you think, Kate? Loyalty aside."

"I don't know either, but I think you should let them decide if they want to."

"And how do I do that?"

"You write a letter of apology to John. You don't have to invite him back. You don't have to encourage him. But you can let him know that you spoke in anger."

"Does Esther want me to do that?"

"We didn't agree to terms before I came up," I said, grinning.

"What if they did marry and it was awful?"

"I don't see how you can protect her from that. She knows what the circumstance is. She may decide, or John may decide that it isn't a good thing. But it ought to be their decision, not yours."

"All right. I agree. I'll write the letter. You were a great comfort to your own mother, I know. You are to me. I spoke of it to Doris—"

"Don't give me a good conduct medal just now, Mrs. Woolf," I said. "I don't feel up to it. You could do me a favor instead."

"Anything," she said, frankly, without gesture.

"I want a job, and I think you know the head of the agency I'm interested in. I've met him, and I think he'd hire me, but I want the job right away."

I left Mrs. Woolf making a phone call and went to my room to shower and change. While I was dressing, you came in.

"Word is that the Lady herself will be down for dinner," you said. "Drinks at six-thirty."

"She's offered to write a letter to John, apologizing."

"White of her," you said. "Doubt must be on my father's side."

"She is sorry, E."

"Oh, I know she is," you said tiredly. "So am I. We do try, you know, but there's just so little to work with on either side. Can you face her and turkey?"

"I think so."

"I made us all Pilgrim hats. Then I thought better of it."

"You're growing up into a very subtle woman, little dog. What happened to your watch?"

"John and I had a discussion about femininity, and we decided I ought to try it."

"Very becoming."

"Remember when I never thought I could make it? I'm not

bad, really, am I?" You were quite ordinarily admiring yourself in the mirror.

" 'For hell too fair; for earth too wise,' " I said, smiling.

"You remember that. That's odd. But sex isn't being wise, is it?"

"I don't suppose so. Sometimes it seems to me downright stupid."

"I'm so glad you're here, Kate. Nothing's ever too awful if I can talk to you about it."

And I was back to being too good to be true, which was guiltily all right with me.

I spent that Friday at interviews your mother had arranged while you waited at home for some word from John. By the end of the day, I had the job I had been uncertainly moving toward for nearly a year, in which I could gather up all the scattered interests and talents that I had, from the languages I had almost inadvertently learned to the painfully acquired knowledge of governmental procedure.

"Little dog," I said with almost as much candid excitement as you might have had, "I'm going to be in New York from the first of the year with a trip to Europe before the summer's over. I'm going to help save the world after all."

"Not if it's nonsectarian," you said.

"Why?"

"You should be doing missionary work."

"Don't be ridiculous!"

"Then where's the moral responsibility? Money doesn't bless anything if God isn't involved. What good is a hospital without a church?"

"Plenty."

"But it's a man's soul—"

"I don't give a damn about a man's soul. It's his own business, and I want no part of tempting him to sell it for bread or medicine or education. I think it's immoral."

"Only if the faith isn't true," you said.

"And yours is the true faith?"

"Yes," you said firmly. "You're the one who said there was no point in being a nominal Christian."

"Right. That's why I don't go to church."

"I pray for you, Kate."

"Well, don't," I said angrily. "I don't want to be prayed for."

"Don't you believe in anything any more?"

"I never did, E., not in your sense. I'm no good at extremes."

"You think I'm being extreme, don't you?"

"No more than you've ever been. I don't want to fight with you about God. Belief isn't really a thing to fight about."

"Why not? It seems to me the only thing worth fighting about."

"Onward Christian soldiers," I said.

"But I believe that activity not rooted in prayer is mere bombast and flurry."

"Don't quote at me."

"Why not?"

"Well, then quote decent English, something like, 'How many other things could be tolerated in peace and left to conscience had we but charity. . . .'"

"No point in quoting that. It supports your argument."

"You used to like Milton."

"You're playing, Kate. I'm serious. You never really talk any more. You never really settle down with an argument."

"I never did," I said defensively. "I've always been frivolous and irresponsible. You're just seeing me in the new light of faith."

"You make fun of me."

"Not really. I just don't want to be bullied. I want you to be pleased with me about the job. I want to be able to talk about it without getting into a religious argument."

"I'm sorry," you said.

"And don't sulk, please."

But you were crying.

"Didn't he call?" I asked.

"No."

"He will, E. I'm sure he will."

"I don't know what I'll do if he doesn't. I'm marooned in this house. When you go, there won't be anyone."

"Monk's here, and I'll be back after Christmas."

"No, she's not. She took Lissa to Calgary on Wednesday."

"Oh, good," I said.

"Is it? Is that marriage any good at all by now?"

"Oh, I think so," I said, trying not to sound uneasy. "If Andy gets his money problems straightened out now—"

"They're straightened. The will was very generous."

"So—"

"What does money cure?" you demanded. "I mean, really?"

"I hope a lot, but let's not get back to that. Why don't we have a game of chess or listen to records or something?"

I was sorry not to be able to talk about God, but I simply couldn't. You weren't really interested in doctrine or history. You were reading the lives of the mystics and martyrs, and you had collected a vocabulary and imagery which were embarrassingly sentimental. I hadn't been raised in a hard faith. I don't suppose any Episcopalian is, but my father treated ritual with more intelligence than emotion. Being in love with God, the only relationship you considered, made me uncomfortable. I was suspicious. I'd been free to be suspicious of all your other enthusiasms. This unnatural respect, inhibition, made real talking impossible. I couldn't settle to critical gossip about Monk and Andrew, either. I was still too rawly involved and ashamed. As for John, I felt required to support him, but I hadn't met him. And, though nothing you told me about him gave me any real opportunity to be critical of him, I still kept coming up to responses I knew I should not make. Embarrassed, I hid in chess, in music, until by

235

the time I left for Washington on Sunday, we were nearly shy with each other and sorry about it. There was still no word from John.

I spent that Christmas alone in Washington. I could have hurried my packing and been with you, but I hadn't the courage to go through your first Christian Christmas, which would be literal with love. I preferred to remember the tree full of pagan promise, on which birth was still represented with Easter eggs and from which no shadow of the cross was cast. In any case, John was with you.

He had accepted first your mother's apology and then her invitation. Meanwhile he wrote to you, as careful as a lawyer in his phrasing, releasing you but not himself from the commitment of the engagement. He did not mention his mother.

By the time I arrived on January 1, John had gone back to Louisville to pack up his belongings. He had decided to accept an offer of partnership in a practice in Boston, the money for which was an early wedding present from your mother. The wedding itself had been postponed until June.

"He said he needed to get settled," you explained, "but I suppose he hopes that maybe, given a little time, his mother may be resigned enough to come. Anyway, there's no reason to rush. As John says, we aren't exactly eager teen-agers."

"And your mother is resigned."

"Oh yes. Once he said he had decided to practice in Boston, she was fine. She could pay for it. That was hard on him. He wanted to borrow the money from her, but she wouldn't hear of it. She told him accepting it would prove that he'd forgiven her. So he did. He can't practice anywhere but Louisville without money. It doesn't really make any difference. Once we're married, Mother's going to turn over all my money from my father to me anyway, so this really meant just having some of it sooner. John's pretty solemn about money. It's a good thing one of us is. And it's nice that, for once, it's going to be useful."

Why did I listen, suspicious? John Kerry was a man with a pro-

236

fession. He was obviously not like Christopher Marlowe Smith or Charlie or any of the others who had never had any intention of supporting themselves, much less anyone else. If he asked for money, it was to make a world that would be possible for you to live in, free of the social capital he had depended on. He was willing to borrow it. He was willing to desert his mother and his world. He was in no great hurry. Maybe, in John Kerry's position, I would have been in a hurry. But he was being protective of you, careful. And surely I should be able to understand that.

"A happier time for us all," your mother said, greeting me warmly.

"It is all right, is it?"

"I think so, Katherine. And what mother can really resist a June wedding? I started dreaming about Esther's before I stopped dreaming about my own. I've had a very rude, very dear note from Andrew Belshaw saying that he intends to pay for the bridesmaids' dresses."

"Are they back then?"

"Yes, they've been back in town since two days after Christmas. Didn't Esther tell you? They're coming for dinner tomorrow night."

Andrew's partner, Dan Karno, had also been invited. You were sorry that John couldn't be there, suggested seriously, until both your mother and I laughed at you, that we set a place for him anyway, but were finally comforted by the promise of another dinner party particularly for him when he got back to New York.

There is comfort and protection in formality, whatever else it stifles. I was glad of an evening dress, of the maid who helped me into it, of my mother's sapphires. I was glad to be a guest of the household so that I could move forward to greet Monk and Andrew and Dan when they arrived with ritual kissing and handshaking, determined by the length rather than the intimacy of relationship. I knew it would take more than an evening like this for Andrew and me to reestablish ourselves in customary friendship, but it was a beginning. Monk, who might have been shy of a party less declaredly costume, could burlesque this occasion with real, if slightly hectic, success.

"One should never dine with friends in street clothes," she announced to us all, then confided to me in a whisper that raised the butler's lapels but carefully not his eyebrows, "I even bought a Maidenform bra. Isn't it grand to be rich?"

Andrew smiled at her, not with the young indulgence he once had, but more easily. He looked very tired, but he did not seem so. He and Dan together divided their attention among the four women with such ease that we must certainly have been a pleasure to them. Dan was particularly protective of you, as if he sensed your new, engaged vulnerability. Andrew, who had found the right balance of impudence and flattery with your mother, talked with her about the gallery, letting Monk describe their discovery of new Canadian painters when they went through Vancouver. And I found myself on Dan's other hand, postponed a little perhaps, but not ignored. We were all enjoying being well behaved because, with the exception of Monk, it was a thing we knew how to do and weren't often enough so encouraged.

At dinner Mrs. Woolf directed our attention to topics obviously already chosen. Monk and Andrew were asked to tell us about their trip to California to visit the Ridleys, a subject which allowed them to entertain us with a plan they had made to marry off Andrew's sisters to Monk's brothers in an orgy of mismatching that was sometimes diabolically inventive. Once we had sketches of each of the characters, it was a game we could all play. There was one sister left over, which led us to choose a brother deserving of two wives until Dan offered himself, subject to discussions of dowry, as a solution. Before we had strained or exhausted that kind of good humor, Mrs. Woolf shifted our attention to several shows in New York.

"I wish someone could explain to me all these twisted pipes and engines and wrecked cars," she said.

Dan had some trouble with them himself. Andrew talked about

the problem of innovation, the influence of professional specula-tors. You spoke with too much defensive energy about the right of the artist to choose his own raw materials. I tried to suggest, less personally, that economics might have something to do with it. Traditional materials were so expensive that perhaps the dump was the only source for some sculptors.

"But you all seem to be agreeing that you don't really like it," Monk said suddenly. "Lissa loves the dump. I don't mean I take her there on purpose for an outing, but in California where you feed the ducks is next to the town dump. Lissa was much more interested in the bits of glass and bottle tops and old bumpers than she was in the ducks. She kept saying, 'Pretty, pretty.' And I looked at it again and thought, 'Well, maybe it is.' It's just that all of us feel guilty about the waste and the mess—"

"But the artists aren't telling us it's pretty," I said. "This kind of thing is social satire, surely, a comment on planned obsoles-cence. We're not supposed to like it, are we?"

"Some of it doesn't seem to be satirical," Andrew said. "That's what troubles me. It's all right for Lissa to think a Coke bottle top is pretty, but once you know what a Coca-Cola cul-ture means, you ought to be satirical."

"Why?" Monk demanded without belligerence but with a kind of bravery to challenge Andrew that I hadn't seen before. "Being critical isn't the only way to live in the world."

"Like the crucifixion," you said. "It's one of the ugliest acts in history, but in painting and sculpture it's often not just tragic but beautiful."

"Do you think we're getting religious insight into smashed cars?" Andrew asked.

"I like that," Monk said. "I'm sure it's time we did. After all, it's the way a lot of us are going to die."

"There's a lot of talk," Dan said, "about the significance of destruction, the aesthetics of destruction."

"I don't like the nihilism of it," I said. "It frightens me."

"Understanding destruction doesn't have to be nihilistic," you said. "That's what you've never understood. It can be part of the cycle. How can you be reborn until you know what it is to die?"

"Some kinds of knowledge I don't risk," I said.

"But it's not all dark, it's not all destruction," Monk insisted. "We've been taught to be suspicious of every bright object. I like the lights of the city. I like the colors in the supermarket. What's so dreadful about Coca-Cola?"

"Well," Andrew said, smiling, "you'll keep us all from being comfortably reactionary, but that's sociologically all wrong. Young mothers are supposed to be the conservative force, not the avant-garde."

"Come on, Andy," you said, "motherhood has nothing to do with it."

"It certainly does," Monk said, refusing your support. "I'm talking about what Lissa knows about the dump."

It was a conversation that went on nearly all evening. Mrs. Woolf commented only occasionally, but she listened with real interest, with a kind of proprietary pleasure. She was offering the evening to you as proof of her ability to produce it. Perhaps she knew, too, that art was the one subject that could keep you from talking too much about religion, a subject about which the rest of us shared her nervousness.

I got not much more sense of Dan that evening than I had the first time I met him. I simply knew that I liked him, not only because he liked all of us, but that was important. When he heard that I was looking for an apartment, he suggested one in his own building that he knew was going to be available and offered to find out about it for me.

"It would be a good location for you," he said, "and it would be nice for me."

It turned out to be nice for both of us in those months I spent in New York. We got into the habit of having dinner together about once a week. I went to show openings with him and to the theater. We were more than socially convenient for each other and our paired friends. We were really companionable, for, though we rarely talked very personally, there was an assumed knowledge that made our friendship possible. We knew how to be discreet with each other without explanations.

Before Dan and I were accustomed enough to each other to admit shared reactions, I met John Kerry, the man who believed in himself. He was a good-looking man, but he was not attractive. He was too spare, his features economical, his body in size and strength utilitarian. And, as he was made, so he behaved with never a wasteful gesture or word, never an emotional extravagance. Yet none of these details which were characteristic of him made him seem either dull or ungenerous because the one imbalance in his nature, his nerves, sang in the wires of his voice, splintered the light in his eyes, and made his stillness of body a demanding tension in the room. I have never met anyone who gave so strong an impression of being under control. My own willfulness next to his was almost comically insignificant, but we recognized each other, refused to react, and withdrew to our assigned roles.

Never let it be said that a southern gentleman, for whom the southern lady is an idiot goddess, doesn't know how to deal with an emancipated woman from the West or the North. He treats her exactly the way he treats his southern lady, and she loves it, not aware that the gentle deference is designed to turn her into an idiot goddess gradually; protection and admiration are habit-forming drugs. I was, of course, in no real danger. You, I could see, had already succumbed. I couldn't resent it. It was too becoming. But how could John Kerry see you so absolutely open to him, so full of desire, and be in no hurry? Will. He wanted it that way. I had to teach myself all over again to be in the same room with you.

That is, I think, the sense I had of John when I first met him, which had, as I look back on it, more to do with you than with him. Perhaps my view of him was always unnaturally colored by your response to him. When you talked about him, you spoke of no more than the spare, practical, confident man he was, but, when you were with him, you were so physically tuned to his tension, so desiring of his will, that I assigned him a sexual power I did not feel. Once I tried to explain my reaction to Sandy.

"And why should you have expected to feel it, anyway? You're not attracted to men," she said, by way of comforting me.

"Not exactly true," I said. "I'm attracted. How I choose to react is another matter."

"You'll always insist on the myth of bisexuality, even when it's not to your advantage," Sandy said with resigned good humor. "I only saw her at the wedding, and, if that was any example of how she'd been for months, I'm glad I didn't have to deal with it. I don't even remember what he looked like."

In any case, after the first evening I spent with you and John, your marriage to him seemed to me inevitable and therefore right. When later I had moments of violent reaction against him, it wasn't difficult to explain them away as pure sexual jealousy. For one thing, I admired him. If he sometimes seemed frighteningly rational, cold in his judgments, he was always sound and never belligerent or ungenerous in an argument. Compared to Andrew, for instance, who could make such extravagant speeches, John seemed so much more trustworthy, so much more responsible. But he was never condescending to Andrew, and he often gave in to an almost boyish laughter when Andrew had taken a point beyond sane debate.

"You win on imagery alone," he'd say.

We only once discussed my work with any seriousness. I was just beginning to understand the scope of the work the agency was involved in, and I was impressed by its success stories. I spoke with enthusiasm about the use of small amounts of money which could and did revitalize the economy of whole villages in Greece, in Sicily, in Korea, and gradually might even in Vietnam and some of the South American countries.

"I don't really approve of that kind of aid," John said mildly.

"Why not?"

"Because while it goes on, we ignore the basic economic problems of these countries. Saving one child or one family or one village really accomplishes nothing while the economy of the country goes unchanged."

"But it's not meant to be a substitute," I protested. "What you're talking about has to be done at a government level and must be done, but that's going to be slow and burdened with political complications. This kind of aid, in the meantime, can go on humanely and intelligently."

"But it's wasted. It's like tending a hang nail of a patient who's dying of cancer."

"No," I said, "because a child isn't a hang nail. It's a bad analogy."

"You protest sentimentally, not logically."

"All right," I said. "Let me give you an analogy which will agree with your point of view. Would you refuse pain killer to a man dying of inoperable cancer?"

"Not if the drugs were available, no, of course not. But I don't give either energy or imagination to men or circumstances that I can't improve. In your situation, for instance, I would rather have a relatively insignificant job in government where important changes could possibly, if not probably, take place than the job you have now which is obviously interesting and emotionally satisfying but finally useless."

"Individual people can't mean much to you, then."

"No, they don't, not as an idea, anyway," he said, but then he gave one of his quick, economical smiles. "On the other hand, I wouldn't like living in a world without people—women, like you."

The idiot goddess of sentiment, waster of the world's resources —God bless 'em all. Just the same, I admitted his view as superior to mine, and I imagined that, if he had to make a choice, John Kerry could have chosen rational significance over a sense of personal fulfillment. He was simply careful not to put himself in a position where that had to be the choice.

Only once, before the marriage took place, did I admit to any doubt about him. We had all gone to the theater together, Andrew and Monk, you and John, Dan and I. Afterwards Dan suggested drinks at his apartment. There was nothing unusual in the conversation. Andrew and John were good-humoredly arguing the social utility of theater, Monk contributing her random and marvelously distracting observations, you laboring the religious point of view. Dan and I did more tending of drinks than talking until after everyone else had left.

"One for the road?" Dan suggested.

"Lovely."

"I'm feeling violently indiscreet," Dan said, but his face showed more distress than pleasure.

"How unusual," I said. "Why?"

"There's something wrong with him."

"Who?"

"John," Dan said.

"What?"

"I don't know, but don't you feel it? Do you like him?"

"I think so," I said. "I admire him."

"Oh yes, that," and Dan shrugged with a slightly effeminate gesture which I saw only when we were alone together or occasionally when I saw him with one of his homosexual friends. "We all admire *men*—sane, responsible, successful, father figures of the world. But what Andy says about him is true—there's nobody there."

"Or something wrong," I said.

"Did you wonder, when you first met him, if he was one of us?"

"No," I said. "That never occurred to me."

"It doesn't to me any more, but it did."

"I don't find him attractive," I admitted.

"Neither do I."

"But Esther does," I said.

"Does she? Does she really?"

"All you have to do is look at her, Dan."

244

"But, honey, she's a bit that way with you, too. I make no parallel really, but part of it for her is that you don't want her. I don't think he wants her, either."

"Why would he marry her?"

"We all have too many answers to that one, don't we?" Dan said.

"I'd like to think you're being bitchy," I said without edge.

"I am. I know it's not in character. I'm scared . . . and not just for Esther. Sometimes, when I forget for a minute how impressed I am with him, I catch myself looking at him and thinking, 'You poor, poor bastard.' "

"Envy compensation."

"I hope so. How are you dealing with yours?"

"Not compensating," I said, "just suffering. Now, get me one more for the road and think of something more cheerful."

"Has Ramona told you that she thinks she can't be in the wedding?"

"No. Why?"

"Positive rabbits. Or is it negative rabbits?"

"Really?"

"Nice, isn't it? I mean, they make such exceptionally good ones."

It's not odd that Monk's expecting another child reminded me that I could have had one of Andrew's children myself. I was delighted for her and not at all envious, but I left Dan for the first time not liking him very much, which was a compensating reaction. Suspicious dislike is the most easily transferable of emotions.

Before Monk had an opportunity to tell me her good news, she heard that her favorite brother—the one who had not been allowed to go to college and had drifted into the city, for a time into Robin Clark's hands—had been killed in an automobile accident. Four days later, Monk had a miscarriage. In the weeks that followed, if she had literally shut herself away, it would have been easier to reach her. Instead, as soon as she was physically strong enough, she accepted all the invitations that were so important to Andrew, continued the house-hunting they had begun soon after they got back to New York, and helped you with shopping for the wedding. She was neither absent-minded nor bleak. But the brisk, attentive cheerfulness was a terrible substitute for the distracting, willful humor we were used to. She was thinner. Her face for the first time showed the strain. In two months, she seemed to do the aging the rest of us had spaced out over the years. We all talked about what should be done. No one had any novel notions: she should be able to cry; she should get away; she should find comfort in the Church. Oddly, none of us spoke to Andrew about it, perhaps because he never raised the subject himself. It was, after all, some part his own grief, too. The change in him was less marked and accounted for also by his coming inheritance. He drank very little, only enough to be polite. He spent more business and less social time at the gallery, which grew now in expectation of capital and was beginning to attract some serious attention. He was quieter, more attentive not only to Monk but to everyone. He never went out in the evening without her.

As we watched, wanting to help and not being able to, each of us could remember a time when Monk or Andrew had been able to confront or comfort or advise. You and I particularly told the stories of those times to each other, but acknowledging the debt only made it seem heavier.

"There isn't anything to be done," Dan finally announced with some impatience. "And nothing needs to be done, that's our real trouble. They have each other."

"In fact, the real trouble is that we're feeling left out. Is that what you mean?" I asked.

"Exactly."

"But people shouldn't be isolated from each other," you protested.

"They're not isolated from each other," Dan said. "I'm developing a new theory—love is not an audience participation activity. 'Our gang' has limitations. And that, for me, is a real step forward."

Gradually and reluctantly we accepted Dan's view. You stopped feeling guilty about accepting Monk's help with the wedding. I stopped making occasions for her to confess her grief or for Andrew to ask my advice about it. They began to be a little easier, a little less withdrawn. It was Dan who finally took a holiday, being the one who deserved it. You found your comfort in the Church. I didn't learn to cry, but I hadn't anything to cry about. I was enormously interested in my job, absorbed and content in a way I'd never been before.

Like the party after your show, your wedding was somehow grander and more hopefully joyous than most. Was it again because people didn't quite believe in it but were caught up in your belief, in your dedicated confidence? It was a large wedding, in expensive good taste, gathering all kinds of people. Your brother Saul came home from Europe to give you away. I hadn't seen him in years. He looked startlingly like you. You could have been Shakespearean twins; I remembered the day of your haircut. But Saul had none of your capacity for arbitrary devotion. He was as wry and detached as he had been at fourteen, as nervous and as fond of you. The only emotional change I noticed in him was his marked courtesy with his mother, who tried very hard, for his sake, not to react with too much proud amazement. Frank and Doris came, able to combine other kinds of commitments as an excuse for the trip. When Christopher Marlowe Smith accepted his invitation, I promised Monk I'd introduce her to him because she didn't believe that he was real. Sandy telephoned several days before the wedding to ask if she might bring a friend. She had just arrived in town. But the parties before the wedding and the wedding itself were not so much gatherings of personal friends as monumental tributes to matrimony itself which, if you had been less religiously involved, might have been horrible. As it was, no social requirement was too much for the tribute you wanted to pay yourself to the vows you were about to take. John guided you through them all with steady good humor and good will. I found that I was as sorry for him as I was relieved when it became obvious that his mother would not relent.

It was an evening wedding, the reception a dinner and dance for five hundred people at the same hotel where, years ago, you had argued with your mother and Saul had sprinkled salt on the table. Mrs. Woolf, I think, owned it or a good part of it.

Did you ever look afterwards at this particular album? I've looked at it often, perhaps because these photographs gathered together so many people I have known and cared about. But I've looked again and again at the pictures of you, too, and of John, trying to see in your faces evidence for a judgment that, at the time, I did not make. The past ought to be a real crystal ball, but it rarely is. None of the photographs caught the images I still can recall, the first of which is your sudden pulling of a grotesque face, eyes crossed, tongue forward under your upper lip, when one of your mother's heavy-handed advisers hurried past the bridal party and on down the aisle just before the wedding march began.

"For God's sake, Esther!" Saul whispered, but he did laugh before his face clicked back into the solemnity (photographed several times) of giving you away.

Then I remember not your face, for I stood behind you, but your strong right hand, resting on John's arm. After you had been pronounced man and wife, I saw you turn your wondering, wonderful face to your spare husband, but for that moment I stopped attending.

The photographs take over from there through the reception. I was busy being in them myself at first, then collecting scraps of other people's concern and gaiety. I was with you again in ritual uselessness when you left the party to change. Your maid was waiting in the rooms your mother had reserved. She helped you out of your wedding dress and into the costume so carefully described in the newspapers the next day. I hardly saw it. I stood behind you at the mirror while your hair was fixed and watched the certain pleasure of the gift you were about to make of yourself.

"Now, Effie, find Mother and find John. Tell them I'm ready." When she left the room, you turned to me. "How do I look?"

"Fair," I said. "Fair enough."

We kissed as sisters do in plays, careful of each other's makeup.

"This is how it should be," you said then. "This is how you told me to do it."

Then John was there and your mother, and the ritual of the night closed in again in crowds and flashbulbs. As the car pulled away, Dan was suddenly beside me.

"All right?" he asked.

"Fine," I said. "Just be a darling, will you, and see I don't go home with anyone else?"

"Had you anyone in mind?"

"No," I said. "Nobody at all."

Sandy and the young woman who had come with her were on their way out as we started back in.

"Going so early?" I said, sorry that I hadn't really spoken to them.

"Not really our sort of party," Sandy said, smiling. "Come see us, will you?"

"Not our sort, either," Dan said to me, "but that's what makes it fun."

We set about then to dance until dawn. Nobody who didn't know us would have found us a less good imitation of the romantic, young couple than you and John had been. We were, perhaps, even better at it, knowing what we were doing.

There were in the days that followed so many parties and excursions involving Frank and Doris, Monk and Andrew, Dan and assorted other people that between such a lively social life and my work, I had hardly time to notice that you were gone. I was getting ready to leave myself for what was intended to be a European tour of agency offices. If I had known then that I would not be back in New York for over a year, I might have been less grateful for the distraction.

A week after the wedding, we were all at the first successful opening at the gallery. It's perhaps ironic that the gallery was able to pay off all its own debts before Andrew received the first money from his inheritance. It did not make him feel independent.

"We couldn't have kept it open to be successful," he said. "My father wanted to teach me what a failure I'd be without money. I grant him that lesson. He was right."

And that show, which marked the end of failure for Andrew, also marked his acceptance of the idiom of violently treated metal. As I looked at one bold assemblage of bright but fractured and betrayed steel colliding up into fountains of light, I heard Monk say, "After all, it's the way a lot of us are going to die."

I turned to find Doris, wanting to explain it to her, but she and Frank were busy receiving guests with so much parental pride that I didn't want to disturb them. It was Andrew's eye I caught instead. I went over to join him.

"If we can just live long enough, Katie," he said quietly, "maybe we can learn how."

Monk came over and said, "That's the tenth red sticker. Don't you feel a little ashamed to be selling all this junk for thousands of dollars?"

"You're the one who liked it," he said in amused protest.

"Liking it's one thing. Paying for it is another."

Dan behind her muttered, "Will you send your wife home before she ruins us?"

"In fact, I've got to go home," she said. "This time I think I'm getting morning sickness at night."

"Oh, Monk, I'm so glad," I said.

"You women who get your satisfaction out of vicarious motherhood!" she said fiercely. "Next time I'm going to buy one at a store."

"Only if it's another redheaded girl," Andrew warned.

"A boy," Monk said. "If this one isn't a boy, I'm giving it back."

The following evening when Doris and Frank were having dinner with young Frank, I accepted an invitation to dinner with Sandy. The apartment was so like the one in Los Angeles that for a moment it was hard for me to believe that I was still in New York. Sandy greeted me and took me into the living room where Lauris waited, but it did not take me long to keep from confusing places and people. Lauris was not another Esther Wilson. She was interested neither in making an impression nor in listening to personal histories. Later I learned that her reserve that night was partly reluctance to be at all involved with anyone Sandy had known before, but Lauris never, even with close friends, gossiped much. It bored her. I learned, too, that she shared my indifferent suspicion about the cause-dedicated magazines that Sandy so faithfully supported. Her attention was engaged when the conversation was about travel or paintings. And she asked a lot of intelligent questions about my work until I felt embarrassed by the amount of talking I was doing and asked her what she did.

"I'm Sandy's manager," she said. "Traveling as much as we do, I couldn't really be anything else, and I like it."

There were no possessive gestures, no private looks or comments. The duties of entertaining were not so rigid an imitation of male and female roles. Lauris fixed the first drink, Sandy the second, and then it was Sandy who stayed in the kitchen to finish a sauce.

Because Sandy wasn't so obviously in command, not at all indulgent, in a way she was less easy than she had been, but the nervousness disappeared as Lauris and I began to make friends. By the end of the evening they were telling stories together of places they had been, things they had learned.

"I have now rationed the number of hairy rugs Sandy can buy on any one trip," Lauris said, laughing. "It began to feel as if we'd been on a hunting expedition instead of a concert tour."

"And Lauris is rationed on paintings."

"You must get on Andy's mailing list for when you're in town," I said.

"Good," Sandy said. "Has Esther done anything lately?"

"A little," I said. "She hasn't had much time."

"Any good?"

"No. It's uncertain and sentimental. We had a wild argument recently about the theater mostly, but about sculpture, too. Esther's theory is that she ought to be able to use all the materials and devices for the dissolving or destroyed form in order to redeem it. We went to see *Krapp's Last Tape*. That's what started it. I told her nobody in his right mind would want to write *Krapp's Salvation*, but she does, sculpt it, anyway. And I didn't have much support from Monk, either, who thought writing *Krapp's Salvation* would be just her sort of thing."

"We saw one of her plays on TV the other night," Lauris said. "I didn't think it was bad."

"Monk's an amazing person," I said. "I think you'd like her, Lauris."

"You know, I never did," Sandy said. "She was such a fool at college."

"You wouldn't find her the same kind of fool now," I said.

"Of course, I was a fool, too," Sandy said. "I guess, one way and another, we all were."

"Well, come to dinner with me one night after I'm back. I'll have Monk and Andy."

After I left them, I found myself thinking of Joyce, but, even if she hadn't had a husband, it could never have been like that for Joyce and me, any more than it could have been like that for you and me. Sandy and Lauris were emotional equals and glad to be. I wondered if that, in fact, was what Andrew and Monk had begun to discover about each other so that Monk could now risk an idea of her own and work of her own, so that Andrew didn't have to keep asserting his freedom.

"So love isn't an audience participation sort of thing, agreed," I explained to Dan, "but it isn't a spectator sport either, is it?"

"It's true I've never seen enough of it to learn how, if that's what you mean. Do you suppose, for instance, that I could finally stop being a dependent, little faggot and grow up into the person I walk around pretending to be?"

"Maybe. Meanwhile, will you promise to look after my parrot and feed my cat and see that the guppies don't eat each other while I'm away?"

"And someday we may be old enough to have real pets, too," Dan said. "See if you can find one while you're away—one that costs too much and hurts too much—a real one."

Frank and Doris and I had arranged to travel together. We were all very tired by the time we boarded the plane, but we hadn't had a real opportunity to talk together since they'd arrived in New York. Yawning, Frank put away the book he would love to have slept over, and Doris asked for black coffee.

"I hope when young Frank decides to get married, he finds a poor Quaker. I don't think I'm strong enough to do this again," Frank said.

"What really amazed me is that Esther so obviously enjoyed it all," Doris said. "And John, too."

"After all my effort to marry her off to a responsible young man. I just shouldn't have worried. Were you surprised by him, Kate?"

"In a way," I said. "Did you like him?"

"Yes," Frank said slowly. "He's a bit earnest, but then Americans are. Certainly Esther is. For her a husband with a developed sense of humor would be like a husband with a second head."

"I didn't like him much," Doris said. "And I can't really say why. Unfair to judge someone under those circumstances, anyway. I felt sorry for him, I think."

"Hard not to," I said.

"You two always do this to me. Just as I think I can give up worrying, you tell me I have to start all over again," Frank said. "You aren't going to tell me that really Andrew and Ramona are still miserable just as I'm feeling really happy for them."

"No," I said. "Anyway, I'm not."

"Nor I," Doris said. "Just think of those television plays!"

The conversation no more than touched on you and John again. It drifted instead from pleasure to pleasure until our sense of well-being made us overwhelmingly sleepy and we gave in to that pleasure as well. When I woke to landing instructions, Doris' head was resting heavily on my shoulder, Frank's on his own developing double chins. A good moment, that kind: the world behind settled and growing, the world ahead full of possibility.

I hadn't time to stay in London. I took a flight out to Rome that day and was in Rome for three weeks, learning everything from office methods to the structure of welfare agencies in Italy. I spent more time in committee meetings than seemed to me useful, less time observing the work that was actually being done until I went to Sicily. There our funds were being handled by local welfare agencies, supervised only to the extent that they must follow basic policies of distribution, which I discovered were so broadly interpreted in some cases that it was hard to find any rational explanation for how the money was being spent; but, if I was sometimes bewildered or disapproving, I was also fascinated to see the way in which one intention is translated into another from one culture to another. Because my Italian was good, I was treated with particular respect, but the social workers were more interested in showing me monuments to their culture than the slum areas I had come to see. When I asked about a particular fishing village, close enough to the city so that several large tourist hotels had taken over much of the sea frontage, I was given a lecture on the economic delights of tourism.

"But what about these fishermen and their families? What are they doing now?"

"We can't deal with everyone. We interview only those families who have steady income. The others aid would be wasted on."

I was invited to be present on the day in which a number of the families came to pick up welfare checks and boxes of food and clothing sent from the warehouse in Rome. When I arrived at the office, coffee and cakes were being served by a young secretary to three social workers. It was obviously a special occasion for my benefit. We talked with formal politeness. One of the women was the daughter of a rich family, another the granddaughter of a famous composer. I had noticed elsewhere in Sicily that social work was not so much a profession as a dedication for wellborn women who had a taste for piety and power. The secretary left us and returned to announce that everything was ready.

We walked across a bleak, little courtyard and into a low, dark building. The door opened to the sound of a great number of subdued voices, but, as we walked in, there was silence and then the scraping of chairs and benches. There must have been at least a hundred women and as many children in the room, all standing now in silence. The women were almost all dressed in black as were not quite so many of the children, all of whom had been dressed in their best clothes. The chief social worker greeted the group, and they chorused a formal greeting in return, the children in the front rows bowing and curtsying. Each of the social workers was greeted in the same way, and finally, when I was introduced with a formal eulogy which made me feel a cross between the Statue of Liberty and the Virgin Mary, the chorus was even louder, the curtsying and bowing deeper. I had not expected to make a speech. The few words I said mildly surprised the social workers and puzzled the audience, for whom Italian was a public language which had little to do with real communication. Fortunately I didn't speak long enough to make any serious social or political mistakes. After that, I watched the lines form before tables of parcels and books of checks.

Soon after the distribution began, a young woman with a very young baby and a little boy of no more than three tried to enter the room. She was told by the secretary that she was too late. I heard the young woman try to explain that she had walked a long way from her village into the city. The little boy had been sick and couldn't walk very fast. But the secretary was firm. The woman must come back next month and see to it that she was on time. She turned away without further protest. I didn't say anything, but I must have looked both puzzled and disapproving.

"They have no discipline," the secretary explained. "If we are not strict with them, they think they can come in any time at all for what they want."

"But she's walked a very long way, hasn't she?" I asked.

"Yes. And next time she will know not to be late and waste so much of her time."

A little girl stumbled into me on her way out with her mother. I righted her and smiled. The child backed away into her mother's skirt while her mother bowed and thanked me a number of times, but behind the almost frantic humility of gesture I felt a deadening hostility. It was very hard to stay in that room until the last mother and child had left.

"That one is our pride," the secretary explained to me about a young boy of perhaps ten. "He stood highest in the city in his class in religion and was sent to Rome to see the Pope. He came back with a signed photograph. A devout family."

I gave you a mindful nod, thinking of our argument about non-sectarian aid. I was not sorry to leave Sicily at the end of ten days.

I had seen so many photographs of the Parthenon that I had not expected to be impressed by it, and at first I was not, but I was not disappointed, either. Seeing it there from the plane window, I had an odd, comforting sense of a familiar skyline, like the skyline of San Francisco from the Berkeley salt flats or the skyline of New York from the deck of a ship. The drive in from the airport increased that sense of familiarity because so many of the trees and flowers were familiar to me in the partial desert of California. Even the air, trembling with the possibility of heat mirage, was part of my earliest memory of California roads and fields. The city itself was, of course, not familiar at all. I disliked it first for its strangeness after so much promise of home. Once I got to know it, I disliked it for other things, but that was later; that is how it is now.

Athens had been planned as the most important part of my trip, not because activity there and throughout Greece was more extensive than it was in Italy but because the woman who ran the Athens office was considered the best informed and most successful of all the regional supervisors. Several times it had been suggested that she return to the States to train younger people, but she had lived in foreign countries too long to feel at home in her own. She had asked to stay in Athens until she retired. Trainees of all sorts were, therefore, sent to her. A man who was about to take over one of the small offices in South America had just been with her for two weeks. I was to stay a month.

Like many women who have dedicated all their intellectual and emotional energy to a job of work, whether it be a school or a hospital or a charitable agency, Grace Hardwick had collected a personal folklore. She had obviously been too attractive a young woman to be dismissed into sublimated spinsterhood. The stories ranged from tragic, young love to lovers in high places. There were rumors of an illegitimate child; there were other rumors of self-sacrificing sterility. Some even believed that she had been in a religious order for some time. What all these stories had in common was their lack of malice. Each one paid its own kind of tribute to Grace Hardwick's personal magnetism.

By the time I met her, she was nearing sixty, and, though she was extraordinarily hard-working, some of the natural energy, which had won her so much admiration and probably at one time strong criticism, too, was gone. The attractiveness was not. She had the kind of dark hair that moves to white without stages of gray. And, though her face was strong-boned, it was gently fleshed, both her mouth and eyes sensitive to and expressive of a narrow, positive range of moods. I never saw her depressed, but she smiled and laughed easily. Though she was absent-minded about combing her hair, often noticed a button or a drooping hemline after she got to the office, she dressed well and was, with good reason, proud of her figure, faddish about diet. Her staff, all of them Greek, liked to indulge her in the few quirks she had, and she let them, with an amused gratitude that did not get in the way of her being very demanding about thorough and accurate work. No one stayed in her office long who did not like to work.

I arrived prepared to like her, and I did, but at our first meeting I felt I had not made a very good impression. When I got back to my room at the YWCA, I nervously went over the questions and answers of that hour, wondering what kinds of mistakes I had made. Oh, she had been kind enough, but something in her manner was reserved, even perhaps disapproving. Had I been too critical of what I had seen in Sicily? I didn't think so. Had I asked too many questions or the wrong ones or too few? Had I been too casual? No, I had probably been too formal. When I could locate no specific mistakes, I was impatient with my own nervousness. I decided that my only mistake was being disappointed that she hadn't recognized something remarkable in me. And, when I came upon that truth, I realized that I had been in love with the myth of Grace Hardwick for several months, was, after one hour with her, in love with the person of Grace Hardwick as well. She knew it. She was used to it. She would not let it get in her way. I decided that it wouldn't get in my way, either.

It was that first evening that I took a bus tour up the Acropolis to see the Parthenon. For a while I stayed with the crowd of tourists and listened to the guide. On the steps of the Parthenon, he delivered a tribute to Athena who was not, he insisted, a primitive image of the Virgin Mother, but the manifestation of both masculine and feminine virtues. This building in its perfect proportions, combining strength and subtlety, was more an embodiment of Athena than any of the representations of her we would see either here or in the British Museum. All the attributes at the center of Greece's unique greatness were here in an aesthetic both rational and humane. . . . I walked away and stood at the wall, looking down at modern Athens, a mean, gimcrack sprawl of crumbling plaster and dirt and noise in the shadow of this great and ancient hill, this perfect intelligence. I was moved as I have never been in church, both awed and required by the truth behind me and the bitterness at my feet.

I didn't carry this revelation with shining eyes into the office the next morning. I'd have to do my own admiring of my winning sensitivity and medal intelligence. This woman honored nothing but successful hard work, and I should not expect stars for that, either. I could hear my father say with some wryness, "The truth is that virtue is not only its own reward, it is often its only reward." At the end of the week, I was so much absorbed in learning the idiosyncrasy of the office routine and reading reports in the spare minutes I had that I didn't notice at first the absence of that arm's length at which I had been kept. I must have reacted to it just the same because my comments about my discoveries were less and less guarded.

"Did you really send this report on the children's villages to the Queen?"

"She asked me for it," Grace Hardwick said.

"Well, if it's possible to say what you think, it's possible to do something about it, isn't it?"

"Yes, and a good thing for you to learn. You're so nearly a candidate for the Junior League, I wonder how you came to be here at all."

"I'm half breed," I said. "Mongrels can't be volunteers. They have to be professionals."

"Really? Well, it's been a long time since I've been home."

"You wouldn't like Washington," I said.

"Do you mean I wouldn't get along there?"

"No," I said quickly. "No, I—"

"Don't be embarrassed. Everyone's a little shocked by the system here at first. You have to understand how elaborate authority is in Greece before you can ignore it, and you have to be a foreigner. People don't usually stay long enough to find that out. I only appear to be reckless. I never am."

That night we had dinner together at a restaurant where Grace Hardwick often ate. As soon as she had done the ordering for us both, she sat back and looked at me with direct but amused regard.

"This is the evening I've set aside for getting to know you," she said. "Shall I ask questions, or will you just talk?"

"I don't really know what sort of thing I should say."

"Do you have an apartment in New York?"

"Yes."

"Do you live in it alone?"

"Yes."

"Tell me about it. Tell me what's in it."

I don't remember another question or command all through dinner. When we had finished and she had paid the bill, she said, "Now, would you like to see mine?"

"Very much," I said.

It was an apartment very like one I would live in. There were a few pieces of family furniture. There were paintings. There were more objects, collected over the traveling years. When I had looked around and asked questions about some things, we went out onto a balcony that looked across the city to the lighted Acropolis. A bottle of brandy and two glasses had already been set out on a small table.

"How do you feel about Athens?" she asked, once she had poured our drinks.

"I haven't seen much of it," I said.

"You don't like it."

"No."

"No, neither do I," she said. "As for the Acropolis, I'm nearly too old for that by now, but I expect you aren't. You would admire Athena."

"Yes," I said.

"I have too much of Arachne in me to admire any of them, or did have at one time. The errors of the gods don't seem that important to me now."

"Is it hard to live for a long time in a place you don't like?"

"Not at all. You see, I love it. Greece. I'm thinking of asking you to come along on a trip I have to make next week. How's your driving?"

"Good," I said.

"Mine's not. It never has been, but I don't like taking any of my Greek staff with me. They're too suspicious, too critical."

For a time then we sat without talking, watching the large, star-lit sky above the distant temple. When I finished my brandy, I got up and said good night.

"Don't show me to the door," I said. "I can find my own way."

The policy of working through local welfare agencies which had seemed an uncertain solution in Italy worked very well in Greece under Grace Hardwick's direction, but she spent a great deal of her time driving around the country to see that the money was being used as it should be. She not only made it her business to know all the local authorities but also kept an eye out for people who might be good in the welfare offices. Her knowledge of regional politics was her knowledge of particular people. On that first trip, I began to keep a notebook of names and comments, hers and my own. We called on villages where money was being used to reestablish pottery factories, wineries, olive groves. I started a second notebook on village industries. We saw particular families, too, sometimes because they were old friends, more often because we had heard about a child who needed an eye operation or a scholarship, things that could not be arranged without permission of the head office. They were long days. We were often on the road by six in the morning, and we never ate dinner before ten o'clock in the evening, usually with at least two other people, but Grace often slept for an hour or so in the car, and she insisted that I take an hour's rest in the afternoon, often simply under a tree by the side of the road after a picnic lunch. At those times, she wrote in notebooks of her own. At first, I found it hard to doze while she was busy at work, but by the fourth or fifth day I didn't have to be ordered to relax. I could fall asleep in the middle of a conversation. Once, when I woke, she was watching me, amused.

"You're still no more than a child," she said. "I wish I could do that."

"I wish I could help it," I said. "It's the air. It has the taste of my childhood."

"You like it here, don't you?"

"I love it."

"I should take time to show you temples, but I haven't got it. You'll find the time one day yourself."

The trip, as first planned, was to take just over a week, but, because the Athens office seemed to be running smoothly and because there was always something else to check on, someone else to confer with, we spent more than two weeks in the Peloponnesus. Grace didn't talk much in general about the work though she answered questions readily enough. She could, anyway, reveal more with a quick comment than most people can in an hour's lecture. She accomplished more over ouzo with two officials than I had seen accomplished all the time I was in Washington.

"Your Greek's improving," she said, as we were on our way back to Athens. "You have a good ear. And you can drive a car."

At that compliment, I passed a burro and rider with more style than courtesy, and she had the good humor to laugh.

"I'm told you're being groomed for executive work in New York and Washington. I'm told you're very bright about policy and government regulations. Also tactful and presentable. Is that what you want?"

"I thought so," I said, "before I came here."

"How would you like to stay?"

"Is there any chance of it?" I asked, my tone of voice answering her question.

"I've been offered the salary for an American assistant for several years, I suppose because I'm getting old. I haven't liked the idea. But I am getting old, whether I like it or not. I haven't more than five years left, maybe fewer. I'd suggest that you be appointed provisionally for a year. After that, we could see how you liked it, and how I liked your work."

"There's nothing I'd like more than working here with you."

"Well, we'll see."

I had only ten days in Athens by the time we got back, but in that ten days arrangements had been made, with some flattering reluctance in New York, for me to stay on.

"I told them there are lots of people with good manners and political connections. You happen to speak Greek," Grace said, pleased with herself. "Now, what are you going to do about your apartment?"

"Sublet it for the time being."

"Good. Finding a place in Athens isn't hard as long as you have money, but there really isn't any reason to spend it. You could move in with me."

"That's kind of you," I said, "but I'd better not."

"Why?"

"Because I love you," I said, as matter-of-factly as I could, "and you might find that a nuisance."

"I'm too old to find it a nuisance," Grace answered, "and you're old enough to put up with it."

So I wrote to Dan, asking him to pack me a trunk, store my paintings, and find a tenant for my apartment. Then I packed the suitcase I had and moved into the spare bedroom at Grace Hardwick's apartment. We were neither one of us in it very often except to sleep. A girl came in early every morning to fix our breakfast, clean up after we had left and do our laundry. She was gone by the time we came back for an hour's rest after lunch. We were often not home again until midnight. Grace took only a

Sunday holiday which she usually spent reading and writing letters. It did not seem to occur to her to fix a meal for herself even then when there was time. After I had been there a month, I was tired of restaurant food and of always eating in public.

"I'm hungry for my own cooking," I announced. "Would you mind if I got you a meal this Sunday?"

"Can you cook?" she asked doubtfully.

"Have the courtesy to risk it just once," I said, "and then you can decide."

"Well, see that it's good. I'm cranky about a bad meal."

"You're not. I've seen you perfectly good-humored after meals I could just barely choke down."

"But on Sunday I don't work," she said.

I had not eaten three meals a day with her without noticing what she enjoyed. Our first Sunday meal was so much a success that there was never a question of eating out on Sunday again. In fact, Grace occasionally complained that she got a decent meal only once a week, but there wasn't time for me to shop or cook during the week. Often we were invited out to dinner, which I enjoyed more than Grace did. She found some of the formality of political social life tedious.

"You'll really be better at this one day than I am," she said late one evening as we were coming back from a particularly solemn evening. "You can be as stuffy as the worst of them."

"That's why I was a candidate for Washington," I said.

"Is that a threat?"

"Of course not."

"I'm glad. You know, I intend to have two tantrums and a stroke if you decide to go back at the end of the year. I might find another assistant, but I'd never find such a cook again."

"You know I want to stay," I said.

"So you see, living with someone you love isn't impossible, is it? That's not a bad lesson to learn, however peculiarly. But will you want to stay after I'm gone? That's what you really have to decide."

264

"Where will you go?"

"I don't know, Kate, my darling, to hell or Italy or some place. I won't stay here. I don't feel guilty about not dealing with your sexual appetites. I'd guess they've been nothing but a problem to you anyway, but I'm not interested in your appetite for martyrdom, either. One dying mother is enough."

"Do you think I could handle it alone?" I asked.

"Sure of it. Oh, I also think you're awfully young and silly, but you'll outgrow that. Do you want to do it?"

"I don't know."

"Good. That's reassuring. But we must set aside an evening or two for talking about what you don't know and why you don't know."

"Make it three evenings," I said.

"Are you really that complicated?"

"No. I'd hoped there would be time for you to tell me what you do know and why you know it and when it happened."

"I think it would only confuse you," Grace said. "We aren't really at all alike."

That night I had the first attack of insomnia I had had since I arrived in Greece. I lay listening to the violent noise of Athens that does not die away until nearly dawn, high-powered sports cars gunning up the narrow canyons of streets, people shouting to and at each other, doors and windows slamming. I tried to think what it would be like to live here alone without Grace, who stood not only between me and the test of the job but also between me and my own desire and loneliness. Finally I got up quietly and sat on the balcony, looking out at the temple built in tribute to perfect balance, perfect self-sufficiency. It rose above the ugly city more a rebuke than an inspiration.

"Can't you sleep, either?" Grace asked, standing behind me.

"I guess not," I said.

"What's on your mind?"

"Athena's a hard goddess," I said.

265

"Then there's some protest in you after all," she said. "I always really thought so."

"A lot," I said. "But there's no point in protesting, is there? We live in our ugliness, simply rebuked by beauty."

Her mouth came down upon mine as if to speak to my grief.

"I'm really no good at this any more," she said, "but I don't see how else you're going to learn. Come to bed."

After that night, which had no sequel, I asked endless questions in my head, occasionally found a moment when I might have asked them of Grace, but somehow I felt I shouldn't. I should discover the answers for myself.

"You worry at the world so, Katie," she said to me one Sunday evening as I sat staring away from a book in my lap. "What is it now?"

"Did you live like this when you were my age?" I asked.

"How can you expect me to remember so far back? I don't think I ever was your age."

"Yes, you were," I said. "I'm sure of that."

"But I was never you, so it can't make much difference."

"But where were you when you were twenty-six?"

"I don't know. In jail perhaps, or maybe that was the year I was writing a book."

"Did you live alone?"

"I don't think so. I didn't often."

"Were you in love?"

"I have never been in love," Grace said, "except with my work. That's just how some of us are made. It's fortunate because there's a lot of work to be done."

"And the big, blond German turns his gun on his wife and shouts, 'Country first!'"

Grace laughed. "It's been my line. No point in taking it out of the script by now."

Grace held a lot of views she felt that way about. If I took issue with her, she would complain good-humoredly that she was too old to change. A new idea in work she didn't let herself be reluctant about, but it tired her. In February, she had a heavy cold which she didn't quite get rid of; I worried at her until she agreed to go away for two weeks at the end of March. While she was gone, I had to make a major decision about the budget and, as a result, had a major disagreement with the head of the clinic. By the time Grace got back, I was thoroughly discouraged.

"Don't think I'm going to bail you out of this," she said. "Oh, I could, but then where do you stand the next time it happens and I'm not here?"

"I don't stand. I run," I said gloomily.

"That's the spirit!"

A virtue of a job that is impossible to do is that there is not time to brood much about any aspect of it. Three days after Grace got back, we left Athens for another tour of the south. By the time we got back, the head of the clinic had resigned himself to my decision and was even pleasant over ouzo when we met by accident. Just the same, I knew that Grace's refusal to interfere had more to do with his mood than any power of my own.

The mail had piled up while we were gone both at the office and at home. News from Doris was that young Frank was going to marry a Quaker, but not a poor one, and they were faced with another American wedding. "Frank's rewriting his will in defiance of the daffodils." There was a letter from Andrew, letting me know that they had a son, born in late March, named Peter for Monk's brother who had been killed—and perhaps for Peter Jackson, though Andrew didn't mention him. I was pleased, but I also found it strange to realize that already the burdens of salvation were being handed on to the next generation. The gallery had now had half a dozen very successful shows. Andrew was beginning to be invited to sit on museum boards. "The charity boys are also after me. Please advise." I did not find your postcard until I got down to bank statements and investment reports. A Mexican under a sombrero on the front, not bad enough to be funny, and printed across the back, "Here for a divorce. Write to me at Mother's." Stupidly I counted up the months on my fingers as if you had been telling me that you were expecting a baby and then was embarrassed for you that the number was nine. I don't know why, an indecently bad symbol, I suppose, like some of your sculpture when you ignored obvious connotations. Why a postcard? Then I tried to imagine a letter full of dashes and faces. I could not imagine the last nine months of your life. I didn't know how to begin.

"Going for a walk," I said to Grace, who was just on her way to bed.

"Why don't you pace up and down the balcony instead and talk to me?"

"Because you need your sleep."

"I wouldn't sleep. I'd wonder if you were doing something silly."

I didn't know whether to protest or be flattered. I remembered Doris saying, "It's the only part of being loved that you've missed. You might even enjoy it." So I poured us each a drink and we sat in coats with rugs over our knees, looking out over the city, while I again tried to tell the story of your life or my life, or whatever this is, for the first time with some candor. I must have talked for nearly two hours.

"Every time, I begin to talk about Esther and end by telling the half story of my own life. It's like a Shakespearean bad quarto —a minor actor remembering his own lines very clearly but paraphrasing the major part," I said finally.

"Maybe you're not minor. You're wondering what you ought to do about Esther. Isn't that it?"

"I don't suppose there's anything to do."

"But you wonder. Why don't you go and find out?"

"How do you mean?"

"I'll give you a week in June," Grace said, getting up. "That ought to be time enough. Now, we have to get some sleep. You *are* getting to be a nuisance."

For the next six weeks Grace seemed determined to face me with all that was dullest and most disheartening about the job. I saw all the people we wouldn't admit to the clinic for lack of funds or on some technical silliness. I was assigned as guide to important American visitors who wanted cheap goods and cheaper night clubs. I was sent north to investigate personal rumors about one of our field representatives, whom I then had to fire. Grace even suggested, in a flair of vindictive humor, that I should attend stunt night at the American Embassy.

"There's enough unavoidable stupidity," I said, refusing to be amused. "You don't have to invent any more."

"I do have to dig for your temper," she said. "I sometimes despair of finding it."

"Well, congratulations."

Two nights later, still in an unforgiving mood, I began to pack for my trip.

"Don't leave too much behind," Grace said. "You may not be coming back."

"What are you trying to prove?" I demanded.

"Nothing, Katie. I'm trying to leave you free to decide."

"Okay, but I got that point about six weeks back. I'm very quick-witted about seeing that I'm free to decide. Nobody's ever wanted to take the blame for what I do. You haven't even been invited." I was shouting and beginning to enjoy it. "You don't have to bail out. You're not even on the trip. Relax, relax, relax!"

She was holding me and laughing at me and telling me to please shut up before I blackened her already mythical reputation.

"You're a witch," I said more quietly.

"There we are," she said. "I've ruined you for the Junior League. I'll take the blame for that."

"You don't have to," I said, sitting down on my bed, feeling so tired that I couldn't imagine ever moving again.

"What's this?" Grace asked, picking up a long, cardboard cylinder.

"I meant to show you. I found a painter while I was up north last week, making things out of string and wax and wool. The people in the village think he's crazy. He probably is, but I bought a couple to show to Andy, to give to him if he likes them."

Grace had opened up the package and was holding up the ragged apron shapes.

"Sick ethnic," she said.

"Yes, and there ought to be more of it and less depressed imitation. 'We have history, but we have no bread'—he gets the two things together."

"Would he know that he does?" Grace asked.

"Yes, I think so."

"You're falling asleep, child."

"Defense mechanism."

"A good thing you've got them. Sleep well."

I did, and I slept well on the plane, too, so that when I arrived in New York on a Saturday morning, I had accomplished the time shift without effort and was met by yawning friends, complaining at the early hour: Dan, Andy, and you. Monk was at home, supervising the children and an elaborate breakfast which began with strawberries and champagne.

"We canceled your hotel reservation," Andrew explained. "You're staying with us."

They had bought a small town house in the Village. Andrew called it small, anyway. It was five stories high, one room wide and two or three rooms deep. It reminded me of Frank's and Doris' house in London.

"It did us, too," Monk said. "That's really why we bought it, but I'll never be any good at running a house, Kate." She looked over her shoulder quickly and then whispered, "I just hate the servants. The first two weeks we had them I just locked myself in my room and cried, but Andy's fired the nanny now so that at least I can play with the children."

Lissa was temporarily a very solemn and uncertain little girl, learning to deal with the obscene curiosity of a baby brother, but there were already healthy signs that she would survive him. That he would survive her was still considered risky.

"Hello, Crow," she said, the first time any of us had heard the name, but we knew it would stick.

That first day was full of drifting conversation and patches of excitement. I had presents for everyone and tales to tell. Andrew and Dan were fascinated by the paintings I had brought home and began to plan a show. Monk decided I ought to be the subject of a television documentary which she described in a thrilling voice, details supplied by an impudently enthusiastic audience if she faltered for a second. You were very quiet, not withdrawn really, but patient. The story you had to tell did not belong to this mood of homecoming which went on through Sunday to a party on Sunday night, which included Sandy and Lauris, who had finally found their way to the gallery, and a number of other old and new friends.

Monday was the day set aside for visiting with you. I discovered that you were not living at home but had an apartment of your own only a few blocks away. I could walk to it for a late breakfast Monday morning, just any time I woke up. Accustomed to your habit of late rising, I spent the early part of the morning reading volumes of new plays that had been left in my room. I didn't dress until about ten-thirty, then realized, as I was putting on my lipstick, that I was nervous. Well, why not? This was the meeting I had come all the thousands of miles for without any clear idea why. And you had seemed to me in the last two days farther away than you had often been in Greece.

The streets of New York are extraordinarily quiet after Athens. That June morning the air was clear and warm as I crossed a wide, clean street free of organic odors and shouting friends. The Village, which had at one time seemed to me an intimate neighborhood, felt huge and impersonal and strange. I had a hard time distinguishing the words of an occasional American voice, being unused to its rhythms. The experience wasn't new to me. I noticed it more for the choice I would have to make before the week was out. I was thinking of that as I knocked on your door.

It was obvious that you had also been up for some time, working perhaps, and then waiting with some apprehension of your own. You were dressed in lemon yellow, a color I always forgot about for you because it seemed unlikely until you were in it. We kissed in what becomes a shy custom for American women by the time they are nearing their thirties, and then you stood back with a gesture as much of showing as of welcoming me in.

"It's very small," you said, "but I have a good workroom out in back."

It was, I think, what is called a Pullman apartment, a name that means little to my generation, most of whom have never been inside anything but a commuter train. It was one long, narrow room, at one end of which was a bathroom and a tiny, open kitchen, one unit containing stove, sink, and refrigerator. All along one wall, which was brick painted white, book shelves had been built under which was a door-sized table that served as a desk and an eating area. It had been set for breakfast with two straight chairs, side by side. On the other side of the room, to the right of the entrance door, there was a daybed, at the far end of the room a comfortable chair, a small table and lamp that obviously served as a bedside table as well. What was remarkable about the room was neither its odd shape nor its smallness but its immaculate order, which had not been achieved by one, grand cleaning gesture but was obviously habitual.

"I wouldn't know it belonged to you, except for the first editions," I said. "What's happened to the antlers?"

"I left most of my stuff at home in the attic. There wasn't room. Anyway, I got tired of the clutter. It was time to simplify."

The meal you presently began to prepare was as much of a surprise. Gone were the greasy fried eggs and burnt toast you used

272

to present without embarrassment, if clumsily. Your gestures were sure, accustomed. A pot of jam and glasses of orange juice were set out before it was time to sprinkle capers into the scrambled eggs.

"Scotch woodcock," you said, "in memory of London."

You had made real coffee, which sat over a candle keeping warm. I was ridiculously impressed by the matching cups and saucers. I felt I should say something, but the change that seemed to me so extraordinary obviously had taken place too long ago for you to be aware of it any more. It was not, in your terms, important.

Sitting side by side to eat made conversation awkward. There should have been a mirror of the sort I so often spoke to you in, as we sat at the counter in a London milk bar. Instead we had to stare at book titles or turn to find our faces much too close together so that we chewed and swallowed with self-conscious daintiness. I felt ridiculous and somehow relieved. I found myself imagining how I would describe this scene to Grace, and I saw her eyes, slightly hooded with age, amused, but there was reserve there, too, requirement: go and find out. When we finished breakfast, I moved at once to the daybed. You cleared away the dishes and brought back an ashtray and fresh cups of coffee. I expected you to sit in the chair, but instead you sat down next to me, and there we were in this awkward side-by-side again.

"Don't you want to look at me?" I asked.

"Not for a while," you said, "not until I've told you the hard things."

And so we looked down at our own hands and feet while you told me the story of your marriage from the wedding night until the day you packed your bags and left for Mexico nine months later, I waiting for the paper flowers and animals which never materialized. Apparently they did not breed in the new, tidy soil of your life.

"I almost didn't go to Mexico. I almost took a plane to Athens instead. I had some melodramatic notion of throwing myself at your feet, telling you I'd given up everything—God, John, the lot. If you wouldn't have me, I'd kill myself."

"Why didn't you come?"

You turned to me, startled. "What would you have done with me?"

I didn't answer. For once I was silent against my welling desire, not from any reluctance in me but from a mood in your face I couldn't read but didn't feel either known or welcomed by. You took that silence for what it had always been before, nothing, and turned back to your telling.

There was no malice in it. There was real sorrow. I tried to forgive you the graphic detail which forced me to imagine what it had been like. I didn't really have to imagine anything but the final scenes. I had known myself what it was like to stand before the open delight of your desire and be incapable of answering it. At least I had had a moral excuse. John had none.

"When I realized that he was afraid he simply couldn't," you said, "I thought I could do something about it. For a long time, I just didn't have the nerve. He's so remote in some ways. There wasn't any way of talking about it. But I thought I could help. I wanted him so much. The longer he avoided it, the worse it was for me. It was about five months after we were married. I simply couldn't stand it any longer. One night after dinner, I just began. At first I thought it was all right. He laughed and told me not to be silly, but he seemed interested, curious anyway. I didn't care what I did as long as it worked. It was quite a performance. And I didn't even know, when he started toward me, that it wasn't all right."

He had nearly killed you. Then he didn't dare take you to the hospital. He tended you himself with absolute gentleness, but in horror of you and of himself that he could not speak.

"I told him we had to talk. I told him nothing mattered. Sex didn't matter, but we had to be able to talk about it. Finally he said I was morally depraved. He'd realized before we were married that I'd had some experience. He knew women did these days, but nobody but a whore knew the things I knew, did the things I did. I tried to tell him. I tried to explain to him that nothing about the body is evil, that nothing he might want or I might want could be anything but lovely if we really loved each other. And I did love him. I wanted to tell him that I knew he was afraid. I didn't dare. We went on for a couple of months the way we had before, twin beds and reading lamps. I was beginning to resign myself to it. There are lots of things besides sex once you decide about it. Then one night he came over to my bed as if he'd made up his mind to try. When, after a while, nothing happened, I began to be afraid for him. I touched him and began to talk to him, nothing crude really, just loving, and it began to work, but he felt to me so uncertain. I took him with my mouth, and he came. Then he hit me. Just once. He told me he never wanted to see me again, and he meant it. Oh, I stayed around for a week. I didn't really know what to do. Finally I went to my minister. He talked with John. After that, he said I really had no choice. I should go to Mexico for a legal divorce. Then I should file for annulment with the Church because the marriage had never been consummated. I'm waiting for that now."

"What's happened to John?"

"Nothing. He wrote to my mother and told her that he'd like to stay on in Boston if she'd allow him to pay back the money over the next five years. Otherwise he'd sell out and go back to Louisville. She said he could stay. She has that little bit of vindictive pleasure at keeping him away from his mother."

I couldn't think of anything to say. I realized that at some point in the story I had taken your hand which I still held very firmly in mine. Now that I knew I had it, I didn't know what to do with it, but you didn't seem to have noticed.

"Well, it's over," you said, "and the odd thing about it is, I'm not really unhappy. In fact, I'm sometimes even . . . glad. There's something very peaceful about giving up all that. Human relationships don't really even interest me very much any more. I

275

don't mean I don't care about people. I do. In a way, I even care more because I'm not involved. I'm getting an answer to that old question of Pete's—we have to be ugly with each other's sins until we're detached enough to accept them of our own free will. Do you understand that? Probably you do. You've always been self-sufficient. I never have. It's something I had to learn about now."

"And you're working," I said, having let go of your hand.

"Yes," you said. "I want to show you."

Your workshop was as uncharacteristically ordered as your apartment had been. There were a dozen sketches pinned up on the wall. In the center of the room, on a stand, was your Crucifix-ion, almost finished. The cross was wooden, the Christ shaped of pieces of metal which had, though not obviously, first been used for other purposes. It must have been fairly heavy, but it was sup-ported by the right number of nails. The figure was life-sized, the head up, the effect not skeletal so much as sketched in three di-mensions, a hanging, straining weight of mortal suffering, unde-feated. It was almost as if the head listened, as your bell ringers had done, to the note sounded above. I stood before it a long time before I turned away, knowing that for me man so tormented into whatever vision of salvation could lead me nowhere but to despair.

"No?" you asked.

"It's powerful, E. It's beautiful in a way—beautiful with the sins of the world. You've done what I said couldn't be done, re-deemed the material. It's just that I don't believe it."

You nodded. "I know. It's funny how far apart we've grown, isn't it? That's maybe the only grief I've got left with knowing how much farther I have to go."

"How far have you got to go?"

"On anyway, as far as I can, as far as I'm called."

Then you talked of the faithful life lived in the imitation of Christ. You read me bits from the lives of saints, but your texts were not often those we had studied together and argued about

276

in philosophy of religion courses. What you were reading now was confessional literature mostly and persuasions of the persuaded. You had one little book called *The Right to be Merry* by a nun in an enclosed order. She wrote of talents given up to be given back, of poverty. "We are just too poor to own our bodies, to exercise over them the proprietorship by which we could lawfully claim the pleasures of the flesh." "We accept the commands of others as alms to our poverty."

"Are you thinking of going into an order, E.?"

"Thinking isn't exactly what it is," you said. "I study and pray and wait."

"A teaching order?"

"I'd take the vow of silence and enclosure," you said.

"Do you want to?"

"How can I explain it to you? In the worldly sense, nobody wants to be a saint, but some of us are called. I may have to be a saint, but I'm not sure I can bear it."

I could hear the disbelieving laughter, the derisive comments, the cynicism of an invisible company of people. You, a saint? First, there was the impossible arrogance of it. Second, there were the doctrinal problems to be solved with particular reference to you: because your only sanctioned relationship was technically unconsummated, your purity could be established for you to take your vows. Finally, your personal history made you such an unlikely candidate. But none of that mattered really. Nor did it matter that I myself couldn't possibly believe in the usefulness of a life spent in prayer for the world. The only honest protest I had to make was for myself. That you might one day shut the door on the world we lived in, leave me in it alone without ever the hope of looking up in a company of strangers to say, "There. There you are," was all I could think of.

"I would miss you," I said.

Later all the others would argue against belief or your motives in belief or your capacity to serve. You had friends more capable than I of denying the truth of Christianity. You had in your life

277

lined up so many psychological clichés that it wouldn't take more than an introductory course for anyone to accuse you of searching for a father figure, of trying to sublimate your homosexual tendencies, of Jewish paranoid appetites and delusions. Nobody needed even the terms to know that you had been, in the simplest, old-fashioned sense, "disappointed in love." It was Saul, apparently, who fought morality with morality. He was to tell you that you were making a completely selfish decision, committing suicide to escape the responsibilities of love for your family and your friends. There must have been lots of people to remind you of the fortune you were giving up. Your mother, for one, for it was the only gift she was certain of giving you. Christopher Marlowe Smith, I'm sure, suffered a sense of shocking waste. For you, giving up the trinkets and toys that had delighted you would be much more difficult than giving away an inheritance you never really believed in and found an occasional nuisance. Did I know that none of these arguments would finally matter to you at all? They didn't matter to me.

"It would be hard to give up children," you said that afternoon. "It would be hard to give up fame, but, if the teaching of Christ is true, the only thing to do is live in terms of it."

"It's a hard faith," I said, remembering how long ago you had said it to me. "Maybe any faith, taken seriously, is."

When I left you that day, I had offered no objection and made no gesture of protest. Perhaps I thought there was still time. But who on earth would have dared or even wanted to take the responsibility of saving you from seeking your own salvation?

I had my own doubts, my own decisions to make. I spent the next day at the head office in committee meetings and conferences until late afternoon when I was to meet the head of the organization for drinks and dinner. He asked a great many questions about our work in Greece. Then he spoke of problems in South America, the political pressures from Washington. We had finished dinner before he was ready to discuss my job.

"Kate, I think you know you're being considered as a replacement for Grace. She's recommended it, but she's not sure you're ready for it. I'm not, either. I'm not sure you wouldn't be more useful to us here or in Washington. Since we don't seem able to make up our minds, I think the answer is for you to make up yours. If we send you back to Greece, we'll recall Grace almost immediately to set up a training program. If you stay here—"

"Does she know she'd be recalled so soon if I accepted the job?" I asked.

"It was her suggestion."

"I see."

Then he outlined the kind of job he had in mind for me if I stayed, and he did make it sound as attractive as he could. I listened to what a year before would have seemed to me nearly ideal. Now, when I tried to think of living a life of committee meetings and political cocktail parties, my imagination simply failed. Instead I could hear in my head the repeating sentences of the Greek language records I had once so dutifully listened to: "In Greece, the sky is almost always blue"; "Hospitality is a Greek virtue"; "Help! Police! Someone has stolen my purse!"; "Get a doctor. The pain is in my stomach." I could feel the dry k's of that language forming in my throat mixed with the sharp, unlikely taste of retsina.

"Let me know on Friday," he was saying.

Monk was on her way to bed by the time I got home, but Andrew was in the mood for a nightcap. I told him about the two jobs, describing them in as unprejudiced a way as I could.

"It sounds to me as if you're going back to Athens," Andrew said.

"But you think I'd be more useful if I stayed here."

"No, Katie. That's what you think. You're bugged by people like John Kerry and their utilitarian arguments. Well, so am I. But if you make the wrong choice for absolute sense because it's the right choice for you, why not? Something's got to be said for loving what you do."

"Well, yes," I said.

"What about Esther?"

I lifted my hands in a Greek gesture.

"She's doing some real sculpture, isn't she? If she keeps it up, I want to give her a show."

"I don't think it will work, Andy."

"She's spoken to you then . . . about the order."

"Yes."

"Did you try to talk to her?"

"I didn't have much to say."

"No," he said. "No, I suppose not. Will you be going back to anyone there?"

"No," I said. "The only person . . . friend I've made is Grace Hardwick. She'll be recalled."

"Will she mind?"

"It's her suggestion."

"Will you?"

"For a while, yes, I'm sure I will."

"But you'll manage," he said, sighed and got up. "I couldn't. I wouldn't want to. I wonder how Grace Hardwick really feels."

"The way I do, I think."

"I'm glad it's the job you want, Katie, but we'll miss you . . . all of us."

I sat up for a while after Andrew had gone to bed, but I didn't get anywhere with his doubts or my own. The choice, technically still before me, had been made. I did not think of Grace. I did not think of you. I was trying to decide what furniture I should ship to Athens.

I didn't really avoid seeing you for the rest of the week. There was a lot to do. We did go to the same parties. I called on your mother. We were simply never alone together. Perhaps everything that could be said had been said.

"Come to see me in Athens," I said to everyone as we waited for my plane to be called.

Then, when the flight was announced, I went down the line kissing people, so many people a stranger could have joined the party and I wouldn't have noticed. You were at the end of the line, wearing a hat because you had just come from church. I had to check an impulse to take it off your head.

"Good-by, little dog."

"I'll pray for you."

"I know," I said.

It was over a year before I received the letter that told me you had made your decision. Shortly after that the box of your belongings arrived. I took a long time over the answer, finally reduced to a note. Nowhere are there directions for the proper form to thank someone for an inheritance. I was not sorry to miss the melodrama of your being taken away. Your mother wrote to say that you had been allowed to take your enameling set, rather as if you were going off to summer camp. I think at first it must have seemed like that to her.

Resignation is always a temporary and easily disturbed condition. Mine was disturbed each time I had any communication from you. During the months you were a postulant, you wrote more letters than I had ever known you to before, perhaps because you had to ask permission. They were dutiful little notes for Christmas and my birthday. You spoke briefly of your life which was simple and hard and happy. You sent prayers for me and my work. I did try to answer them, but it wasn't any use. My concern about earthquake damage in three villages, my most recent trip to England to see Frank and Doris, the concert Sandy had given in Athens all seemed beside the point. I wrote a couple of paragraphs after I'd seen the new cathedral at Coventry with its faint flights of saints and strong, unattractive Christ, but they were irrelevant comments. You could no longer be concerned with the things of this world. It felt to me as if I were trying to conduct a private séance, and I've never been any good at communicating with spirits. I have a hard enough time with what I know to be the real world of people around me.

I suppose I can explain why all this began, though I don't know why it has gone on and on through these months of my living and the years of our life. It was after Monk and Andrew had been here in Athens with me for a week last spring. They had just seen you as a bride of Christ and watched the doors close behind you, shutting you off from them for the last time.

"I always thought it was odd that you didn't see her again at least once before she went in," Monk said. "I think she expected you to come. But maybe, in a way, she was just as glad you didn't. She said a funny thing—she said she thought you had taken paganism just about as far as it could go. I was expecting to find you involved in some kind of cult of Athena. I guess she didn't have vestal virgins though, did she? Wasn't that Diana? But here you are, as rational as ever. What do you suppose she meant?"

"That I'm as rational as ever," I said, "worshiping what is political and humane and worldly."

"But you're really not that cynical, are you, Crow?" Monk asked. "Don't you sometimes feel the prayers of the nuns?"

"Do you?"

"Oh yes. If I hadn't married Andy . . ." she began, "but we're all committed by now, aren't we? Here you are with your Greeks. I have motherhood and television. And Esther's with God."

"Oh Monk," I said, laughing, "you do make us sound a tidy, mad lot."

"I think we are. Did you hear that Andy sold Esther's Crucifixion for a fabulous amount of money to some religious fanatic in Connecticut? We gave the money to Esther's order. It will keep them from starving and begging for a while. I did find out that, though you can't send individual presents, you can send things for everybody. Esther always liked olives. You could send them all olives."

Andrew and I walked up the Acropolis one afternoon while Monk was resting. She said it was either the seafood or she was pregnant again. We listened to the same guide I had listened to when I first came to Athens, then stood where I had stood, looking down on the city.

"It's a good life you have here, Kate, isn't it?"

"Yes."

"We see Grace quite often, you know. She said you'd be happy. I think she gets homesick for Athens occasionally, but she likes what she's doing."

"She would," I said. "She's a good teacher."

"It was as if she had a part in a play," Andrew said after a moment, and I knew he was speaking of you. "It was as if, after it was all over, she'd come out again dressed in her own clothes ready to go off with us for coffee or a drink somewhere. When we drove off, I somehow felt we were deserting her there. That isn't the way she feels, I know. The trouble all along for Esther was that nobody she met was ever God."

"How did her mother take it?"

"Quietly. Ramona says she was proud. I hope so. It's the only good choice she has."

"Do you believe in it?" I asked. "In what Esther's doing?"

"No," he said. "I believe in this," and he nodded down at the city. "I believe in art and in failure. But Esther couldn't ever have settled for that, could she?"

"I'm not sure I do, either," I said.

"Oh, I think we kill a few of our dragons before one of them gets us. I believe that. Were you in love with Esther, Kate?"

"Yes."

"She didn't know."

"Probably not," I said.

"Surely that's a failure masquerading as success."

"That's your decent answer," I said.

I am not guilty, and Joyce is right: it is a limited way to live. Yet I don't see how I could have afforded any other. It's a happy enough ending surely, even for me, vindicated of a crime I didn't commit, an evil I don't believe in. Andrew is right too: there may be something wrong with the argument, with the whole concept of self-sufficiency, but it has been expedient. If I have been incapable of loving you well enough, I've made a virtue of loving you badly. Pray for me if you will, Sister, beloved of God. This is not for you.

Publications of
THE NAIAD PRESS, INC.
P.O. Box 10543 • Tallahassee, FL 32302
Mail orders welcome. Please include 15% postage.

This Is Not for You by Jane Rule. A novel. 284 pp.
ISBN 0-930044-25-8 $7.95

Faultline by Sheila Ortiz Taylor. A novel. 140 pp.
ISBN 0-930044-24-X $6.95

The Lesbian in Literature by Barbara Grier. 3rd ed. Foreword by
Maida Tilchen. A comprehensive bibliog. 240 pp.   ind. $7.95
ISBN 0-930044-23-1   inst. $10.00

Anna's Country by Elizabeth Lang. A novel. 208 pp.
ISBN 0-930044-19-3 $6.95

Lesbian Writer: Collected Work of Claudia Scott
edited by Frances Hanckel and Susan Windle. Poetry. 128 pp.
ISBN 0-930044-22-3 $4.50

Prism by Valerie Taylor. A novel. 158 pp.
ISBN 0-930044-18-5 $6.95

Black Lesbians: An Annotated Bibliography compiled by
J R Roberts. Foreword by Barbara Smith. 112 pp.   ind. $5.95
ISBN 0-930044-21-5   inst. $8.00

The Marquise and the Novice by Victoria Ramstetter.
A novel. 108 pp.
ISBN 0-930044-16-9 $4.95

Labiaflowers by Tee A. Corinne. 40 pp. $3.95

Outlander by Jane Rule. Short stories, essays. 207 pp.
ISBN 0-930044-17-7 $6.95

Sapphistry: The Book of Lesbian Sexuality
by Pat Califia. 195 pp.
ISBN 0-930044-14-2 $6.95

Lesbian-Feminism in Turn-of-the-Century Germany.
An anthology. Translated and edited by Lillian Faderman and
Brigitte Eriksson. 120 pp.
ISBN 0-930044-13-4 $5.95

(continued on next page)

The Black and White of It by Ann Allen Shockley.
Short stories. 112 pp.
ISBN 0-930044-15-0 $5.95

At the Sweet Hour of Hand-in-Hand by Renée Vivien.
Translated by Sandia Belgrade. Poetry. xix, 81 pp.
ISBN 0-930044-11-8 $5.50

All True Lovers by Sarah Aldridge. A novel. 292 pp.
ISBN 0-930044-10-X $6.95

A Woman Appeared to Me by Renee Vivien. Translated by
Jeannette H. Foster. A novel. xxxi, 65 pp.
ISBN 0-930044-06-1 $5.00

Lesbiana by Barbara Grier. Book reviews from *The Ladder*.
iv, 309 pp.
ISBN 0-930044-05-3 $5.00

Cytherea's Breath by Sarah Aldridge. A novel. 240 pp.
ISBN 0-930044-02-9 $6.95

Tottie by Sarah Aldridge. A novel. 181 pp.
ISBN 0-930044-01-0 $5.95

The Latecomer by Sarah Aldridge. A novel. 107 pp.
ISBN 0-930044-00-2 $5.00